Gabriel's life ground to a halt some time ago, but he's still running—from his past, his family, and now the new man in his life. A man who just won't get the message that Gabriel isn't interested in love anymore.

Laurie won't give up on the beautiful man who is broken and intent on running away. Even though he doesn't know what Gabriel is running from, he's determined to be at his side no matter what.

When Gabriel's past finally catches up, they both stop running and find themselves plunged into something Laurie could not have dreamed of, and Gabriel never stopped having nightmares about.

Reader Advisory: This book contains a scene of attempted suicide.

This book is a work of fiction. Names, characters, places, and incidents either are products of the author's imagination or are used fictitiously. Any resemblance to actual events or locales or persons, living or dead, is entirely coincidental.

Lab Rat
Copyright © 2019 Cheryl Headford
ISBN: 978-1-4874-2165-6
Cover art by Martine Jardin

Published by eXtasy Books Inc or
Devine Destinies, an imprint of eXtasy Books Inc

Look for us online at:
www.eXtasybooks.com or www.devinedestinies.com

LAB RAT

BY

CHERYL HEADFORD

Dedication

To Steph who was the first to take a chance

Chapter One

Gabriel

Life sucks. I mean really sucks. I'm a good person, so why do bad things keep happening to me? While I'm not the type to help old ladies across the road—I'd probably scare them into a heart attack—I don't go out of my way to hurt people either. And yet . . .

My family has pretty much disowned me, and I don't blame them. They can't cope with me, never could. Hell, I can't cope with myself. They kind of tried for a while, in their own way. The thing is—it wasn't my way. It wasn't a good way. It wasn't the right way.

When I was thirteen, something bad happened to me—really bad. They never got over it. Neither did I, but that didn't matter. I got into drugs and alcohol in a big way. I became dark, too dark. Then, when I was fifteen, it all got to be too much. I couldn't hold it all in anymore—the memories, the pressure, the . . . problems it left me with.

They say I had a breakdown. I don't know what that is, but I ended up in hospital. I don't know how long I was there or what happened to me there. I only know that I felt safe. For the first time since *it* happened, I felt safe. I didn't want to come out. I wasn't ready to come out, but they pronounced me *cured* because I could string sentences together and go for days without screaming or hiding under the bed.

My parents knew, though. They knew I wasn't cured, that I never would be. They tried for a while, but they couldn't cope. Not with the screaming in the night. Or the staggering in at three in the morning, either high or pissed—to stop the screaming in the night. They couldn't cope with the physical conditions, the mental problems, the attitude, the violence. They couldn't cope with watching the child they loved change into a monster.

When I was sixteen, I moved out and went off the rails. Surprisingly, I still managed to go to school now and again, and I got decent results in my exams. This led to the headmaster persuading me to go back for my A levels, and even more surprisingly, given what I was doing to my body by that time, I got three A levels in one year. And thus ended my academic career.

There was talk about going on to university, but to be honest, I couldn't be bothered. I still had the nightmares, and I was afraid to go out into the world. I felt vulnerable and exposed in unfamiliar places and situations. I guess I was—I am—a complete nut job.

At the moment, I'm living in a grotty room, in a grotty house, on a non-descript street, in a second-rate town, that is . . . nowhere. I have two housemates who are used to me and know when it is and isn't safe to talk to me, and who ignore the screams.

Tonight, I'm going out. It's Saturday night. I always go out on Saturday nights. I go to the same place, see the same people, and do the same things. You'd think I'd get bored, but it's safe.

I give myself a last look in the mirror and am reasonably satisfied with what I see. I need a haircut, and I'm way too pale, but at least the shadows around my eyes are camouflaged by the kohl, and where I'm going the vampire look is par for the course. The black lips in the mirror smile at me, but there isn't any humour in them or in the piercing blue eyes that stare coldly at me when I allow myself to catch their gaze.

Ah well. This is the best it's going to get tonight. I close my eyes and take a deep breath. I don't feel up to going out. I'm not myself at the moment, mentally or physically. It's not as if I can even get pissed anymore. I learned the hard way that alcohol and my meds don't mix, or do mix. Blegh.

But then, today hasn't been a good day. If my head's anything to go by, it's not going to be a good night either, so what's the point in being good? What's the point in trying to look after myself? Fuck it.

I check my wallet to make sure I have enough for taxis and plenty of booze. Then I flick my hair over my shoulder and stalk out of the room.

I intimidate people easily, and I don't know why. I'm a nice person—to everyone but myself. Okay, I'm not the most sociable. I have friends, but I don't let anyone get too close. What's the point? I'm not a good friend to have. I try, but good friends don't turn cold for no reason. They don't run away, don't get so angry they have to hit the wall so they don't hit you, for no reason at all. Real friends can be relied on, can give, can communicate and don't drag you down.

Surprisingly, I do have real friends. Even though I'm such a bad friend, there are people who somehow seem to like me despite it all. I'm a shit to them. I spend all my time trying to push them away, and they spend all theirs trying to save me. I wish they wouldn't. Although . . . sometimes it's nice to have someone hold my hand when I wake up in hospital, or on the floor, or . . . worse. Sometimes it's nice not to be alone. But it's not safe.

"Hey, Gabe!"

Sigh.

I turn around and force myself to smile at two girls who are running down the street toward me. The taller of the two reaches me first. She jumps at me, flinging her arms around my neck. I've no choice but to put my arms around her to steady her as she presses herself against my chest and kisses me.

I don't kiss her back. She doesn't expect me to. I don't kiss anyone. That's getting too close, and I don't do close. I draw back and smile at her, setting her on her feet. The other girl catches up, and they both link arms with me.

"You look awesome tonight, Gabe."

"Thanks, Carrie. You don't look so bad yourself."

The other girl, Sophy—the bossy and pushy one—tosses her candy floss pink hair and grins at me with purple lips. Her striped top and net mini-skirt are the same colour as her hair. She strokes her hand down the softness of my coat sleeve. "This is nice. Is it new?"

"Yes. It's cashmere. Very expensive wool. Another guilt offering from the 'rents."

"You shouldn't be so hard on them, Gabe," Carrie says softly. "They do their best."

"Yeah. They've always done their best. Shame their best was never good enough."

"Maybe if you gave them a chance. If you didn't keep pushing all the time . . ."

"Don't!" I snap in my cold don't-fuck-with-me-right-now voice.

She blushes and turns her head away.

I feel bad. Carrie doesn't deserve that. She doesn't deserve me being a twat to her. But I can't help it. Some places just don't bear examining, and my relationship with my parents is one of them. If I'm being honest, they aren't that bad. They did their best, they really did. I was completely out of control. No one could've helped me. No one can.

Shaking my head, I smile at Carrie. "Sorry. You're probably right, but you know how it is with me and the 'rents. It's not a place I want to go right now. Right now, I want to go out and let my hair down. I want to dance and sing tunelessly at the top of my voice, songs I don't even know, and get completely and horribly pissed."

"You're not supposed to drink."

"There's a lot of things I'm not supposed to do."

"But Gabe . . ."

I turn to her, suppressing the desire to slap her. "Carrie, you're one of my best friends, but tonight I don't need a lecture . . . about anything."

"Had a bad day, hun?" Sophy innocently quips. I wince and turn away. I know she'll have *that* expression in her eyes and I don't want to see it. Not now.

The club's hopping. There's a long queue of kids outside, pretending to be something they're not. Trying to look dark and deadly when the darkest thing in their lives is the makeup they slap on their faces. The place is saturated with teenage angst. Not one of them knows what it's like to look into your heart and find only darkness looking back. Not one of them gazes in the mirror and sees hell staring back through unfamiliar eyes.

I sigh and close my eyes. Today's been a bad day, and tonight's going to be a bad night. I need a drink.

Sophy drags us to the front of the queue, eliciting cries of complaint that she ignores. Those who know her don't bother. She's a natural force, like the wind or the tide. When she sets her eyes on something, nothing gets in her way . . . almost.

The bouncer knows us. He smiles and steps aside to let us pass. Then the sound envelops me. I love it. The pounding beat I hear with my heart. The stress leaks out of me, and I relax for the first time in days.

The writhing mass of bodies in the middle of the floor is as enticing as the sea on a hot summer day, and I can't wait to go swimming. It takes a while to undo all the buttons on my coat, but it's a relief to take it off and hand it to the check-in desk. I thrust the ticket into my trouser pocket. I can just about get my hand in there.

Sophy and Carrie have disappeared into the crowd, and I'm so glad. I don't want to be with friends tonight — friends who accuse me with their eyes of things I'm very well aware I'm guilty of.

Skirting the edge of the dance floor, I decide to give the pleasure of the dance a miss. Just for now. It'll be all the better for the anticipation. I really need a drink.

The bar's busy, but not unusually so. I can be patient. I lean on the counter, waiting for the barman to catch my eye . . . but something else does. At the far end of the bar, where it curves, there's a group of boys I haven't seen here before. One of them looks up as I glance in their direction. Just for the briefest instant, a spark of electricity arcs between me and the biggest, brightest, bluest eyes I've ever seen.

I don't see the rest of him — the face, the hair, the clothes. Just the eyes. With something dangerously close to panic, I make a point of turning away. The barman appears in front of me. I order two straight JDs on the rocks — doubles, of course. I down the first in two gulps.

Ah. That feels good. I didn't even taste it, but the warm feeling as it goes down makes me close my eyes in pleasure. Sipping carefully on my second glass, I weave through the crowd to an area where a forest of Grecian pillars cluster together. Some are encircled by shelves at elbow height, perfect for setting down drinks.

I'm not a fool. I never put down my drink — not anymore. There was a time when I didn't care, when I was pretty much hoping for someone to spike it so I could get free drugs and a good hard screw. But I left that behind some time ago. I carefully cradle my drink and scan the dance floor.

There are plenty of familiar faces. Many of them smile or wink when they catch my eye. Most of them would give their right arm to go home with me — and that's not conceit. In fact, it's depressing because I haven't taken anyone home with me for months. Shit, it's been years.

I people-watch as I sip my drink — refusing to allow myself to admit that I'm actually watching for a particular person. Of course, I'm not. That's ridiculous. I don't do that kind of thing. It's too dangerous. Way too dangerous.

Annoyed, I realise my glass is empty. Feeling a little light-headed, I head back to the bar. The group of boys has gone. Of course, they have. Why would they linger at the bar? Why would I even care?

After gradually consuming another JD, I decide it's a good time to start dancing. If I don't, I'll be far too pissed, far too quickly, and I don't want to go home yet.

Leaving my empty glass on the shelf, I step onto the dance floor and allow myself to be absorbed. I close my eyes and slip into the stream of energy, my body picking up the basic rhythm of the dance and moving with it.

This isn't the kind of place where people dance a foot apart, in couples. If there are couples, they're locked together, usually engaging in sexual acts of one kind or another, some more . . . adventurous than others. Oh, I'm not suggesting anyone's stripping off and having sex in the middle of the dance floor, but it's surprising what two people can get up to, fully clothed in the middle of a crowd. That's part of the reason I keep my eyes closed.

It's not difficult to lose myself in the music. This is the only time I ever feel completely relaxed, in control, safe, real. I don't dance, not as such. I just let myself be taken over by the music, allowing my body to move as it will. Somehow, I never seem to bump into anyone and often find myself swaying in someone's arms. I always dance away as soon as

I realise what I'm doing, but it makes me smile . . . unless they try to hold on. Then I panic. I'm not a good person to be around when I panic.

Tonight's a good night after all. The alcohol's hitting my system big time. I haven't eaten today. It wasn't deliberate — I just wasn't up to it. I had neither the focus to prepare it nor the appetite to eat it. As you can imagine, after three double JDs and no food I'm pretty mellow and also quite light-headed. That's not a good thing. Not for me.

The light-headedness develops into a feeling of detachment. I love this stage in the inebriation process. It's as if I exist in my own world. Everything and everyone else is on the outside, and I'm completely safe. Nothing bad can happen to me. Nothing sad can reach me. I'm at perfect peace.

I become aware of arms around my waist, and the smell of someone I've never smelled before. I know it's strange, but scent is important to me. I recognise people instantly by their scent, even with my eyes closed. So I know this scent is new. It's earthy and powerful, but in a good way.

I open my eyes and immediately go into shock. The intense blue eyes that smile down into my own, from behind a curtain of glossy and wild red-and-black hair, are familiar to me. Under normal circumstances, I would have panicked and run away, but this is different. I don't know why it's different, it just . . . is.

"Do you have any idea how beautiful you are?"

I was kind of thinking the same thing myself — not about me — but I'd never have said it, never in a million years. How dangerous would that have been? How dangerous is this?

I've stopped dancing, and so has he. We stare at each other. He's smiling and I'm not. I should move. I should move now . . . run . . . move . . . get away . . . get out of here . . . danger . . . Danger! But I don't move. I can't.

I'm going to faint. I can't breathe, and the lack of oxygen, along with the alcohol, is making me dizzy. I have to get away from here. Oh shit, something's happening, like wind rushing down a long tunnel. I can't escape. I close my eyes and try to steady myself. I knew this would happen, of course I did, but I didn't think it would be so soon. Still, with my eyes closed, I feel warm breath on my face, lips brushing mine. My eyes snap open in shock. A feeling of strangeness sweeps over me. I have to get out of here. I have to do it now.

I can't head for the door. The door is too far. I can't see anyone . . . anyone I know. Breaking away from him, I push through the dancing bodies, which are suddenly hostile, blocking my way when I have to . . . I have to . . . The toilets. They're close, and I can lock myself in a stall. I'll be okay when I'm on my own. It'll be okay if no one sees — if no one knows.

Why the hell are there so many people in here? Surely there shouldn't be so many people? It's wrong, all wrong. I'm finding it hard to breathe. It's so hot. I'm panicking. I know I am, and it's making everything worse, but I have to . . . I have to . . .

The door bursts open, slamming into the wall with the force of my thrust. There are a couple of people in the toilet. In the act, so to speak. They're startled by my explosive entrance. I head for a cubicle, but it's hard to see. There's a pounding pain in my left temple. I stumble and go down on one knee.

Someone calls my name, but it seems to be coming from a long way away. Someone puts their arms around me. I open my eyes and find myself gazing into vivid blue eyes. Then it all just . . . goes away.

I'm used to waking up in strange places, strange situations. Sometimes it's a hospital bed, but it isn't bad enough for that, not this time. My mouth is dry. I keep licking my lips, but it doesn't seem to be doing much good. Where's my drink? Didn't I have a drink? My head hurts. Something's telling me to open my eyes, but I'm in no hurry. It's nice here. It's warm and comfortable and . . . and . . . .

"What? Where am I?" I blink open my eyes and find I'm in a car. "Fuck." I turn my head. Why am I surprised to find myself looking into eyes that are rapidly becoming way too familiar? "How'd I get here? Where are you taking me?"

"I carried you," the warm chocolate voice states simply and mildly. "And I'm taking you home."

"How do you know where I live?"

"Your friend Carrie. She was concerned about you. She said she'll be round in the morning to check on you. She'll bring your coat."

It's the first time I realise I don't have my coat. That's the least of my worries. "Who the fuck are you?"

"No one. Just some guy you met in a bar, a guy who happened to be the designated driver tonight and to have a car parked nearby."

"I . . . Why? I'm not used to being picked up by strange men."

He chuckles. "Well, I'm not used to picking up strange men, so I guess that makes us even."

"Look . . . I'm not thinking clearly at the moment. I'm . . . I don't . . . I'm grateful and all but . . . ."

"But you just want me to drop you off and leave you the hell alone?"

"Yeah." I'm feeling too sick to be nice to him. The pain in my head's a bitch, and I can't be doing *nice* right now.

"We're nearly there, I think. Is it this block or the next?"

"The next. Just there, by the red car."

I'm extremely relieved when we pull up outside my

house. I open the door almost before the car stops. I freeze at the firm grip on my arm. I turn, shocked, and the boy smiles at me. "I'm Laurence ... Laurie ... and you honestly are very beautiful."

What does he expect? Why is he saying this to me? What does he want from me?

He must see something of my confusion in my eyes, because he lets go of my arm and smiles gently. "I'm not going to hurt you, you know. You seem so scared every time you look at me. I swear I'm not going to hurt you. But I *would* like ... I mean ... I *do* like you, despite your unfortunate tendency to run away. I'd like to see you again."

Fuck. No, not now. I can't cope with this now. I guess I've been lucky. Maybe my friends warn people off. Maybe my ... persona scares them away. But I haven't heard those words in a very long time. I shake my head.

"No. I ... I don't ... No. No."

I force my uncooperative legs out of the car and back away. I watch Laurie's face, with his blue eyes staring at me out of the open door. He looks surprised, shocked, disappointed? I turn to the house and take a step ... then ... then ... Oh shit. Not again.

CHAPTER TWO

It's the lights. I hate the lights — they're so bright. I don't like bright. I want to go back to my room. It's not bright in my room. It's dim and cool and safe. I don't want to be here. I don't want to talk. I don't want to think. I don't want to . . .

"Good morning, Gabriel. Are you going to be a good boy today? You weren't yesterday, were you?"

"I want to go home."

"All in good time. We have work to do today, and the sooner we get it done, the sooner you can go back to your room. One more day. Just one more day."

"Can I go home then?"

"We'll see. Relax now, Gabriel. You know it's easier when you relax. I'm going to give you an injection, and I want you to relax and let your mind open. Relax now, Gabriel. I'm going to start now. Remember to relax."

The lights. I hate the lights. I hate the lights. I hate them. I hate . . . I hate . . .

It's the screaming that wakes me every time. This time, though, it's different. The screaming is still there, the absolute panic. But this time I'm not alone. There's someone here with me. My housemates never come near when I'm screaming — they know better. It scares them. It scares me.

I prise open my eyes, and shock stops the screams. It almost stops my heart. I try to push him away, but he holds on. He's in my bed. He's . . . dressed, but I . . . I'm not. What the fuck happened last night? Was I that drunk?

"Get away from me."

"When you stop shaking."

"Fuck that. Get *away* from me."

I manage to push him back, and he stretches out like a cat, propping that head with its glorious hair on one hand.

"What the fuck are you doing here?"

"That's okay. I wasn't expecting thanks. Not from you."

"Thanks? What do I have to thank you for?"

"Well, I could have left you unconscious on your doorstep, but I thought you'd be more comfortable in bed."

"I . . . What? I . . . You undressed me?"

Laurie shrugs. "You threw up."

I groan. I'm not worried about passing out or throwing up—that's not unusual for me, especially after alcohol—but the thought someone saw it, saw me, and took off my clothes . . . I'm horrified. No one sees my body. No one.

"Get the fuck out of here."

"Just as well I wasn't expecting thanks, isn't it? Otherwise, I might be feeling crushed right now."

"I don't give a shit. Get the hell out of my room."

Laurie's face turns introspective. He reaches out and runs his finger over my arm. The touch sends shivers through me, and for a moment I freeze, staring at his hand. It's been a long time since anyone has touched me, especially there.

Stunned, I raise my eyes and gaze into the deep blue orbs. "Is it because of that?" he says softly. "It's all right. It doesn't bother me."

My heart is pounding. I'm overwhelmed. I can't cope with this. I shake my head. "Get out of my room. Get out . . . get out!" I'm acting unreasonable, but I can't help it. I'm getting hysterical, but I can't help that either. By the end, I'm screaming at him.

Looking completely shocked, he does what I ask.

I collapse back on my pillow, shaking . . . and not because

of the alcohol or the fits. What the hell just happened? No one, *no one*, sees me naked. No one sees. But Laurie . . . Laurie is . . . I turn onto my side and hug myself. I'm hardly aware of the tears until they overwhelm me, and I sob until I'm exhausted.

Eventually, the smells of coffee and bacon break through my self-inflicted misery coma and make me salivate. God, I'm hungry.

I get out of bed carefully. I have a pounding headache, and I think it's going to turn into one of those weird migraine-y things I've been having ever since . . . Ah well, I'll just get some coffee and maybe some toast. Then I'll come back to bed. I feel like I haven't slept in a week.

I glance at the clock. Seven-thirty. Shit. It's rare for one of the boys to be up at this time of the morning on a Sunday. To them, it's still the middle of the night. Unless . . . I smile. It'll be Andy then, coming home.

I pull on some pyjama bottoms and a long-sleeve t-shirt and stagger out onto the landing. Swaying, I lean against the wall for a moment to get my balance. Maybe Carrie's right, and I should stay away from the booze. Perhaps it would be better to go back to bed. My stomach rumbles and threatens to rebel. Maybe not.

After paying a visit to the bathroom to take care of business and swallow my meds, which lie like hot coals in my empty stomach, I carefully make my way down the stairs. God, my head hurts.

I open the kitchen door and have to grab the frame to stop myself from falling flat on my face in shock. It isn't Andy. Of course not. Why wasn't I expecting this? I should have expected this.

"I thought I told you to get out."

"Yeah, out of your room, not out of the house."

"Damn, I'll have to remember to be more explicit next

time."

"So, there's going to be a next time?" Laurie turns and smiles at me while putting two plates of bacon sandwiches on the table.

"No, I didn't . . . I never . . ." I'm confused now. Confusing me isn't difficult when I'm like this.

"Sit down. How do you like your coffee?"

"Black with no . . . no . . . sugar." Numbly, I sit down. Everything has taken on a surreal quality. I'm sitting in my kitchen, in my PJs, with a stranger who slept in my bed last night making breakfast. This doesn't happen to me. This never happens to me.

Automatically, I take a bite out of my sandwich. It tastes good. I peer at Laurie through narrowed eyes. Somehow, he seems to fit in my kitchen. He's cheerful, though. I can't take cheerful in the morning. He puts my coffee down, then sits and enthusiastically tackles his sandwich.

After a while, I glance up and catch him watching me. He has grease or butter on his chin. I wonder if he knows.

"What?" I ask irritably. My headache's not getting any better.

"You look like shit."

"Thanks," I say sarcastically.

"Seriously, though, you really do. I mean, you're still beautiful but—"

"Stop saying that," I snap.

"Saying what?"

"That I'm b-b-beautiful." Dammit. When my brain goes haywire, my speech goes to hell, and it drives me crazy.

"Why?"

"Because . . . because pe-people don't . . . d-don't say that to me."

"Why not? They should. You *are* beautiful."

"Stop. P-p-please do-don't." I stop, frustrated.

"What's the matter?"

"Nothing. Ju-just shut up and . . . and . . . and go."

"No," he says softly.

"Why are you . . . you tormenting me?"

He gazes at me for a moment, a soft expression in his eyes. "Because you aren't well, and I'd be a pretty poor knight in shining armour if I abandoned the damsel still in distress."

I stare at him. Did he just call me a girl? "A . . . d-damsel?"

"Figure of speech. All part of the metaphor. Don't worry, there's nothing remotely girly about you."

I swallow. The bacon suddenly tastes like cardboard. I'm utterly confused. There's something about Laurie—his calm confidence perhaps—that makes me feel . . . safe. His blue eyes are concerned, and cloudy like a stormy sea. They're darker than mine. Dark as the night sky, but definitely blue, completely blue.

"Gabriel?"

"Huh?" I tear my attention away from his eyes and blink at him.

"I asked if you're okay. You've stopped eating."

"I . . . I'm not . . . not . . . hungry any m-m-more." Damn. I hate this. It's the last thing I need right now. "Will you please go away now?"

"Is that what you want?"

I want to say *no*. It's been a long time since anyone's been there for me. Anyone who's been prepared to stick around when I . . . When . . ."Yes. Please just . . . just go."

Laurie looks disappointed, but he nods and gets up, taking his plate and mug to the sink. I should get up, too. I know this, but my mind won't let my body do what it needs to do to get there. I sigh and run my shaking hand through my hair. Ow, that hurts my head.

Cautiously, I manage to get to my feet and somehow follow him to the front door. The pain in my head's kicking up a notch and I'm getting that unreal feeling I know is going to explode into a full-scale Armageddon very soon. I have to get rid of him . . . and fast.

I practically throw him out the door, but before I can close it, he does something unthinkable. He turns and puts an arm around my waist. I freeze at the contact, which allows him to murmur, "Your friends warned me off, you know? Told me I'd be in a world of pain if I let myself get involved with you. But you know what? I think you're worth it."

Before I can say a word or make a move, he lowers his head and kisses me. It's just a brief touch, a gentle brush of his lips across mine, but it's enough. My whole body stiffens as my brain goes into hyper-drive. Sensations, feelings, lights, colours, and memories flood me.

Then my head explodes.

The pain is unbelievable. It paralyses me. I can't see, can't hear, can't scream. I'm locked in darkness, pain screaming through every fibre of my being. I hate them. I hate them for doing this to me — but I'm helpless.

The pain subsides slowly. First, the darkness becomes tinged with light — red and pulsing, burning me, blinding me — then fades to pink, then gold. I become hyper-aware of the beating of my heart and concentrate on that, holding on to the steady rhythm like a lifeline. It stops the spinning, stops the pain, and slowly draws me back. Then the same hypersensitivity that hit me with Laurie's kiss washes over me again. It swamps me, but if I lie very still and just let it flow through me, I know it'll stop soon and take most of the pain with it.

This hasn't happened for a long time, a really long time. Usually, it's just the headache. I take a deep breath and start to become aware of my body again. It feels heavy, but for some reason, I feel . . . safe. That's unusual.

As the light grows, I hear a voice call my name. At first, I think it's a voice from my dreams or from the past, but as I surface, it becomes more, not less, clear. Where the hell am I? Am I in bed? Oh hell, I hope I'm not in hospital again.

"Gabriel. Gabe . . . are you there? Can you hear me?"

Oh no . . . no . . . no. Not him. Anyone but him. For a while, I can't move, and I use the time to get royally pissed. Why won't he just go away?

"Because I'm worried about you."

Shit. Did I say that out loud? I open my eyes. The light stabs into my brain, but the pain is manageable now. At least I still have my clothes on this time. He reaches out his hand, and I shrink away.

"No. Don't touch me."

"I'm sorry, Gabriel. I–I didn't mean . . . Are you all right? I was so scared. If you hadn't come 'round soon, I would've called an ambulance. You've been out for ages. You were barely breathing. What the fuck happened? That wasn't a seizure. You were screaming."

"No. Not . . . it wasn't . . . I don't . . . It . . . happens sometimes. Sensory overload. It's part of it."

"Part of what? What the hell's wrong with you, Gabriel? Does this happen often?"

"I . . . Sometimes," I say defensively.

His hand is shaking as it reaches for mine. I jerk my hand away. It would be a very, very bad idea to let him touch me now.

"Is it something to do with what happened to you? When you . . . when you got hurt?"

I'm terrified. He's going down a road I haven't walked in years, and I'm walking it barefoot on glass. I wrap my arms around myself and whisper, "Go. Please go."

He stares at me for a moment. I'm shaking again. He

looks as if he wants to put his arms around me, but I draw back.

He sighs, looking so sad. Then he gets up and walks to the door. When he gets there, he turns.

"I don't know what happened to you, Gabriel. I know it must have been bad and you're still hurting. I don't want to push you. I won't ask you about it, but if you ever want to talk, I'll be here."

Then he's gone.

I lie down on the bed, covering my eyes with my arm. The light hurts. I'm so tired. This always wipes me. I can't keep my eyes open. I can't stay awake.

When I open my eyes it's dark, I sense someone in the room with me.

"Gabe?"

"Laurie?"

"No. It's me, Bobby."

I groan and sit up, blinking at my housemate. "Wassup?"

"Carrie's here. She brought your coat."

My first reaction is that I don't want to go down. I want to curl up and go back to sleep. My head feels better, but I'm exhausted, totally washed out. I don't feel up to the guilt trip. But then I sigh and give way to the inevitable. It's Carrie.

Carrie's waiting anxiously in the living room. She seems so small. When she sees me, she gets up and runs to me, throwing her arm around me, then steps back, embarrassed. She lowers her head, and I scuff the carpet with my shoe, not wanting to look at her.

"You okay?"

"Yeah."

"You sure?"

She looks up and meets my eyes for the first time. Carrie

would never call me out, not overtly. She wouldn't even mention the alcohol or the fact that she'd told me not to drink. But it's there in her eyes.

"I'm sorry, Carrie. I should've listened to you. I shouldn't have got drunk last night. I knew what was going to happen. I've been ill since Thursday. That's why I did it. I just wanted . . . I wanted to be . . ."

"Normal?"

I shake my head. That isn't it. That isn't it at all. If I wanted to be normal, would I dress the way I do, paint my face, pierce my body? No, it wasn't about being normal, not at all. I look directly in her eyes. "No. Free."

"Oh, Gabe, why do you do this to yourself? You look so . . . so . . ." She lifts her hand to my face. "I'm scared for you, Gabe. Last night was . . . Last night was awful. If it hadn't been for that man . . . You were . . . You were . . ."

I can't help but smile. "Just say what you mean, Carrie. I look like crap and made a major fool of myself last night spazzing out in the middle of the club."

"That's not what I mean. You know that's not what I mean. No one gives a damn about that, but they do give a damn about you. I was half frantic not knowing. I wanted to come with you but that boy . . ."

"Laurie."

She gives me a strange look. "I never caught his name."

"You warned him off me though." I can't help but smile at the expression of horror on her face.

"Um. He seemed . . . he seemed a bit . . . and I thought . . . He . . . You wouldn't . . ."

"Carrie, since when have you not been able to tell me anything, and by that, I mean everything?"

Carrie laughs. "I know. It's just that he seemed . . ."

"What? Freaky? Creepy?"

"Into you."

I'm completely shocked. Of all the things I'd expected her to say, this was about the last. "You warned him off because he was into me?"

"No. I warned him off because I know what happens when someone tries to get close to you."

"You do?" I raise my eyebrow.

"Yes, I do. I've watched it happen, and I don't want to watch it again."

"Watched what happen?"

"You. Slowly destroying both of you."

"What?"

"Tell me it isn't true, Gabriel. Tell me that's not what happened to Daniel and Michael."

"I . . ." I can't look at her because I know she's right. I loved them both, in different ways, but love nevertheless. They both tried so hard. Danny was my boyfriend before I . . . When we were kids. When I . . . When it was over, and I came back, we picked it up, and it was good for a while. Then I went off the rails and pulled him down with me. He was a great kid, full of fun and fire, and I destroyed him. As far as I know, he's still in the hell I created for him. I haven't seen him for years.

Michael, on the other hand, was as dark as I was in his own way. I met him in the mental hospital I was sent to—no, committed to—when I had my *breakdown*. He was schizophrenic but great fun. We had good times together until he fell in love with me. He wanted to share my pain. He tried to get close to me, wanted me to let him in. But there are some places no one goes, not even me. He took it very personally, and it hurt him badly. He didn't survive my love.

I sigh deeply and sink down on the chair, my head in my hands. I want to curl up in a corner, with walls on either side, enclosing me, protecting me. I want to hide in a deep dark hole. I want to crawl into a coffin and bury myself deep. I want this to be over. I want this hell to be over. I want to be me again, and if I can't, I don't want to . . . be.

"Did I do the right thing?"

"I don't know. I don't know anything at the moment. I'm just tired."

"I know, hun. I can see it. I hated to leave you last night. I was worried, but he . . . uh . . . Laurie was so adamant he was going to take you home and you'd be okay. But you weren't okay, were you?"

I hadn't meant to say anything. I know she worries, but I shake my head before I have a chance to do anything about it. Then there wasn't anything else I could say. "No."

"Did you have another seizure?"

"Yes."

"More than one?"

"No but . . . I . . . my headache."

She knows all about my headaches. She's nursed me through quite a few.

"Ah hell, Gabe. I shouldn't have left you alone. I can't bear to think of you going through that alone."

"I didn't," I whisper. "I wasn't alone."

"What do you mean?"

"He . . . he stayed with me."

"That boy? He stayed here?"

I nod awkwardly.

"But why?"

Now there's the question. "He said . . . he said it . . . it was because I'm worth it."

Chapter Three

I don't know quite what hurts so much. I don't know if it's the words I said, or the memory of the feelings I'd had, or the knowledge I probably won't see Laurie again. Whatever it is, it hits me like a brick, and I slide off the chair onto the floor sobbing, barely aware of Carrie throwing herself to her knees and taking me into her arms.

"Oh, Gabe, Gabe. Why do you do this to yourself? Why do you keep on hurting yourself? I'm scared for you, Gabe. You're getting worse again, and I'm scared."

I can't speak. Not only because I'm beyond speech but because she's right. The decline has been gradual, so gradual I've barely noticed it, but it's been happening nevertheless. The listlessness, the headaches, the attacks, the depression . . . they've all been getting worse, and I've been hiding it, even from myself.

I'm not scared, not of this. Why would I be afraid? I want the pain to stop. I want the dreariness to end. I want to die. It's taken a long time to admit that. Even when I was living it, I didn't admit it.

"I don't care."

"Gabe, you have to care. You have to. There are people who love you. Love you so much. You keep pushing them away, but they still love you. They want to be there for you. I want to be there for you. I love you, Gabe. I've always loved you. I know you can never love me back, not in the way I'd like, but that doesn't stop me loving you. I'd do anything for you. If I could take away your pain, I would, even if it meant that I had to take it on myself."

I look up at her, feeling exhausted, and try to make sense of what she's saying. "You . . . you love me?"

"Always."

"Oh."

"Is that all you're going to say? Oh?"

"What do you want me to say? You're my best friend, Carrie." I laugh bitterly. "Almost my only friend. I love you, too, but . . . not . . ."

She smiles brightly and rests her cool hand against my hot face. "I know that, hun. I've always known it, and it's okay. I just want what's best for you. I want to help you."

"No one can help me," I whisper.

"They might be able to if you just opened up a little. You're so . . . shut in. We can't help you if you won't let us. Please, Gabe, let me in. Talk to me."

"Talk? I'm too tired to talk. Just so tired. And even if I wasn't, what could I talk about? No one knows the truth about me. No one. How can I talk to anyone about the way I feel, about the things that are eating away at me inside, when there's a huge part of it that I can't talk about? Not don't want to . . . can't?"

"That's bullshit, Gabe. If you want to, you can."

I shake my head. "I can't." I sound as exhausted as I feel. I can barely keep my eyes open. I rest my head on her shoulder. I think she gets the message, because she stops talking and just strokes my hair until I fall asleep.

When I wake up, I'm lying on the settee and Carrie's gone. There's no way she could have got me up here, so one of the boys must have helped her. I feel bad about what she said. I know she loves me. I know she wants to help me. I know it hurts her when I shut her out, but it's so much better than the alternative.

I'm dangerous—dangerous to myself and dangerous to

everyone around me. Dragging myself to my feet, I haul my sorry ass to my bedroom and am asleep almost before my head hits the pillow.

It's Wednesday, and I'm going out. I haven't been outside the door since Saturday, and I'm getting stir crazy. On Wednesdays and Fridays, I take an art class at the university. It's not just about painting. It's about art history and art appreciation, too. We have regular field trips to galleries and showings. In the summer, we're going to Paris. They're going to Paris. I haven't decided if I'm going to go yet. I want to, but for me, it isn't that easy. Paris feels too exposed. I won't feel safe there.

It's very cold. I thrust my hands into my pockets. It's one of those winter days when there's frost on the ground and a deep blue sky above. There's a kind of brittle silence in the air that makes you feel as if all your senses have expanded, and you occupy all the space around you. It's an opening up day, not a closing down one, like the dreary, miserable, rainy days that have become the norm recently.

Although I appreciate the clarity, the purity of the day, my mood would better have matched a dreary, rainy one. I've pretty much shaken off the physical effects of the weekend, but the depression and fear cling to me like a bad smell I'm not able to shake.

Since Sunday, Carrie's stayed away. I think she's embarrassed. I should have called her, I would have only . . . She was right in everything she said. I do shut people out. I do push them away. I do hurt them. It would be better if I drove them away altogether. Then I wouldn't keep hurting them. Why do they keep coming back? Why don't they just get the message and stay away from me?

I'm in a gloomy mood as I climb the steps into the main university building. There've been many times when I've walked up these steps and wholly appreciated the beauty of the architecture—the Gothic arches over the windows, the delicate columns, and the deep red colour of the stones. Not today. Today I'm too wrapped up in myself to notice anything.

The art class is on the second floor. The building has been extensively refurbished, and the inside shows none of the architectural beauty of the outer shell. It's all about chrome and glass, corners and edges. Still, it's light and airy, and if it doesn't lift my mood, at least it doesn't darken it.

We're going to be sketching today. I like sketching. It's in preparation for a painting. We're putting on an exhibition at the end of the term at a local art gallery. They're making a room available just for us. It should be an exciting prospect, but it's hard to get excited about anything these days. I love to paint, but it's all about losing myself in the work. What happens after the painting's completed doesn't interest me at all.

There's a lift up to the second floor, but I seldom take it. I like to climb the stairs. They're a distraction. I'm not particularly fit, but two flights of stairs are nothing to me. I could run up if I wanted to. Sometimes, if I'm feeling scared and frantic and on edge, I do. But today I'm down, not manic.

It's been suggested that I'm bipolar. I have to smile at that. It's also been suggested that I'm schizophrenic, but they're wrong there, too. The doctors have proposed a lot of things to explain why I am like I am. They don't have a cat's chance in hell of getting it right. It's true there are times when I'm up and times when I'm down, times when I'm lethargic and times when I'm manic. What they don't realise is that they equate to the times when I remember and times when I forget. I just take what medication they give me and hope for the best. I know it won't help. None of it will help, except maybe to make me numb for a while.

I usually have the headaches and fits when I'm in a manic phase, so I should be okay today. I've never had an episode in art class . . . not of anything. I feel safe here, relaxed, calm. I'm relaxed and smiling by the time I reach the correct corridor and enter the familiar room.

The easels have been pushed back against the wall. We don't use them when we're sketching. The chairs are set in a semi-circle around the central podium. Some of the students are already here. They smile and nod in greeting. The teacher is setting up items on the podium.

"I thought we were going to be sketching a model today?" one of the students, a lecherous old bag who only comes to class so she can ogle the young men, pipes up.

"Unfortunately, our model fell ill, so we're going to have to make it a still life. If we leave it another week before we start the sketches, it won't give us enough time to properly work on the paintings. You're going to try out different mediums until you find the one that suits you and the painting, and that will take time. There are only three months until the exhibition, and that doesn't give us as much time as you think. Especially when you factor in our visits to the museums and galleries that I've scheduled for you to study form."

I have to admit to being disappointed when I look at the motley selection of articles set up on the podium. They singularly fail to inspire me.

"I'll do it." A voice speaks up from the doorway. I freeze and can't turn around—couldn't if my life depended on it. I know that voice.

"I beg your pardon?"

"I'll model. I intended to join the class to paint, but I reckon I can do my work and pose for it at the same time."

The voice is like melted chocolate and seduces the teacher instantly. I can tell by the blush on her face and the stammer in her voice.

"I . . . um . . . I don't usually take students in the middle of a term."

"Oh, I'm not a novice. I brought my portfolio."

He walks past me to the front of the class. I keep my eyes firmly fixed on my sketchbook, which I've taken out of my bag and perched on my knees.

"Oh, my . . . these are very good . . . very good indeed. I think you're a little too advanced for this class."

"Not at all. There's always something to learn, and I just love to paint. I've never had any formal training, and I haven't done any art appreciation or history, which I'm very much looking forward to studying. In the meantime, I'm happy to pose for your class. I've done it before."

"We . . . erm . . . I was planning for . . ."

"When I offered, I assumed it would be nude. I don't have a problem with my body. I'd be happy to show it if you're all happy to sketch it. I can always use a mirror later on to do my own sketches."

The teacher giggles nervously, and I choke down the urge to scream.

I sit like a statue until I sense someone sitting next to me. I don't have to look up to know who it is.

"What the hell are you doing here?" I growl.

"Apparently posing for a painting."

I raise my head and glare at him. "You know what I mean. What the fuck do you think you're doing? Didn't you get the message?"

"Did you leave me a message?" he says smoothly, a twinkle in his eyes. "Sorry, I didn't pick it up."

"Have you been stalking me?"

"Only in a manner of speaking."

"What manner of speaking?"

"Oh, you know, the one where I hang around on street

corners with a sandwich board and a picture of you saying *have you seen this boy?*"

I stare at him. Is he serious? He grins and starts to laugh. I can't help but join. He has a very infectious laugh.

"Seriously, what are you doing here?"

"Your friend told me you come here, so I enrolled in the class. I wasn't actually planning on posing, but I'm never one to miss an opportunity."

"So, you *are* stalking me."

"I suppose I am." He feigns surprise, and I laugh again. "Why?"

He shrugs. "Pick a reason . . . because you fascinate me, because you're beautiful, because I was worried about you, or because there hasn't been a minute since Sunday when I haven't thought about you." He pauses and looks up at me through the tumbling mass of his hair. "Because after I kissed you the only thing I've been able to think about is kissing you again."

I stare at him, lost in the depths of his deep blue eyes, which are only a few shades darker than the sky I can see through the window. Then I shake my head. "It isn't going to happen."

"Why not?"

"Because —"

We're interrupted by the lecturer, who coughs nervously at Laurie's shoulder. "We're ready. If you're sure?"

"That's fine. I'll be right there."

The lecturer smiles and walks away. Laurie turns to me with an intense expression in his eyes. "Have a drink with me after class . . . a coffee," he specifies.

"I don't . . ."

"My treat."

"But . . ."

He doesn't give me a chance to say *no* because, grinning,

he gets to his feet and saunters away.

The lecturer leads Laurie behind a screen in the corner of the room, then leaves him to prepare as she settles down the class, which is now full. When everyone's fairly settled, she calls to Laurie, and he strolls out completely unconcerned. He steps up onto the podium to a chorus of gasps and murmured comments. As I suspected, Laurie has an incredible body, not too muscular, but nicely defined, with a firm six-pack and tight, rounded buttocks.

When he's been arranged in a reasonably comfortable position by the lecturer, he freezes. He's truly spectacular, with his beautiful body and the shocking spill of multi-coloured hair pouring over one shoulder. My stomach feels tight and unsettled, and I briefly consider getting up and walking away, but I can't. Who am I kidding? From the moment I heard his voice, I knew I wouldn't be leaving without him.

After staring at Laurie's body for far too long, memorising every curve, every line, every . . .

"Gabriel. That's wonderful work, the best I've seen you do."

"It is?" I glance down at the sketch pad I didn't even know my pencil had touched. It is.

Blinking, I look up at Laurie again. He winks at me.

The lecturer has Laurie take up two different positions before the end of the class so everyone can have three sketches to choose from for their final work. I'm pleased with all my drawings, but the latter two just don't have the passion of the first. Satisfied with my work at least, I pack away my sketchbook while Laurie disappears behind the screen to get dressed.

"Don't forget that on Friday we're going to the museum to study the way the Masters have treated the human body, and to consider medium and style. Would you all please gather outside the museum at six o'clock with your sketchbooks? Thank you. Good class, people."

Laurie comes out from behind the screen, still looking unruffled and cool. He's immediately surrounded by students and the teacher. He gives me an apologetic glance over their heads, and suddenly I panic. Grabbing my bag, I head out of the room.

I walk fast and don't look back. My heart's pounding and I can't breathe. Getting outside is my only focus. When the cold air hits me, I realise I left my coat inside in my rush to get the hell out of there. Oh well, I'll walk fast and warm up.

I get to the gates, and a wave of dizziness sweeps over me. I grab a pillar to steady myself. I know it doesn't have a physical source. It comes from the panic, the overwhelming feeling of wrongness, of unworthiness, of self-loathing. If only he knew. If only he knew about me, he'd be the one running, but there's something about him, something I've never seen before, never felt before. I'm so torn. I want to run, but I'm not sure in which direction.

It's so cold. I'm going to have to start moving soon, or I'll freeze where I stand. I have a headache starting. It's not one of the big ones, but all the same . . . I'm starting to feel sick, and I know that doesn't have a physical cause either.

I push myself off the pillar and start walking down the street. I hear running footsteps behind. Then someone falls into step beside me. I almost pass out. Why didn't I move faster? Why didn't I run? Because I didn't want to. Because I was hoping, even as I was dreading and fearing.

"You left your coat behind," he says at last.

It's what he doesn't say with words, but with the tone of his voice, that hits me like a brick.

"Thanks," I mumble, not stopping.

"Don't you want to put it on?"

"I'm not cold."

"Dude, you're turning blue. I'd rather not have to carry

you home again."

I'm not cold now, I'm boiling. Anger slices through me like a knife, but I keep it in check. Pausing, I take the coat and slip it on, taking my time fastening the buttons. While I'm doing it, I sense him watching me. When I'm done, I turn and carry on walking. Laurie falls into step beside me.

"There's a nice cafe just up ahead. Would it kill you to let me buy you a coffee?"

"No thanks."

"What about the pub, then? You don't have to drink. You can have a *Coke*, although I think they sell coffee there, too."

"No."

"Well, how about you buy me a coffee, then? To say thank you for rescuing you the other day."

"I didn't ask you to." I'm getting angry again. If he thinks I owe him . . .

"Whoa. No need to snap my head off. I was only joking. You don't owe me anything. I'd do it again in a moment."

I stop and turn to look at him. He's smiling at me, but there's something more than a smile in his eyes. He means what he's saying.

"Why?"

He seems slightly shocked. "Well, for one because it's what anyone would do for someone in trouble. And for two, I . . ." He pauses and smiles gently. "I'm captivated by your awesome beauty and your intriguing personality."

He smiles brightly, but the way he said those words, he isn't joking. For a moment I'm stunned, and something stirs around my heart, something warm, but I slam down on it. What am I thinking?

"I told you not to say that." I carry on walking. He carries on following.

"I'm anarchistic. I never listen to anything or do anything unless I want to."

"Well, neither do I."

"I know. That's why I like you so much."

"Fuck off."

"Nope. Not listening. Look, I don't know what it is with you. I don't know what you're scared of or what's eating you up inside, but hell, Gabriel, all I'm asking for is one drink. One coffee. Half an hour out of your life. Would it kill you?"

Would it kill me? He has no idea. Maybe it would kill us both . . . slowly. But he . . . I glance at him out of the corner of my eye. He knows I'm looking, and he knows he's won. I sigh and shrug. "One drink. But it's not going to be a *Coke*."

Chapter Four

The pub is busy for a Wednesday. It's not packed, though, and we easily get a seat in a dim and secluded corner. Laurie leaves me there and goes for the drinks. The crowd seems to part for him. He has this air about him—not swagger or arrogance, but a kind of grace and self-confidence—that's as repelling to some people as it is attractive to others.

What the hell am I doing here? The urge to get up and walk out is strong, but the urge to stay is stronger . . . for now. I'm afraid to explore my feelings for him because, quite frankly, they scare the hell out of me. I'm honest enough to admit to myself that I'm attracted to him, very attracted, and that's part of the problem.

He has the face of an angel and the body to go with it. Thinking about his body makes me feel hot, literally. I fan my face with a beer mat. He has a body to kill or die for. But that's not it. Okay, it's part of it, but not *it*. He has this way about him, a golden light that surrounds him and spills out of his eyes . . . oh God, those beautiful eyes.

Thinking about his eyes makes me shiver, and the ghost of a smile passes over my lips, as much for my poetic turn of thought as anything else. I'm the least fluffy person I know, and here I am thinking thoughts like *a golden light that surrounds him and spills out of his eyes*. What the hell am I thinking? I know what I'm thinking about. I'm thinking about his eyes.

No. I can't. I can't think about his eyes. I can't think about *him*, not in that way. My track record with boyfriends is appalling — one dead and one who might as well be. Loving me is poison. But . . .

"Here you go. JD and *Coke*. I was determined to get you drinking *Coke* whether you wanted to or not. I know you won't waste a perfectly good JD just because of a little *Coke*."

I stare at him, confused.

He grins. "I can be very single-minded when I want to be."

"I've noticed," I say sarcastically.

Laurie is unperturbed. "But you love it."

I open my mouth to say something but close it again at the self-mocking gleam in his eyes. I turn away and take a sip of my drink, leaning back into the shadows.

"Can I see your drawings?"

"What?" I almost choke on my *Coke*.

"The sketches you made of me today. Can I see them?"

"No."

"Why not?"

"I . . . They . . . they're private." I frown deeply. It's strange. I feel as if he's asking me to expose myself, but he's the one who was exposed today.

"You show me yours, and I'll show you mine."

"What?" My eyes widen until I see him patting his portfolio case. I smile with relief.

"Wow."

"What?" His eyes are wide, and it's hard to concentrate on anything else. In here, in the dimness, they're a more concentrated blue. They remind me of the sky at night, when there's a full moon and it's not completely dark. They are . . .

"You should smile more often. It suits you. You have very beautiful eyes, and they light up when you smile."

"Don't." I wince, covering my embarrassment by rummaging in my bag for my sketchbook.

"Why do you do that?"

"Do what?"

"Get upset when someone tells you that you're beautiful. Or is it only me you get upset with?"

"No. It's . . . It's just because I'm not."

"Well, we'll have to agree to differ on that point, but even so . . . Why does it matter whether you are or you're not? To me you are. That's my perspective, my right. I can believe you're beautiful if I want to. Most people, whether they're beautiful or not, like to be told they are sometimes. Especially by someone who means it." He regards me thoughtfully over the top of his pint, making me feel very uncomfortable. "But you . . . It's almost as if it hurts you."

I'm getting more and more uncomfortable and irritated as the conversation progresses. If only he knew. If only he could see how ugly I am on the inside. Corrosive—like acid, eating away at my soul and contaminating anyone who touches me.

"I just don't like it, that's all." I shove my sketch pad into his hands, hoping it'll distract him. He gives me a long look, then starts flicking through the book. When he comes to the ones of himself, he examines them more closely, more slowly.

"Some of these are very good. This one, in particular, captures the moment well. It has movement." It's the first one I'd done that morning, and I'm glad he likes it. "It might not be technically perfect, but with a bit of work, it could be very good. You've got real passion, and it comes out in your work."

I'm stung. Who the fuck is he to criticise my work? *Not technically perfect! Needs some work!* What gives him the right to be so condescending? I snatch my book out of his hands and stuff it back into my bag. "Your turn," I snap.

Looking startled and a little guilty, he opens his portfolio and spreads some sketches and finished paintings on the table. I stare at them in shock. If I'd seen these first, I'd never have shown him mine. I feel sick.

"Why the fuck did you join a poxy little art class? You could be a professional."

He looks a little uncomfortable. "I am."

"What?"

"I am a professional. I'm an illustrator. I have my own business. I've recently gone into partnership with a friend in a small gallery. That's why we were out Saturday night, celebrating our opening."

"Then . . . then why did you join the class?"

"Well . . . for one thing, I wasn't lying about the fact that art appreciation and history interest me. I truly think that examining other people's work—the Masters, you know, their technique, mediums and stuff—will be good for my own work."

"And the other?" Damn, why'd I say that? Why'd I have to ask? It's not as if I don't know the answer.

"Is because there's an angel in the class," he murmurs softly. "And it's not too often you're touched by an angel."

I shake my head reflexively, feeling sick, but he's got me by the eyes, and I can't look away. Slowly, he moves closer. Although I'm panicking like crazy, I'm caught like a deer in headlights. I can't move. I'm utterly frozen as he leans forward, closer and closer, until our lips touch.

This time there's no information overload. I'm not hypersensitive and wide open. But still, the touch of his lips and his hand on my waist, the earthy smell of his cologne . . . My eyes flutter closed, and I couldn't move if my life depended on it.

When his tongue begs entrance, I let my lips part, but I don't respond. I can't. My whole body is rigid and shaking. My heart is pounding, but it's with fear and not passion. Laurie seems to know the score. He doesn't draw back or get pissed with me for my lack of response or take it personally. He doesn't push me or try to overwhelm me. He just kisses me . . . gently.

When Laurie breaks the kiss, I remain frozen, with my eyes closed as I struggle to bring myself back under control. My eyes fly open when his hand brushes my hair and touches my cheek. I wince and turn my eyes away.

"Oh, Gabriel," he says softly. "Beautiful Gabriel, what are you so afraid of? You're the most beautiful boy I've ever set my eyes on, but you seem to hate yourself. Why? What's hurt you so badly?"

"You . . . you promised." It comes out like a groan, and now it's Laurie who flinches. He drops his hand, and I take a large swig of my drink. Damn, the glass is empty, and I need more. When I get to my feet, Laurie looks up, startled, as if he's expecting me to run away. I won't deny I'm thinking about it.

"I need another drink. Do you want one?"

Smiling with relief, he drains the last of his drink and hands me his glass. It's such a relief to get away from him. The intensity is killing me . . . literally. My head's hurting like crazy, and I want to go home and lie down. The thought of running is appealing, but something's holding me back. I'm sick of feeling sick.

At the bar, I knock back a double JD, no *Coke*, knowing it's a bad idea and not caring. I'm in that very familiar vicious cycle. Switch off mind — commence self-destruct sequence.

As I stand patiently waiting for my second JD and Laurie's pint, someone grabs my bum. The *brain-off-self-destruct-on* impulse goes into overdrive, as I turn and strike at the same time. The man, who fortunately I don't know, goes down like a sack of potatoes, but unfortunately, he's not alone.

I'm grabbed from behind as someone punches me in the

stomach. Suddenly, the red mist descends. I'm out of control. I know I'm out of control, but sometimes there's nothing I can do about it, and this is one of them. I completely flip, and the bar explodes around me.

At some point, the fight bursts out of the front door, and that suits me. I can be deadly when I have room to move. But someone grabs me from behind, pinning my arms to my sides. I can break the hold easily enough, but something stops me, something cutting through the mist.

"Gabriel, calm down. Gabriel. It's okay. You're okay. It's me."

It's the name that does it. No one calls me Gabriel, no one except . . ."Laurie?"

"Yeah. Is it safe to let you go now?"

"Yeah."

I stagger when he lets go. He steers me to the side and leans me against the wall.

"Are you safe there for a minute while I go get our stuff?"

I nod dumbly. Now that the red mist is passing and the adrenaline fading from my system, I feel exhausted, not to mention battered. I half collapse against the wall and raise my hand to touch my cheek, which hurts. I wince. I'm going to have a bruise there tomorrow. My ribs are sore, too. My hands are the worst, though. Shit, I must've really laid into someone. My knuckles are bleeding. Oh, great . . . and this evening started so well. I have a gift for being sarcastic even to myself.

Laurie appears in the doorway with our bags and coats. He looks anxious. "Come on. We'd better—" But he doesn't get to finish the sentence because five somewhat battered and very angry men come spilling out behind him.

"Fucking freaks." They spit in our direction. "You wait. We're going to rip your fucking heads off."

One of them pushes Laurie, and he stumbles. The red

mist rises again, and I shove off from the wall to run head-long at them . . . only to find myself swinging round to slam face first into the wall. It isn't a hard blow, but unexpected, and it winds me. An arm across my back pins me to the rough brickwork.

"I think you'd better get the hell out of here before I let him go."

"Fucking freak. He's a psycho."

"Maybe he just doesn't like being sexually assaulted."

"What the fuck?"

"I saw exactly what happened, and if you don't get the hell out of here right now, I'm going to call the police and see what they have to say."

I wish I could see their faces, although maybe that wouldn't be such a good idea right now.

Amid grumbles of *freak* and *faggots,* the voices recede and a sweeter one speaks gently, close to my ear. "For the second time tonight . . . is it safe to let you go?"

He doesn't sound pissed or shocked. In fact, he sounds amused. I nod, and he steps back, releasing me.

"I'm sorry about that. I didn't mean to hurt you, but I didn't want you to flip again. Someone would've called the police, and you might have got into trouble."

"Do you think I give a fuck about that?" I retort. I try to push his arm away. He steps in again and touches my face where I can feel the bruise emerging.

"Does it hurt?"

"No."

"Liar," he says huskily, leaning forward to kiss the spot. I go stiff, just as I did before, my heart pounding. The adrena-line that had made me high is pumping through me again. I'd done the *fight,* and now the *flight* was calling me.

"Come on." He takes me firmly by the hand and drags me around the corner into an alley next to the pub. He slams me into the wall and pins me there with his body. I panic and try to struggle, but my ribs hurt and I'm tired and . . . and . . . it's not as if I want to. It's not like I don't want him to . . .

Laurie ignores my struggles and lowers his face to mine. I can't help it. I let my head fall back until it hits the wall. My eyes close on their own, my lips part, and my body moves to mould itself to his. It must be shock from the fight, but suddenly I'm flooded with . . . with . . . something. No longer am I frozen, frightened, and unresponsive. I'm hungry . . . starved . . . desperate.

Throwing my arms around Laurie's neck, I pull him into me and kiss him violently, while grinding my body against his. He's trembling, breathing hard, and I . . . I am. I. Am . . .

"No. Stop."

I cling to Laurie, but he firmly pushes me away. "Stop, Gabriel."

"But . . . I thought . . . I thought you . . ."

"I do. You have no idea how much I do, but this is all wrong. When I kiss you, and you kiss me back, I want to be sure it's because you want to kiss *me* and not because you're desperate and shaken and shocked and just clinging to anyone. I don't want you to do something tonight that you'll regret tomorrow."

"But I . . . but I . . ."

"No, Gabriel. It doesn't feel right. You're shocked and hurt and . . . I'd be taking advantage of you, and I won't do that. Come on, I'll take you home."

If I was shocked before, it's nothing to what I am now. I'm so confused. He's been pursuing me for days. He's the one who kissed me. He's the one who pulled me into the alley, then . . . then . . . What did I do?

Suddenly, I know. I know what I did. I let myself care. I should've known. If it seems like it's too good to be true, then it usually is. It's better this way. It's better if he hurts me before I hurt him. I deserve it, and he doesn't.

Fortunately, my house isn't far. By the time we get there, my head's pounding, my ribs are sore, and my cheek and eye are throbbing. I'm beginning to think I won't make it. My head's spinning.

"I think it'd be better if you went in alone. I'll see you in art class on Friday."

I hang my head and nod. He can't wait to get away from me. Who'd blame him? I'm not pretty when I lose control. I expect he hates me now. There's no way he'll be coming to art class again, no matter what he says. Why would he?

"Gabriel."

"What?"

"Look at me, Gabriel."

"I can't." I turn to fit the key in the lock, but Laurie catches my arm and turns me around.

"Look at me," he repeats gently.

I can't. I can't bear to see the expression in his eyes—the shame, the disgust, the regret. Laurie puts a finger under my chin and tilts my head up. He smiles as my gaze crawls up to meet his. He's not frowning, and he doesn't look disgusted.

"Gabriel. Don't do this."

"What?"

"Don't convince yourself the reason I wouldn't kiss you, and . . . take it further was that I don't like you, or you're not worth it. The only way I was able to control myself at all was because I care for you so much that when I kiss you, I want to know you're kissing me back because you want *me.* Not just some desperate comfort that could come from anyone. I'm not going to give up on you, Gabriel."

Laurie brushes my sore cheek with his fingers, then leans in for a last gentle, sweet kiss before he lets me go and walks away.

I stand for a long time staring after him. I want to believe it. I want to believe him. Can it be that he really does see something in me? He did go to a lot of trouble to find me. He kissed me . . . twice. Then he . . . left me.

But he left me because he cares about me. But if he cares for me, he wouldn't leave me. And why do I care anyway? Because I don't care about him. Laurie isn't real. I'm falling for a dream, and dreams hurt. He's going to hurt me, and I hope he does it before I hurt him. He's so sweet and gentle and pure—everything I'm not. I can't allow him to sink into the black hole around my heart. I'd rather die.

My head hurts. There's too much pounding around in there. My cheek and ribs hurt, and my hands are beginning to swell. I feel wretched. I just want to crawl into bed and stay there. But I can't move. I'm just standing here looking after him, feeling his kiss on my lips, and watching him slowly disappearing.

CHAPTER FIVE

It's ridiculous, I know, but . . . well . . . it's Friday, and I'm excited. I'm like a teenage girl about to have her first date. I've spent all day getting ready. I'm putting the finishing touches to my makeup when Andy sticks his head around the door.

"I thought you were going to an arty place."

"The museum."

"Wow. Do you always dress up so much to go look at dusty old books and broken china?"

"Not always, no."

"So, what's so special about today, then?"

"Nothing."

Trying to ignore him, I brush my hair and fasten some silver bracelets around my wrist, over the leather straps. I never go out without straps around my wrists. They make me feel safe. They hide a lot.

"Is there any particular reason why you're lounging in my doorway, watching me get dressed?"

"Maybe."

"You should've brought your camera. Then you wouldn't have had to stand there for so long."

"It's more fun watching you preen."

"Watching me what?"

"You know . . . preen. Like birds do, fluffing out their feathers."

"Yeah, right."

"You're not going to wear those, are you?" he says as I

pull on my boots.

"Why not? What's wrong with them?"

"You're going to a museum. You'll scare the dinosaurs out of their cases."

"They don't have dinosaurs in cases."

"Okay, then. Give the curator a heart attack, whatever. But don't you think you're going a little overboard for a museum? Even I'm scared of you."

"I'm not scary."

"Well, I know that, but anyone who doesn't know what a pussycat you are is going to run for the hills when they see you. Why do you have to be so . . . obvious?"

I shrug. "It's the way I am, the way I've always been."

"Not always." There's something strange in his voice. I look up sharply.

"What do you mean?"

"When we were kids, before . . . before you . . . When we were kids, you were just like everyone else."

For a moment, I stare at him. Andy and I have history. We go back a long way. I smile. "Who wants to be like everyone else?"

"You have a point. Are you ready yet?"

"Almost, why?"

"No reason." He shrugs. "I just thought your friend might be getting bored waiting for you."

"My friend? Laurie? Laurie's here?"

Andy smiled and shrugs.

"How long's he been here?"

"A while. That's what I was coming up to tell you."

"Then why didn't you tell me?"

"Because I like messing with you. It's so much more fun."

"Git."

Laughing, I throw a screwed-up tissue at him, and he ducks out of the door. I'm suddenly incredibly nervous.

How stupid is that? Nevertheless, my fingers are trembling as I finish doing up the many buckles on my boots.

The look Laurie gives me when I walk into the room both excites and scares me. I blush and lower my eyes.

"Wow. I'm going to the museum. Where are you going?"

He's not looking too bad himself. His hair's loose around his shoulders, and it shines like silk—the red streaks glowing. He has a little kohl around his eyes, and heavy silver gleams at his neck and hands. I'm captivated by his wristbands. They're decorated with dulled embossed silver. I so want to touch them, to run my fingers over the embossing and not stop until I'm stroking the long fingers and . . . Ugh.

"I thought we'd . . . um . . . I was thinking maybe . . . well, we usually go to the pub after a field trip, so I was thinking . . ."

Laurie smiles. "Sure. Why not? As long as you promise to behave yourself and not start any fights."

My blush kicks up a notch, and my face starts to burn. "Uhm, okay."

Grinning, he picks up his soft leather jacket, which matches his trousers, and slings it over his shoulder. I want to touch—his jacket, his trousers . . . him. No. Bad idea. I need to stop thinking about him like that. But as soon as we get out of the house, he puts his arm around my shoulders, and it's the most natural thing in the world to put mine around his waist.

As we walk along the pavement, Laurie starts kidding around, bumping his hip against me and grinning. At first, I get annoyed, until I realise what he's doing and respond. Suddenly, we're like a pair of school-kids, messing around, bumping each other, tickling. By the time we get near the museum, I'm giggling, and trust me I *never* giggle. I'm scared, but it's the *best* scared I've been in ages.

We're almost at the museum when Laurie grabs my arm

and pulls me into a narrow alley between two buildings. Before I know what's happening, I'm up against the wall, pinned by his body, and he's kissing me. This time there's no hesitation in my response, even though my mind is screaming at me. *What the fuck do you think you're doing?*

In far too short a time, Laurie pulls away and walks toward the street, leaving me staring after him, stunned. Laurie turns, grinning. "Are you coming?"

I stumble after him, my head spinning. Frankly . . . any more of that and I think I might well have.

The whole class is here, standing on the steps, staring at us. We're still messing around, and I'm not sure whether the stares are because of the way we look or the way we're behaving. Probably both.

"I didn't realise you two knew each other," the lecturer comments, smiling.

"We do now," Laurie comments back with a brighter smile.

I was expecting the trip to be boring, yet it's anything but. A huge part of that is due to Laurie. He's unreservedly enthusiastic about every piece we look at, examining and commenting on everything from composition to style to brush strokes. Everyone is impressed, and, by the end of the evening, I think they're all a little in love with him.

All except me. I'm hopelessly, completely, and disastrously in love with him.

As expected, we move on to a nearby pub. It's absolutely packed.

"Are you sure I can trust you to go to the bar?" Laurie teases when I offer to buy him a drink.

"I promise to behave myself," I say with a mock pout that makes him laugh.

I manage to navigate the bar with no mishaps, and by the time I get back, the class has commandeered a table in the corner. They're discussing what we've seen and how it might translate to their own work. As usual, I sit back to sip my drink—a straight *Coke*—and listen. This time, however, there's a whole new dimension because I'm listening to *him*, and every time I glance up, he's looking at me with a blatantly flirtatious look in his eyes.

I can't believe it. I'm flirting. I'm actually flirting. I'm looking up at him from under my hair, licking the rim of my glass and my lips, flashing eye signals. God, I'm good. I'd forgotten how good I am at this, and how good it feels to be doing it. Laurie seems a little stunned and quite flushed. What the fuck am I doing? I really shouldn't be doing this. I really, really, *really* shouldn't be doing this.

Struck by the horror of what I'm doing and where it could lead, I lower my head and stare morosely into my drink.

"Do you want another *Coke*?"

Laurie's voice startles me, and it appears that when I raise my head, the expression on my face startles him.

"No. Get me a JD."

"Are you sure?"

"Yeah."

Laurie shrugs. "Okay."

I watch him disappear into the crowd, and I feel empty.

"So, Gabe . . ." Someone calls out, and I drag my eyes back to the group. "Is there something going on between you two?" They nudge each other and giggle. I feel the tips of my ears turn red.

"Why are you asking me?"

"Because we asked him when you were at the bar."

My eyes widen. "What did he say?"

They giggle again. "He wouldn't. That's why we're asking you."

I shrug and smile in what I hope is an enigmatic way.

"Oh, come on, Gabe, we're not stupid. We've been watching you ever since class. You two are so together."

"If you're so sure, why'd you ask?"

"Well . . . you know." Their snickering continues.

"No, I don't know."

"Well . . . because it's awkward, isn't it? It's . . . not right to assume." Dave is a big man, not the kind you'd expect to find in an art group. He's a big, cuddly bear and doesn't have a subtle bone in his body.

His equally straightforward wife nods. "We could be wrong."

Nancy, the third in their merry band — a lecherous, dirty-minded sixty-something — leans forward, her grin slack, and winks. "And it wouldn't be . . . umm . . . appropriate, if we were wrong."

"You mean you've been snickering behind your hands on the assumption we're together, but then got worried, because if you gave in to your insatiable desire for teasing and insinuating, then found out you were wrong, we might get offended, or worse, based on a perceived assault on our sexuality. So you tested the water with Laurie, and when he didn't shoot you down in flames, you decided you'd just come out and ask me, whether I was offended or not."

I speak in a quiet and friendly voice, and I can see everyone trying to work out what the heck I've been talking about and whether it's offensive or not.

"What he means is" — a familiar voice cuts in — "that you didn't want to suggest we're gay in case we weren't and got pissed about it."

"Oh." Everyone nods and grins as Laurie puts our drinks on the table and slides in next to me. He settles his arm around my shoulders. I glare at him, but I don't push his arm away.

"So, does that mean you are, then?" a particularly dim and persistent artist asks. I glare at her, but Laurie . . . well,

I'm learning that Laurie likes to be in the spotlight as much as I don't, so instead of answering, he turns toward me, and before I realise what his intentions are, he kisses me tenderly on the lips.

I freeze instantly. What the *fuck*?

"Oh. Wow. So, does that mean you're like boyfriends now?"

The slow anger that's been building in me since this conversation began peaks. I stand up, down the JD in one mouthful, and glare at Laurie.

"No, we are *not* boyfriends, and if he carries on like this, we won't even be friends." Slamming my glass down on the table, I get up, walk away, and lose myself in the crowd.

As quickly as I can, I make my way to the door. It's suddenly hot and claustrophobic, and all I care about is getting out of there.

Bursting out of the pub and into the cool evening air is glorious. I take a deep breath before striding off . . . fast . . . toward home. I'm absolutely fuming. How dare he? How dare he make assumptions like that and make a fool of me in public. How dare he?

I decide to take a shortcut through the park, and it's while I'm walking through the wooded area near the far side that I hear footsteps behind me on the path. They sound furtive, and I'm immediately on high alert.

I don't make any attempt to speed up, hide, or run. The way I'm feeling right now, I'd welcome the prospect of beating someone to a bloody pulp.

The heavy breathing and soft footfalls are coming closer. I tense, waiting for the attack I'm now sure is imminent.

"Gabriel. Wait."

I groan and speed up. I'd have preferred a mugger. But no . . . I'm not that lucky. I want someone I can justifiably beat up and what I get is the last person I could ever hit, although he's the one I most want to pulp right now.

"Gabriel, please wait."

Yeah, right. No chance.

Laurie has an almost uncanny knack of catching me off guard. Before I can even turn, he grabs my arm and swings me off the path, against a tree. He plants his hands either side of my head and presses his body against mine.

"Wait. Talk to me. What happened? Why are you so upset?"

"You bastard. Get your fucking hands off me." This time it's Laurie's turn to be surprised as I slip my hand down between us and grab his balls . . . hard.

He gives a sharp cry and steps back, holding himself.

"Don't you ever do that to me again!"

"Do what?" he gasps. There are tears in his eyes.

"Where do I start?" I count them off on my fingers. "One, I'm not your fucking boyfriend, and you do not . . . I repeat . . . do *not* have the right to kiss me whenever you feel like it, especially in public. Two, do *not* follow me through the woods and expect me not to rip off your head. I get twitchy when I'm followed through areas like this. Three, never, *never* pin me against a wall, tree, or any other inanimate object.

"Who the fucking hell do you think you are? How many times do I have to tell you that I'm not interested in you, in your stupid games, in your . . . in your . . . I'm not interested." I peter off and finish lamely because I'm looking into his eyes.

Laurie smiles a slow smile. He steps toward me again.

"I'm warning you. One step closer and it'll be my knee and not my hand, and it *will* seriously damage your reproductive capability."

Laurie just smiles and takes another step.

"I'm warning you. Not another step." I wonder why I haven't moved. I keep warning him, but he ignores me, so why don't I just get the hell out of here? All I have to do is dodge around him and run. We're not far from home. I can beat him there with no problem. I should move. I really should.

This time, when Laurie pushes me back against the tree, I don't resist. I'm breathing hard, and my heart's about to burst out of my chest. How many more times am I going to be in this situation? He's like a drug. I have to get him out of my system. I have to . . . I have . . . I . . . I . . .

I sigh as his lips find mine and my arms automatically go around him, one burying itself in his hair and the other finding the small of his back, pulling him toward me. He smells wonderful, and his hair is so soft and . . . oh *God*, he's a good kisser. More than good, he's fabulous.

"Are you sure you're not interested?" he whispers, kissing the corner of my mouth, my cheek, my ear.

Oh God. Oh God. Stop. Stop. "Stop." With a moan, I push him away from me. "Please don't," I gasp. "Please."

"What's wrong? I thought you were enjoying it."

"I was. I am. It's just . . . I can't, Laurie. I just can't."

"Why not? I want to, and I *know* you want to. So where's the problem?"

"The problem is that I can't. There are so many reasons why I can't . . . and . . . and I don't have to explain them to you," I say defensively. "I just can't, okay?"

"Okay. I'll back off. I know I can be too full on at times. Look, I'm going to the club with my friends on Saturday night. Why don't you come? You can meet my friends. We can chill together. No pressure. I'd like to be your friend, Gabriel. If that's all it can be, then . . ." He shrugs. "I'll be disappointed, but it's your choice."

My mind takes a huge backward step. He . . . he's . . . But I want . . . I don't want . . ."Okay. Why not?"

"Meet us at eight outside, yeah?"

"I'll be there."

"Promise?"
"I said I'll be there. I'll be there."

Chapter Six

Are you all right, Gabriel? The strap's not too tight?"

"I want to go home."

"I'm sorry, that's not possible right now. Be a good boy, and we'll see . . . maybe sometime soon."

"But I want . . ."

"I'm sorry, Gabriel, but what you want isn't relevant. You know that."

"My arm hurts."

"I know it does, but it won't be for long. If you cooperate with us, it won't hurt so much. You know that you have to, Gabriel. You know that you can't leave until we say you can, and we won't say that until we're sure you're ready to go out there."

"But I am. I'm ready. Please, let me go . . . please."

"There's no point in having hysterics, Gabriel. There's no one to hear. You can't keep on fighting us. The sooner you stop fighting and start concentrating, the sooner you'll be through with all this and can go home."

"I don't want to do it, it hurts."

"I know it hurts. I know that. You don't think we want to hurt you, do you?"

"Yes."

"That's just silly, Gabriel. We should be working together. I don't want to be fighting you every step of the way. I don't want to hurt you. If you cooperate, it'll be over much sooner, and it won't hurt so much."

"My head hurts."

"I know."

"But it hurts bad."

"I know, Gabriel. Just relax. Try to concentrate on opening your mind. I need to see inside your mind, Gabriel. I need to see what's going on with you, why you're causing us so much trouble."

"But . . . but . . . please . . . please stop . . . please stop. It hurts."

"Yes, I know it hurts, but it won't for long. We're almost done. Just stay still for a little while and focus on the light. No, Gabriel, don't go to sleep, not yet. It's too soon to go to sleep. Just concentrate and – "

"It hurts. Stop . . . stop, it hurts. Stop . . . stop . . . stop . . ."

"No . . . no . . . no . . . stop . . . stop . . . stop . . . no . . . *No . . . No!*"

The screaming wakes me again. Even though the night is chilly, I'm sweating. The sheets are tangled around my legs, and everything's wet. My pyjamas are soaked through. Oh shit, that isn't sweat. I groan. Not again. My head hurts too much to get out of bed, but I have to.

I strip the clothes off the bed and stagger to the bathroom to throw up. I manage to leave the toilet long enough to drag the bedclothes down to the kitchen and stuff them into the washing machine. I strip off my pyjamas and throw them in after. It occurs to me that it would be a good idea to have a shower before I go back to bed.

When I'm in this condition, thoughts tend to surface sluggishly, and in a strange, disjointed order. I think about Laurie, and the way I was feeling on Friday night when he held me in his arms. Time means very little to me at the moment. I've only a vague idea of how much of it has passed since then. The pain of those thoughts brings me abruptly back to the dream. I shudder and my stomach rebels again. While I'm throwing up — which is not a nice experience as I spent most of yesterday in bed and have only eaten sparse mouthfuls of the food my housemates left periodically on the nightstand beside my bed — I think about Laurie's kiss, and it makes me smile and feel better.

I turn on the shower and step under the cool water, not waiting for it to heat properly. Apart from the fact that it makes my headache kick up a notch, it's very pleasant. I remember that it's Saturday and I'm supposed to be going out with Laurie tonight. Ah well . . . it's a long time until tonight.

My head hurts. I'd better get out of the shower. I'd better . . . better . . . Ah hell . . . I fall to my knees again and heave into the toilet. This isn't an unusual occurrence when my head's playing up, which is pretty much all the time now.

Something weird is happening, and it scares the hell out of me. Recently, when I have one of my headaches, just before the pain hits, I seem to . . . hear . . . something. It's not like I imagine voices in my head, because I can't actually hear what they're saying. It's like someone's having a conversation in the next room—I can hear them speaking, but not what they're saying.

But as I sit with my head over the bowl, the pain in my stomach and head too much to even think about trying to stand up or crawl back to bed, I hear the voices. They're clearer but broken.

. . . it seems they missed the fact that neural connections . . . unusual intensity . . . obscuring . . . and therefore some of the strongest . . . not recognised . . . mistake . . . dangerous . . . track down . . . eliminate . . .

No . . . no, I will not . . . I cannot . . . I don't want to . . . I won't.

I try to get up. I try so hard, but I've left it too late. The pain comes screaming as it always does when the voices fade. Maybe it's listening to the voices that . . . that . . . Agh . . . the pain . . . I can't . . . I can't . . . Ah, what . . .

I wake up shivering and naked, still on the floor of the bathroom. I need to lie still for a while—a long while—as my sensory overload fades and reality begins to creep back in.

With reality comes the cold, a chill so deep that it feels as if my bones have turned to ice.

The pain in my head isn't going away. Shouldn't it be going away by now? I try to sit up, but the room spins. There's water all over the floor. Bugger, I must have left the shower running and it overflowed. Oh no. There's a lot of it. It's going to leak out under the door. I have to turn off the shower. Oh no, not any time soon.

I'm so cold. Why do I feel so sick . . . so shaky? What's going on? Everything fades in and out. My head hurts. I lift my hand to touch the side of my head. It hurts. My fingers come away sticky. Blinking my eyes, I peer across the room. There's blood on the toilet seat and on the floor, swirling in the water. Just great. I close my eyes, feeling tired and seriously weird. Something is crawling in the back of my head, telling me that I should be moving, getting up, getting warm, but I ignore it. It's too much effort to —

"Gabe? Gabe, are you in there? Gabe, there's water coming under the door. Are you okay? Gabe?"

Someone's hammering on the door. It's a long, long way away.

"Gabe, if you don't open the door, I'm going to break the fucking thing down. Open the door, Gabe."

Tired now. So tired . . .

Crash. The door bursts inward, in an explosion of wood and water, closely followed by Andy and Bobby.

"Fuck, Gabe, what the hell?"

"Gabe?"

Something touches my face, and I force my eyes open. Andy looks scared. Bobby, crouching behind him, is more practical.

"Get him into bed, Andy. He's freezing. I'll clean up in here."

"But his head . . . he's bleeding."

Pushing Andy out of the way, Bobby takes his place and peers into my eyes. "I think he's okay. He just needs to get warm. If he's still out of it in an hour, we'll call the doc. But I think it's just the usual, with a bang on the head thrown in. I heard him screaming in the night."

"So did I. I wish I'd checked up on him."

"You know he doesn't like it when we do that."

"Bobby—"

"Don't ask."

"How do you know what I was going to say?"

"Because I'm scared about it, too. I know it's getting worse. All of it's getting worse, and I don't know where it's going to end."

"Bobby—"

"Just get him warm, Andy."

When Andy yanks me to my feet, the world spins and fizzes, then disappears.

"Aww." I wince as fingers press hard against the side of my head. When I open my eyes, an unfamiliar figure comes into focus.

"How is that feeling, Gabriel?"

"Great. That's why I said *aww*."

"Can you sit up?"

It transpires that I can. My headache seems to be back within manageable levels, and I'm warm again.

"Who the hell are you?"

The stranger smiles. "Ah, I see you're feeling better."

"The question remains. Who are you and what are you doing in my bedroom?"

"I'm sorry, Gabriel, I should have introduced myself. My name is Doctor Sherman. Your friends were worried about you and gave me a call."

My gaze flicks to Andy and Bobby, who are hovering,

anxiously and sheepishly respectively. "How nice of them. You're not my doctor. Where's Doctor Bryce?"

"I'm a locum. I come out when your own doctor isn't available."

"How interesting. Can you leave now, please? As you can see, I'm fine. I've had a hell of a night, and I just want to sleep it off."

"Are you feeling sleepy?" the doctor asks, peering at me in the way doctors do.

"No. I'm feeling sore, tired, and seriously pissed off, so it would be a good idea if you left now."

"Do you have any idea why you passed out in the bathroom?"

I shrug. "It happens."

"How often?"

"Sometimes."

"You're not being very helpful, Gabriel."

"I've heard that before."

"I bet you have. Now, if you want me to leave you alone, maybe you should answer some of my questions."

I sigh again and settle back against the pillows, bringing my knees up to hug. "You're not going to let me rest until I do, and I'm not up to physically throwing you out so . . . what do you want to know?"

"Have you been seeing anyone about these blackouts?"

"Have you read my notes?"

"I've told you, I'm a locum on emergency call. I haven't had time to read your notes."

"Then yes . . . yes, I'm seeing someone . . . several someones, to be exact. I've been seeing someone for years."

"Are you taking any medication?"

"Shedloads."

"And are they doing any good?"

"Possibly."

"What's that supposed to mean?"

"It means that maybe things would be worse if I wasn't taking them, but in my perspective, no, they're not working, because everything has been getting worse for months."

"Everything?"

"The weird headaches, the blackouts, the shaking . . ."

"Have you been tested for epilepsy?"

"I've been tested for everything, and they still don't have a name for it. It's not epilepsy. I don't have seizures. They're something else."

"Something like . . . what?"

"You tell me."

I'm bored with this now. "You know what? I'm sick and tired of doctors and their tests, language, and condescending manners. They start off thinking they have all the answers, telling me that this time they'll fix it. New doctor, a new set of promises. I've had every test you can imagine, and they all say the same thing, which is precisely nothing. There's absolutely nothing physically wrong with me . . . except for the fact that I keep passing out and I have headaches that are so bad I become completely non-functional and freeze up for hours. So, tell me how *you* think you're going to find the miracle cure when no one else seems able to."

The doctor starts off looking shocked. Then he smiles. "I don't think there's anything much wrong with you, Gabriel, at least not from this incident. As for the rest . . ." He gazes at me for so long it makes me acutely uncomfortable. "Have you thought that perhaps your problems might have a . . . less physical source?"

"You mean am I a complete nut job and it's all in my mind? You're not the first one to think that either. Six months in a mental hospital didn't help, so I guess the *thera-py* I keep getting offered isn't going to either."

"It must be very hard for you, living with something like

this."

"Sometimes," I say, suspicious of his seemingly caring tone.

"You're very angry about it."

"Partly."

"Partly?"

"I mean, yes, I'm angry, but only partly about this."

"What else?"

"Lots of things. Look, none of this is relevant to my medical condition. I've answered your questions. You can see I'm not about to explode or turn inside out. Will you please go away and leave me alone now?"

"I appreciate how you're feeling, but if what happened to you tonight happens often, it could be dangerous. You were lucky tonight. If that blow had been to your temple, you could easily have been killed."

"Do you think I don't know that? Do you think I haven't been told a thousand times? What am I supposed to do? Wrap myself in cotton wool and lock myself in my room for the rest of my life? What kind of life would that be?"

"Well, maybe you could be a little more careful until they find out what's happening to you and find a medication that will control it."

"I told you. They're not going to find what's wrong. And I'm not going to spend the rest of my life locked in a room. Not in a hospital or here."

"So you push yourself until something happens, then throw it in our faces as evidence that we don't know jack shit."

I stare at him. Did he really just say that? Andy and Bobby gasp. "I-I live my life the best way I know how. I'm not going to let this beat me, and I'm not going to put my life on hold. I live how I want to live, and if something happens . . . well . . . at least I won't have to live with this anymore."

"Is that what you think? That if something happens, it'll end the pain? Are you trying to make something happen?"

I have to laugh at that. "If you're asking me whether I'm trying to kill myself, then the answer's no. Been there, done that." I rub my arm. I know the doctor's seen. Damn, that's why he asked. "But if you're asking me if I care whether I live or die . . . well, now . . . that's a whole different question, isn't it?"

The doctor drops his gaze. He can't look at me. Well, that's no surprise. He sighs and closes his bag. "Well . . . I don't think the incident tonight has done you any lasting harm, but I am concerned about you, Gabriel. I'm going to recommend to Doctor Bryce that he refer back to your consultant to see if they can help you get some better control of your condition."

"Do what you want. It won't do any good."

"You're very sure about that."

I stare at him for a moment. *If only he knew.* "I am."

"Well, I'm going to try anyway."

"Knock yourself out."

"Take care of yourself, Gabriel."

I watch the doctor leave. Worms are writhing in my gut. I have names for all my worms—these two are anger and fear. I also have despair, hatred, emptiness, loneliness, and frustration, but they're out at the moment.

Andy gives me an anxious look as he follows the doctor out. Bobby remains. He regards me thoughtfully.

"What?"

"Isn't it about time you stopped feeling so sorry for yourself?"

"Whatever."

"Why do you have to keep locking everyone out? Why won't you let anyone help you?"

"No one can help me."

"Oh, fuck off, Gabe. You don't know that. You don't be-lieve it. You just . . ."

"Just what?" I say coolly.

"It's what you said, isn't it? Only you lied. You said you don't care if you live or die, but that's a lie. Fuck, Gabe . . . You scared the hell out of us. This time we thought you might've actually crossed that line. Andy's a fucking wreck. We can't keep picking you up off the floor. One of these days—"

"You don't have to *pick me up*. You don't have to do any-thing for me. We're not friends. We're just housemates."

"Cut it out, Gabe. Stop talking your bullshit. We care about you, and we know damn well you care about us, so just shut up with the crap."

"Fuck off, Bobby."

"Yeah, I will. But . . . you've got another razor blade in your hand, Gabe. Put it down."

The heavy glass ashtray is the nearest thing to my hand, and it smashes into a thousand pieces as it hits the door.

Chapter Seven

I'm so tired, so very tired. I can't keep my eyes open. Andy makes me eat at some point, but I don't wake up properly even then. I can't find any energy.

The first time I wake up to any level of consciousness is a huge disappointment. It's dark outside. I've missed seeing Laurie again. He probably would've waited at the club and thought I stood him up. I'm absurdly disappointed. Most absurd of all is that I'm trying to convince myself it's missing a night out at the club I'm disappointed about.

I feel heavy and tired, and my head hurts, but only from the bump. With some effort, I get out of bed and drag my aching bones to the airing cupboard to get fresh linen for my bed. It's a pain making up a new bed, but it's lovely to slip between clean sheets and lay my head on a cool pillow. However, I resist the temptation for now. My stomach's growling. I need to eat, and I need to make sure the dirty bedclothes are washed. I don't want my housemates complaining that I'm causing them hassle again.

I must admit to an uncomfortable, guilty feeling in the pit of my stomach about the way I treated Andy and Bobby. I'll have to make it up to them when I'm feeling better.

There's no one in the kitchen. I check the washer. Someone's washed the bedding and put it through the dryer. It's not completely dry, but dry enough to get out and hang on the airer. A couple of days and it'll be ready to put back in the airing cupboard to start the cycle all over again.

I look at the clock. It's eight-thirty. Laurie would've realised I'm not coming by now. He'll be laughing with his friends. They'll probably be drinking, maybe dancing, having a good time. Maybe Laurie's dancing with a hot guy. He deserves it.

I sit at the table and chew on cardboard toast. Yeah, I'm feeling sorry for myself. I'm feeling bloody sorry for myself. Don't I deserve to? Aren't I entitled to be a little sorry for myself after everything that's happened to me? Don't I?

There's a knock at the front door. I glance at the clock again. Just before nine. It'll be Shannon for Andy, then. She always comes at this time. She works at a local supermarket and comes straight after her shift. Well, dammit, Andy can open the bloody door.

There's no movement from upstairs. Ah, fuck it. I get to my feet and drag my sorry ass to the front door.

Laurie stares at me for a long, long moment. I'm so shocked at seeing him that I just stand and stare right back.

"Are . . . are you okay?"

"I'm fine. I'm sorry about standing you up."

"Who gives a fuck about that? When you didn't turn up at the club, I rang the house phone. I had to look up the number, as you didn't bother to give me your mobile number. Your friend said you've been ill. He said that last night you . . . That you could've . . ." He's about as uncool — in the flustered and upset way, not the cute and awesome way — as I've ever seen him.

"Yeah. I fell and hit my head. It's okay."

"It was more than that, wasn't it?"

I shrug.

"I was scared. I ran all the way. I didn't . . . I didn't know if . . ."

"I'm fine."

"So, are you going to ask me in?"

"Would it make any difference if I told you to piss off?"

He grins, looking relieved. "No. I'll kick in the front door and rugby tackle you to the ground if I have to."

"Well"—I say as I step aside to let him pass—"with everyone treating me as if I'm made of glass, it would make a refreshing change."

Laurie shakes his head and precedes me into the kitchen. He glances at my half-eaten piece of toast, then goes straight to the fridge and starts taking things out, seemingly at random. I watch with interest, leaning against the doorframe.

He works in silence, and soon the smell of cooking assails my senses. I'm still quite dizzy, and after a time of watching him from the door, during which he doesn't even glance at me, I sit down.

"What are you doing?"

"I'm making you dinner."

"I kind of figured that much."

"You look as if you don't eat enough. In fact, you look like shit. So just for tonight, just this once, I want to make sure you have a good meal."

"What makes you think I'm going to eat it?"

"Well, the sounds your stomach's been making for the last couple of minutes gave me a clue."

A bubble of mirth brings a smile to my lips, then bursts out in a laugh. It's been a shit week, and now here I am with a practical stranger—make that a damn hot, sexy stranger—cooking me dinner while I sit, half naked, with my hair still stiff with blood, and watch him. Once I start laughing, I can't stop. In the end, I'm clutching my sides and rocking, tears streaming down my face.

Laurie turns around with his back to the cooker and folds his arms. "What exactly do you find so amusing about this situation?"

I shake my head, still laughing. Shovelling stir-fry onto plates, Laurie turns and puts one down in front of me. It smells good. I start to eat while Laurie sits and looks at me.

"Aren't you going to eat yours?"

"I've already eaten."

"Then why'd you make a plate for yourself?"

"So that if you finish yours, you can have more."

I put my fork down and look at him. I'm confused. I'm always confused when I'm with him.

"Eat, Gabriel."

"Why do you call me that?" I ask him as I start eating again. This is good stuff.

"Call you what?"

"Gabriel."

"Um . . . because it's your name?"

"I know, but no one calls me that, except . . . you know . . . doctors, lawyers. Everyone else calls me Gabe."

"Gabriel is a beautiful name. It suits you. Gabriel is one of the four archangels. He's the messenger of God, the only one of the four who walks among us lowly creatures on Earth. Gabe is the name of an ordinary human being, but Gabriel . . . Gabriel is an angel. Heaven on Earth."

I gaze down at my plate, biting my lip. For God's sake! I have tears in my eyes. What the hell's that about?

"I'm no angel."

"A fallen one, maybe. Remember, I've seen you fight."

I look up, sniffing, embarrassed. "I'm sorry."

"Sorry?"

"I was a complete arse. I shouldn't have done that. I-I get so . . ."

"It's okay. Actually, I don't think I ever told you that you were actually pretty bloody awesome."

"I was?"

"Fuck yeah. You do know there were five of them?"

I shrug. "When I get in that kind of mood, I don't care. I don't know what happens. Something flips and . . . I can't stop myself."

"For a skinny kid, you sure can fight."

"Skinny kid?"

"Yeah, well . . . you're pretty skinny, and you're what, seventeen?"

"Shut up. I am *not* skinny, and I am *not* seventeen. I'm almost twenty."

Laurie's eyebrows rise. "Seriously? I thought you were younger."

"People do."

"You'll be glad of that one day."

"Yeah."

"So, what happened last night?"

"It's none of your business." I sigh and shake my head. "I'm sorry. I'm a bit . . . raw right now."

"That's okay. Want to talk about it?"

"Want to? Maybe. Able to? No, not yet."

"Fair enough. Can you at least tell me what happened last night?"

"Kind of. I have . . . headaches. You saw it before, on Sunday."

Laurie nods but remains silent to let me talk.

"I can't describe what it's like. It starts with a kind of un-real feeling. As if I'm detached from everything, and nothing from the real world can get through to me, but at the same time, I'm hyper-aware of everything—every touch, every whisper, everything.

"Then the pain hits. It hurts so much I completely seize up. I can't see, can't hear, can't feel . . . only the pain. After a while, I either come down or pass out. I've . . . not been well since Wednesday . . . before that. Last night, I had a dream. It was a nightmare. I woke up screaming. I do that all the time.

"I'd . . . I needed to change the bedclothes. My head was . . . I knew I was going to have an attack, but when I get like that, my thoughts don't make sense. They don't join up, so instead of going back to bed, I went in to have a shower. I got sick instead and threw up.

"When the pain hit, I passed out and hit my head on the toilet. I guess I was out cold for a couple of hours, long enough to flood the bathroom. Andy and Bobby found me and got me into bed before I died of hypothermia, and here I am. Living to fight another day." I didn't mean for my voice to sound so bitter and helpless.

"Do you have to fight? I mean, fight so hard?"

"Oh yeah, I have to fight. If I stop fighting . . ."

"What? What will happen if you stop fighting, Gabriel? What will happen if you just lay down your burdens for a while, and let your friends take care of you? Will the world end? Will it make your medical conditions any worse?"

"I . . . I don't . . ."

Laurie gets to his feet and walks slowly around the table. He reaches for my hand, and I can't resist when he draws me to my feet. I shiver when he puts his hand on my waist. I don't want this. I don't want him to kiss me. I want him to leave me alone. I want him to stop asking me difficult questions, to stop asking me to talk and stare into the darkness within. No, I definitely, definitely don't want him to kiss me. But I think I'll die if he doesn't.

Laurie doesn't kiss me. He just stands, with his hands on my waist, gazing into my eyes. "Do you still believe you're not beautiful?"

"Laurie, don't . . . please."

"Don't what? Don't tell you what's clear for everyone with eyes to see, everyone but yourself."

"You don't understand. You only see what's on the outside."

"I know. But what's on the outside is so beautiful, so pure and so . . . What's on the inside can't be that bad, Gabriel."

"But it is. What's on the inside is poison, Laurie. It destroys everything. It's destroyed everything and everyone I've ever loved."

"So you won't let yourself love again, or believe you're capable of it?"

"Yes. No. Don't confuse me. It's not fair. I'm confused enough already."

"I'm not trying to confuse you, Gabriel. Far from it. I'm trying to get you to see clearly."

"Don't. I don't want to see clearly. I've spent a lot of time fogging the glass."

"Then it's about time to de-mist the window. You don't have poison in you, Gabriel. You're the least poisonous person I know. You'd never hurt anyone but yourself. You're shutting your eyes to the beauty that's you. The only one you're poisoning is yourself."

"No." I turn away and sit down, resting my elbows on the table and my head on my hands. "You don't understand. I've hurt everyone, everyone I ever loved. I drove my mother to a nervous breakdown, my father to the verge of divorce, my sister to a grotty house with a grotty husband she ran off with just to get away from me. I drove one boyfriend to drink and drugs, and the other to suicide. No one I've loved has ever escaped me unscathed."

"Tell me about them, Gabriel. Tell me about your boyfriends. What happened to them?"

He draws up a chair and sits next to me, stroking my back while I tell him as much as I can remember. I tell him about how my life went off the rails. About the drink, the drugs, the casual sex, and about Daniel, the bright star who made it all worthwhile . . . until I extinguished his light. I tell him about my breakdown and about Michael. I tell him everything that happened . . . almost everything. What I don't tell him is why.

Laurie's expression shows he senses there's something else—something I'm holding back—but thank God, he lets it lie. I'm exhausted and in no shape to be pushed on what it might be.

I can barely lift my head when he says quietly, "Daniel and Michael made their own choices, Gabriel, and you weren't and aren't responsible for any of them. You didn't force Daniel to drink or Michael to stop taking his meds. You didn't hold the needle for Daniel or the gun for Michael. None of it was your fault, Gabriel."

But it was. I can't tell him why . . . but it was.

With a huge sigh, I shake my head and let it fall on my arms. Laurie becomes business-like.

"Come on. It's getting late and time you were in bed. You didn't sleep last night, and you look completely exhausted."

I let him help me to my feet and steer me toward the stairs. I expect him to say goodnight in the hall, but he doesn't. He shoves me up the stairs and follows me. After checking to make sure I take my meds, he watches me get into bed, then sits next to me, stroking my hair. I stare up at him. He's the one who looks like an angel, outlined in brightness, the red in his hair catching fire and burning like flames. His eyes are pools of light in the darkness, bleached of colour against the fire, almost silver.

Laurie freezes and stares down at me, drawing me into his eyes, falling into mine. Slowly, he leans down, and when he's close enough, I bury my hands in his hair, drawing him down faster. This time the kiss is a two-way street. I'm not frozen and unresponsive. Neither am I hungry and seeking to overpower. This kiss is gentle and sweet, our first exploration of each other.

When Laurie raises his head, he has stars in his eyes. "You're so beautiful."

I guess I'm getting desensitised to him saying that, because it doesn't hurt this time. Laurie runs his hand up my arm, the tips of his fingers brushing my skin, making me shiver. When he gets to my hand, he covers it with his own, then turns his head to kiss my wrist—gently, softly.

At first, I close my eyes and surrender to the sensations—the tickle of his breath on my skin, the warmth of his hand over mine, the touch of his lips on... Suddenly I realise what he's doing, and it feels as if he's spitting acid on me. I jerk my arm away and hold it protectively across my body.

Laurie doesn't seem startled, and he definitely doesn't look sorry. He just looks sad. "You're tired, and you should sleep. I'll leave you alone in a minute to get some proper rest. I'll come back in the morning. But first, it's vital to me that you know how beautiful you are... how beautiful you are to me.

"I want you to know that no matter what happened to you, no matter how hurt you are, how damaged you think you are, it doesn't matter. Nothing matters except that you're here and I'm here, and I'm not going anywhere. You're an amazing person, and I think I'm falling in love with you. I want you to know that, to know that I think every... single... part of you... is beautiful."

As he speaks, in a low, hypnotic voice, keeping my eyes entrapped by those glowing silvery orbs, he gently takes my arm.

At first, I resist, but I've neither the strength nor desire. Something inside me is screaming for release, begging me to let it go... let it all go... praying he won't hurt me, that this won't tear me apart.

He punctuates his words by planting small, tender kisses on the inside of my wrist, caressing the deep, angry scars with his lips.

I close my eyes and let the scorching tears flow. I feel weak, so weak. I'm shaking all over, and the hand that Laurie's holding is clenched into a fist but . . . but . . . For the first time, I don't care. I don't care that I'm weak. I don't care that I'm shaking. I don't care that I'm hurt and damaged and doomed. I don't care because here, with him, I feel safe. And . . . and part of me—a very small part—feels . . . beautiful.

"Laurie," I whisper. He lifts his head. Now he seems a little anxious, and I try to smile. "Will you stay with me?"

The smile that breaks over his face almost breaks my heart. What have I done? What the hell have I done? I don't let people in. I don't let people touch me, and there's a bloody good reason for that and now . . . and now . . . Laurie's lips find mine, and I lose my train of thought. I forget . . . I forget it all. There's nothing before, there may be nothing after, but right now . . . right now everything's perfect.

Chapter Eight

I test the world by cracking open one eye. Nothing hurts. I haven't been screaming, I don't have a headache, and I'm not sick. Hmm, seems pretty good. So why does everything feel wrong? As consciousness returns, the feeling of strangeness grows. Something isn't right. Something . . .

Oh hell. There's an arm across my stomach. And the arm's attached to a body — a naked body. Slowly, I turn my head. Laurie's fast asleep. His hair is spread over the pillows, his eyes are closed, and he's breathing gently, his chest rising and falling in hypnotic rhythm. For a moment, a smile breaks over my face, and I reach out to touch him.

Then I freeze. What do I think I'm doing? What have I done? He's sweet and caring and beautiful. He kissed me as if . . . as if he loved me. But I can't. I can't let him love me. He sees only beauty in me, but it's a lie. It's all a lie.

Thank you, Laurie. Thank you for making me feel beautiful for one night. But it's over now. The night has gone, the morning's here, and I have to go. I watch him for a while, tears streaming down my cheeks. I was happy. For a few hours, I was actually happy . . . and that's why I can't do this anymore. I remember what it's like to be happy and I can't . . . I close my eyes, and I'm swamped by the emptiness inside.

Carefully, I slip out of bed and rummage in my wardrobe for my favourite clothes. I take the whole box of jewellery and choose what I want, sitting at the kitchen table. I take a last look around the kitchen, then sadly walk out of the house without a backward glance.

I walk fast. I don't know where I'm going, and I don't care. I'm not walking *to* anything—I'm walking away, far away.

I'm hurting worse than I can ever remember. Part of me is telling me to turn around and run back into his arms. He's the first person who's ever truly loved me. He's the first person who's even come close to making me love myself. For the first time, last night, there was a moment when . . .

But I can't think like that. I can't go back. I can't ever go back. I love Laurie. Yep . . . I admit it. I love him. And that's exactly why I can't be with him. If I go back, he won't give up. He'll always be there, chipping away at my defences, and I'll let him in. I'll always let him in, and I can't do that. He doesn't understand. None of them understands. It's not safe to love me. It's just not safe.

I feel exposed and glance around nervously. Everything seems sinister—the whole world. What am I going to do? Where am I going to go? There's nowhere I'll be safe, nowhere. One day . . . one day they'll find me. One day I'll look up, and they'll be there, they'll take me back, and anyone who's near me will be crushed. I can't do that. I just can't.

The pain comes from nowhere. It's a double assault and drives me to my knees. One sliver of pain slices into my heart, and it comes from Laurie. Why'd he do that? Why'd he keep pushing? Why'd he work his way into my heart? Now it hurts. It hurts so much. I've always thought that the phrase *broken-hearted* is stupid. I mean, how can a heart break? And even if it were possible to actually break a heart, you'd die. Of course, you would, because a broken heart couldn't beat.

Now the pain in my chest is so intense, so real, that I know my heart's broken and that it can never be healed. I understand. Part of me dies at that moment. Part of me just disappears, and the great black hole that spins in my core gets bigger and sucks in all the light that remained in the darkness of my soul.

At the same time, pain slams into my head. I hear the voices. They seem to be close by . . . so real.

Urgent recall . . . dangerous deterioration . . . possible consequences . . . immense power . . . total destruction . . . uncontrollable discharges . . . external damage . . . exposure . . . unacceptable risk . . . immediate neutralisation.

It's like trying to listen to a CD that's jumping over a scratch or a radio programme plagued by static. I hate the voices. I hate them because I know where they're coming from, and I don't want to know they're still there. I don't want to know what they're talking about. Somewhere deep inside, I feel I should be scared, terrified, but there's nothing new in that. The fear is just sucked into the general terror that reaches for me out of the black hole as I go spinning into it.

This time there's something else, something strange. As I lose consciousness, there's a feeling as if my mind expands, and something . . . something bursts out.

I'm aware of people, lots of people, all around. I can hear them. They're talking about me. I know they're talking about me. I can't move yet. I can't open my eyes, but I can feel them touching me.

Oh, the poor boy. Is he all right? . . . freak, probably on drugs . . . Should we get help? . . . Maybe we should call an ambulance . . . Maybe he's going to die, cool . . . Did he have a fit or something? Wish I'd been here . . . Can I help? Should I do something? . . . I'm going to be late for work, but I want to see if anything interesting happens . . . I wonder what's for tea tonight . . . This is better than the telly.

Then a new voice overrides all the others.

Why . . . why did he run away? I know he wasn't coming back. I thought . . . after last night I thought we had something. I thought I was finally getting through to him. Why won't he let me in? Why won't he realise how beautiful he is? How much I love him? Why? What have I done wrong? What did I do to scare him away? Why is he so scared? Why won't he reach out to me? Why won't he let me reach out to him?

"Laurie?" Why did he say those things to me here? Why was he so open in front of all these people? Why? *Oh shit. No.*

My eyes snap open, and I sit bolt upright. There are maybe ten or fifteen people clustered around, some looking concerned, some interested, some hungry. I gaze at them. I can still hear them but . . . but no one's speaking.

"Did you say that?"

"What? Gabriel, are you okay?"

"Tell me. Did you speak?"

"Gabriel—"

"Did you *speak*?"

"No. No, I didn't speak. I was too nervous, too scared."

"No," I whisper and close my eyes, letting myself fall back to the ground. I don't care about the stares. I don't care about the people. I don't even care about Laurie. All I care about is the stabbing pain in my head, a fizzing, popping, creeping pain and all I can think is . . . *Oh no . . . no . . . no. Not again.*

"Gabriel. What is it? What's wrong? Please, Gabriel, speak to me, or I'm going to call an ambulance."

"No." I sit up again. "I can't . . . It's not . . . Just help me up. I'm all right, just . . ."

"I don't know if that's such a good idea, Gabriel. You look—"

"Did I ask your opinion?" I snap. "If you won't help me, I'll do it myself." For the first time, I actually take notice of my surroundings. I'm in the park. There's a bench nearby. If I can crawl over to it, I can . . .

"You're so fucking stubborn. Here."

I look up, blinking in the sunlight. With a sigh, I take his hand and let him haul me to my feet. The pain stabs me, and I stagger. He puts his arm around my waist, and I rest my head against his shoulder. It feels good. "I'll help you get home."

"No." That's the last place I can go now. This is . . . Now I know—know for sure—I'm not safe. No one near me is safe. I glance down at the ground where I'd been lying. Nearby is a holly bush. There are other holly bushes in the park, but unlike any of them, this one has no leaves. Underneath the bush lies a robin. It's dead.

I push away from Laurie, stumble and almost fall. It's as if two realities are superimposed over each other, and I keep switching back and forth between them. I can't exist in either. I take a deep breath and let it out slowly, but the world keeps flickering. I can't do this on my own.

"Why are you so hell-bent on running away? What are you running away from?"

I lift my eyes and look at him. Can I tell him? Can I? I shake my head. "Myself."

"You can run away from yourself when you're better . . . when you're well. In the meantime, please, *please* take care of yourself. Let me take care of you."

I want to run. I need to run. Laurie doesn't know it, but *he* needs me to run. But I can't. I know that . . . he knows that. Maybe it would be all right for a while. After all, I can't fight them. I can't fight anyone like this.

"All right. I'll come home, but you have to leave. You have to walk away and never come back. You have to promise me."

People are drifting away. Now they're sure I'm not imminently about to die or have a fit, there's nothing to interest them anymore. We're almost alone. Laurie comes close and puts his arms around me. I'm too weak to pull away.

"I won't promise that, Gabriel, I can't. I don't know what's wrong with you, why you're so frightened, but I know one thing. I suspected it before, but after last night I know it without a shadow of doubt. I love you. That can't be denied. I'll never leave you. You can push me away with all your strength, and I'll keep coming back. You can curse me, and I'll let you, but I won't listen. You can beg me, threaten me, abuse me, beat the crap out of me, but you'll never . . . ever drive me away."

"Please."

"I know you're scared, Gabriel. I know you think that by driving me away you'll somehow protect me from whatever you're afraid of, but I don't want to be protected. I want to protect you. I want to make you feel safe again."

I shake my head. "You can't. You don't understand."

"Then help me. Make me understand. Talk to me. Tell me what's going on."

Again, there's that flash, that moment of weakness when I almost tell him. But I can't. I can't put him in danger. If he knows, he's a threat to them, and I won't do that. I won't put him in danger just to ease my burden. I'm selfish, but not that selfish. No. I'll let him help me for now, but sooner or later I'll be strong enough to run away, and I will.

I can see that's exactly what he's afraid of, what he expects. He's going to be on guard now, and next time I'll have to be more careful, better prepared, have a better head start. He can be as watchful as he likes, as cautious as he can. He can tie me to the bed if he wants, but he won't be able to hold on to me because I'll always be one step ahead. I'll always know what he's planning, what he's thinking. My bonds are breaking, and that's exactly what I'm most scared of.

"I-I'll come home with you."

"For now?"

"Just take me home, Laurie."

I'm too tired to fight, too sick. The two worlds, two parts of me, are coming back into alignment. The fact that I'm aware of it at all proves that. I've been half asleep for so long, and now I'm waking up. But it's disorienting . . . and painful. It saps my energy and makes me weak, and that's precisely why this is when they'll come for me.

My mind is working overtime. Sensory overload is threatening again. This time there are more senses to overload, which is why I can't let it happen. I'm putting my friends in enough danger as it is. I won't put them in more . . . from me.

When we get to the front door, I'm surprised to find it open.

"I didn't have time to shut it. I woke up and you weren't there. I knew something was wrong, and when I came down to the kitchen and saw your things spread all over the table. I knew you'd gone and weren't intending to come back, so I just ran."

I nod, too tired to speak. It's too hard to hold on to everything, and he's making it worse. His touch, his voice, his smell, his thoughts, they're overloading me. The essence of him touches something so deep, so powerful within me, and that alone is hard enough to cope with.

In the kitchen, Laurie stops and turns me around to face him. He puts his arms around me and looks deep into my eyes. I shiver. It feels as if he's looking inside me, as if he can see . . ."Don't."

"Why not? What are you afraid of? What are you afraid I'm going to see in there?"

"Don't."

"I meant what I said, Gabriel. I'm never going to leave you."

"I know."

"Why do you make that sound like such a bad thing? Tell me you don't care about me. Tell me that you don't feel the same thing I do, that you haven't felt it from the moment our eyes met in that bar."

"I . . ."

"Think about it, Gabriel. Think carefully. Because if you tell me truthfully that you feel nothing for me, I'll walk away."

I think back to that moment, the moment of complete clarity when our eyes met. I think about the way he looked at me the first morning when I woke, and he was lying on my bed. He'd been there all night, uncomfortable, cold . . . waiting, making sure I was all right. Then he'd tracked me down to the art class and joined when he so clearly doesn't need to. He kissed me . . . so gently. He's put up with my crap and kept coming for me, saving me. I remember last night, the way he made me feel.

"No. I can't. I can't tell you that. I do . . . I do care for you."

I feel the tension leave Laurie. He thinks he's won. Maybe he has. Maybe I've lost the battle. Perhaps I've doomed us both. The smile on his face is almost worth it. Almost.

Slowly he lowers his head, and this time I'm not frozen. Tired as I am, I lift my face, close my eyes, and surrender myself to the sheer pleasure.

Laurie's hands roam my back and mine rest on his hips. I feel as if maybe . . . maybe I can be safe here . . . with him. Maybe I can keep us safe. Maybe.

I feel dizzy. My head's hurting again. It's all concentrated in one spot. It's going to happen again, and it's going to happen soon.

I try to break away, but Laurie won't let me. He holds on tight, holds me close. I try to turn my head away, to tell him . . . to warn him. But he imprisons my lips as much as he imprisons my body. I'm lost. It . . . it's . . .

"Laurie." I moan into his mouth. He thinks it's with desire and pulls me close. Part of it is. Part of it *is* desire, and that's the problem. I shouldn't be feeling strong emotions right now. It only makes it worse. I shouldn't be letting him get this close. I should pull away and run. I should . . .

The dizziness is coming from a different source now. His kiss is . . . it's awakening parts of me that have been asleep for so long. I truly loved Daniel, and I thought I loved Michael, but this . . . I've never felt like this before, never been with anyone who could . . . just with a kiss . . . just with a kiss, just with . . . with one . . .

I moan again and surrender. I can't fight it. I'm too weak, too confused. I'm lost, hopelessly lost. My eyelids flutter, and so does my heart. I open myself to him completely and let myself go. *Oh no. Bad move — very bad move.* I should never have done that. I've lost control. I try to fight. I try so hard, but it's too late. I'm helpless.

The pain builds as I try desperately to regain control. It's hopeless. It's slipped from my grasp, and it's already overwhelming me. But wait. There's a feeling . . . a strange, unfamiliar feeling. At first, I can't place it. I can't work out what it is, what it means. Then it bursts over me. I love him. I love Laurie, and I want to protect him. With every fibre of my being, I want to protect him, more than I've ever wanted to protect myself.

I let the knowledge flow through me. I smile against his mouth and allow myself to completely relax. For one moment of beautiful, pure clarity, my worlds combine and I'm whole. I'm one. It's only for a moment, but a moment is all I need. I focus everything on that feeling, pour all my energy into it. It builds inside me, flowing through me. Then . . . then . . .

Everything coalesces into that one point. Pain flowers in

my head and bursts through my fallen defences to consume me. My body shakes with the effort of holding it all in, and so I stop trying to hold it. It flows out of me in a wave of energy that ripples through my body, through both of us.

All I'm aware of is the kiss, the touch of Laurie's lips on mine. I feel him tense, hear him gasp as the energy leaves me and I fall.

Chapter Nine

When things start coming back, they're . . . strange. I can tell instantly, even before I'm aware of my surroundings, that something's not right. For one thing, there are voices, and I know they're not in the room with me.

We've located the last one. There was a discharge of energy that should have torn him apart, but it's been shielding him, so he must still be alive. I didn't think any of them were capable of that. We still can't locate him through usual means, but a discharge like that should have killed him, so it's bound to have done some damage. We've been monitoring hospitals in the area. The shield was very effective in . . . unusual ways. We've only just received the intelligence. There's a car on the way. He must be neutralised, or he will present a danger to us all.

Shit. I expand my awareness, not failing to recognise how easy and effective it is now. I feel Laurie close by. Then, as I widen the scope, I sense lots of people, strangers. No, no, no. I sit bolt upright and get a startled exclamation from Laurie.

"What the fuck, Laurie? I told you . . . I *told* you not to bring me here. Fuck, Laurie."

"Calm down. What do you expect? We've all been scared stiff. You've been out for more than two days."

"Fuck. But I have to get out of here."

Panic screams through every fibre of my being, and I'm half out of the bed before Laurie pushes me back.

"Whoa, Gabriel. You can't wake up from being unconscious for almost three days and walk straight out of here. You can't."

"Like fuck, I can't! Laurie . . . you don't understand. I'm in danger. It's not safe here. It's not *safe*."

"Of course, it's safe, Gabriel. It's a hospital."

I try to calm down, but it's not easy. The panic is swamping me, consuming me. "Nowhere's safe. Here least of all. They're coming. They know where I am. I have to get out of here."

"Who's coming? Who do you think is after you?"

"Not *think*. They're coming, Laurie, coming now. Please. I have to. I *have* to get out of here right now."

My head's killing me, and I can't shut out the voices. They won't go away now. If I concentrate, I can understand what they're saying. If I don't, they slide into the background, but they're like an itch I can't scratch, a background fizz that's always there, and it makes my head hurt.

"Look. I don't know what's going on, but you can't just walk out of a hospital after being unconscious all this time."

"Watch me," I grind out, glaring at him.

"You're naked," he says softly.

"Shit."

Laurie presses gently against my shoulder, pushing me back. "Listen. I don't pretend to know what's going on here, but that night, the night you kissed me . . . Something . . . something happened. The world . . . changed. Because of that, I'm prepared to believe there's something bizarre going on. But you still can't walk out of here. You need to find out what's wrong with you. Before—"

"I know what's wrong with me." I can't look at him. I know he doesn't believe me. He thinks I'm acting stubborn. There's an internal battle going on between the part of me that's begging me to trust him and the part that's screaming *run, run, run.*

"Gabriel—"

"No. It's true, Laurie. I do know what's wrong with me,

and it isn't something they can help me with here. I know I haven't given you much reason to trust me but . . . But I . . . Look, I'll give you all the information you want. I'll tell you everything, I promise, only please, *please* believe me that we're in danger, terrible danger, and it gets worse every moment we stay in this place. I *have* to get out of here."

Laurie gazes at me for a few minutes, and I can see the conflict in his eyes. It's nowhere near as bad as the conflict ripping through my mind. The voices are buzzing like angry bees, and I know it's because they're discussing me. Every now and then I tap in, and I know from what I feel and what they say that they're getting closer. Some of the other things they're saying are equally terrifying. People are dying, and if they get here before I leave, I'm going to be next.

Eventually, he nods. "All right, but you still can't walk out of here naked. I have your clothes in the car. They gave them to me when they brought you in, and I haven't thought about them since. Damn, I've spent almost every moment here." He stops, looking uncomfortable. "I'll get them. Just don't do anything stupid before I get back."

Grinning with relief, I nod.

I should've known better. As soon as Laurie walks out the door, the panic sets in again. I tune in to the voices and check where they are. Close. Too damn close. For the first time, I realise I'm surrounded by the usual medical paraphernalia. It's crazy I didn't notice it before, but the panic blinded me to everything but getting Laurie to understand.

Needless to say, once I start freeing myself, alarms go off. I make sure to deal with the non-alarmed stuff first, and by the time the first nurse comes bursting through the door, I'm clear of the bed and ready for a fight. I'm quite prepared to physically fight them if I have to, but I'd rather not. The pain in my head's blinding, and the adrenaline's not going to do it any good at all.

I force myself to stay calm as a nurse built like the side of a house tries to manhandle me back to bed. Surprising myself with how soft and clear my voice is, I stare him in the eyes and say, "If you don't take your hands off me *right now,* I'm going to call the police, and have you charged with assault."

The nurse backs off but continues to assault me verbally. I respond quietly and respectfully, but to the effect of *Fuck off and get out of my way. One way or another I'm leaving here right now, and if you try to stand in my way, I'll put your head through the wall.*

In the middle of it all, a doctor arrives and tries to reason with me. Is he crazy? I'm not feeling particularly reasonable at the moment. What the hell does he expect? After making all this fuss, I'm hardly likely to say *okay, then, just because it's you, I'll get back into bed, now shall I?*

"Look. I know you mean well, but can we cut the crap? I'm not hallucinating, delusional, or mentally ill. I'm doing this of my own free will, knowing it's against medical advice and could result in a prolonged and horrible death. I'm not going to sue you, and I'm quite happy to sign a form to that effect. We could stand here all day and argue, but wouldn't it be better if we just pretend we've gone through all that and skip to the end where I leave?"

The doctor regards me closely for a few moments, then asks everyone else to leave.

"Can I at least put a dressing on your arm?"

"My arm?" I glance down and am truly shocked to see blood dripping off my fingers. "What the fuck?"

"It's generally considered to be a bad idea to rip out something that's going to leave a hole in part of your body that bleeds a lot."

"Ha, ha." I sit down on the bed and allow the doctor to clean up my arm and press a dressing over the place that's bleeding—profusely. I swear he's deliberately trying to make it hurt as much as possible.

"It would've been a lot better if you'd taken it out carefully, and in the right direction."

"Yeah, yeah, lesson noted. Next time, I'll be more careful."

"So, you're acknowledging there's likely to be a next time?"

I sigh theatrically. "I was *trying* to be sarcastic."

"You failed, because we both know there *is* going to be a next time."

He changes the pad for a less gory one. I'm relieved to see the bleeding's slowed down.

"Please. Spare me the lecture."

"It's my job." Then, without even looking up, he says softly, "Does this have anything to do with the telephone call we had half an hour ago?"

"What?" My heart stops, and my blood runs cold. No problem with my bleeding now, blood doesn't flow when it's frozen. "What call?"

"Do you realise we're supposed to keep you here by whatever means necessary?"

"Fuck that," I snarl, yanking my arm away, and making a lunge for the door.

"Wait," he calls as I reach for the door handle. "I'm not going to do that. I . . . there was something about that call that made me uneasy. Just let me finish taping your arm, and you're free to go."

"You know you're going to get into trouble for this? More trouble than you can imagine."

"Leave me to worry about that. Just get out of here—fast."

"I intend to."

At this point, Laurie appears in the doorway with a bag in his hand. He's panting and looks nervous to see the doctor, who simply smiles and nods to him on his way out.

"What have you been up to now?"

I'm too nervous to respond. My heart's thudding and every beat sends a hammer into my brain. I just grab the bag and start throwing clothes on. Thank God I was wearing trainers and not boots.

When I'm done, I grab the bag and practically run out the door, leaving Laurie to follow. No one gives us a second glance, at least not overtly. I feel exposed, unsafe. I keep expecting to see them come out of a lift or around a corner.

When we get outside, I breathe in the fresh air gratefully and head off, away from the front door. I don't know where I'm going, and I don't care. I just know that I have to get as far away as I can, as fast as possible. If I disappear, it'll be harder for them to find me. I have to keep moving. I have to —

"Wait. Where are you going?"

"Away."

"Wouldn't it be better if you get away in the general direction of the car?"

"No. That's where they'd expect me to go."

"Gabriel, you're making me very nervous."

"You should be. Go get the car and meet me."

"Meet you where?"

"The cafe."

"What cafe?"

"Go out of the main gate and turn left. It's a few hundred yards away. Park outside, and I'll come to you."

"Gabriel . . . what's all this about?"

"I'll tell you. I promise I'll tell you, but we have to get away from here. Please, Laurie. We have to get away right now."

"Okay. I'll meet you, but you better have a good reason."

"I do. Now go."

Looking over his shoulder as if he expects me to run out

on him, Laurie walks away. I feel empty and exhausted. If it wasn't for the unbelievable terror that fills me from head to toe, I wouldn't feel anything at all. I watch until he's out of sight. Then I run out on him.

There's no way I can let Laurie get caught up in all of this. I'm on the run now, and it would be unthinkable to ask him to leave everything behind and follow me. I cut through the industrial estate next to the hospital, and from there across the fields.

It would probably be best to stay away from the road. I'll have to take it eventually for at least a short distance. Otherwise, the only option is to strike out across open countryside, and I'm definitely not keen on that. It's not the weather to be sleeping out of doors without a tent or even a sleeping bag.

No, it's better to get to the station and take a random train to a destination that's a long way away. Oh no. Ah hell. I stop and all but fall to my knees. I have no money, no cards, no phone. Oh shit. I have nothing.

Right. I have to go back to the house, just to pick up . . . No, once they realise I'm not at the hospital, they'll go straight to the house. The boys can truthfully tell them they have no idea where I am, if not at the hospital.

But they won't get to the house yet. They haven't even arrived at the hospital. I can feel it. The voices are not talking about it. So what if I sneak into the house the back way? If no one sees me, they can't tell them anything. But what if they're watching the house?

My head's pounding. I can't think. I don't know what to do. While I'm trying to work it out, I start moving again, just because it has to be better than standing still. It's very cold, and I don't have a coat. I keep going over and over things, trying to find something I've missed—a chink of light, some way through. As usual, I miss the obvious. This time it's because I want to.

I'm barely aware of pavement under my feet instead of grass. I start walking along the road, my mind racing.

Suddenly, a car door opens across the pavement in front of me. My heart stops, and for a moment I'm frozen. Run . . . run . . . my mind screams at me, but my body's so scared, it's practically shitting its pants.

"Get in the car, Gabriel."

Relief floods me, and I almost collapse. I grab on to the door to stop myself from falling. "What the fuck are you trying to do to me? How'd you know where I'd be?"

"It wasn't too difficult to work out. I know you so well."

He's joking, but I'm in no mood for humour. I'm so torn. I want to get in, God, how I want to get in, but I can't. I can't get Laurie involved. It wouldn't be fair. It's so screwed up. But can I do this on my own? Can I? I know I can't. My head hurts, and I'm exhausted. How far will I get on my own? How soon will they track me down? To be on the run, alone, forever?

"Get in, Gabriel. If you don't get in, you're going to fall over, and I'm going to carry you in."

He's got a point, but I'm not going to give up without a fight. "Laurie, I can't. I can't let you get involved. You don't know what it would mean to you."

"I don't care. There's no way you're getting away from me without a proper explanation."

"But if I give you an explanation, you'll be involved, and it'll be too late."

"Get in the car, Gabriel."

The internal struggle is rapidly exhausting what little energy I have left. For the first time, I feel like someone who's been unconscious for two days. My stamina is disappearing fast. Maybe I should get in. Maybe I can get him to take me to the station and lend me money for a train. I could get a long way away, then hitch further. Then I could get a job and . . . God, I'm tired. What was I thinking about? I . . . I can't go with Laurie because . . . I just can't go.

I get into the car. As soon as I close the door, I say, "Take me to the station. I'll get a train."

"A train to where?"

"I don't know. It doesn't matter. Anywhere. It's best you don't know."

"You still don't understand, do you?" Laurie says softly.

"Understand what?"

"I think I fell in love with you the very first moment our eyes met in the club. It's only got worse since then. You kept falling, and I kept picking you up, and every single time, instead of getting weaker, you got stronger and I was so—impressed, astonished, proud—I don't know what the word is, but I do know that every time, I fell a little more in love with you.

"Sitting by your side these last few days, watching you sleep and wondering if I'd ever see those incredible eyes again . . . They were the worst days of my life. I thought I'd lost you. No one knew what was wrong with you, and they kept coming up with these crazy ideas, but everything they did only made things worse. I've never been so scared, and nothing that happens now could possibly scare me that much.

"I'd do anything for you, Gabriel, anything. You only have to ask. If only I can be with you, I'd give up everything."

I look at him. We're stopped at a traffic light. Our gazes lock. "You'll have to," I say, and in that moment, both our fates are sealed.

A cacophony of car horns alert us to the fact that the lights have changed, and Laurie takes off again.

"I don't think you fully realise what this means."

"Then tell me."

"You'll have to leave everything behind. Everything. You won't be able to see your family or friends, use your cards, even your name."

"Fuck, Gabriel, what the hell are you involved in . . . the mafia?"

"Worse, the government."

"Right. Wait here."

He pulls the car into a space in an Asda car park and disappears. When he comes back, he's laden with bags, most of which he throws into the back of the car. One, he tosses at me. It's a mobile phone, pay as you go.

"Ring everyone you need to ring, then throw it out the window. There's another in the back. I just need to stop off at the bank to empty my account. Then we're good to go."

"You're far too good at this."

Laurie grins, but it's a strained one. "Misspent youth."

After we visit the bank, Laurie makes several calls, then stops a stranger in the street and gives him his phone, suggesting they get a new sim card. It's a teenager, and it's an almost brand-new iPhone, so by the time we walk away we have a new best friend. I toss the cheap phone Laurie bought in a rubbish bin. Then we fill up with petrol and drive.

Chapter Ten

"Why are you doing this?"

"Doing what?"

"This . . . all of it. Why have you just walked away from everything for someone you don't know and have only just met? And don't give me any bullshit about me being beautiful and being in love with me, because that's all very well and good, but it's not enough to give up your life for."

Laurie shrugs and smiles. "I could ask you a similar question."

"What do you mean?"

"You're clearly in a lot of trouble and a lot of pain. Why would you trust someone you've only just met, who frustrates the hell out of you, who you can't decide whether to even like, and who seems to find the whole *walking away from everything* rather too easy?"

My blood runs cold. Laurie's smile is suddenly feral, and fear flashes through my head. Is he part of this? Is he one of *them*? Or something worse? Just who the hell is Laurie and what does he want with me?

"I . . . I hadn't thought about it until now."

"You should have."

Laurie lets me suffer for a few minutes, then laughs. "Relax. You're scared of enough things as it is. You really don't need to be scared of me. Yes, I did find it easy to walk away, because I've done it before . . . more than once. I travel light, and all my friends know how to help me disappear when I need to."

I don't know what shocks me most—that Laurie's felt the need to disappear before, or that he's talking so calmly about it now.

"Why?"

Laurie glances at me from the side of his eye. "I've been on the run since I was twelve. Initially, it was from Social Services. I don't know why they had such a problem with me living on the streets, to be honest. I was far safer there than I had ever been with my family."

That knocks the wind out of my sails. The thought of the strong, competent man I know being hurt so badly he ran away at twelve comes like a belly blow. "I'm sorry. I didn't . . ."

"Of course, you didn't. Why would you? It doesn't matter. It's old history. Just like the shoplifting, prostitution, and drug dealing that led to other . . . erm . . . disappearances. To be honest, this is the first time in my life I ever thought I'd actually put down roots and stay a while."

Another body blow. I groan aloud. "And I screwed it up for you. I'm so sorry."

Laurie's hand warms my thigh. "You've nothing to be sorry about. You haven't spoiled anything. You have no idea how much you haven't spoiled it. My past has been full of running away, and yeah, this time was supposed to be different, but when I ran before it was because I had no choice. This time I'm doing it because I want to, and I'm not running away from anything. I'm running toward something— the future, with you."

I don't know what to say to that. What can I say? *Thank you* would be so trite and so pathetically inadequate. Besides, I don't think Laurie is the kind to accept thanks easily. I'm certainly not the kind to give it, and he knows it. He likes me as I am, so . . .

"Stop thinking so much. Where do you want to go? South

Coast? Wales? Ireland? Scotland?"

"Ireland's out because by the time we get to the port, they'll be looking for us and we won't get through. North. Scotland. We need to stay away from populated areas. By tonight, our faces will be all over the news, and we'll be wanted for something nasty. Well, maybe not yours, not yet, but it will be. And they'll know about you emptying out your bank account and the calls you've made. We need to go somewhere remote, at least for a while."

"Okay. We'll just drive north."

"They'll probably get the police to look out for the car."

Laurie gives me a hard look. "No problem. I have a friend who'll fix that."

We drive in silence for maybe fifteen, twenty minutes. Suddenly there's a wall between us. The knowledge of what we've done and what we intend to do weighs heavily, and we're both lost in our own worlds.

Finally, we pull into a fairly small garage. We park outside the office, and Laurie turns to me and says, "Wait here. I won't be long."

"But—"

"Just wait, okay? I won't be long, I promise."

It's utterly ridiculous, the way my heart's pounding. When did I get to be such a coward? When did he get to be my rock? I don't know. All I know is that somewhere along the way he turned into my safety blanket, and the thought of him leaving me alone is terrifying. He must see something of that in my face because he smiles gently.

"It'll be all right, Gabriel. I'll take care of you. You don't have to be afraid anymore. I'm here now."

If only that were true. If only he could make me safe, but not even he can do that. There's nowhere and no one who can do that. Still . . . I feel . . . scared when he disappears into the office.

I'm so jumpy, so nervous, sitting here all alone. People walk by, cars whizz past, mechanics eye the car as they go about their business. I'm scared by them all. I feel so vulnerable, as if every eye is watching me — watching me *for them.*

Time stretches, and my stomach ties itself in knots. I'm actually shaking with the tremendous pressure of feeling so exposed and so scared of every sound, every movement outside the car. My head starts to pound, and the voices begin to intrude again.

We're getting close. The energy trace is weak, which could mean any number of things. We feel the fear, but that could be more to do with his surroundings and what's happening to his body than an awareness that we're closing in. However, we cannot exclude the possibility that he does know, as his awareness is certainly expanding, and we believe the implant has come fully back online. We're not sure how far he's controlling it, or how far it's controlling him. We'll be at the hospital within the next half hour. We've arranged for him to be detained there should he recover consciousness before we arrive, although we have been reliably informed this is unlikely.

So, they haven't got to the hospital yet. Where the hell are they coming from? What do they mean about the implant? Can't be that. Anything but that. Is that why the pain has got so much worse? What if it is? What if the nightmare is beginning again? I don't want to go through that again. I don't think . . . *Oh God. Oh God.*

I find myself rubbing my wrist. It feels naked without my wristbands. The ridges probably feel more pronounced to me than they really are, but what they represent has never been so raw, so present. I find myself staring at them and remembering back to the first time.

I'd almost done it then, nearly escaped, but they had to bring me back. Even so, they almost made it go away. I'd thought their treatments had turned it off. The voices went away, and I only heard them as a buzz in the background when one of my migraines hit. That's what I thought they were then—migraines. At least that's what I convinced myself to believe, what I wanted to believe.

Now I know different. Now, when it's too late. I think I always did. Oh God, what am I going to do? I can run from them, but I can't run from that, and if I could, they'd follow. I need to find a way of shutting it down. I have to.

The urge to get out of the car and run is almost unbearable. But there's nowhere to run to. I look down at my wrist and stroke my scars with the tip of my finger. There's one place I can run. I can escape. I can be at peace. I close my eyes and remember. I'd been so close . . . so close to ending the nightmare. Just a few more minutes and . . .

My eyes fly open when I hear Laurie's voice. He isn't talking to me, but his voice is clear. He's standing too far away, and speaking too softly, for me to hear, but I do hear. I hear as clearly as if he was shouting in my ear. What I hear is inconsequential. It's the fact that I *can*. God, is everything going to scare me from now on? I know the answer to that one, and I don't like it.

Laurie's talking to a young man, probably about four or five years older than me. He looks a bit . . . dodgy. Smiling and nodding, Laurie comes back to the car and gets in.

"It's all fixed," he says proudly. How can I tell him he's wrong? I smile, but he gives me a strange look, as if he knows. "Is everything all right?" he asks anxiously.

Somehow, I make myself smile and nod. But again, he knows, and he stares at me for long, hot moments, as my heart feels as if it's going to escape from my chest and tears burn my eyes.

Eventually, shaking his head, he starts the car and drives it around the back of the showroom and into the workshop. Almost as soon as we get ourselves and the shopping bags out of the car, another man gets into it and it's whipped away.

Laurie leads me into the office by a different door. The man is sitting behind a desk, and he's speaking animatedly on the phone. He makes a gesture with his hand. Laurie nods and leads me back out into the workshop.

"What's going on?"

"Don't worry. I've got it all covered."

"What, Laurie? What's going on?"

"We're getting a new car."

"But what'll happen to the old one? What if someone talks? What if they find the car?"

"Don't worry so much, Gabriel. After today, the car won't exist anymore. A paint job, a new set of number plates and the only way of identifying it as the original car will be to check the serial numbers, and I don't think they're going to be doing that for every car on the road."

"No, but—"

"Gabriel, I think it would be better if you didn't ask too many questions. Let's just say my friends aren't all . . . umm . . . law-abiding citizens and there are things going on *behind the scenes*, so to speak."

"Oh."

"Don't worry so much. I told you I'd take care of you, and I will, in ways you can't imagine. It's going to be all right. Trust me."

"No, it's not." I think my heart's going to break. I want to believe him. I so want to believe him, but he doesn't know . . . he doesn't *know*.

Laurie puts his arm around me and feels the shaking. "Are you okay?"

"No. I'm scared."

He turns me so he can gaze into my face and lays his hand against my cheek. "You have nothing to be afraid of. I'm going to take care of everything."

I can see from his eyes that he believes it, and I wish with all my heart that I could believe it, too. But I know. Maybe . . . maybe I should tell him. I look into his eyes and see the love, the protectiveness, the belief. I don't know. Maybe . . . maybe I can . . . maybe I can trust him.

Pain slams into the back of my head, so hard that I stumble forward into Laurie's arms. There are no voices now, but an explosion of anger that has the world spinning around me. I try to raise my head to look at Laurie, but it's like a ball of lead. My legs give way under the weight. Laurie grabs me around the waist and pulls me against him, but I can't stay on my feet, and I pull him down with me.

For a moment the world goes dark, but only for a moment. I blink heavily, and his face comes back into focus. He's cradling me in his arms, looking anxious.

"Gabriel, what's wrong? Are you all right?"

"They . . . they're at the hospital. They know I've gone."

He brushes the hair out of my face and smiles. "That's all right. They won't find us. They don't know where we've gone. In a few minutes, we'll have a new car, and we can go anywhere. They won't find us. They won't know where to look."

"They'll know where to look."

"No. We'll disappear. We'll go wherever you want. They won't find us."

"I . . ." I want to tell him the truth, right here and now, but I don't have the energy. That explosion of anger is still ringing through my head, and I'm completely open, hypersensitive to everything—every sound, every sight, every feeling. I can't close it out. I can't control . . . I can't . . .

"I can't," I whisper before merciful darkness covers me like a blanket and I sink gratefully into it.

Waking up is hard. The pain hasn't faded much at all. The

only relief is that the voices seem to have stopped. At least, I'm not hearing them anymore. It takes a while to realise we're moving. I crack my eyes open and see the world sliding by outside the car window. It's getting dark.

"Where are we?" I whisper as I try to sit up.

"On the M-six, just passing Kendal."

"Where's that?"

"Less than an hour from the Scottish border."

"How'd we get here?"

"In a car."

"Ha, ha," I say, in no mood for sarcasm. If Laurie wasn't here, I'd moan aloud. Fuck, my head hurts.

"You've been . . . asleep . . . for hours."

"How'd I get in the car?"

"I carried you. I'm getting used to that." He has a smile in his voice, but it can't hide the concern.

"Thanks."

"What happened to you?"

"I . . . It's a long story."

"I'm expecting it all tonight, Gabriel," he says softly. "I think, considering I've given up everything for you, the least you can do is tell me why."

He's right of course. I know he's right. He deserves to know. But I . . .

"I don't know if I can."

"Why not?"

"I suppose . . ." I try to sit up straighter, but the pain lances through me again, and it defeats me. This time I groan and press my hand against the back of my head.

"Are you all right?"

"No."

"Gabriel. I'm scared . . . not for me. Not about getting caught by whoever the hell is after you, but for you. I don't know what's happening to you, but I know it's bad, and it scares me. Do you know what's wrong with you?"

For a moment I toy with the idea of lying. It would be so easy to say no but I can't, not with him.

"Yes."

"Oh," he says simply. "It's getting worse, isn't it?"

"Yes."

"Is it dangerous, Gabriel? Is it going to . . . Will you . . ."

"I don't know. It's dangerous, for sure—for both of us. But . . . I don't know what's going to happen. The last time it happened, I didn't . . . I didn't get the chance to see how it ended." I'm unconsciously stroking my wrist again, and he doesn't miss the gesture.

"Are you hungry?"

"What?" The question takes me by surprise. It's an unexpected change of subject.

"You haven't eaten all day. Come to think of it, you haven't eaten for three days. Shit. How are you still functioning?"

"I'm not. Yes, I'm hungry."

"Okay, we'll stop at the next services and fuel up—us and the car. Then we'll look for somewhere to spend the night. When we're settled, you can tell me everything."

"I want to get over the border before we stop for the night. It's still early."

"Whatever you want, sure. Just food for now, then."

The services aren't far, and it seems like no time before I'm jerking awake after not realising I was dozing. I climb out of the car on trembling legs, but at least my headache has abated enough to let me stand and walk, if not think or speak.

"Come on. You've been sleeping all the way, and you still look exhausted. Are you sure we can't just stop here? I'm worried about you."

You should be, I think, but I don't say anything. What can I say that won't make it worse? I just smile and shake my head, which is a mistake.

The services are a big surprise. They're not the bulky, characterless places I'm used to. The buildings are wooden, and the whole area is very pretty. We sit by a huge window that looks out over a lake—with ducks and lilies—to a green vista of gently rolling hills.

"This is nice."

"Hmm." I have no energy for talking. What little I have is being concentrated into eating. Now the plate's in front of me, I'm not hungry. No . . . I am hungry, but I'm too tired to eat. I can't believe how tired I am. Everything's an effort, and my eyes feel like someone has thrown grit into them. I'm completely exhausted, want nothing more than to crawl under a table, curl up, and fall asleep right here.

It isn't natural. I know that. I know why. I know what comes next, and I don't want it to. Maybe I should just let them catch me. Maybe I should let it happen. At least then it would be over. But it wouldn't be. It wouldn't be over. It would just go on and on.

I need help. I can't do this on my own. I glance at Laurie. The sun is shining through the window and blazing off the red streaks in his hair. His blue eyes are sparkling, and he's smiling at me. He's beautiful and I'm tired.

"I'm going to tell you. I'm going to tell you everything. I need help, Laurie. I can't do this on my own anymore."

There are tears in my eyes. I put down my knife and fork to dash them away. Laurie leans across the table and puts his hand over mine. "You don't have to do it on your own. You're not alone any more, Gabriel."

I look up at his face, and it shimmers through the tears. For the first time in ages, I smile a genuine smile, and the ice around my heart melts a little.

When we've eaten—and he makes sure I eat the whole

meal, with dessert and two bottles of water—we visit the clean and impressive toilets, then go back to the car. After filling up with petrol, we're on our way again.

I don't know why, but it's an enormous relief when we cross the border into Scotland. It isn't a different country, but it feels like it. It feels, if not safe, then safer.

After driving for about half an hour, we find services with a Premier Inn, near Lockerbie, and Laurie books us in for the night. It's cheap and cheerful, and best of all, impersonal and anonymous.

The first thing I do when we walk through the door of our room is crash, but Laurie's not going to let me get away that easily. He shakes me awake and helps me prop myself up on pillows so I can rest my head. Then he sits on the bed, his back against the wall and his knees drawn up, a look on his face that says . . . *okay, I've kept my side of the bargain, now let's hear it — let's hear it all.*

I sigh, close my eyes so I won't have to look at him, and sink into the past.

CHAPTER ELEVEN

"When I was thirteen, we studied the paranormal as a concept in our sociology classes. We reviewed all the usual stuff—ghosts, auras, ESP, telepathy. One day, some people came to class, and they set up a series of tests that we were told was to teach us about conducting controlled experiments in ESP.

"It was all a huge joke, just a laugh because no one believes in any of that, right? My friends and I giggled and wisecracked and treated it as nothing more than a way of getting out of our regular lessons. It was a bit of fun. We did it. We laughed about it. We forgot.

"It must've been about two months later when I came home from school, and there was a big black car parked outside my house. Two men in suits were talking to my parents, and the only word I can think of to describe them is sinister. They were all smiles and seemed to have impressed my parents, but they scared the hell out of me. It was the way they were looking at me . . . as if I was a piece of meat on a butcher's block."

I take a long drink of water from the bottle Laurie put on the bedside table and try to slow the pace of my heart. Even now—after so long and everything that's happened in between—I can smell their cologne, see the way they were perched on the edge of the *best* sofa in the *front room*. That's what my parents used to call the lounge, the place that was only used for parties or when important people came. It smelled of polish and incense. My mother was a bugger for that.

"Gabriel?"

I glance up. Laurie's face is sympathetic but resolute. I can tell that he isn't going to let me get lost in the story, any more than he's going to allow me to stop telling it.

"Sorry. They were very pleasant, very polite, very respectful, but they still scared me. After a while, they left, and I didn't really understand who they were or what they wanted. I just knew I didn't want to see them ever again.

"When they'd gone, my parents explained they'd offered me a place on a government-run program for gifted children." I snorted. "That kinda surprised me because I'd never considered myself gifted in any way. I was pretty average, really. I tried to ask exactly what I was supposed to be gifted at, but they were vague. I got the impression they didn't know either. They were impressed that the men were from the government and the rest didn't even matter. I'm not sure they even knew what part of the government they were from. Education authority? Ministry for gifted children? Department of bullshit?

"I told them straight away I didn't want to go. The prospect terrified me. I didn't want to move away from my parents, and I certainly didn't want to go with those men. But the 'rents had stars in their eyes, and what I wanted didn't matter."

I glance at Laurie to test his reactions so far. He's gazing at me with a strange expression on his face—cautious, concerned, and carefully non-committal. I think he has an idea where this may be going, but he can only be, at best, partly right.

"In the end, I had to go. It was a great honour, a wonderful experience, an exciting adventure, blah blah. And in the beginning, it was. There were twenty of us altogether, from different schools, different parts of the country, different ages. I was one of the youngest. We all met up and were taken onto a huge bus. It had all sorts of good things built in, like televisions, video games, DVD players.

"Everything was awesome. So awesome it didn't matter that all the windows were blacked-out so we couldn't see through them. We had no idea where we were being taken. I think most of them didn't even notice . . . but I did. I was already nervous, and that made it a hundred times worse.

"When the bus stopped, we all got out. We were in a courtyard in front of a huge old building with other more modern ones on both sides. I had no idea where I was, but I had the feeling I wasn't going to enjoy it there.

"When we got inside, we were divided into four sets of five and taken off in different directions. We were shown to separate rooms and asked to meet up in the common room in half an hour.

"The room was pleasant enough, small, but so new it still smelled of pine. There was a window looking out over lawns and a neat garden, a narrow bed that looked as if it had never been slept in, a desk and chair and a wardrobe. We'd been told that there was a common bathroom, kitchen, and relaxation area, just for the five of us, and that the other three groups would have the same.

"In the wardrobe was a uniform, a short-sleeved tunic top with a symbol embossed in gold over the left breast, and loose, elastic-waist trousers. It was weird, but it was soft and felt nice to wear. I figured it was there to wear, so I put it on, then went to join the others in the relaxation area. I never saw that room again."

I glance up at Laurie. His eyes are wide, but he doesn't seem to be laughing at me, disbelieving. Not yet.

"Are you okay?"

"No, but you want to hear it, and after all this time I want to tell it."

"Okay, but . . ."

"What?"

"You don't look so good, Gabriel, and you're shaking. I know I said I wanted to hear it, but not if it's going to make you ill."

"It's not about you now, Laurie. It's about me. I *have* to tell you."

Laurie nods but moves to sit next to me. He pulls me into his arms and draws my head down to rest on his shoulder. I feel safer and actually begin to relax a little. The words come more easily.

"Everyone was dressed in the uniform and we joked about. Then someone came and told us we were going to have a medical, just to make sure we were healthy, because part of the program would be physical training, and they needed to know if we had any issues that might get in the way.

"I was uneasy from the start, and it got worse as, one by one, the others disappeared and didn't come back. I was the last. They took me to a room that looked like a normal doctor's surgery and did all the usual tests—blood pressure, height, weight, reflexes. I was beginning to relax when the doctor told me they were going to give me a shot.

"That sent my comfort level through the roof. I tried to get him to tell me what it was, and what it was for, but he was vague, and I got scared. I tried to run away. It was stupid, I know. By then I was deep inside the lair, and there's no way I would've been able to find my way out, even if I could've got through the locked doors. Still, I tried. I had to try."

I glance at Laurie and he nods. He seems to understand that I had to try, that he would have done the same.

"There were two men in white uniforms waiting outside the door. They dragged me back and held me while the doctor gave me the shot. Almost the moment the needle went into my arm, I was unconscious."

Laurie hugs me close. I'm so lost in the story, I don't even realise how much I'm shaking, although I can still taste the fear that gripped me at the time when I realised how I'd been tricked, how helpless I was, how stupid.

"When I woke up, I was in a strange room. It was all white and had only a bed, which I was strapped to, and a couple of cupboards. I spent a lot of time in that room, and for a fair amount of it, I was unconscious. Not always, though. In between experiments and treatments, I did sometimes have nights of natural sleep, and there was even a place where we could relax. I saw those who'd come with me during those times. They were all silent, hollow-eyed, like walking ghosts. No more fun, no more laughter. I didn't realise at the time, but I was the same, and it only got worse.

"No . . ." It's so easy now that I've started. The words are running away from me. I'm getting muddled, telling things out of order. Things that aren't important. "I need to tell it in order. Almost as soon as I woke up that first day, they came and took me away. They went over and over the same tests I'd had at school, the basic ESP and telepathy tests with flashcards, drawings in sealed envelopes. It was boring and tedious, but safe. I did what I was told and then they let me sleep because I'd been tired from the moment I opened my eyes.

"The same thing happened every day for I don't know how long. Not that I was always a willing participant. I was thirteen. There were tears and tantrums, but they were patient and unrelenting.

"And then . . . And then . . ." I squeeze my eyes shut. This is the point. This is where it all changed, where my life went to Hell. My heart's pounding, my mouth's dry, and I'm sweating. Laurie tightens his arms and whispers into my hair.

"It's all right. I'm here. You're not that helpless little boy anymore, and you're not alone."

"I know." I take a deep breath. "One day . . . one day I woke up and everything was different. I was lying on a bed but moving. There was a drip in my arm, and I felt drugged. I tried to speak, to ask what was happening. I was scared, I was . . . No one spoke to me, and I got more and more afraid.

"Then they wheeled me into something that looked like an operating theatre, which it was. Someone—a doctor, a nurse—leaned over me and told me that I had to be a good boy, and if I was good and relaxed, it would soon be over, and I'd be back in my room.

"I was terrified. I tried to get away, but I was strapped down. I started to scream, and the person came back and tried to soothe me, saying that I had been such a good boy and I just had to be brave for a little while and then it would be over, and I could go to my room and rest.

"They gave me something, and I started to drift. I stopped screaming, but I didn't stop being scared, especially when I heard someone in the background talking about an implant. I didn't want them putting things inside my body, but I couldn't fight them. I tried. Oh God, I tried, but I was only thirteen. The last thing I remember is someone lowering a mask over my face and telling me to relax and that's it."

"Shit, Gabriel. What did they do to you?"

"I didn't know for a while, not for a long time, because they never mentioned it again, not until months later when the headaches got so bad I was convinced I was dying. I begged them to take me to the hospital because I was sure there was something in my head that was killing me. They told me not to make a fuss and that it was only the implant *bedding in.*"

"What? They . . . they put something in your head?

They . . ."

"Yes."

"And that's what causes the headaches?"

"Yes."

"And all the rest of it?"

"Yes."

"Even now?"

"Yes."

Laurie tries to shift so he can look into my eyes, but I resist him. I don't want him to look at me. I don't want anyone to. I can't meet his eyes. It feels as if a boil has been lanced — a relief, but the poison has to go somewhere, and I'm scared it will have poured right into him. What will he think of me when this is all said and done?

"But why? What does it mean? What's it for?"

"If you listen, I'll tell you."

"Sorry. It's just . . . It's hard to hear, hard to believe. Who were these people? How'd they get away with it, stealing children like that, doing God knows what to them?"

"Because they're part of the government. They're a secret research project aimed at helping to create a super soldier. The implants are meant to tap into the psychic centres of the brain and enhance latent psychic ability.

"Almost from the moment I came 'round after the operation, they started the experiments. Sometimes they were the same as before, hour after hour guessing cards or trying to read minds. More hours watching videos with electrodes stuck all over my body. The difference was that now I had the implant.

"I don't know to this day whether they controlled it or whether it did its own thing, but it certainly had an effect. I don't know how to describe it, but sometimes it made me feel like my mind was expanding outside my head, a long way outside my head. Like I was speeding down a tunnel that opened out, wider and wider.

"I could do all sorts of things—hear people talking all over the facility and even outside—until they realised I could do it and shielded it. I could perform better in all the tests, communicate telepathically with everyone else who had the implant, and the testers, all sorts of things. The only problem was that every time the implant activated, it provoked the headaches, which always ended in me passing out. Sometimes for days.

"After a while, the experiments changed. They would take me into a dark room and strap me into a chair." I shudder. Oh God, *The Chair*. I can't . . . I just can't talk about that, not even now. Not even to Laurie. It makes me sick to think of it . . . to think of what they did . . . what they . . ."I . . . they did . . . things . . . tests. They tried to make me . . . to find out what the implant was doing, whether the implant had triggered any talents."

I take another drink, to wash the bitterness from my mouth. It doesn't work. The taste of the past is a bitterness nothing is going to sweeten. May as well get it all out there.

"Then there was a time I don't remember very well. I think I must've been drugged or even unconscious for most of it, and I have no idea what they did to me. I think something went wrong because I have fleeting memories of anxious faces and whispered conversations that might not even have been in the same room. I don't remember the content, but I remember the general feeling. They were worried, almost panicking. Looking back, I think I came pretty close to dying, although I don't know why.

"I . . . Laurie . . . they . . . they did things to me in there. They changed me. Some of it I don't remember, and some . . . There's some I don't *want* to remember, and I can't . . . I just can't talk about. It hurt me. It . . ."

Laurie drew me to him and squeezed me tight.

"It's okay, you don't have to. Is that what you dream about? The time when you were at the facility?"

"Yes."

"No wonder it makes you scream."

"Yeah."

"What happened in the end? I mean there must've been an end, or you'd still be there."

I have to smile at that. "What makes you think I'm not? What happened was that one day I woke up . . . woke up properly for the first time in ages. They came for me and took me home. There was no explanation, no reason, nothing. No one spoke to me or even said goodbye. I was beyond being scared by then, beyond even being curious. I just went along with whatever they told me to do.

"They put me in a car with those same blacked-out windows, presumably so I wouldn't be able to tell where we were going. That was a laugh. I don't know whether or not they realised, but I was hyper-aware. I knew what the driver was thinking, what he was feeling, what the man who was sitting in the back with me was thinking. He thought I was a failure, and the sooner they got rid of me, the better.

"I did get a little twinge of fear at that. What did *get rid of me* mean? I needn't have worried. They practically threw me out on my doorstep and left me.

"My parents were absolutely beside themselves. I'd been gone for almost a year, and they'd spent most of that time going frantic trying to find me. I'd just disappeared into the ether, and they'd tried everything, to no avail. I tried to tell them what had happened, but no one would believe me."

I look up into Laurie's face, a tinge of panic in my heart. "You believe me, don't you?"

"I can't lie to you, Gabriel. It's tough to take in. A secret government project that steals children. Paranormal activities . . . ESP . . . it's all science fiction stuff."

He must see the panic and pain in my face because he leans down and gently kisses me, then says, "But I've seen what happens to you. I felt the energy that came from you that day. I've seen the genuine fear in your eyes. And above all of that . . . I trust you. I know you wouldn't lie to me so . . . yes, I believe you."

Relief floods me, and I stretch up to kiss Laurie desperately.

"What happened next?" he prompts gently after a time.

"I tried to settle back into my old life, but it wasn't happening. I was fourteen with a whole year missing out of my life. My friends had moved on, but not as far as I had. I had nothing in common with them anymore. Just about the only friend I had was Daniel. He'd been my boyfriend before I was taken, although no one knew that . . . just us.

"The headaches were happening more and more often, worse than they are now. Sometimes I'd be in bed for days. The doctor said they were migraines, and prescribed medication that didn't touch them.

"But . . . it wasn't just the headaches on their own. When they came, other things came with them. I started to hear things, voices in my head. Except the voices didn't come from inside my head—they came from all around me. I was spontaneously listening to other people's thoughts. At first, it was people around me, people who were close to me, and I learned, painfully in some cases, exactly what they thought about me and what I'd been through. No one believed me.

"I was desperate to fit back into my old life, but my experience in the facility had changed me, destroyed part of me, awoken another I couldn't control, didn't want to control. I tried to silence it with drink and drugs, and to hide the physical wreckage it left behind—the blinding headaches, attacks of uncontrollable shaking, blackouts, and muscle spasms. Not to mention the psychological damage—panic attacks, paranoia, self-abuse.

"I went deeper and deeper into the spiral of drink, drugs, and self-harm, and I dragged Daniel down with me. He was sweet and gentle and kind, and he was there for me, pulling me back every time I got to the brink, holding me when I fell apart. I know he didn't believe me when I talked about what happened to me, but he believed I was hurt, sick, and needed help.

"The thing was, he stuck by me so well that when I descended into Hell, I took him with me, and once down there neither one of us could get back. I was dragged away by events, but as far as I know, he's still there. The last I heard, he's a hardcore heroin addict, working tricks to sustain his habit, and two steps away from a prison cell. In a way, I hope he is in prison, and not . . .

"He was beautiful, Laurie, truly beautiful in every way, and I screwed him up and left him there to slowly rot."

"It wasn't your fault. You were dealing with things in the only way you could. You didn't force him to do any of the things he did. It wasn't your fault."

I stare up at him, conflicting emotions tearing me apart. This is the first time I've even tried to tell anyone all of it, and it's an enormous relief to get it off my chest. I feel safe with Laurie in a way I never have before, not even with Daniel, but . . . but still . . .

"I want to believe that. You've no idea how much I want to believe that, but I can't. I *was* responsible for what happened to Daniel because if it wasn't for me, he never would've gone down the path he did. He was as straight as they come, figuratively speaking, of course, a model student, on course to be head boy. He was popular and pleasant, squeaky clean, the boy-next-door type. He didn't even swear, and would never have started drinking and smoking, definitely not drugs.

"Then he started to do all those things . . . for me. I was scared of what was happening to me. It was all getting too much. I couldn't control what I was thinking, feeling, knowing what everyone else was thinking and feeling . . . I was scared of how I was when I was sober and more scared of what would happen when I was drunk, and *he* had to drink to cope. I was scared the first time I took drugs, so he did it, too, so we'd go through the experience together. Step by step, we walked together into Hell. I got out. He didn't."

"So how'd you get out?"

"I tried to kill myself," I say simply. "It was all just too much. Nothing stopped it. Nothing shut it out. The drink and drugs helped a little. They dulled the edge of whatever it is the implant does to me, but they couldn't stop it altogether, and I just couldn't cope anymore. I couldn't cope with what it did to me, and I couldn't cope with what I was doing to try to stop it.

"One day it was particularly bad. I'd passed out at school, twice in two days. In between, the voices were there, constantly. The students, the teachers . . . I couldn't shut them out . . . any of them. And most of them were thinking the same thing . . . *freak*.

"I came home from school with a headache screaming in the back of my head. I knew what was coming. This was about as bad as it had ever been. I knew that within half an hour or so I'd be in pain so bad I couldn't even scream, locked in torment until it decided to release me, which might be hours or days. I didn't want that again. I didn't want the pain anymore.

"I went straight to my bedroom and got the razor blades I hid under my bed. I used them to cut myself, which was the only release I had from the voices. I went into the bathroom and sat in the bath with a razor blade in my hand. The headache started to build, and I knew if I didn't do it, then I'd never be able to . . . so I did. The pain came screaming into my brain, but it didn't have power over me anymore because something else was happening that made it all just slip away."

I'm rubbing my wrist again. I hadn't noticed until Laurie stops me, lifts it to his lips, and kisses it gently.

"How can you even bear to look at it, let alone touch it?"

"Because it's part of you, part of your life, of what makes you the person you are. I keep telling you how beautiful you are, and you keep not believing me . . . but it's true. You're beautiful, and, because they're part of you, these scars are beautiful, too."

I can't believe him. I don't. And yet . . .

"What happened next?" he asks softly, somehow knowing how hard it is for me to hear him say those things, nice as they are.

"My parents found me. They were almost too late, and part of me will always hate them for that—for not being too late. I was admitted to a mental hospital, committed so I couldn't leave. It was almost as bad as being at the facility. They couldn't help me, of course, because they wouldn't believe or accept the truth. They talked about paranoia, schizophrenia, delusions. They treated me with drugs, therapy, electric shocks—anything they could throw at me—but they couldn't cure me because they didn't know what was wrong in the first place. They wouldn't believe me. On the other hand, they did, albeit accidentally, manage to dull the pain. I don't know if they took the implant offline or just suppressed its effects, but whatever it was, it worked . . . kind of.

"In the end, they had to let me go. But I'd changed—changed completely. The treatments and the drugs I've continued to take suppressed the worst of the symptoms, but solving one problem only created more. My parents were terrified I was going to hurt myself again, or with my uncontrollable rages, hurt them. They were scared of me, of what I'd become, and were relieved when I moved out. They felt guilty as hell and compensated with material things.

"I tried to find Daniel, but he'd disappeared. I had a new boyfriend, Michael. I met him at the hospital. He was schizophrenic but really cool. We'd got close when we were in there, and when he came out, we started going out."

"What happened?" Laurie sounds concerned. He must've heard something in my voice. "I mean, you said you'd told me everything, but I don't think you have, not really, and I need to know it all."

"He couldn't handle the outside world . . . or life . . . or me. Most of all me. We were together for maybe four months. For the first three it was good, but then it all started falling apart. He got more and more paranoid, and every time I passed out or got one of my headaches, he'd be convinced I was possessed. And he tried all these crazy ways to exorcise me.

"I couldn't handle it, and we both got more and more frustrated and angry—with ourselves and each other. I suppose you could say we brought out the worst in each other."

"Can I assume it didn't end well?"

I look up at him. He's smiling, kind of, trying to lighten the heaviness, trying to make light of what he thinks happened. I close my eyes, feeling completely exhausted. "It ended when we had a huge argument. He accused me of hiding things from him, and he was way out in left field with what he thought it was. So I told him. I told him everything, just like I told you.

"He went very quiet, and we had the best sex we ever had. We fell asleep in each other's arms. When I woke, he wasn't there. I went looking for him and found him in the next room. I walked through his blood and apparently spent half a day staring at the thing that used to be his head before someone found us. I didn't even know he had a gun."

"Oh, my God, Gabriel. I'm so sorry. That must've been . . . must've . . ."

"Yeah . . . yeah, it was. I ran. I ran far, far away, but I couldn't take it. I couldn't cope with being so far away from everything familiar. I couldn't deal with what was happening to me and with all the other stuff going on in my life . . . and the new people I met weren't used to me and freaked when I passed out or had a shaking fit or got wiped by my headaches. So I came back. I was lucky. I got a room with Andy and Bobby, who I swear are just about the only two people in the world who would've been able to cope with me for so long. And that's it.

"The medication they gave me at the mental hospital suppressed the worst symptoms, and I had a few years when I could pretend to be normal, but lately it's all started again, and it's been getting worse and worse."

"Shit, Gabriel."

Chapter Twelve

Closing my eyes, I snuggle my head into Laurie's shoulder so I won't have to look into his eyes. "When I get one of those weird headaches, I can hear them. For ages, it was just a buzzing, like they were outside the room with the door closed. I could hear the voices, but not what they said. And then, the other day, I started to hear them more clearly.

"They were talking about the implants activating again. They said they were more powerful—or maybe *we* were more powerful—than they thought or expected. I'm not sure what they meant, to tell you the truth. In the beginning, I only got snatches and didn't understand most of it.

"One thing I did understand, though, was that they want to *neutralise* me . . . us, all of us. They said we're dangerous, and that most of us have already been neutralised. I'm the last. I'm the only one left alive, and they're coming for me. I'm scared, Laurie. More scared than I've ever been before. They want to kill me, and they can track me from the implant. Every time it activates, they know where I am."

"Then we have to stop it activating."

"But that's the point. I can't . . . I can't control it. That's always been the point." Laurie's arms tighten around me, and I feel . . . safe, almost safe, safe enough to cry.

Laurie strokes me gently as I cry, and it feels so good. The storm is over quickly, and I'm left feeling strangely calm. Here we are, on the run, fleeing people who are trying their best to track me down and kill me—kill us both—with no home, no future, and no hope, but for now, for this one moment, this one night, none of it matters because I'm here . . . with him.

No! I have to stop. Stop thinking like this. Stop relaxing. Stop believing. Stop hoping. This is not going to work. I poison everything. I hurt people. I'm a freak, a monster. I'm going to get us both killed. If I care for him at all, I have to leave him. I have to walk away and make damn sure he doesn't follow me. I can't let him be dragged any further into this.

But I can't. I can't walk away. I can't leave him. I can't do this on my own anymore. I can't, and I don't want to. I don't want to be alone. I'm too tired, too empty. If I walk away from him, I walk away from life.

Why not? I'm going to die anyway when they catch up with me. This way at least it'll only be me, not him. I'll just walk away. Walk away from it all. End the pain. Finally get to rest. Lay down my burdens. Give up.

And as easy as that, it's done, the decision made. Tomorrow, I'll walk away from Laurie, and I'll walk away from everything and everyone else. From the fear, the loneliness, the struggle, the endless confusion, and pain. Tomorrow it'll all end. I don't know how I'll do it, but details like that can be worked out later. It's a huge relief to know that I only have one night. I just have to live through one more night, then it'll all be over. I'll be safe at last.

Exhaustion is creeping in at the edges of my consciousness, and my headache is still there, although somehow talking about the whole crazy situation seems to have relieved the tension somewhat. The headache's getting better rather than worse. That's a good thing, isn't it?

"Are you okay?"

"Yes. No. I don't know."

"Care to pick one?"

"No. But I think maybe I will be. If they don't catch us

and wipe me out first."

"No one's going to do that. I swear to you, Gabriel, I will save you. Give me a few days to work on it, and I'll fix it."

He looks so sincere, as if he means it, as if he really thinks he can do it.

"I . . . what about your life, your art, your gallery? I can't ask you to give all that up for me."

"I'm not."

"But . . . You do understand, don't you? You can never go back. You can't speak to your family or friends ever again. You can't use your cards or phone. They'll trace you, find us."

"We've already been over this. I'm not leaving anything important behind. Don't worry. Things will happen. I'll get my paintings shown. I'll get the proceeds of the sales and the profits of the gallery. How it happens isn't your worry. Just know that none of it will ever be traceable to us."

"I don't understand."

"No, and you're not meant to. Just trust me, okay?"

I stare into his eyes, and what can I say?

"Okay."

Smiling, Laurie lowers his head. I close my eyes, melting into the kiss. Somewhere, something in the back of my mind is screaming at me. At some point, I'm going to have to listen to it. I know that. I know this can't last. I can't do this anymore. I'm exhausted, truly and utterly exhausted, and no matter what Laurie says, what he does, I'm too tired to go on. Tomorrow . . . tomorrow I'm going to do something about that, but tonight . . .

I relax in his arms and surrender completely to his kiss. His hand strokes my hair, so gently, while his other arm supports my back. Slowly—ever so slowly—his kisses trail from my lips over my cheek and chin down to my throat. I let my head fall back and moan softly as his lips touch the sensitive skin between my neck and shoulder, while his hand travels down to rest lightly on my waist.

Carefully, he lowers me back onto the pillows, twisting slightly so that he's half lying on me. He pauses and gazes down at me. There's something in his eyes, something I've never seen before, and it makes me breathless.

He remains motionless, and I'm mesmerised by the expression in his eyes. No one has ever looked at me like that before. "Laurie?"

"Ssh, it's all right. Everything's going to be all right. I'll take care of you, Gabriel. You're safe now. I'll make you safe. I love you." For a moment he seems surprised. Then he grins. "That sounds so good. So good." He strokes my hair and my face. The grin fades and his eyes shine, softer than any eyes I've ever seen. They're so blue. "I love you, Gabriel. I really do. I've never said that to anyone before, not like that, not like this, and it feels so fucking good. I love you."

I just stare at him. I think I'm in shock. What can I say? It feels good to me, too, or at least it did — until I realise what it means. I can't say it back. It would be so easy — to say it, to let it be true. So easy . . . for now, but . . . Although, what difference does it make now? Tomorrow I'm going to die, so what difference does it make what I do tonight?

I find myself relaxing at the thought. It doesn't matter. It doesn't matter anymore. I don't have to hold it all in anymore. I don't have to be afraid of saying what I want to say, of feeling what I want to feel. I smile. It's a smile that starts deep inside, deep in the realisation that it doesn't matter anymore, that I'm free. For this one night I can be who I want, say what I want, and it doesn't matter.

Laurie misinterprets my smile, and I might feel bad about that if I wasn't feeling so damn good. I raise my hand and touch his face, in utter wonder of the feelings I'm finally allowing myself to feel. "I love you, too."

For a moment, when he starts to undo the buttons on my shirt, I freeze and put my hand over his to stop him. I close my eyes and fight a battle with myself. It's not that I don't want this. I think I've wanted it since the first moment I saw him but . . . He says I'm beautiful. He thinks it, I'm sure. But he won't when he sees my body. I don't know if I can bear it. I don't know if I can bear to see his face when he sees . . .

Laurie lays his hand flat on my chest, over my heart, my own still lying on top of his. He leans down and gently kisses me with small, butterfly kisses, teasing my lips.

"It's all right, Gabriel. You can trust me. It's going to be all right, I promise."

But it's not. It's not going to be all right. I'm going to have to watch his face change. I'm going to have to lie here and have his words thrown back in my face. Just like all the rest. But none of them has looked at me like Laurie does. What difference does it make? He's not in love with me. He's in love with who and what he thinks I am. He thinks I'm beautiful.

"I'm not going to hurt you, Gabriel. I'd never hurt you. You're beautiful, so beautiful, even if you don't see it. I see it, Gabriel. I've always seen it, right from the start."

Oh, no. Oh, God no. If only he hadn't said that. If only he hadn't said I'm beautiful. I close my eyes and try to shut out the truth. I'm going to see it. I'm going to see that look on his face, the one that always comes before the withdrawal, the accusations, the desertion. Sometimes there's even violence. And always I'm left feeling violated.

Once there was someone, not long after Michael. I needed someone to hold me, someone to tell me that it wasn't my fault, that I was still alive, still worth something. He saw, and he didn't turn away. He smiled at me and made me feel it was going to be all right. I let myself believe it was going to be all right.

All the time he was fucking me, I believed. Even though he didn't want intimacy, even though he wasn't making love to me, just screwing me, hard and fast. Even then I believed.

But when he finished, his eyes changed. When he'd got what he wanted from me, he stood up and threw the used condom on my belly and laughed at me.

"Thanks for the fuck," he said. "It was just what I needed — a throwaway with a pretty little whore. All the better that I didn't have to pay for it."

"But . . . but I thought . . ."

"Thought what? That I cared? Don't make me laugh. Who the fuck would care about a freak like you? We all know the story. A sad little fucker who couldn't even succeed in killing himself. You managed all right with that freak of a boyfriend of yours, though, didn't you? They say you were fucking him when he died. Is that true? What's it like . . . to be fucking someone in their death throes? Does it feel good?"

"No, I . . . it's not true."

He shrugged noncommittally, then gave me a look so cold it made me shrink away from him.

"Do the world a favour and make those cuts deeper next time. I'll hand you the blade if you want to."

He was laughing when he dressed. He didn't give me a second glance as he walked out the door. He might as well have handed me the blade right there and then. It couldn't have cut me deeper than his words had. I felt like the condom . . . used and discarded.

He was the last. I've never trusted anyone to come near me since.

But Laurie isn't the kind of person who would do that to me. Hasn't he just given up his life for me? Or has he? He said he's going to keep exhibiting his paintings, that he's going to get the money. What if he's going to leave me here?

What if he's . . . But he said he loves me. He said . . . His eyes are . . . different. He doesn't look at me as if . . . But he hasn't seen. But I told him, I told him everything and he . . .

I remind myself that it doesn't matter anymore. If I trust him and he screws me over, it won't matter. The pain won't last long. In fact, it'll just make tomorrow easier.

For a moment, I think I'm going to pass out, then I relax and let my hand slip down to my side. Slowly, painfully so, Laurie undoes the last of the buttons and slides his hand inside my shirt and over my ribs. He strokes my chest, stomach, and side, and I let my eyes flutter closed, forgetting with a sigh.

Shifting his position slightly, Laurie lifts my arms away from my sides so he can tug up my shirt, exposing my body. Not giving me any chance to think about it, he lowers his head and bites my nipple, gently, but enough to make me gasp and arch my back. I can feel him smiling.

Still stroking my side, he starts kissing his way down my chest and over my stomach. His tongue laps at my skin and makes me shiver. I find myself moaning softly, losing myself in the sensations as he works down toward my belly button and . . . and . . .

"No. No, Laurie. I . . . I can't."

Pushing him away, I grab at my shirt and try to pull the two sides back together again. Laurie is immovable, but he does wriggle back up my body, lying to one side so he can carry on stroking my side through my shirt.

"It's all right, Gabriel. Please don't close down, not now. Let me in. Let me please you. Let me make love to you. You have a beautiful body. Why are you so afraid of me seeing it?"

I shake my head. I don't want to speak. I don't want to tell him my shame. I don't want him to see it. All I want is to crawl away and hide.

"Gabriel. I've seen."

"What?" He raises his hand to touch my face.

"I've seen you naked, remember? The very first night. I undressed you and put you to bed. Your body is as beautiful as the rest of you. You have nothing to be ashamed of."

I almost choke with shock. I'd forgotten. "But . . . the scars . . ."

"Every inch of you is beautiful to me, Gabriel, and the scars are as much part of you as your beautiful eyes and soft lips." As he speaks, he strokes my lips so sensuously I have no choice but to open them and let him slip his finger inside.

Keeping my gaze locked with his, Laurie tugs my shirt away and slips his hand under it to stroke me, running his fingers lightly down over my ribs and side, along my hip bone, and across the top of my jeans to dip down under the waistband as he bends to kiss my stomach. I tense but force myself not to freeze up.

After a few minutes, he pulls away and stands up. My eyes snap open as something akin to panic grips me. I've scared him away after all. No matter what he said he can't — I'm pulled up dead by the look in his eyes. I stare at him, mesmerised as he slowly undresses, the sexiest smile on his face. By the time he's naked, I'm literally drooling.

"Now you." His voice is a husky whisper, and I shake my head from habit as much as anything else.

He smiles and reaches out his hand to me. Shaking with fear but resolute, I take it and let him draw me to my feet. I cling to him, feeling our bare chests pressed against each other, his heart beating underneath mine. I barely notice when he nudges my shirt from my shoulders and lets it fall to the floor.

For a while, he holds me against him, running his hands over my back, letting me rest my head against his shoulder. I'm trembling all over, partly because of his touch, partly because I'm still so scared, and partly because I'm exhausted. It all combines to be somewhat overwhelming, and Laurie seems to realise this, allowing me time to just be there in his embrace, letting my body relax and my heart calm.

Finally, Laurie moves me gently away from him and turns me around, so my back is against his chest. I lean my head back, and he nudges it aside to kiss my cheek as he runs his hands over my chest and stomach.

"You're beautiful, Gabriel," he whispers in my ear. "Everything about you is beautiful. Your hair is beautiful. Your face is beautiful. Your chest is beautiful. Your stomach is beautiful."

As he works his way through the litany, he kisses or strokes each part of my body, making me tremble even more, but this time only because of the way he's making me feel. Nothing else matters anymore. Nothing else exists anymore.

Even when he runs his fingers over the ridges of old scars — some self-inflicted and others souvenirs of my time at the research facility — I don't close up. I don't feel ugly and defaced and defiled anymore. I feel . . . beautiful.

I barely notice when he releases my jeans and peels them down over my hips. He leans forward to reach lower as he buries his fingers in the soft fur that nests my rapidly hardening cock.

"Laurie."

"Shhh. Don't speak." He kisses my cheek, and I turn my head to meet his lips as he moves away and turns me again, gently lowering me onto the bed and slipping my jeans and pants over my feet, discarding them.

I lie there, completely naked and exposed, as he examines every inch of me with hot, hungry eyes. I've never felt so vulnerable, so open. With one word, one glance, he could tear me open and gut me. Instead, he smiles and lowers himself onto me.

"Thank you," he whispers against my chest as he kisses his way downward again.

I would like to say it was the most wonderful experience of my life, that we made love all night and I fell asleep sweetly in his arms and had the best night sleep of my life, but it wasn't like that at all. I couldn't relax, not completely, and as hard as Laurie tried—and he really did try—I couldn't stay . . . hard. Even though his touch inflamed me and brought me to life, as soon as he tried to take it any further, I deflated like a burst balloon.

Laurie told me over and over that it didn't matter, that he understood—and I'm sure he did, at least to some degree. It wasn't him. It was me. After about half an hour, I turned over on my side and shut him out completely as I cried, feeling as wretched as I've ever felt in my life.

After a while, he just curled himself around me and put his arm over me, holding me gently. At some point, my body finally relaxed, even though my mind didn't. I melted into his arms and he simply raised his head and kissed me once, then hugged me close as I drifted off.

Chapter Thirteen

And I wake up screaming.

"Gabriel. Gabriel, what's wrong? Gabriel, please . . . please. It's all right, I'm here."

The words filter through the pain, and the screaming stops. It isn't a conscious decision. It just . . . stops. My head's on fire. The pain is awful, worse than ever before. What's happening to me?

I barely feel Laurie's hand on my face, stroking me, trying to soothe me. My vision is blurred, red-tinged. It flickers with the pulse of my heart, the throb of the pain in my head. I've never had anything like this before.

"What's happening to me?"

"I don't know. Tell me what's wrong. Where do you hurt?"

"My head. I . . . I . . . Please."

I grip his hand, and he pulls me to him. He's scared—I can feel it—scared for me. Somehow the thought gets through the pain and makes me smile. The pain's still bad, but it's bearable. I don't even remember having dreamed.

Slowly, the pain fades to a dull throb, and I push Laurie away. Not far, but so I can look up at him.

"Are you all right?" he asks.

"Better."

He gives me a smile that's shaky around the edges.

It's the first time I've seen him look so uncertain. Somehow it makes him even more . . . precious. "You're not going to hurt me, *are* you." It's not a question, and I surprise even myself with the certainty in my voice, the wonder.

Laurie flinches. "No. I'd never do that. Is it only now you've realised it? Didn't you think I meant it when I said I love you? Didn't anything I've done mean anything to you?"

"Yes. Yes, it meant something, but . . ." Tears pour down my face, and the only way I notice is because Laurie absently wipes them away. "I've heard it before. *It's all right. Don't worry. I won't hurt you.* And then . . . It's not that I didn't believe you, that I don't believe you, but . . . I've learned not to let myself . . . not to let the pain in."

"God, Gabriel. I didn't . . . I didn't realise how much you've been hurt. I'm sorry. I won't put any more pressure on you. I'll just . . . I'll just be here for you. In time you'll see, you'll know I'm here for good. That I meant what I said. I see now. Words can't do it. There've been too many of them. Words can't get in there anymore, so I'm going to have to show you. Just give me time."

My stomach turns over. Time. That's the one thing I can't give him. That I won't give him. I can't, not now. I force myself to smile and nod, then snuggle into his arms so I won't have to look at his face. He holds me close and strokes my back. I feel better, but not . . .

A wave of dizziness sweeps over me, and a buzzing starts in the back of my head. It's encouraging that it's only buzzing. They're not focusing on me, not talking about me. They're not close. For a moment, I have a surge of hope. Maybe they've given up. Maybe they're going to leave me alone. Maybe . . . What am I doing? I'm getting soft, letting myself relax, believe. I can't do that. I can't afford to do that. They'll use it.

"Are you okay?" Laurie asks softly.

How can I tell him the truth? "Yeah, at least . . . better."

"Well, better's good." He kisses me gently on the top of my head.

Suddenly I have to get out of there, get away. "I'm hungry." Great. That's the last thing I wanted to say, the last thing I want to do. I don't think I could eat now if my life depended on it. Ah, well.

"Come to think of it, I could eat."

I can hear the smile in his voice. He thinks it's a good thing that I want to eat. He thinks it means I'm getting better, but I'm not. Now what? Well, I suppose this is as good a time as any to get away. I'll go to the restaurant. Then I'll tell him I need the loo and climb out of the window. What if there isn't a window? Then I'll sneak out the back way. I only need a few minutes' head start, and he'll never find me. There's a huge lake outside and lots of fields and trees. Actually, the lake wouldn't be a bad choice of destination. The water would be cool. Cold, probably. Maybe I wouldn't even need to drown. Maybe I could just lie in the water and die of cold.

Laurie gets up enthusiastically and heads into the shower. I have absolutely no spare energy for showering, so I sit gingerly on the edge of the bed to wait for the spinning to stop, then pull on my clothes, which are thankfully scattered around the bed, quite close. When I'm dressed, I lie down again and close my eyes.

The buzzing is still there, but it seems far away—good. I'm feeling strange, detached as if I'm floating above the bed. It's almost like the feeling I usually get before I pass out. But this is different. I don't have the usual sense that something is coming. I find myself drifting, and my mind expands. I hear Laurie humming in the shower, but over the humming is something else. Then there are other voices, other songs.

"Oh, shit." My *Oh, shit* is for two reasons. Firstly, what Laurie is thinking about is me . . . just me. His thoughts are saturated with me. He really does love me. And secondly, the fact that I'm hearing him—that I'm hearing any of them—is a very, very bad thing. It means the implant is online, and I have no idea how to turn it off again.

The buzzing starts to resolve into voices, which join the general cacophony in my head.

. . . heading north.

Do you think he knows we're looking for him?

Of course he knows we're looking for him. Why else would he have run away from the hospital? He seems to have disappeared into thin air. If it wasn't for the implant, we would have no idea where to look.

His notes say he has always been the most difficult to control. I have no idea why they let him go in the first place.

They simply didn't recognise the raw talent. The notes record him as a failed experiment, and yet he's the only one who has been able to effectively shield, the only one who has evaded us for so long.

Not for much longer. One way or another he's coming to the end of the line.

I hope we find him before it's too late. I believe he's learning to control the implant, at least unconsciously. He—

Doctor. We have information coming in.

Good. The implant's online. Get a lock on the coordinates.

It's going to take a few minutes.

We don't have a few minutes. He . . . Goddammit. It's impossible. He can't be. Gabriel? Gabriel, if you can hear me, you have to . . .

I sit bolt upright. "Jesus Christ!"

Laurie's coming out of the shower, rubbing his hair with a towel.

"What is it? What's wrong?"

"I heard them. I heard them, and they know I did. They know where we are. We need to leave. We have to get out of here . . . *right now!*"

"All right, Gabriel. Calm down. What's wrong? What happened?"

"I told you. I *heard* them. They know we're heading north. The implant. The implant came online, and I heard them talking. But that means they can get a lock on it. They can find us. Please, Laurie. Please let's go."

"All right. All right. Let me get dressed."

I pace about the room, frustration and impatience tearing me apart inside. "I can't stay here, Laurie. I'll meet you in the car."

"But I won't be—"

I'm already out of the door. The fresh air hits me like a towel in the face. I take a deep breath and realise I'm shaking. I lift my hand and watch it vibrate. It's all right. I just need to calm down. It's not a fit. It's not an attack. They're not going to get me. Not yet. They're not here . . . yet. It's just fear. Just . . .

A moment of clarity almost knocks me off my feet. It's now. The time is now. By the time Laurie gets here, I could be long gone. It could all be over. Just a few minutes . . . well, an hour, maybe, to make sure he's not going to find me. Then . . .

But they know where we are. What if Laurie doesn't leave? What if he keeps on looking, and they find him here? But they won't know that he was with me. They'd have no way of knowing. But what if . . . what if he's so upset, he goes to them . . . or after them? What if . . .

While all the *what-ifs* are going through my head, time runs out, and Laurie comes hurtling through the door.

"Gabriel. Thank God. I thought you were going to run out on me."

Oh, how right he was. I sigh and push myself away from the wall. I hadn't even realised I was leaning on the wall. I feel dizzy again. Shit. Is that the implant? How do I stop it? How do I switch it off? I drag my feet as I follow Laurie across the car park. The buzzing is furious. It's not me this time—it's them. They're doing this. They're trying to activate the implant.

The dizziness increases, and I fight with every ounce of strength. I have to stop whatever's happening. I can feel it now. It's like an itch I can't scratch, a vibration in the back of my head that's altering everything—the whole world. I stop as waves of energy radiate from me like ripples in a stream. The ripples meet resistance and come flowing back. I don't know what I'm doing or what they're doing. Am I the ripples going out or the ripples coming back? What are the ripples? How can I control them?

I see them clearly now. It's as if the whole of reality is shivering and warping. Through it all, I see Laurie's face and his eyes are wide, his mouth gaping. I realise—with something of a shock—that this is not all in my mind. He can see them, too.

The waves are getting clearer and clearer, and . . ."No!"

I'm being sucked in, and the more I try to stop it—the more I struggle—the faster I seem to fall. Then the world winks out. I close my eyes, and when I open them, I'm in a room. It looks like some kind of control centre. Consoles line one side, reminding me of the cockpit of an aeroplane. Three people—a man who's sitting in a chair in front of the consoles, and a woman and man who are leaning over his shoulder—are poring over data and having a muted conversation. They haven't seen me yet.

Strange, but I can still see the car park and Laurie, his eyes wide, his mind buzzing with indecision. He wants to run to me, but he's afraid, afraid he'll hurt me. He has no thought for his own safety.

"Where am I?"

The three people turn, and their faces are shocked. The woman takes a step forward and the whole image wavers and fractures before settling down again.

"Gabriel. Please don't run. Please . . . just listen."

"Oh my God. He's here. How?"

"Shut up, Garfield. If you startle him, he'll run again."

"But it's impossible. He can't be —"

"Garfield, shut up or get out."

"Yes, ma'am." The sarcasm is obvious, and the woman smiles, including me. I don't want anything to do with that smile. It's feral.

"Why are you doing this to me?"

"We aren't doing anything to you, Gabriel. You're doing this all by yourself."

"Not this. Why are you chasing me? Why can't you leave me alone? You stole my life from me. You fucked me up and threw me away. Isn't that enough for you?" Wow, that felt good. The anger is . . . freeing. There's no room for fear in there. "For the last seven years. I've been living in Hell. I've staggered from one disaster to the next. I've lost everyone I ever loved. I tried to kill myself and regretted every day since that I didn't succeed. You've taken away everything — my family, my friends, my health, and damn near my sanity. Why?"

She actually seems sad. "I can't answer that, Gabriel. Saying it was a mistake — a huge and unforgivable mistake — doesn't give due respect to what you've been through. The whole project was ill-conceived, clumsily executed, and thoughtlessly terminated. You and the other test subjects were let down in the worst ways imaginable. You should never have been thrown back out there into the world without at least some kind of debriefing, someone to contact if things went wrong."

"Test subjects? Is that all we are to you? Lab rats. We're people, people who had lives, futures. You destroyed that, ripped it away from us. I was thirteen years old, for God's sake. I was a child. You drugged me, operated on me without my consent, put me through months of painful experiments, scarred my mind and body, then just . . . just threw me away.

"And now you're hunting me down. Why? I haven't done anything to you. I haven't given away any information about your project. How could I? I don't know anything. I've never done any-

thing to you, so why do you want to hurt me? I've been waiting for this. I've always known you'd come. Why? Why don't you just leave me alone?"

"We're not trying to hurt you, Gabriel. We never have been. We're trying to help you."

"Don't lie to me!" My anger lashes out, and they all wince, thrown back against the console. They all seem worried now. Did I do that?

"We're not lying to you. You have to believe me."

"I don't have to believe anything. I heard you. I heard you talking about me. You want to kill me."

"No. No, Gabriel. That's the last thing we want to do. You've got it all wrong. We want to help you."

"Help me? Liars!" Again, a wave of energy sends them all flying backward. "I heard you. You want to neutralise me. Just like you've neutralised all the rest. They're all dead. I'm the last."

"No. You've misunderstood. We don't want to neutralise you. We want to neutralise your implant. It's unstable. It's always been unstable. That's why you've had so many problems, but it's reaching a critical stage. It's going to burn out, Gabriel. It's going to kill you. That's what killed the others, not us."

"What?" It feels like I've been hit in the stomach. Is it true? Is what she's saying true? Or is it a trick? I've been running from them for so long, afraid for so long. How can I trust them now?

"We've been trying to track you all down for years. The others were easy. We tried so hard to get to them all before their implants turned critical. We succeeded with five of them. Just five, Gabriel, out of fifty. Forty-four men and women have died . . . because of us. Can you imagine how we feel about that?"

"How you feel? Who gives a fuck about how you feel? What about how I feel? What about how they felt?"

"I understand why you're upset and angry but – "

"No. You don't understand. You don't even come close to understanding. How could you?"

"I'm sorry. That was a stupid thing to say. You're right. I don't understand. None of us understands. But one thing we do understand is that you are dying. Even as we speak, your time is slipping away, and we don't want that to happen. All we need is for you to trust us . . . just a little. Let us help you."

"How can I trust you? How do I know you're not lying to me?"

"You don't but . . ." One of the men tugs on her sleeve and she half turns, keeping her gaze on me. He whispers something in her ear, and she turns back to me, her eyes wide. "Gabriel, you have to go back. Right now. The energy you're using to maintain the connection is destabilising your implant even more. It's burning out, and you have to turn it down as much as you can."

"How do I know — "

"You're burning out, dying. If I wanted to kill you, all I'd have to do is leave you alone and wait. You'll die. Very soon."

"You're lying."

"Think about it, Gabriel. Feel it."

She's right. I can feel it. Now that I think about it, I've been feeling it for a long time, and I can feel it now.

"Yes." It's just a whisper.

"Go back, Gabriel. Go back and wait for us. We'll send someone to get you as soon as we can."

"What makes you think that I want you to save me?"

"What?"

"Didn't you listen? You've taken everything I ever cared about away from me. I tried to kill myself once, and I'd decided to do it today, to do it right. I don't want to live anymore like this. And I don't want to live inside some facility as part of another experiment. I won't be a lab rat again."

"That's not what we're asking, Gabriel, I swear it. We can't give you that part of your life back, but we can give you the rest of it to do whatever you want with. I promise you we will take you in, remove the implant, debrief you, and let you go. I swear it."

"What does debrief mean?"

"Make sure you know how to deal with whatever effects there are left afterward."

"And there won't be any more pain? No headaches or blackouts? No voices in my head?"

"I'm afraid there'll still be voices in your head, Gabriel. That's part of who you are, and all the experiment did was open you up. But we can teach you how to control them, how to shut them out."

My mind's in turmoil. I can feel the implant fizzing in my head. The pain is starting to spread out from the base of my skull, short-circuiting my brain.

"All right. Can you find me?"

The woman turns to the man working the console. He nods. She turns back to me and nods.

"Okay, I'll wait."

That's all I can manage because the room's spinning around me, and the waves are coming thick and fast, and I can't hold on and I can't . . . I can't . . .

"Gabriel."

Laurie's anguished cry welcomes me back to reality, and I have just enough time to gasp, "We have to . . . have to . . . wait. They . . . they . . . help . . . me," before I collapse in his arms.

Chapter Fourteen

Laurie

When Gabriel just stopped, I wondered what was wrong. Then, when I turned around to ask him, everything was weird. I know it sounds crazy, but everything was—wrong. The air around him was shimmering. Like a heat haze, but more intense. I tried to get to him, but it was as if there was a barrier there, solid as an invisible wall, and I couldn't get through. I couldn't touch him.

He looked . . . fragile. He's never been what I would call robust. He's strong but vulnerable, and he's always seemed so, I don't know—delicate maybe, but not in a frail kind of way. Crazy, I know, but it's something that comes from the inside rather than the way he is on the outside. Even when he's snapping at me, and blazingly angry, he's still so . . . fragile.

God, I wished I could go to him because I knew instantly he was in trouble. His face had gone blank, and his eyes were wide and weird. I battered against the wall—or force field or whatever the hell it was—but there was nothing I could do.

Then it disappeared, and he swayed. I ran to him and caught him as he fell. He said we had to wait, that they were going to help him, and I didn't know what to do, what to think. I couldn't ask him because he was out of it. What changed? Why were we suddenly not running anymore? I didn't feel safe. I didn't feel he was safe. But what could I do?

I waited for a while, but he wasn't showing any signs of coming 'round, and I had two choices—take him back up to our room or put him in the car and drive. I wanted to put him in the car. I wanted to run. He'd infected me with his paranoia and deep-rooted fear, and it wasn't easy to force myself calm.

He'd said to wait. He must've had a reason. So wait we would, although it wasn't easy. I was struggling. I must have sat there in the car park, holding him, for at least half an hour, until people started walking past, giving us the kind of looks that spoke of complaints to the manager. They clearly thought he was drunk.

I think probably four or five groups of people passed us. Two families hurried their children away. A group of old ladies tutted and clucked and skirted us at a *safe* distance. And two couples, lost in each other, barely noticed us—so homogenous, they may have been the same couple. I was fairly incoherent at the time.

Then these two bikers appeared from behind us. Glancing over my shoulder, I caught a glimpse of two chrome monsters across the car park. I blinked up at the man-mountains, and my mouth went dry. Their beards alone were scary—they could've housed a family of squirrels.

"Ye all right mate?" one asked in a broad Scottish accent. I nodded, scared.

"Yer friend looks a wee bit out o' it there."

"He ... he's not well. He has ... Sometimes this happens."

"Do yer need a doctor?"

"No. He'll be all right. He ... it happens sometimes. He'll be okay."

"Aye. My brother's like that. Can we give ye a hand, laddie?"

"I . . . I'm not sure what . . . what to do."

"Well . . . he's no goin' far like this, eh? I'll tek him back to yer room. Gie us the key."

Still stunned, I put my hand in my pocket and took out the piece of plastic that acted as a key.

"Tek the laddie to reception, Rory, and see he gets another night, or they'll be kicking them out at ten."

"Sure thing, Jamie. Come on, lad."

The great bushy biker helped me to my feet while his friend scooped Gabriel up in his arms as if he were weightless.

I was in a dream as I followed Rory to the reception desk and he talked them into giving us a second night for half price. I'd no idea why, but I wasn't paying much attention. It wasn't that I thought Jamie was running off with Gabriel or . . . well, doing anything bad to him, but . . .

I didn't know what had happened to Gabriel, or what was going to happen to him, or when they were coming for him. I wanted to be there. And I certainly didn't want Gabriel to come 'round looking up at Jamie. As nice as they seemed, Rory and Jamie were still scary.

I was almost relieved when I got to our room to find Gabriel sprawled on the bed, still very much unconscious, with Jamie peering at him with what appeared to be a concerned expression on what I could see of his face.

"Are ye sure he's gonna be okay? He looks totally out of it."

"Yes. He gets like that. He'll be all right. We'll be okay now. Thank you." God, I wished I believed what I was saying. Jamie peered at me doubtfully.

"Are ye sure, laddie? Look, if ye're running, mebbe we can help ye."

"No. No, it's nothing like that. Honestly, it's not. We . . . we're all right."

Jamie took one last long look at Gabriel, then squeezed my shoulder. "Come away 'en, Rory. I do believe it's yer turn te pay."

And just like that, they were gone, and we were alone.

Almost as soon as the door closed, I started to feel nervous again. Jamie was right. Gabriel was out of it this time. I don't know how, but somehow, I knew something had happened, was happening — something bad.

Gabriel was so still and . . . lifeless. I started getting paranoid that he'd die or stop breathing. After I'd checked a couple of hundred times, I got up onto the bed and sat against the wall, pulling him between my legs and resting his head against my shoulder so I could wrap my arms around him, feel his heartbeat, and look down into his face at the same time.

And here I am still.

God, he's beautiful. Philip warned me about that. He told me one day I'd be brought down by a pretty face. He said that a lot. Mainly, I think, because I never had been — at least not since the first time, and not even Philip goes there. Even I don't go there — not anymore. I'm out of it now. I have a new home, new friends, a new life.

If it hadn't been for Philip, I would never have had the courage or strength to start my own business, to use my art. Of course, Blossom helped. If it hadn't been for her and her money . . . I shudder. No, it's best not to think about that. Still, it's taken a lot out of me . . . out of all of us opening up the gallery.

Philip's a worrier. Thank heaven for Ruth. Without her, he would've gone insane . . . or at least lost all his hair years ago. She tamed him. He was a wild one. We both were. We've been friends since our first day at school, and, even after everything that happened later, he was still there for me.

I had a crush on him once. Maybe that's traditional for gay boys with straight best friends. He accepted it without a qualm, even though he made sure to make it very clear from the start that he wasn't interested in me as a lover, only as a friend.

The crush ended when Ruth came on the scene. She's just too nice to hate. She's been Philip's saving grace, and he's been mine.

We were pretty crazy when we were younger. Nothing like I was later, of course, but enough so that when I came back, he understood, and more than that, he forgave. Ruth was a little more reserved. I don't blame her, but in the end, they both took me in willingly, and they helped me get back on my feet again.

I wish Philip were here right now. He'd know what to do. He always knows what to do. I'm the one who drifts through life, and he's the one who directs me.

It was Philip who dragged me into that bar the night I met Gabriel. He and Shay are as straight as they come, although I have my doubts about Cory. They didn't put up too much of a fight. Not that the bar was exclusively gay. It was . . . unusual. It wasn't the kind of bar we would've normally been seen within a mile of. I suppose I fit in fairly well, but the others were far too conservative. On the whole, we all stood out like sore thumbs.

We were actually thinking about leaving when I saw him. I don't know what it was, but in that instant, I saw his eyes, and I knew. I didn't even see the rest of him, not that I remember . . . just two blue eyes, so wide and bright and looking straight at me, straight into my soul.

I've never believed in love at first sight, and it probably was just fascination at first sight, but there was no way—no way at all—I was going to leave it at just one glance.

Philip laughed when I told him I was staying at the bar

and not leaving with them.

"I've told you, Laurie, a pretty face is going to bring you down one day. And that one? That one's going to be standing over your bleeding body laughing."

I'd laughed at the time, although there have been occasions since then when I've wondered if he was right. Except that it isn't Gabriel looking down on me . . .

No. I can't think about that, not now. I can't think about why I'm sitting here looking down at him. If I think about that, I'll go insane.

He feels cold. I frantically press my hand over his chest, and I can't feel his heart. I panic — total blind panic — until I feel for the pulse in his neck, and it throbs, strong and steady, under my fingers. I relax, weak with relief. I'm letting my own fears get the better of me, and I know better than that.

He is cold, though. I grab the edge of the quilt and tug at it, slowly inching it toward us, wrapping it around both of us. Gabriel sighs and nestles his head into my shoulder.

"Gabriel?"

There's no further response or movement, so I get back to reminiscing. The first time I saw Gabriel — I mean saw him properly and not just his eyes — I was so totally knocked off my feet, I was literally stunned and couldn't move. He was awe-inspiring. Not only was he beautiful, but he was . . . I thought he was so free.

He was dancing, his eyes closed and his arms raised over his head. He was a primal force, and everywhere he went, everything seemed to pause and hold its breath until he moved on again. He was all black and white and silver and so, so beautiful.

I watched him for a while — what else could I do? I couldn't take my eyes off him. Then I was moving. I didn't intend to, but suddenly it was as if my body had a mind of its own and I had no choices left, only one inevitable path, straight into his arms.

He felt almost insubstantial. A faery creature—too slender, too delicate, too beautiful to be human. Of course, I've since realised that is nowhere near the truth of this amazing creature I hold in my arms. He's very, very real—a fiery, passionate, and above all warm, human being. Warm? Maybe *hot* would be the better word . . . in every aspect.

I have to smile when I think of all the times I've been subjected to that heat—the blazing eyes, the temper, the passion. It's burned me, to be sure, burned deep into my heart, but it's all to the good. Absorbing that heat has helped me survive the cold. I didn't know that in the first moment of intense heat, or the second, when I held him, and we stopped dancing, and he opened his eyes and blasted my soul.

He looked so . . . stunned . . . so pure . . . so delicate . . . as if one breath could blow him away, one hug could snap him in half, and yet there was a sense of such strength about him. I have to smile. I've seen both of those things many times since that day—the strength and the frailty. I never know which I'm going to get. That's one of the things that fascinates me. There was never a question of walking away—it was never an option for me.

And it was never an option for him either, even though he wouldn't acknowledge it. I saw it in his eyes, that very first instant and every time I've looked into them since. He's tried so many times to drive me away, and if I'd thought for one second it was what he truly wanted, as hard as it would've been, I'd have let him go. But it was never what he truly wanted. It was always fear that made him push.

I tried so hard to take that fear away from him, but it was never in my power. Maybe now, at last, he can find peace, one way or another.

I look down into his face, and my heart stops as his eyelids flutter. I hold my breath as the beautiful blue eyes that have been gazing into my soul since the first moment I saw them open and stare up at me.

He looks completely spaced out. He doesn't know me. He doesn't know anyone. He blinks and licks his lips. Then he smiles, and it makes my heart hurt.

"Gabriel?"

"Laurie?"

"What happened?"

"I'm not sure."

His voice is weak, and he looks . . . distant . . . as if he's still behind that invisible wall. That scares me. "I was scared, Gabriel. It's as if you were locked away and I couldn't get to you. I thought I'd lost you forever."

He gives me a strange look and shakes his head.

"I went . . . wherever they are. They . . . they're not . . . not trying to kill me. They're trying to save me. The . . . the implant is . . . I don't know . . . breaking down, going haywire. It's going to kill me if I don't do something."

"Oh shit, Gabriel." My heart's pounding. I'd been so scared something like this would happen, frightened that one day when he had one of his . . . attacks . . . he wouldn't wake up. I'd been right. "Do you think they told you the truth?"

He gives me the most direct look he's given me yet. "No, but I don't think I have anything to lose. I can't go on like this. I know I'm dying, I've known it for a while, but I didn't know why. I wasn't sad. In fact, if that hadn't happened, I was going to . . . going to . . . Today, I was going to leave you. I almost did."

"I knew it. I was so scared when you ran out of the room, because I knew you were going to keep running. I was surprised when I saw you waiting."

"Not as surprised as I was. I'd made up my mind. I was

so close. I don't know why I didn't. I was thinking . . . about you . . . running through what if's, and I suppose time just ran out."

"No. Time did not run out. My time did not run out. I was so scared, and as soon as it hit me what you were doing, I ran like I've never run before."

"I don't think you did, Laurie. I don't think you did know what I was intending." He speaks in such a dull, flat voice that it sends shivers through me. My mind struggles with what my heart's telling me.

"No."

"I wasn't going to run away. I was going to finally stop running away. It's all I wanted, Laurie, to stop running, to stop feeling this pain, to stop ruining your life . . . to just stop."

"No, Gabriel. I'll help you. I'll help you to stop running. I'll save you. I'll . . ."

He smiles, but it isn't a nice smile. "You can't, Laurie. You can't save me. You never could. I know you tried, and I know you love me. As far as I can, I love you, too, but I'm too damaged. The only reason I opened to you last night was that I thought it wouldn't matter. That after today, nothing would matter. And that even if you hurt me, it wouldn't matter . . . just make it easier."

"But I wouldn't hurt you. I'd never hurt you."

"I know. And that's why, in the end, I couldn't do it. I couldn't . . . It was because I didn't want to hurt *you*. It wasn't a conscious decision. It was just . . . I knew I was going to leave you today."

"But you didn't. You didn't leave me."

"Not yet."

"You're not still planning . . ."

"No. But I don't know what's going to happen when they get here."

My heart thuds in my chest, and my mouth goes dry. "Maybe we should—"

"We can't, Laurie. I can't. I know that. If I don't let them help me, I'll die. If I do let them help me, maybe I'll die anyway, but if I don't... They promised to take it away, to stop the pain. No more headaches, no more fits, no more running. I don't know if I believe that. Maybe what they're promising is a lifetime of being a living experiment, but one way or another, there'll be no more running."

"But you can't let them—"

"I can, Laurie. I can because in the end, I don't want to die. I want to live... because of you. Whatever happens, if I have to die, it won't be running away. For you, I want to stop running away."

Oh, hell. He had to say that. Why did he have to say that? "Gabriel. I don't want you to do this for me. I want you to do it for yourself or not at all."

Gabriel smiles and nods. With a sigh, he pulls himself up to sit next to me, leaning his head on my shoulder. He seems so weak.

"Are you all right? You seem... You don't look well."

He laughs softly. "Don't you ever listen to anything I say? Of course, I'm not well. I'm dying. I think if they don't get here soon, they'll be too late."

"How soon?"

He turns toward me, twisting across my body to bury his hand in my hair and pull himself up to kiss me. It's the most honest kiss he's ever given me. Reflexively, my arms go around him and draw him close.

I hold him gently, and he presses himself close to me, and it is... How can I describe how I'm feeling? In all the time I've known him, Gabriel has never been so relaxed, so open. I know with absolute clarity that in this one instant, this one kiss, he's given himself to me entirely. There's no more hiding, no more holding back, no more running away. It's the most bittersweet moment of my life.

For a while, I just hold him and let him kiss me, responding gently, allowing him to explore, to take his time. He can't keep it up for long. I sense him tiring and gently push him backward across the bed. He lies there, looking up at me with stars in his eyes.

"You should rest."

"I don't want to rest. I want to kiss you, and I want you to kiss me, and I want . . . I want what I should've had last night, what I should've given last night. I want—"

"Ssh." I silence him with a kiss and lower myself onto him, sliding one hand under his head to tangle in his soft hair, raising it so I can kiss him deeply. This time there's no tension, and his only response is a sigh.

Rolling to one side, I raise his t-shirt and draw lazy patterns on his skin with my finger. He's lost weight and condition since I first met him. Not much, but it shows in the prominence of his ribs and slight inward curve of his stomach. It makes me sad, and I slide down to kiss it. He closes his eyes and sighs again.

I know he's ashamed of the scars that cover his body, but to me, they're truly beautiful because they're part of him. I lick and tease them until he's trembling and moaning softly.

Making love with Gabriel is sweet. It's everything I ever imagined or wanted it to be. I would never have shown him, but as I held him to me last night and watched him fall asleep, there were tears on my cheeks. I'm almost afraid to touch him, waiting for him to tense, to pull away, to run from me, but he doesn't.

Beneath my hands and lips, Gabriel sighs and moans. He buries his hands in my hair and gives himself to me absolutely.

When it's over, he lies with his head on my chest, and we

both cry. It was too sweet to be borne without tears.

After a while—a time in which we stroke each other and kiss each other gently on whatever part of the body we can easily reach—Gabriel looks up at me. He's tired, I can see that. There are dark smudges under his eyes, which are dull and heavy, but he looks happier than I've ever seen him.

"We'd better get dressed."

"Why?"

"They're close."

I restrain myself from asking how he knows. "This soon? It's too soon, Gabriel."

"It would always be too soon."

"You're right."

We dress in silence. There's nothing else to say. We both know the score. Our first time might well be our last, and there's nothing either of us can do about it. I can't protect him, and he can't run away anymore.

When we're dressed, we lie down on the bed and simply hold each other. Looking into Gabriel's eyes, I'm complete in a way I've never been before.

I stroke his hair until his fingers grow still on my back and his heavy eyes flutter closed. Then I watch him sleep.

CHAPTER FIFTEEN

I wake suddenly to a strange sound. I can't work out what it is. Even when consciousness returns, I still can't understand what the throbbing thrum means or where it's coming from. I sit up and Gabriel stirs, blinking sleepy eyes at me.

"What's happening?"

"I don't know. You tell me. What's that noise?"

Gabriel pauses for a moment. Then he seems to fold inward, a frown tugging down the corners of his mouth. "We'd better go outside."

"Why?"

"It's them."

"What do you mean?"

"Look out of the window."

I comply and am absolutely astonished to see the huge, sleek black shape that is descending vertically into the car park.

"A helicopter."

"Yeah." It's a sigh. I turn to see Gabriel slowly dragging himself off the bed.

"Are you all right?"

He turns to me and gives me the ghost of a smile. "I just . . . These last few hours have been the best of my entire life. I don't want them to end."

"Everything ends."

Our eyes meet, and he nods slightly, his smile turning introspective. He holds out his hand and I take it, allowing him to precede me out of the room and down the stairs. We don't bother with any of our things. One way or another, we're not going to need them anymore.

As we step out of the door, the helicopter lands. It seems huge, looming over us like some giant black scorpion, waiting to strike. It's drawing a lot of attention. People are spilling out of the services, getting out of their cars, standing around staring. They're fascinated, spellbound, excited. For many, this is the highlight of their day . . . not for us.

We hang back on the porch, and I put my arm around Gabriel. He's shaking. For all he says he wants this, that it's the right thing to do, I know he isn't sure. I know he's terrified by the decision he's made, to face the thing he's been running from for a third of his life. I'm so incredibly proud of him. Apart from the shaking, which only I can feel, he stands erect and proud, waiting for his fate with dignity.

As we watch, the shiny black side of the crouching creature splits, and a set of steps unfolds. A woman dressed in a smart black business suit and a podgy man with wild red hair descend and make their way confidently toward us. I draw myself up, preparing to defend him with everything I have if the need arises.

The woman smiles. The man seems less sure of himself, and he glances around as if he expects danger to come swarming from all sides.

Gabriel draws back a little, holding on to my waist so hard his fingers dig into me, causing me to wince. I make sure he isn't aware of it.

"Hello, Gabriel. My name is Elena. We've met, remember?"

"I remember," Gabriel says quietly, ignoring the hand she offers. She smiles graciously and drops it.

"I don't blame you for not trusting us. If I were in your place, I wouldn't trust us either. I very much hope that by our actions, we can change your mind. We really do want to help you. *I* want to help you."

"Why?"

She pauses and drops her gaze. "I wasn't part of the original experiments. Hell, I wasn't out of college at the time. When I came to work at the facility, the files were closed. The whole thing was glossed over and hidden away, and they tried to pretend it had never happened."

Gabriel winces, and his lips draw into an angry line, which Elena acknowledges with a sympathetic nod.

"But then . . . people started getting twitchy. Something happened, and suddenly old files were being pulled, closed files were being opened, and there was a general air of doom and disaster.

"I was brought in as an expert in neurological enhancement technology. I was working on prototypes of far more advanced versions of your implant, and I was shown the files and the schematics of the technology used at the time."

Gabriel looks blank, struggling to understand, and Elena gives him a small, understanding smile.

"What I'm trying to say is that they realised things were going wrong, and they brought me in to try to fix them."

Gabriel nods. I can feel him fading, and I wish they'd just get on with it.

"Only I couldn't fix it," she says sadly. "I wasn't surprised it was all breaking down. It was crude and invasive and largely ineffective.

"People were dying. By the time I got involved, some of your fellow test subjects had already died, and we were given the task of tracking down the others and stabilising the implants. We very quickly discovered it was impossible to do that . . . stabilise the implants, that is. They've degraded beyond any possibility of repair. They were never suitable for the job and should never have been used—not on anyone, especially not on children. Not against their will."

She raises her eyes and meets Gabriel's for the first time. "I have no reasons, no excuses, no explanations for what was done to you. I can apologise, but I appreciate it would be hollow and probably offensive. I can't excuse my colleagues, but I can assure you of my own commitment and integrity.

"I can't tell you I haven't failed you, all of you. In the beginning I–I couldn't . . . I lost six, one after the other. There was nothing I could do to save them. They were like you . . . bitter, angry, hurt. I promised them I'd do what I could, that I'd try to help them, and I did. I did try. I tried as hard as I could, but it wasn't good enough.

"As I began to learn more about the implant, the experiments, the procedures and processes, I started to understand the complexities more and became more successful. I saved one and then another, and I tried harder and harder. I still couldn't save them all. Some died, some lived, some we didn't find in time, but . . . I tried my very best with every one of them.

"I can't offer you guarantees, Gabriel. I have to admit that I'm very nervous about you. I've read your file from end to end many times, and what's written there just doesn't make sense with what I've learned about you since." She smiles, but there's no smile on Gabriel's face. He's holding my hand so tightly it hurts, and I have to admit I'm gripping back almost as hard. The things she's saying make me feel decidedly queasy.

"I can understand when they record you were difficult to manage—disobedient, uncooperative, strong-willed. I've heard that said of you from many sources. But they recorded your experiment as a complete failure. They discarded you and washed their hands of you long before the end of the project."

A stab of anger shoots through me at the way she's talking about Gabriel. *Discarded? Washed their hands of?* I know

Elena is only trying to convey what had happened at the time, but still . . .

"You weren't the only one. There were others who were terminated at the same time." She glances at him and proceeds hurriedly. "By *terminated* I mean taken out of the programme. After having read your files—not just yours, all of you—I couldn't work out why they'd done that. I've come to the conclusion that those who were interpreting the data had no idea what they were looking for.

"I believe the reason they considered your experiments to be failures was that your results were so different to everyone else's. Your baseline was nowhere near the one they were looking for. Your reactions were off their scale. They read that as being non-effective, and it never seemed to cross their mind that you were over the bar, not under it."

I glance at Gabriel to see if he's as confused as I am, but he's staring at Elena, wide-eyed, and I have no idea if it's because he doesn't understand or because he does.

"Out of all the subjects I've been tracking and bringing in, you were the only one able to effectively shield. I don't know if you were conscious of it, but you were doing it nevertheless. The only time we were able to get any kind of location from you was when the implant activated, and it was doing that more and more as it became unstable and degraded.

"I'm not ashamed to say this, but I've become totally fascinated with you, Gabriel. Your mind is extraordinary, and when you were able to communicate, even projected into the room . . . There's no way I'm going to let that mind be scrambled by a shoddy piece of crap. Not if I can do anything about it.

"I want to help you. I promise I'll personally take care of you and do everything in my power to save you. And I promise that afterward, I'll ensure you're given whatever help you need to come to terms with what happens next . . . and to pick up your life without any more ill effects."

"What do you mean . . . come to terms with what happens next?" Gabriel asks.

She smiles. "I thought you'd pick up on that. You know the experiments were about tapping into latent psychic abilities. The implant was supposed to enhance your own natural abilities, and with some it did. However, with you, it had the opposite effect. Instead of magnifying the effects of what the experiments were doing to you, you had already surpassed its capabilities when it was implanted and from then on it actually suppressed your abilities. That's why they've been getting stronger and not weaker as the implant degrades. When it's removed, those abilities will kick in full strength, and you're going to need help to learn to control them."

"What abilities?"

"You've already been using them unconsciously, Gabriel. The voices you hear in your head are the thoughts of the people around you. The more you concentrate, the clearer the sounds, and the further away you can pick them up. That will become a good deal more intense, and you'll need to learn how to consciously shield.

"Then there are the energy fields you've been generating. So far, they've only extended a very short distance from your body, but without the dampening effects of the implant they'll become far stronger and more wide-ranging, and if they're left uncontrolled, they'll be extremely dangerous to those around you.

"It isn't hard to learn to control them if you're committed and cooperative. I swear to you there'll be no strapping you down and forcing you to do things you don't want to do, things that are painful and distressing to you. No drugs, no invasion of your body. The exercises and techniques are simple and just take a lot of practice and concentration."

"If I survive the removal of the implant."

"Yes."

"And I might not."

"No, you might not."

"How likely is it?"

"That you will die while we're removing the implant?"

"Yes."

"I'm not going to lie to you, Gabriel. Your strength is not your friend in this. The harder you try to resist—and you will try to resist because the implant will make you—the harder it will be to save you. The bottom line is that it's highly likely we'll lose you, but if we don't try, then no one and nothing can save you."

"I know."

"Will you come?"

"I don't have a choice."

"There's always a choice, and it's wholly yours. If you say no, we'll go away and never bother you again."

"And leave me to die."

"If that's what you want."

"No. No, that's not what I want."

Elena smiles gently and motions us toward the helicopter.

"Can Laurie come?"

"Of course. I wouldn't have dreamed of asking you to come alone. You need your friends at times like this."

"He's not my friend."

Elena smiles. "Good."

The inside of the helicopter is plush and comfortable, but somehow, as the steps are withdrawn and the door closes, it feels like a coffin.

Gabriel holds my hand tightly, and I feel him shaking. He doesn't show it, though, not on the outside. I steal glances at him. He's staring straight ahead, not meeting anyone's eye. Occasionally, Elena makes a comment or asks a question, but he ignores her. He's good at ignoring things.

The journey isn't very long, about half an hour. I'm glad it's no longer, as my hand is cramping and I'm beginning to feel positively airsick. As I step out onto the asphalt, I wonder for the first time how we're going to get home. Oh well, it's a little too late now.

Still holding my hand, Gabriel walks toward the imposing building that looms before us. His back is ramrod straight, and he's staring straight ahead. I wonder, uncomfortably, whether he's remembering what happened to him the last time he was here.

"Are you okay?" I whisper. He doesn't answer. "Gabriel?"

Elena, who is preceding us toward the building, setting a fast pace, stops and turns.

"Is everything okay?"

"Sure. I think Gabriel might be getting nervous, considering his history with this place."

"Oh. I'm sorry, I didn't think. Are you all right, Gabriel?"

He still doesn't answer.

"Gabriel?" I turn to face him, and he's still staring straight ahead, his eyes wide, his face still and deathly pale. "Gabriel, what's wrong?"

Slowly, very slowly, his eyes orient on me. They're strangely blank but at the same time full of conflict.

"Are you having trouble overcoming your memories of the bad experiences you had here?" Elena asks, but Gabriel makes no move to acknowledge, let alone answer her.

I put my hand to the side of Gabriel's face and stroke his cheek with my thumb. "What's wrong? Are you scared?" There's an almost imperceptible shake of the head. "Then what is it?"

His lips move, forming words that he doesn't have the strength to voice. Then he shakes his head again, jerkily, and winces. He moves his lips silently, then licks them and tries again, with no success.

Elena puts a hand on his arm. "Gabriel," she says softly, "is it the implant? Do you hear something from inside the building?"

He nods briefly and whimpers.

"Is it hurting you, Gabriel? Is what you can hear hurting you?"

"Mmm. Not . . . hear . . . feel . . . pain," he grunts.

"You can feel something? Something from inside that hurts you?"

Slowly Gabriel turns his head toward Elena. He nods, opens his mouth to speak, then starts to sway and before anyone can do anything, he collapses. Both Elena and I are on our knees in moments. It's not hard to see that Gabriel's completely out of it. His hand has slipped from mine, and I miss the pain of his grip.

"What's wrong with him?" I demand. "What happened?"

"I'm not sure, but I think the implant recognised the emissions from some of the equipment we use to deactivate it. I think it's fighting back already."

As she speaks, Gabriel begins to writhe, gasping for breath, his head thrown back. Strange whimpers fly from his throat, and I don't know what to do.

"Stay with him," Elena commands. As if. "I'll be right back. Protect his head."

Before I can ask what she means, she's up and running toward the building. Fuck! Now what? Well, for one thing, I find out pretty quickly what Elena meant about protecting Gabriel's head because, before she even reaches the door, his body starts to shake, and it quickly turns into a full-blown seizure. Shit. She knew this was going to happen—why the hell did she leave me alone to deal with it? *Because she's gone to get help,* the reasonable part of my brain supplies, but I beat it down and continue to be angry with her as I shuffle around and try to support Gabriel's head and shoulders on my lap. It isn't easy.

It doesn't take a moment to realise this isn't a seizure, because Gabriel's well aware of what's going on and is sobbing with shock and pain, sounds of extreme distress wrung from him in a never-ending tumult. I hear my name in there and bite my lip. All I can do is stroke his face and burble nonsense in the hope some of it gets through and somehow soothes him.

Before Elena gets back, Gabriel calms down and curls on his side, still sobbing. I rub his back and shoulders, feeling completely helpless. "Gabriel . . . I . . . I want to do something to help, but I don't know what to do."

"Make it stop. Please . . . please just make it stop."

"Make what stop?"

"The pain, Laurie, the pain in my head. I can't . . . I can't . . ." He chokes on his words, and his body starts to shudder again, but it doesn't do what it did before. He just lies there, shaking and sobbing and begging the ethers to stop his pain. I want to scream, cry, rant, cradle him in my arms, and make everything better. I don't do anything because I'm paralysed by the strength of the emotions, and can do nothing but sit and stroke him, hoping he knows I'm here.

Just as Elena appears with three men in white coats and a gurney, Gabriel starts to scream, and I've never heard anything like it. I know it'll haunt my dreams for years to come. Right now, I'm completely frozen with shock, and I don't know what to do.

"Gabriel. Gabriel." It's the most I can say.

Elena reaches us and draws me backward, to my feet, away from him. I gaze up at her, stunned. "It's all right, Laurie. Let them take care of him now. I'll show you to somewhere you can wait comfortably.

"I don't want to leave him."

"I know you don't, but you can't stay with him while we work on him—you know that."

"Yes, but . . ."

"Come with me, Laurie. I'll take you somewhere you can wait."

"How long?"

"As long as it takes."

"And you'll tell me—"

"As soon as I have something to tell. I promise."

Reluctantly, I follow her. The three men are gathered around Gabriel, and I can't see what they're doing. I don't want to go, but I'm not in a position to argue. The logical part of me knows they have to move quickly to help Gabriel. Anything I do to slow them down might make all the difference to him.

Elena leads me into the building and along a corridor. A door opens into a canteen. It's comfortable and cheery, and I hate it instantly. There are a few people scattered around the tables in ones and twos, talking quietly, and the smell of food is . . . very nice, actually.

"If you're hungry, you can help yourself in a moment. Let me show you to your room first."

My room? I follow Elena through the canteen and a door at the other end. Another short corridor and another door that opens into a room, which seems comfortable and functional. There's a minimum of furniture, but it's built for comfort. There's even a bed. When I see it, I glance up at Elena. She shrugs. "Who knows, Laurie. We'll see. Make yourself at home, then go and get something to eat."

The food's good, but I hardly taste it—my mind's elsewhere. I can almost sense him, somewhere. There's something indefinable in the back of my mind that feels as if it's somehow a link to him. Puzzled, I go back to my room and lie on the bed. Closing my eyes, I concentrate on Gabriel. I don't know why. Some of his weirdness must be rubbing off on me.

I smile, relaxing as I think of his smile, his lovely eyes. Then . . .

"Oh shit." Sitting upright, I rub the side of my head where a sharp pain had stabbed me. "Okay, let's try again."

Lying back, I try to focus my mind on Gabriel, and pain lances through my head again. This time I grit my teeth and bear it. It slowly fades. Then there is . . . . . . Gabriel. He seems unfocused and completely lost. I know he's unconscious, but he is . . . there.

"Gabriel," I say, out loud — and realise how stupid it is. *Gabriel,* I say again, inside my mind.

Lau-Lau-Laurie . . . The echo comes back. I almost jump off the bed in shock. It's him. It's Gabriel, and he's here, in my head. Why does that surprise me? Well no, the fact that he's in my head doesn't surprise me, but the fact that he's able to be in there does, given the current circumstances. Where is he? What's happening to him?

Gabriel? I say softly again, projecting my mind to the place I feel he's coming from. *Gabriel, are you all right?*

Lau-Lau-Laurie is all that comes back.

Okay . . . I know you can't talk, but I'm here. I'm here for you. I'm waiting for you. I'm not far away, and I'll be with you as soon as I can.

Laurie . . . Laurie . . . The call is stronger, and this time I share his pain and confusion. He's afraid, I can feel it. He's afraid, but what can I do about it?

Don't be afraid. You're in good hands. They'll help you — do what they can for you. I'm here. I'll always be here. Something strange happens, a kind of constriction in my head. It hurts, but not overly. It feels something like . . . *It's okay, Gabriel, I have you. I'll never let you go.* The grip tightens and the pain increases, but it's okay because I know what it is. It's Gabriel's only way of holding on to me. He can't hold on to my hand, so he's holding on to my mind instead. As long as the grip's strong, I know he's okay, so I hold on with everything I have. This is new to me, and I'm very weak in the mind department, but I try . . . oh God, I try.

It seems to be a long, long time that I lie here, holding on to Gabriel for all I'm worth. I feel his fear, his pain, his confusion, but it's all right because for as long as I can feel him, I know . . .

Oh no. Oh God, no. He slips out of my hold and it's gone—it's all gone. The hold, the touch, the contact . . . Gabriel. All gone.

"Gabriel!" I scream on the inside and the outside, but there's no answer, no one there.

Chapter Sixteen

After a frantic search of twenty minutes, I realise I've no idea where to go. Beyond the canteen, I'm completely lost, and even if I did know where I was, I'd have no idea where to go. It occurs to me that if I'm wandering around the corridors, they wouldn't be able to find me if there was news.

Fining my way back isn't so easy. When I was searching for . . . wherever . . . it didn't matter where I was going, and I took twists and turns for no reason other than that they were there. Now I'm looking for something familiar in corridors that all look the same.

I pass people occasionally, usually in small groups, chatting amicably. No one challenges my presence, and indeed I get warm smiles from everyone. I stop the next group of technicians and ask the way to the canteen. Instead of trying to explain the directions, one of them, a young woman with long hair tied back in a ponytail, volunteers to show me.

"Oh, I can't ask that. You must be very busy."

"You didn't ask, I offered, and we're not busy right now. In fact, we've just left the canteen. We're going to get changed and go home, so no hassle."

Reluctantly, I follow her the short distance to the canteen. At the door, the woman pauses. "You're the one who came with Gabriel, aren't you?"

"What? I . . . How do you know?"

"Everyone knows. It's all we've been working on for weeks. Elena's kind of obsessed. We were starting to . . . Oh.

Um . . . we were starting to think she'd never find him."

"What were you going to say?"

"Um . . . nothing. I wasn't going to say anything."

"Liar."

The woman smiles warmly. "I'm sure it'll be all right. It's not as if they haven't had plenty of practice and Gabriel's — Oh . . ." A look of horror appears on her face, and I don't understand why.

"That doesn't reassure me."

"No. Sorry. But . . . it . . . it's different this time."

"Really? How?"

"Because it's Gabriel," she says as if it's self-evident.

"And?"

"He's the strongest." Again with the tone that suggests I should know what she's talking about. I shake my head.

"I don't know what that means."

"Well . . . Elena's been searching for him from the start, as soon as she read the files. I'm not entirely sure why, but there's something about him that's special. She was looking for him because she hoped if they fixed him before the others, he could've helped us fix . . . Oh . . . bad choice of words, huh?"

"Bad choice of everything. I still don't understand, and this is my boyfriend you're talking about."

"Oh. I'm sorry, I didn't know."

"Now you do."

"Look," she says carefully. "You have to remember I'm just a technician. They don't tell me everything, and a lot of what I know has filtered down."

"I understand that."

She nods. "There's something special about Gabriel. That's all they've been talking about — that there's something special about him. In the original tests, they thought he wasn't strong enough to bother with. They tried everything they could, but he didn't respond, so they dumped him . . . um . . . removed him from the programme and sent him home.

"When Elena was studying the results of the tests, including medical data, she realised the reverse was true. That he was stronger than everyone else and . . . different. Instead of amplifying psychic activity, like with the rest, the implant was dampening his . . . I mean, instead of turning it up, it was turning it down."

I felt like telling her I wasn't *that* stupid but kept quiet as I didn't want to interrupt her flow, and the last thing I wanted was for her to change her mind about talking to me.

"Elena thought that if she could deactivate the implant, he'd be able to protect the others . . . isolate the implant from their brains so it was safe to remove." She shrugs. "They didn't find him in time. They couldn't wait."

"So does that mean . . . does it mean it'll be easier for them to . . . that Gabriel has more of a chance . . ."

"Um . . . no. Well yes, but . . ." She shakes her head and takes a breath. "It could be. If he . . . He'd need to be taught how to use his energy to isolate the implant. He doesn't know how, but there's a chance he might work out how to do it himself. If he does, it'll be okay."

"And if he doesn't?"

"It'll be just the same as everyone else."

"You mean he'll die."

"Um . . . maybe." She seems very uncomfortable now, perhaps realising she shouldn't have said as much as she has.

"Thank you. I appreciate your honesty."

"What's he like?"

"Sorry?" I think that's the last thing I was expecting.

"Well, his name's all we've been hearing around here for weeks. It's all everyone's been talking about. It's just that . . .

well, there's a person behind the name, isn't there, and I was wondering what he's like."

Why does that make me feel warm? At least someone here cares. At least someone sees there's a person behind the name. I can't help smiling.

"He's angry. He's always been angry. Angry with the things that were done to him—angry about what's been happening to him because of it. And he's afraid. But . . . behind the anger and the fear there's a beautiful soul. He's an artist and a singer and someone who wants to live life to the fullest. He doesn't want anyone to know it, but he's sweet and kind and . . . I love him."

For a while, she simply gazes at me. Then she smiles and nods. "He'll be all right."

"I don't know. He was . . ."

"Was what?"

"Is it possible for someone who isn't . . . psychic . . . to hear someone who is . . . inside their head?"

"Yes, if the person who's transmitting is strong enough, they can talk to just about anyone. Was it Gabriel? Is he talking to you?"

She looks eager, and I have to stop myself from getting angry with her. She's not interested because of who he is. It's professional interest only. But there's no one else to talk to. "He was. He was kind of . . . holding on to me. Then he stopped. I'm scared. Why'd he stop?"

"There are lots of reasons. Lots of things can interrupt a transmission. Maybe . . . maybe he passed out."

"He was already unconscious when he spoke to me."

Her eyes widen. "That's awesome. Oh . . . I'm sorry, I'm so used to thinking of him as . . . well as—"

"As an experiment?" I can't keep the sarcasm out of my voice, and she winces.

"Yeah, kind of. I'm sorry, but if he was projecting when

unconscious . . . that's pretty special. Not many people can do that. Not many trained people can do that, let alone wild talents. Um . . ." She glances at me nervously. "That . . . that means people who haven't been trained."

I nod encouragingly. I'm interested now.

"Usually there has to be some kind of conscious focus, or it's scattered. Too scattered to make sense. You must be very important to him. And he . . . he's . . ." She looks uncertain, then she shrugs. "He's awesome."

"Yeah, I know." I sound sad now. I *am* sad. She puts her hand on my arm.

"There are lots and lots of reasons why he might have stopped. Maybe he went deeper under. Maybe the implant interfered with the signal. Maybe something else took his focus. It doesn't mean that . . . that he switched off."

"Thank you." Why doesn't it make me feel any better?

"Elena will come and get you. She's good like that."

"Is she the one . . . Is she . . ."

"Yes. Well, one of the ones. She won't be able to do the surgery, but she'll deactivate the implant."

"Like she did with all the rest."

"Try not to think about it."

"Thank you. I'll let you get back to your friends. Enjoy your time off."

"Oh, we're not going anywhere. We're waiting to hear . . ." She stamped her foot in frustration at her inconsiderate words. "Oh, why don't I just go and cut out my tongue?"

"There's no need for that. You've been very honest. It helps."

She smiles and disappears. I think she's glad to get away from me. She has a lot to tell her friends.

Having nothing better to do, I decide to eat. The food's good. I choose a table by the window. It looks out onto a small but well-kept garden, with a modern sculpture at the centre that's supposed to be . . . well, I'm not exactly sure what it's supposed to be. Trying to work it out uses up a bit of time.

I jump when someone slides into the seat opposite me. My stomach turns over when I realise it's Elena. I can't read her face, but she looks very tired. Something tinkles on the table and draws my eyes. It's a small metal object about five centimetres long that looks like some kind of crazy bug. The top is ridged in a smooth mound that extends all the way along its spine, and protrusions run like little legs along both sides. At one end a deep V makes it look even more like an insect with its antennae or feelers extended.

"Is that it?"

She nods wordlessly, and I stare at it. I can't touch it. I wouldn't be surprised if it scuttles across the table.

It's fascinating, though. I can't take my eyes off it. I can't stop staring. I can't imagine . . . It was . . . This thing was . . . was inside Gabriel's head. And now it's out, and . . . and I can't . . . I can't take my eyes off it because if I do, I have to look up. I have to find out what it means . . . what it implies that it's on the table and not . . .

Elena covers my hand with hers, and I stare at it for a moment before following her arm up to her face. Her eyes are kind but grave. What does it mean?

"Please." I can't bear it any longer. Why doesn't she say something?

"It . . . didn't go quite as we expected."

"What does that mean?" I can't stop myself shaking. I feel sick. The implant is in my hand, and I'm turning it over and over, unaware I'd even picked it up.

"We couldn't turn it off. With the others, as soon as the implant sensed we were deactivating it, it triggered self-preservation programs and fought back. Essentially, it was a battle between the implant and the subject as to what shut down first. We can't remove the implant while it's fully functional because of its deep connection to the brain. If we take it out while it's still connected to the brain, then we take half the brain with it. Not physically, of course, but still with devastating consequences."

"I understand, but . . ."

"We tried to separate the implant from Gabriel's mind as much as we could. Remember we're not talking physically here. We sedated him as deeply as we safely could, so the implant had as little as possible of his consciousness to grab on to and use to fight back, but there was nothing we could do physically to submerge his consciousness deeply enough. We . . . took it past safe—a long way past safe—but he wouldn't let go. He was clinging to something, and it was preventing us from separating them."

"Oh shit." I feel sick. I want to run. "It was me. He was holding on to me and . . . I didn't know it was a bad thing. I held on to him, too."

Elena squeezes my hand. "It wasn't your fault. It all came from him. He was unconscious, vulnerable, scared, and confused. What else was he going to do but hold on to the one thing that was familiar to him? And what else were you to do but hold him close as long as you could?"

"What . . . what did it mean? What did I do?"

"You didn't do anything wrong," she says firmly. "You did what you felt you had to do. What it meant was that it took us longer to achieve the separation we needed and we . . . we had to resort to drastic measures." She takes a deep breath.

I don't know if she's preparing to give bad news or simply getting her story straight in a way I might have a chance of understanding.

"We weren't able to shut down the implant, so we had to

remove it still activated."

I feel sicker than ever. My stomach is trying its best to squeeze itself up into my throat, and I fear that if I try to speak, I'll literally explode. "What . . ."

"Easy, Laurie. Take some deep breaths. You won't help anyone if you pass out."

"No." More easily said than done. Actually, I do feel distinctly light-headed. "Please. Just tell me. Is he . . ."

"He's not dead, but he should be. I've never removed an activated implant. It should have killed him long before it saw the light of day. It should certainly have killed him as we removed it. We shouldn't have been able to take it out without taking half his brain with it."

I lost her after *he's not dead*. Relief floods me, and I feel faint again for an entirely different reason.

"Laurie . . . you need to listen to me."

"I'm sorry." I can't keep the grin off my face.

"Laurie . . . listen. I believe we were able to remove the implant because Gabriel somehow managed to isolate it himself . . . or more correctly, isolated himself from it. Somehow, and I have no idea how, he shut down his conscious mind completely and withdrew, not giving the implant anything, metaphorically, to hold on to."

"So that's why he let go. Oh, thank God. I thought . . . I thought it meant he . . ." My grin just keeps getting wider.

"Laurie, please. Wait. So far, everything I've told you has been extremely positive. There was a time when I almost walked away. I didn't see that there was any way he could survive . . . but he did. That's . . . amazing. I've never met anyone like him and . . ." She sighs deeply and closes her eyes, massaging the bridge of her nose. "But it's not all positive."

A twinge of disquiet tugs at my stomach and makes the smile waver. "We had to anaesthetise him. We took him down deep, more than was safe, and then when he shut himself down . . . he withdrew so far inside himself he doesn't seem able to find his way back."

"I don't understand."

"Although this is technically a surgical procedure, there's very little physical invasion. It's more psychological, and a good proportion of the anaesthesia is very short term. What I'm trying to say, Laurie, is that once the procedure was over, Gabriel should have recovered very quickly. He should have been pretty much back to normal by now — but he isn't. He's not responding at all."

"I . . . don't understand."

"In simple terms, Gabriel should be awake, but he's not. He's not showing any sign of waking up, and we don't know why."

"But . . . but he will. I mean he's not . . . He will wake up, won't he?"

"I wish I could tell you, but I just don't know. There's doesn't seem to be any physical reason for it. We've run every test we can think of, but there's nothing. His brainwave patterns are normal. His vital signs are steady. He has no physical injuries or traumas. There's absolutely no reason whatsoever why he should still be unconscious, but he is . . . and more than that, he's not showing any responses to stimuli."

"What does that mean?" I have to ask. I know what it means. I've watched enough medical dramas to know.

"It means that he's not asleep, Laurie. He's not just unconscious. He's in a coma."

"So, what . . . what are you going to do?"

"For the moment . . . nothing. We'll wait until morning and see what happens. If nothing has changed, we'll have to transfer him to the local hospital. We can deal with emergencies here, but we're not equipped for long-term care. We just don't have the facilities here."

"So you're just going to leave him?"

"For tonight."

"But—"

"There's nothing we can do for him. We know there's nothing physically wrong. He doesn't need medical intervention at this point. He's breathing normally, and his heart's beating strongly. The only time he's going to need medical help is if he goes for more than a day or so without eating or drinking."

"Um . . . I'm not really taking all this in. Can I . . . can I just be with him?"

Elena smiles sympathetically and nods. My legs feel like rubber as I follow her. I wasn't lying when I told her I wasn't taking it in. From start to finish, this whole thing has been a nightmare. If I had known this would happen from the start, would I still have involved myself with Gabriel? Did I wish I'd never met him? Oh, who am I kidding?

I was expecting a hospital room, but this is very much like the one Elena assigned to me. There's no medical equipment anywhere, and a colourful duvet sits cheerfully on the bed. Gabriel's asleep. She must have got it wrong. He's just sleeping. He wouldn't look like this if he weren't just sleeping.

"Are you sure?"

"I'm sorry, Laurie. You can stay as long as you like. We'll leave you alone. If you're worried, open the door and yell. Someone will come."

"But—"

"There's nothing more I can do. There's nothing anyone can do."

"You're not a doctor."

Smiling ruefully, Elena shakes her head. "No, but the physical part of the procedure was carried out by a doctor, and he's in touch with the hospital now, making arrangements—just in case."

There isn't anything else to say. I watch her until the door closes.

Gabriel's lying on the bed, on top of the covers. He looks like he's just taking a nap. In fact, he looks better than he has since I've known him. He's completely relaxed, and there's colour in his cheeks. He's not stressed, or in pain, or trying to run away. It occurs to me that he doesn't have anything to run away from anymore. Does he know that?

I don't know what to do. It's such an unreal situation. His hair is so soft and his skin so smooth, I'm drawn to touch him, but I'm not sure if I should. He's never been so beautiful. Oh hell, I love him. I never thought I'd ever . . . I want to spend the rest of my life with him. I want to wake up every morning and watch his eyes open. I want to fall asleep every night listening to his sighs.

Hell . . . where did that come from? I don't *do* love. Obsession, yes, I've been guilty of that, but love? Hell no. Not that I haven't professed love. It's easy to say, isn't it? Especially in the height of passion, or when you're trying to get into someone's trousers.

I think I might have said it to Gabriel, but I didn't mean it, not then. Besides, it's too soon to be talking about love. Despite everything, I hardly know him, and I didn't run away with him because I love him. It's just that life had got boring, and I wasn't about to let the most exciting thing that had happened to me for years slip away. That had nothing to do with love. None of it has anything to do with love. But when I thought I'd lost him . . .

Cupping his face in my hand, I let my thumb stroke his cheek and brush his lips.

Yeah, I've told people I loved them before, and maybe at the time I meant it. Maybe I meant it when I said it to Gabriel. I was a fool. I didn't love them, any of them. I know, because the way I feel right here, right now, is so much more terrifying than anything I've ever felt before, and if this is love, nothing else compared.

"You're safe now," I tell him, just in case he doesn't know. "It's over. It's all over. You don't have to run anymore. There's nothing to run from. We can go home. We can make a life together."

I want to hold him. I've never wanted anything so badly. Well . . . why not?

It's even more surreal lying next to him, his body close to mine. I have his head nestled into my shoulder and my cheek pressed against his hair. I put my hand on his chest, under his shirt. His heart is beating strong and steady. He's just asleep. He has to be.

There are so many thoughts and feelings running through me that I can't identify any one of them.

"Do you have any idea how much you've screwed me up? I could cope with the freaky behaviour, the intrigue, even giving up my life to run away with you, but . . . I can't handle not knowing. You've pushed me away from the moment we met, but I've always managed to keep hold of you, to pull you back. This time I don't know how.

"I know you touched me, came to me in my head. I know you were trying to get back then, but I don't know what you're doing now. You don't like me saying it, but you're beautiful. I've always thought it, from the moment I first laid eyes on you. You were angry and hurt and confused, but I could see the beauty in you, going all the way through. It was in your eyes. I wish I could see your eyes now.

"Oh hell . . . What am I supposed to say? What am I supposed to do?"

I love you.

"What? What . . . Gabriel? Did you . . . are you . . ."

He hasn't moved. His eyes are closed. He's still asleep, so how . . .

I love you.
Wait, that wasn't . . .
Gabriel? Are you there? Are you . . .
Laurie.
I'm here. Can you feel my arms around you?
Help me.
How? How can I help you? Tell me what to do.
Help me.
I don't know how. I don't know what to do.
Help me.
I will . . . I will, Gabriel. I will help you. Tell me what to do.
Help, help, help, Lau-Lau-Laurie.

This is so freaky. He's lying here in my arms, still and silent, but I can hear his voice as clearly as if he were standing right beside me, shouting.

Please, Gabriel, tell me what to do.
Hold me.
I am holding you. Can't you feel me? Can't you feel my arms around you?
Hold me. Hold me.

With a jolt, I realise he's not talking about my arms. He doesn't want me to hold on to him physically, but to somehow hold on to his mind. Where do I start?

Wait. Just hold on.
Lau-Laurie.
I'm here. I'll be back.
Laurie. Laurie.

Aw, that hurt. I suppose it's because he's shouting . . . kind of. Gently laying him back on the bed, I slide my arm out from under him. *I can't do it, Gabriel. I don't know how, so I'm going to get someone who does. Just hold on.*

Laurie . . . Lau-r-i-e.

The cries are now whispers in my mind, and they don't stop when I leave the room. They're as clear as ever, and I realise I don't need to be close to his body to hear his mind.

Thankfully, Elena hasn't gone far.

"Elena, he's talking to me, and I don't know what to do."

Lau-ri-e.

"Is he awake?"

"No. No, it's not physical. His body's still asleep, but he's talking to me in my head."

"What's he saying?"

"That he wants me to hold on, but I don't know how."

"Try projecting to him."

"You what?"

"Sorry. Close your eyes and picture Gabriel in your mind. Push your mind toward him, into his head, and . . . think to him."

"Well . . . I could try."

"Do it. Maybe you can bring him back."

"No pressure, then."

Elena smiles sadly. "Laurie . . . we've done everything we know how, and I think Gabriel's done everything he knows how. If you can't bring him back, I don't think anyone can."

"Okay." So . . . I close my eyes and call out to Gabriel. I don't know what I'm doing. *Gabriel? Umm . . . I don't know if I'm doing this right. Help me out here. Can you hear me? What should I do?*

Laurie.

It's just a whisper, a breeze through my mind, not like before. It seems distant as if he's moving away from me. Shit . . . he *is* moving away, slipping away.

Shit, Gabriel, don't do this. Hold on. Just . . . hold on. Please, babe . . . I . . . I don't know what to do. Tell me what to do.

Shhhhowww meee.

Show you? Show you what?

Sssssssssshhhhhhhhhowwwwwwwwww.

"Oh God . . . help me, please. I don't know what I'm doing and he's . . . I think he's slipping away."

"Has he said anything at all?"

"*Show me*. He said *show me*. What does that mean?"

"I'm not sure, but I think he's asking you to open up your mind to him completely, so he can find something to hold on to."

"I said I love him, isn't that enough?"

"No words are enough. This isn't about words anymore. This is about feeling. He needs to feel you."

"But I *was* holding him, and—"

"You're not getting this, Laurie. Gabriel needs to *feel* you, not with his arms but with his mind. You have to open up completely."

"What does that mean?"

"It means that you have to give him complete access to your mind. Draw him in, show him everything. You need to find the touch and then draw him in."

"Everything? I-I have to show him everything?" Yeah right, like that's going to happen. There are things in there even I don't see anymore—that I don't want to see.

"Not exactly, but you have to fully and completely open to him, so he'll see everything. You won't be able to hide anything from him, if that's what you mean."

"No. That's impossible. No way." No way. I can't. I love him, and he loves me. There are things I can't let him see. I can't bear to let him see—to watch him change, to see him look at me with loathing, to see him hate me. But if I don't . . .

"Of course, it's up to you, Laurie. You can do whatever you want to do. In fact, you *must* do what you want to do. But you know . . . you must know, that if he gets too far away, slips too deep, no one and nothing can bring him back."

"That's not fair. That's really not fair. I can't do this. I can't. There are things in my past I'm not proud of, things I can't even think about anymore. I can't . . . It's not fair."

Fuck it. Fuck him. It's too much. Even for him. It's not fair. I can't remember those things. I can't . . .

"No, it's not fair. Of course, it's not fair. It's a choice I wouldn't want to have to make, but you do have to make it. Either you open your mind, or he closes his . . . forever. I think you need to come to terms with it in your own way. I'll leave you alone. If you want to, you can just walk out of here and never look back. No one will blame you. If you need me, you'll find me."

CHAPTER SEVENTEEN

I watch her walk down the corridor and suddenly feel very alone. I almost call her back but . . .

Laurie.

He sounds a bit stronger but scared, desperate. I think he's fought his way back to find me, but there's a sense that he's holding on by a thread.

Laurie, please . . . please . . . I . . . I . . . Oh.

There's so much pain in that last thought. He knows. He knows what I'm thinking. Of course, he bloody knows.

Gabriel, don't . . . don't go. Don't leave me. I . . . I'm scared. Elena said I have to open up to you and I want to. God, I want to, but . . . Gabriel, there's things in there . . .

Laurie, please. I won't . . . I won't look at anything that hurts you. Please. I need . . . I need to find . . . something.

Find what?

I don't know. I don't know how . . . I've never . . . I've tried . . . tried to . . . to hold on. I've tried to hold on to you, but it keeps . . . it keeps . . . slipping away.

I'm . . . I'm trying. I'm trying to do this, but I don't know what I'm doing either.

I'm scared. His voice is just a whisper.

Oh hell, what can I do? He's scared. He's all alone, and he's worried. What will it cost me if I do it? What will it cost me if I don't?

I . . . don't know. I've done . . . bad things.

I don't care. I love you, and I don't care what you've done. I've done bad things. I don't care.

I find I've been walking, and I'm in Gabriel's room again, looking down at him. He's still and peaceful. It's hard to believe that there's so much going on in there. Why am I angry? Why am I so angry with him? It isn't fair. It isn't his fault.

I'm sorry. You're . . . angry with me. You're . . . right. I shouldn't have . . . shouldn't have . . . let you in . . . to my life. Please . . . go. Go. Don't look . . . back. At least . . . at least I'll know . . .

"No. No, Gabriel, don't say that. I'm not going anywhere. I . . ." Oh fuck. Why'd I have to hold his hand? Why'd I have to feel how cold it is? When did it get so cold? And . . . oh God, oh God . . . his lips are turning blue. What if . . . Okay, so his heart's still beating, but it's so . . . fluttery.

"Okay. All right. I'll do it. I can't lose you, Gabriel. Not like this. Not knowing I could've saved you. If you . . ."

Oh, I'm talking out loud.

Gabriel . . . I'm going to do it. I'll do anything. If . . . if you hate me, I'll understand. I didn't want you to . . . but I can't let you go. I can't let you die.

I can't do it like this, not like this. I lie down on the bed and put my arms around Gabriel again. He's so cold. It feels like he's already dead.

Show me . . . sh-show . . . meee.

Fuck, he's fading again. I don't think he'll be able to come back again. He's using his last strength for this. *I don't know what to do, but I'll try . . . I promise I'll try.*

Struggling to relax, I try to open my mind . . . and nothing happens. I try again . . . and nothing happens. What am I supposed to do? I'm screwing this up. I'm trying so hard, but it's not working.

Too hard, Laurie. Don't . . . try . . . so . . . hard . . .

No, Gabriel. Don't go . . . don't . . .

I'm in a garden. I remember it — it was a house we used to live in. It was a very nice garden, a beautiful house. I hated it. It was too big and too cold. Too cold, like my mother. Oh . . . now there's a memory. I haven't spoken to her for years – to either of my parents. They weren't impressed by my choices.

But when I was six, the garden was beautiful, full of adventure. There were lots of places to hide, and my favourite was under the willows down by the river. The sound of the river was soothing and it was dark and . . .

Okay, I'm not six anymore. I can't be because he is there. David Cross. He looks as if we're about sixteen. Oh hell, here we go.

The feel of his lips on mine, so soft – my first kiss. His hands on my back, my chest . . . all over my body. He isn't gentle, he never was. He was my dirty secret – not the kind of person my parents would want me to associate with, especially not in this way.

He took me right there, right then – under the willows, down by the river . . . and then we smoked a joint. It was the first time, but it certainly wasn't the last. David liked sex, and he didn't like being told no. He never raped me, not exactly. There were times I didn't want to, and he didn't force himself into my body, but he certainly raped my heart. Nevertheless, I loved him.

We went to a lot of parties and . . . oh no, not this one, not this one. It was loud and smoky, the air filled with the smell of weed and sex. People were everywhere in various stages of undress and copulation. I wasn't used to this. It simply didn't happen in my comfortable life, and I tried to pretend it wasn't happening now. I skirted a sofa where a boy had a half-dressed girl pinned down, one hand grasping a breast and the other between her legs. She was obviously enjoying herself.

In my attempt to studiously ignore them, ignore everything, I almost tripped over a couple on the floor who were clearly high as kites and having a good time.

When I finally heard David call my name, I was so relieved I felt weak. We'd been separated, and I was looking for him. There was a kitchen with a table on which various drugs were being cut, rolled, and snorted. David held out his hand with two blue pills, and I remember backing away until my back hit the worktop. I've never tried so hard to pass through a solid object. I kept shaking my head, but in the end, I took the damn pills.

They didn't make me pass out or zone out. I wish they had. My mind was clear as a bell, just not my own. I let him take me by the hand and lead me up the stairs. I didn't complain when he undressed me and laid me on the bed. I lay quiet and quiescent as he took me. Then I couldn't get up, turn away, or fight back when his friend took me, and then another and another. I have no idea how many men fucked me that night. After a time, I zoned out, then passed out.

I tried to avoid going to parties, but David was insistent. Sometimes he was the one who took the drugs and provided an altar for the night. After the first time, I stayed well away. It was awful seeing him so . . . when they . . . But he didn't seem to mind. In fact, there were more parties when they used him than when they used me. I hated myself. I hate myself.

It wasn't your fault, Laurie. You were so young . . . I've done worse.

Gabriel . . .

Go on . . . go on . . .

His voice is so breathless, so desperate. He hasn't found it yet. He hasn't found what he needs. How much more . . .

The parties went on and on, and we progressed to harder drugs. I stopped caring about anything but the parties, the drugs, and David. My parents became angrier and angrier with me. They did their best, but their best wasn't anywhere near good enough because it was without love, and it followed the same formula they used with everything else. Ask . . . order . . . dispose of.

In the end, they disposed of me, which meant sending me away to a very expensive boarding school for the last year and a half of my education. I was way behind because I'd spent the previous four months in a drug-induced haze.

I hated the school with a passion. Despite everything, I made good friends in my time with David. Some of them remained friends all my life . . . like the guy at the garage. Others . . . not so much.

I soon got a bad reputation at my new school. It didn't help that I was simply shipped off in the middle of one night, still high from the evening before, and I had to go quietly insane withdrawing from all sorts of things with no help at all.

In the beginning, my reputation isolated me. No one dared mess with me, but no one wanted to associate with me either. But then I got a second reputation, and I got plenty of attention . . . at least for one night.

I don't know how many times I tried to escape, but they always found me and took me back. It was like a prison — physically, and in my mind.

Then David found me. We started taking advantage of the boys at the school, blackmailing them, I suppose. We got whatever we wanted, but David got greedy, and I was caught and sent home. My parents were mortified and washed their hands of me.

After a time on the streets, David found us a squat, and we made new friends. Although they really weren't friends. They got me hooked on drugs again and used me as their own personal whore — not just for their own needs either. For about six months, I was literally a whore. I hated myself. I hate myself.

It wasn't your fault. I've been there, Laurie. I had my own flirt with that kind of life. I ended up in a psychiatric hospital with a dead boyfriend. You didn't do anything to be ashamed of.

He sounds so much stronger now. Maybe I can stop, avoid the next bit. Maybe . . . but I can't. Whether Gabriel needs it or not, I can't stop now. He's opened the Pandora's Box, and I can't get the lid back on.

I was in a room — a dark, filthy, smelly room. Someone had been sick in a corner, and it wasn't fresh. He was fat and sweaty, and he had bad teeth and bad breath. I was high as a kite, so it didn't both-

er me as he rammed into me, his saliva dripping off his chin onto my belly. I'd been used so many times, it meant nothing to me anymore.

Then he put his hands around my throat and started to squeeze. At first, I thought I'd done something wrong, that he was angry with me. But he was still staring at me with lust and something in his eyes that scared the hell out of me. He slowed down, sliding in and out of me slowly, and with every thrust, he squeezed harder. I fought him, of course I did, but he was a big man and had me pinned. As time went on — a ridiculously long time — the edges of my world grew dark, and my eyes rolled.

I thought I heard a crash. I thought I heard a voice shouting — David's voice. I thought I heard a fight. I thought I heard a scream. I knew that the pressure had gone from my body and throat, but by then it was way too late to stop me passing out.

When I woke up, David was shaking me frantically. The first thing I noticed was that he was covered with blood and I got scared. But when I sat up, I could see the blood wasn't his. The room was splattered with it. It looked like a slaughterhouse, and it was the sweaty john who provided the meat. He was dead. Absolutely, definitely, and bloodily dead.

I was in shock as David dragged me from the house. I was naked, but I didn't stop to get my stuff. We ran until we got to an abandoned warehouse that had been taken over by scum like us. They gave me clothes and fed us soup that was little more than water. David didn't eat. He crouched in the corner and wouldn't let me go near him.

When I'd finished eating, I took a bowl over to David, and he looked at me as if he didn't know me. I figured he was in shock because of what he'd done. But then I saw the blood. It wasn't just soaked into his clothes. It was dripping onto the floor at his feet.

Eventually, I made him take off his top. I discovered there'd been a fight with the big man — that's why there was so much blood splashed all over the walls. He'd stabbed the man in the back but hadn't killed him. The man was big, and David wasn't. He managed to get the knife and stabbed David in the side before David got the knife back and stabbed him over and over in anger and pain.

He was bleeding so badly that by the time I found out it was too late. I wanted to do something. I wanted to help him. I wanted to save him . . . but I couldn't — I didn't. He made me leave before he died. He made me run. And I did run. I took one look back and saw him raise a hand to wave, but it didn't get that far before it fell back, and that was the last I ever saw of him. I did hear later, though, about how he died, how he was found, how he was blamed for killing the john, and that was that. One more whore off the streets.

After that, I wandered. I was still only seventeen, and pretty. I never had any trouble picking up men — and women, too. One of them became a regular. He took a great liking to me and set me up with a place to stay and a regular cheque. That's when my artistic talent came to light, and from there on I went up and up. Within two years, I had my own place, with nice clothes, nice friends, and my own business. How fragile it all is — everything I've built. It was all froth on a cake that was rotten and stinking.

That was it, wasn't it? That was what he'd needed — the core of me. The real Laurie who was hiding under the thin veneer. He needed to know the truth about me, and that's what he had to hold on to. Well . . . he has it all now. The whole stinking mess. I'm directly responsible for the deaths of two men. One of them I loved and left alone to die. I'll never forget, and I'll never forgive.

Yes, you will. I'll help you.

Gabriel. My relief is palpable. He sounds so normal, so strong. It's as if he's standing in the room with me, talking out loud.

Are you all right?

No . . . but I'm better. Thank you.

Do you hate me?

Hate you? Why would I hate you?

For what I did.

You didn't do anything I didn't do. Well . . . I never killed a client. And I didn't watch my lover bleed out physically. But I watched his soul bleed, and by the time I left him, he may as well have been dead. And that was my fault. He was a beautiful, sweet person, and because he loved me, when I took his hand, he followed me into Hell.

He fell silent for so long I panicked.

Gabriel, are you all right?

Sorry, yes. I was just thinking. Remembering. We've both made mistakes.

You don't hate me? You're not going to leave me?

As strange as it may seem, I feel Gabriel smile. I feel his love flowing through me. For the first time since I was seventeen, I feel light and free. There's always been a shadow behind me, as if David's been looking over my shoulder and sneering, but he's gone now. I've finally let him go. There's no room for him anymore.

Without quite realising what I'm doing, I open my eyes and look down into Gabriel's face. It's still slack, but his lips are rosy, and there's a blush over his cheeks. He's warm. Oh, thank God . . . he's warm.

Tired . . .

Gabriel's thought is light and breezy again, but it's okay. It's different. He's just tired now. I hug him close and nestle my head into his shoulder. I'm breathing his scent, feeling the beat of his heart, the warmth of his body next to mine, when I fall asleep.

I dream of David, but it's okay. Because this time I'm not saying sorry. I'm saying goodbye. I think he's happy to see me go . . . relieved, at least. I never realised how tightly I was holding on.

Gabriel? I'm not really awake, but I just need . . .

Sleep.

Okay. And I do.

Chapter Eighteen

Gabriel

Mmm ... where am I? It feels ... different. I'm warm. It's dark, but not the bad kind of dark. I'm aware of my body now. I'm not living in my head. Living? Well ... sort of. It's been strange. I remember flashes of ... something. It's all jumbled. There was a helicopter—at least I think there was. It was outside the window, then ... somewhere else.

Whoa, wait ... wait ... I can't wake up, not yet. I need to work this out first. Where am I? I don't ...

I remember a building—a big, beautiful building. It's only a brief memory but ... Oh no, no ... it was ... it was ... I'm back. They brought me back. Or is it a memory of before? But Laurie was there. I'm fairly sure Laurie was there, so it can't have been before.

Why did Laurie let them bring me here? Why ... but this is different. What's different? What the hell's happening? Argh ... my mind ... My head hurts, and why does my mind have to go haywire when I need to think? I'm not in pain. Not really. Not like I usually am. But the voices are there, and that can't be good.

But they're not the same. Nothing's the same. I'm not afraid. I'm not afraid of them anymore. I'd grin, but I have to be careful not to show anyone that I'm awake, not yet. So I keep coming back to the questions—Where am I? What happened? I think the first question's pretty much answered now. But the second . . .

There's a dull pounding in my head that should mean something, and it's there in my mind, the answer—but it won't come out. There's something wrong—something missing. Shit. Shit! I remember. I remember coming here. What the hell happened? What did they do to me?

My body is . . . my mind . . . my mind is . . . is . . . free.

I remember feeling like I was drowning, disappearing in the darkness. I remember thinking it was ironic now that I'd decided to kill myself and it was being handed to me on a plate and I could've just let it happen, that I didn't want to die after all.

I remember being desperate, trying to find a way through the darkness. I called and . . . and he came. He was there. Ah hell—it was Laurie. He showed me . . . showed me everything . . . and I found . . . something, and now . . . now I'm here and he's not and I want him to be here. Where is he? Maybe if I focus, concentrate really hard, maybe . . .

Ah hell, that hurts. Ah, that hurts so much. There's too much . . . too many. Voices everywhere. Burning pain. Sensory overload. Too much . . . too much . . . too . . .

Oh . . . oh, that was . . . I try to breathe deeply, to calm myself. Sensory overload like that always overwhelms me. Things have changed, but not that much. It still makes me pass out, but . . . the pain is gone. When I wake up from something like that, there's always pain—always screaming, blinding pain. But this time it's very different. It feels like I'm swimming through treacle, but I know I'm going to get there. After all those times, all that pain, it's good to wake like this.

Only I'm not awake, am I? My body feels strange. My heart's beating too slowly, pumping sluggish, thick blood around my system, and my mind . . . my mind is . . . Oh, okay. I know what to do. I can . . .

No! Something screams *Stop!* Not here ... not here. They're going to hurt me if I stay here. It's going to happen all over again, and I don't care what she says; she's not in charge.

I dare not try to hear again. I think there must be something about this room that stops it all crashing in on me unless I go looking for it. When I pushed through, it hurt. It hurt a lot, but ... I heard something. Actually, I hear a lot of things—tiny parts of many minds, but there was one thing ... something. I'm not sure what it was. I didn't get words, not really, but there were feelings. A warm feeling, somewhere close.

But farther away ...

They want me. They want to experiment on me again—to find out what I am, what I can do for them. They want to use me. I won't do that, not again. I'd rather die ... and if I have to, I'll find a way to bring the bastards down with me. I hate them. Now the fear's gone, all that remains is anger, and I'm damned if I'm going to let them have me. But how the hell am I going to get out of here?

Wait. I'm more aware of my body now. I can feel—allow myself to feel—and what I sense is that there's someone there ... here. I can smell the sweet muskiness of him. If I open my eyes, I'll see him, and I know what I'll see in his eyes. He's holding my hand, and I can hear his pain. I mean ... Have I gone so far that I don't know the difference between hearing, feeling, or thinking anymore?

"Gabriel, why ... I thought we'd fixed it. I thought you were going to be all right now. Why? What else can I do? I thought ... Please talk to me, Gabriel. Let me know you're there, that you're okay. I shouldn't have gone to sleep. Something happened when I was asleep, didn't it? Something happened, and I wasn't here. I wasn't here to help you."

He sounds tired. I suppose I would be, too, in his place. I suppose I am. I hate this. I hate lying here and listening to my . . . my . . . to Laurie being in such pain because of me. I can hear it with my ears and with my mind. Wave after wave of pain, guilt, fear, and . . . and . . . . Okay, not ready to think about that right now. Maybe I could wake up for a little while, just to tell him . . .

"Laurie?"

That's her . . . that woman . . . Elena. Shit, I'm glad I didn't wake up. She's the last person I want to know I'm awake. Although . . .

Okay, I don't know how to do this. It isn't like I do with Laurie, because this time I have to make sure she doesn't know. Their thoughts are like a constant buzz in my head. When it's only the two of them, it's okay. It doesn't hurt, doesn't overwhelm me, and with Laurie, it's different anyway.

I take a breath and relax, focusing on the buzz, separating out the part of it that's Laurie and the part that isn't . . . careful, careful.

I can hear her dilemma. She wants to be professional. She wants to keep her distance. But she . . . she . . . she cares. She cares about me? Great. This is just great. Why isn't anything simple? Why can't I just get a chance to think things through? I have no time. But she doesn't seem to know about . . . Is that good? She's not being told the truth, but she believes . . . She's moral, and she believes—in the project, in herself, and in me. Maybe . . .

I could lie here forever. Well, not here. They're going to ship me out eventually. Oh. I get good ideas sometimes. I have to admit it's not often, but here's a good one. If they think I'm sick . . . dying . . . they're going to have to take me to a hospital. They have to take me out of here, and once I'm out of here . . .

Laurie.

Gabriel? What —

Ssh. Don't let her know I'm talking to you. Don't let anyone know you're talking to me.

The pressure on my hand increases. Relief flows through it, and I have to admit it's released a lot of tension from me, too. I'm getting into the habit of thinking that if Laurie's here, everything's going to be all right . . . but that isn't me. That's way too optimistic for me.

They want me, Laurie. They're still here . . . the people who hurt me. They're still here, and they want to hurt me . . . to experiment on me again. They won't let me go.

No, Gabriel. Elena promised. She promised no one would hurt you.

She didn't lie. She doesn't know. But they're here. I've felt them. My mind is . . . I'm opened up. I can hear . . . feel things a lot more. I can hear them. I know they're here.

Okay. I–I have to believe you, Gabriel. I don't understand any of this, so I have to go with whatever you feel . . . whatever you say. I'll do whatever you want.

"Laurie . . . I can't give you any more time. Don't beat yourself up over this. You tried. You did your best. You didn't fail. Whatever went wrong — whatever's making him like this — it isn't your fault."

"I know."

"He needs to go to the hospital, Laurie. You know that, don't you? He'll be better off there . . . They'll know how to take care of him."

Yes, Laurie. That's what we have to do. I can't escape from here, but when I get to the hospital, there won't be anything to stop me.

Are you sure?

What else can we do?

"I know. Thanks for everything. I know you did your best. I just don't know what . . . what to do. I didn't expect it to be like this. I just can't bear to see him . . ." *And that's true, you know. I can't.*

Why? You know I'm okay, so . . .

But you're not okay, Gabriel. You're talking to me inside my head, and I know . . . No, in fact, I don't know. I don't know if this is real or if I'm just imagining it because here, on the outside, I'm looking at you and you look . . . dead. Do you know your lips are turning blue again?

Oh. Sorry. I'll fix that.

Fix it? I . . .

I don't know how, but I can feel my body, change things like how fast my heart beats and . . . the way my mind's working. I can wake up if I want to, but I don't and . . . I can kill myself, too, if I want to. I can stop my heart. His hand squeezes mine hard. *But do you want to know something crazy? I don't want to die . . . not anymore.*

What do you mean . . . anymore? I thought we'd . . .

Can we talk about this later?

No . . . okay, later. But you have to fix your lips, or I'm going to completely freak.

Okay. So, tell her to do it . . . to make the arrangements to take me to . . . Oh Shit!

What? What's wrong?

I can't. I can't go to the hospital. I can't get out of here. I can't leave this room.

What do you mean?

There's something about this room that stops me hearing. I tried to find you, and when I pushed outside . . . There was too much, too many voices. It overwhelmed me, and if I hadn't pulled back, I don't know what would've happened. It made me pass out. I think out there it might kill me.

Fuck. Isn't there any way —

You have to tell her. You have to tell her that we're talking. We have to trust her. I hate this. I didn't want to involve anyone else, and I don't completely trust her, but I think I need her. I'd forgotten, but she's right. I need to be trained how to deal with this — how to stop hearing. I can't think of anything else we can do. I have to get out of here and I . . . It's the last thing I want, but I'm going to have to let her drug me. At least until we're somewhere safe.

Are you sure?

No. Of course, I'm not sure. I'm scared, Laurie. This is a crazy situation. I've been running for so long . . . and then I thought I could stop . . . and later I nearly died . . . and now . . . Now I'm pretending to be in a coma so I can escape from the people who started all this in the first place. I have to get out, Laurie. I have to get away. I've never been in this position before. I don't know what to do.

Okay . . . okay . . . Are you sure we can trust her?

I can read her, and she's genuinely concerned, but whether she's prepared to go against her superiors, or prepared to deceive them, I don't know.

Once I've told her, there's no going back.

No, but . . . Tell her that if she doesn't give me what I want, I'll kill myself.

I can't tell her that.

Yes, you can, because it's true. I was thirteen when I was brought here, Laurie. I was drugged, tortured, abused, had brain surgery . . . I'm not going through that again. There was nothing I could do about it then . . . but I'm damned if I'm going to let them do that to me again. They want something from me, Laurie, and it isn't just to know how my mind works. They want me to do something for them. I know it. I just don't know what it is. I won't let them have it. I have control. I'll end it if I have to. I don't want to, not anymore, but I will.

Gabriel, don't say things like that. Please don't . . .

Laurie, I . . . You're very special to me, but . . . you don't know what we're up against. Neither do I, but I do know something is going on, something no one's told us. I don't think they've told her either. I think she's moral enough, that she cares enough to help. But if she isn't . . . If she doesn't . . .

Gabriel . . .

Look, can we worry about this later? It might not happen.

Okay, but we are going to talk about this later.

I promise.

Good job with the lips by the way. You're warmer, too.

Don't get used to it. I'm going to get a lot colder before they take me out of here.

What do you mean?

I have to make them think I'm dying. If they don't, they won't let me go.

Don't be too convincing.

I wish I could smile right now.

So do I.

"Elena, there's something I need to tell you."

"What is it?" She sounds startled.

"I need to know I can trust you. Do you promise to listen? That you'll help us if you can?"

"I . . . don't know. It depends what's going on."

"This is going to be pretty unbelievable, so can you please bear with me?"

"I'll try. What's going on?"

"Gabriel's not ill. He's not . . . He's talking to me, and he can wake up if he wants to, but he won't do that here. He thinks there are people here who want to hurt him."

"That's ridiculous. No one here wants to hurt Gabriel. Laurie, if what you're telling me is true, then he has to end this. He's making himself very ill. He can't—"

"Yes, he can. He's doing it on purpose. He has some kind of control over his body, and he can make his heart beat faster or slower and he can . . . he can stop it. He says that if . . . if he doesn't get what he wants, he'll kill himself."

"That's ridiculous. He can't—"

"Yes, he *can*. He says that there's some kind of . . . shield around this room?"

"Yes, that's right. All the rooms can be isolated by an electromagnetic field that disrupts the part of the brain that has the psychic receptors. That means he can't *hear* outside the room."

Oh yes, I can.

"I'm doing my best, Gabriel . . . that's not helping. It's distracting me."

"Is he talking to you now?" She sounds incredulous, and for some reason that makes me feel good—powerful. I haven't felt like this for a long time . . . powerful. Yeah, it makes me something of an arse, but who cares.

"Yes. Look, he says that he can listen outside, but it hurts. It overwhelmed him and made him pass out, but he heard something."

"What?"

"That there's someone here who wants to hurt him."

"That's ridiculous."

"Are any of the original scientists who were involved in the initial tests still here?"

"No, my team's made up of people who were nowhere near here when those tests were being carried out."

"Are you sure?"

"Yes, but . . ."

"But what?"

"When things started going wrong, while we tried to track down the subjects . . . Some of the scientists in charge of the earlier project were brought back to help."

"Brought back?"

"Became involved again. They're not really scientists. Well, not hands-on scientists. They're . . . higher. Oh God, he's right, isn't he? They came back to check if any of the subjects had progressed . . . survived. None of them did— until Gabriel. Now they know how unique he is. No one's interfered yet, not that I'm aware of, except . . ."

Oh shit. I mean, I knew, of course I knew, but . . . but to hear it, to know it's real. God, I'm scared. Can I keep this up? Can I let her . . . If I let her drug me, I won't have any control. I'll be at her mercy . . . in their hands. When I wake up, where will I be? What will they do with Laurie?

I'm scared, Laurie.

I know, so am I. She looks scared, too.

What do you think she's going to do?

I don't know. She's gone very pale. She's thinking, but I don't know exactly what she's thinking about.

I hope she's thinking about getting me out of here. Laurie, I'm . . . I'm really scared. Am I doing the right thing? What's going to happen to me? What has happened to me? What am I now?

It's a relief to get that off my chest. I know that on the outside I'm peaceful and serene, but here, on the inside, in my mind, I'm scared to death. Okay, maybe not quite the right choice of words. When I get scared, I get angry. I always have. To be truthful, that's probably what caused most of my many bad decisions. As long as I can remember, which is back to about thirteen years old, I've been angry, and when I'm enraged I go cold. I hit out at people. I hit out at myself. I release the anger by doing stupid things . . . taking drugs, having wild and violent sex, getting into dangerous situations, which get my blood pumping and chases the anger away.

Recently, most of my anger has been at myself, and one of the things that makes me the angriest is that people care about me. I've spent so long pushing away everyone who could possibly love me. That happened with Daniel and Michael. It starts well . . . well, it usually starts with the violent sex and drugs. But when they want to get close, I push them away. I shove them away so hard and so far, they eventually run away from me, hurt and damaged.

My friends are the ones who refuse to run. I guess that's because they don't try to get close enough to be hurt by the shoving and the coldness. Carrie makes me uncomfortable because she sees behind the mask and still refuses to run. I'm horrible to her, and I know that sometimes it hurts and that upsets me, which makes me angrier than ever.

Right now, I'm angry at the people who did this to me in the first place. Mad at myself for letting them, for allowing them to ruin my life with the fear that is, yet again, paralysing me. I feel sick, but it's mentally sick. My body is so turned down it isn't capable of feeling sick, let alone being sick.

I'm angry with Laurie, too. I let him get too close. I let him fall in love with me and look where that's got us. Would I have done this without him . . . supporting me? I did this because I wanted to get away from the fear, but would I have done it if it had just been me? Would I be alive now? Would I have done for me what I did for him? Dammit . . . he gave up everything for me, even his secrets. I don't want that kind of responsibility. I have enough trouble taking responsibility for myself.

But I can't stay angry with Laurie. I feel bad about being angry with him, and I realise this anger, too, is coming from fear. I'm scared. I'm horribly, mind-numbingly, paralysingly scared, and that's my way of dealing with fear. I turn it into anger and direct it at someone, anyone, and right now I'm too scared to be angry with myself, but I . . . love . . . um . . . like Laurie too much to let myself be angry with him, and I'm too tired. So what can I do? There's only one thing I can do. I have to do something I've never done—not to anyone, not ever, not since . . . I have to admit to another person how scared I am. I need let someone else share the burden.

I'm so scared, Laurie. I don't know what to do. I don't know how to make this right. I don't know what's happening to me. I don't know how I feel. I don't know how I think. I don't know anything.

"You know I love you. Isn't that enough to hold on to? I know you're scared, but you don't have to be scared alone. I'm scared, too. I don't want you to be hurt anymore, and I'm so afraid you will be—that you'll be hurt so badly you won't survive, and I can't bear to lose you. I'm scared because I'm looking at you and you aren't here. You're not looking at me with that fire in your eyes. Most of all, I'm scared that I'm holding your hand and you're not holding mine back."

For a moment I'm slightly disoriented until I realise he's switched back to speaking aloud.

But I am. I'm holding on so tight, Laurie. Can't you feel it?

Shit. I can't help it. The feelings overwhelm me so much that no matter how I try, no matter how shut down I am, I can't stop the tears falling. Laurie touches my cheek, and the panic lets go of me. The fear doesn't. That's still here. It's still squeezing me and twisting me, but it's an old friend, and I can get past it. I can get past it even though I'm not angry with him anymore.

"Yes. I can feel it," he whispers.

Somehow, the fact that he says it aloud, that the sound caresses my ears as well as my mind, makes it all the more beautiful.

Chapter Nineteen

"We can't take him to the hospital. If we do, he'd have to be sedated the whole time. He couldn't stand the noise. We'll have to take him somewhere else, somewhere quiet," Elena says.

I'm literally holding my breath. Does this mean she's going to help us? Laurie's grip on my hand tightens. It hurts. Good.

"I . . . I think I know somewhere . . . somewhere we can be safe. It's a long way away. Maybe that's a good idea. We can use the helicopter for the first part. I think I can trust the pilot. We can't take it all the way, though. We can't risk anyone knowing where we are."

"Does this mean you're going to help us?"

"It means I don't have a choice. As far as I'm aware, there's absolutely no reason for Gabriel to be kept here. If he was well, he could've walked out any time he wanted. He's not a prisoner, so there was no legitimate reason for him to stay unless he wanted to take me up on my offer to train him.

"As no one's given me any alternative instructions, there's absolutely no reason why I shouldn't offer you the services of the 'copter to take you wherever you want to go. I'm due some leave now my part in all this is ended, with Gabriel being the last. My project's going to be shut down, and until I'm reassigned, there's no need to be around. I'm not at all sure that Gabriel's right in his suspicions . . . He's not exactly in a condition to be clear about that right now."

Cheeky bitch. What does she know about my *condition?* Oops.

"What the hell . . ."

It's almost funny, how surprised she sounds. Hasn't she been listening? *Well, I don't know why you're so shocked. Hasn't Laurie been telling you all along?*

"Well, yes, but . . ."

"He's talking to you, isn't he?" I can hear the smirk in Laurie's voice, and I love it. "I suppose you haven't got the hang of it yet."

"No. No, I suppose I haven't."

So will you help us?

"Yes. Of . . . of course I'm going to help you." She sounds a bit dazed. Then she seems to pull herself together. "Don't worry. I-I'll make this work. Will you be all right here for a while?"

"Of course we will, won't we, Gabriel?"

Easy for him to say. *Don't be long. I hate being like this.*

"You don't have to be like this, Gabriel."

No? Well, just in case this isn't clear in your mind yet, I'm not even thinking of opening my eyes until I'm safe — far away from here. And if anyone tries to make me, or to trick me, then I promise that I have enough control over my body to make sure that I never open them again.

"Gabriel, you can't . . ."

"Please, Gabriel, don't even . . ."

Cool. I got them both.

I don't want to die. I really don't want to die, but I can't go through that again. And now I've . . . I've heard them, and I know . . . I know what they want, and I'm not going to let them have it. I'll die before I let them take me again.

"No one's going to take you. I promised you, Gabriel. You're safe here. But if you don't feel safe here, if you're that serious about the situation, then I'll make sure you're safe somewhere else. I promise no one will hurt you. I promise

I'll take care of you. Just don't do anything hasty."

She sounds sincere, but she doesn't know what they're like — the others.

Don't worry, I won't do anything hasty. There's nothing hasty about my decision. It's one I made a long time ago, and I can assure you that a lot of thought went into it.

"Gabriel, please . . ."

Damn, I hate that tone in Laurie's voice.

Okay, I'm sorry. I won't do anything unless I have to. Just don't betray me.

Someone squeezes my shoulder, and the door opens and closes. Then there's silence. I can feel Laurie. I know he's there, but he's so still and quiet. I wish I could see him. I want to speak, but somehow it doesn't feel right.

He's quiet for a long time. In some ways, it suits me. Much as I hate to admit it, even to myself, I'm struggling. It was all so easy last night. Last night? Was it last night . . . or the night before . . . or . . . Whatever. It was easy when I was going to die. Nothing mattered. Now everything matters, and it's making my head ache.

It's Laurie. He complicates everything. He makes me feel . . . He makes me . . . feel. Damn him. I told him not to get close to me. I thought it was to protect him. It wasn't.

I'm tired. I'm so tired. I'm too tired to do this anymore. I just want to get out of here, get away and . . . stop. I want to stop. Maybe it won't be the complete stop I intended it to be, but still . . . no more running. Hell, I'm tired, and I don't think what I'm doing to my body is helping at all.

This morning, when I woke, when I realised I didn't have to wake at all, it had all seemed so sensible and easy — it's been anything but. It's surprisingly hard to keep your body switched off while your mind is switched on.

Initially, it was hard to keep everything shut down. When Laurie said my lips were turning blue, I'd overcompensated and swung the other way — my heart racing and my head pounding. Since then, I've been finding it hard not to sink back . . . all the way. Then there's all the mental activity. That's draining me, and I have to admit, right now there's a temptation to just let it all go and sleep.

I'm not sure what would happen if I went to sleep. I'm pretty certain I'd lose control. The question is, how? Would I lose control and wake up, or would I lose control and . . . not?

"Are you okay?" Laurie asks. "Are you there?"

Laurie sounds tired, too—tired and scared. I'm less afraid now I know things are happening. Elena's going to help us. I know because I saw it in her mind.

I'm here. It's a struggle to keep the weariness out of my *voice.*

"Are you okay?"

I'm fine.

"You look like hell."

Thank you. I thought I was beautiful. There's no way I can keep the sarcasm out of my voice.

"You are, but you look ill. Can't you just wake up for a little while, so I can just feel you holding my hand? So I can kiss you?"

If I do, I don't think I'll be able to come back here.

"Then why . . . You're just being stubborn."

Now he's the one who's angry, and it puts me on the defensive. I can't help it. Anger is an easy emotion for me to fall back on. I'm always angry. I'm familiar with anger, comfortable with it. When I'm angry, I don't have to care.

Stubborn? I'm trying to get out of here with my mind and body intact. You have no idea what happened here, what they did to me.

"No, I don't. You haven't told me, not really."

What the hell do you expect? I barely know you, and I've already told you more than I've ever told anyone.

"I expect you to trust me." He doesn't sound angry now, just tired. "I gave up everything for you and . . ."

Oh please. It's not as if I asked you to. If I remember rightly, I did everything I could to stop you, to drive you away.

"I know."

So don't play that card. You walked away from your life to follow me – but you did it because you wanted to. I didn't have that choice.

"I worked hard to make that life, Gabriel. You know how hard I had to work. For the first time, I had something stable. My own place, my own identity. A reason to not run. I didn't have to fight anymore. I didn't have to run anymore. And I left it, I walked away, I gave it all up . . . for you."

And I'm supposed to feel . . . what? Guilty that I took it all away from you? Grateful? Sorry?

"No," he says sadly, sounding as exhausted as I feel. "I just want you to know how much you mean to me, how much I love you. I want you to know that you can trust me."

I . . . Shit, what am I supposed to say to that? I feel like a deflated balloon or burst bubble. The anger drains away, and I'm just . . . so tired.

"Are you okay?"

His words shock me. I hadn't realised I was dozing. I couldn't help it. The argument drained my last reserves.

Yes.

"I get scared when you go quiet."

I'm okay, Laurie. I'm not really ill. Try to remember that. I'm not ill, just hiding.

"You've been hiding since the day I met you."

Please, Laurie . . . please don't. Not now. I'm too tired.

"Okay. I'm sorry. I shouldn't have been such an arse."

Neither should I. I need to learn how to stop being angry.

"You don't need to be angry anymore."

Need hasn't got anything to do with it.

"No, I suppose."

I've been angry for a long time.

"I know."

I wish I could speak out loud. Speaking like this is exhausting me. It never did before. Maybe I overused my mind, or perhaps it's because I'm doing too many things at once.

"Gabriel? Gabriel, are you okay?" He sounds scared. "Your hand is getting cold again."

Cold? Am I cold? Oh yeah, I'm shutting down again. Shit! Is that what's going to happen when I sleep? Will I stop being able to hold my head above water and drown? Am I going to die? Do I care? It's hard to care, but . . . but well, there's Laurie and . . . and I want to be with Laurie.

"Gabriel, answer me. Are you all right?"

Just give me a chance, will you? I can't . . . I can't talk and . . . and . . . talking takes up so much energy and I need . . . Yes . . . yes, I can feel it now. Everything's speeding up, and my heart is beating stronger. I can hear it. Maybe I should . . . maybe it would be safer if I . . . No, I can't. I can't wake up. What if Elena betrays us, or if their doctors want to examine me before they let me go? I don't know if I can get here again.

But this isn't right. I'm exhausted, and I'm scared to rest in case I die, and I so want to rest. I want to hold Laurie. "I don't know what to do."

"Gabriel, oh Gabriel." His arms are around me. Despite being so tired, I manage to hold him, too. "I've been so scared, Gabriel."

"You're a big boy now, Laurie. You should man up." I'm joking, and he knows it.

"Gabriel . . ."

"I know."

"But why'd you decide to wake up now?" He pulls back and looks me in the eyes. I'd almost forgotten how beautiful his eyes are, and for a moment I get lost in them. "Gabriel?"

"Sorry. I was . . . I am . . . tired. I was afraid if I went to sleep, I'd lose control over my body and wouldn't be able to wake up."

"Oh my God. Is that why you went so cold?"

"Yes, and I hadn't realised I was getting cold, that I was slowing down again. It scared me. It made me think about what was going on, and that if I didn't stop, I might get to the point where I couldn't stop."

"What if they find out?"

"Laurie, make up your mind. Five minutes ago, you were begging me to wake up, and now you're saying maybe I shouldn't have."

Laurie grins ... he really does have the most beautiful blue eyes. "I'm a man of contradiction. Are you going to be all right now? I mean, you're not going to die the next time you go to sleep, are you?"

I keep getting lost in his eyes, the brilliant blue and the expressions that fly through and over them. I remember I need to speak. "I'm sure. I'm out of it now, and I don't even know if I can get back."

"Don't try it now," he says sharply, and it makes me smile.

"No, I won't. I'm too tired."

"I'm tired, too."

"Let's just rest for a while. I don't expect she'll be gone long. We can just rest for a while."

As soon as Laurie gets up on the bed and puts his arms around me, I'm fast asleep.

CHAPTER TWENTY

I must have slept deeply, because I wake suddenly with a hand over my mouth and a sharp voice in my head. *She's coming. Don't show her you're awake.*

Okay, I get it. Stop suffocating me.

The hand withdraws. *Sorry.*

When Laurie lets me go to sit up, I feel cold and empty. I have to stop thinking like this. I can't afford to rely on him, no matter how much I love . . . um . . . like him. I could admit that I love him when it didn't matter — when I thought it wasn't going to last — but now . . . now what? Well, everything's changed. I can stop running. I can settle down, stop being afraid. Stop looking over my shoulder . . . just stop. Can I? Will they let me go so easily?

I felt what it was like when I went outside this room. I've felt it before, in the hospital when the implant was starting to break down. I know I can't go out there alone. I need help, but it's the kind of help Laurie can't give.

I can take care of myself. I've been doing it since I was thirteen. Not very well, but . . . but now it'll be different. I won't have to put up with the pain, the headaches, the fits. I'm free . . . but am I? The physical problems may have gone, but the mental scars are still there. The scars on my body are still there. I'll still be the person I've become. I'm damaged. Laurie has no idea how damaged I am. I gave in to him because I was tired, and because I couldn't go on alone anymore. But I'm stronger now.

He's been through so much. He needs someone full of

light to fill up his darkness—not someone who's even darker. I can't love him . . . I can't . . .

I have to learn to control my mind, then get back my life. Hah. Life? I don't have a life, never did. Damn . . . why did an image of Carrie flash through my mind with a stab of guilt?

Maybe I can make a new one. A new life. Maybe I can go to college, settle down, get a job. God, I'm getting so good at deceiving myself. The truth is I've no idea where I'm going to go from here. I don't have a life to go back to, and I have no idea where or how to make a new one. I have an uncomfortable feeling I know where I'm going, and it's not a place I want to take Laurie. But I'll let him tag along for now. It suits me to have him with me until I know I'm safe. Until . . . until . . . well, until I can work out how to get rid of him. For now—

"All the arrangements are in place. We're ready to go."

Do they *know?*

Elena's taken aback. I can feel it. I thought she'd have got used to it by now.

"I've been as careful as I can. I can't promise they don't know, but no one's tried to stop me."

How do I know you haven't told them? That they won't be waiting for me? That when I go to sleep, I won't wake up in The Chair?

"You don't know, but you don't have much choice, do you? Without me, as soon as you walk out of the door, or wake up where there are people around, you're going to be in excruciating pain that can't be stopped. You'll probably go insane or be forced to kill yourself."

Oh. Well, if you put it that way.

"I'm sorry, Gabriel, but this just isn't going to work unless you trust me. Not only do you have to put your body in my hands to get you out of here, but if you want to stand a chance of being able to live anywhere near other people, you're going to have to put your mind into my hands, too."

Wait a minute. I never . . . .

"Figuratively speaking, Gabriel. I've promised I won't lay a hand on you and I mean it. But you have to trust me to work with me. To do the exercises. To open yourself to me."

Damn, she's got me by the short and curlies, doesn't she? *Okay. I don't have a choice, do I?*

"There's always a choice, Gabriel. Even if it's between life or death, it's a choice."

Yeah, right, sure. So what happens next?

"Well, I've been thinking. Do you have a car back at the hotel?"

Yes.

"Good." She sounds relieved. I can see the relief in her head, too. It's strange. I can't actually read thoughts unless they're formulated, but I can read emotions well. I can't see into her head to read whether she's being completely honest, but I know she's telling the truth, at least for now. "I'm not saying I wholly believe you're in danger here, and I'd much prefer to be able to train you in this facility, but I suppose there's no harm in taking precautions just in case.

"The helicopter's too easily traceable, so I thought that if it could take us back to the hotel, we could pick up your car and drive to my cabin."

Where is it?

"Better you don't know."

But I do know. She's thinking about it so strongly that I can't help but see it. She loves it there, and she has happy memories. But she shakes them and brings herself back to the present.

"Gabriel," she says carefully, and I know exactly what she's going to say. Even if I couldn't see it, I'd know. I could make it easy for her, but why the hell should I?

What's wrong?

"Nothing. It's just . . . This room is protected electronically. It interferes with brainwave patterns, blocking out thoughts from outside. Once you pass the barrier, you won't be able to block them. Not yet. You'll be flooded and overwhelmed."

Uh-huh. I'm not brain dead. I've figured that one out for myself. So?

"So I can't just take you out to the helicopter."

God, is this woman ever going to stop procrastinating? Hasn't she got the message yet? Doesn't she realise that I can *hear* what she's thinking as clearly as what she's saying out loud? For God's sake, isn't that what this is all about?

Just say it for God's sake!

I feel Laurie flinch and hear her gasp. Oops, I must make a mental note about shouting my thoughts.

"Say what?"

I can't help the frustrated sigh. *I don't know, do I?* I say slowly as if I'm speaking to a child. *Because you haven't said it yet.*

I'm practically grinding my teeth, but I'm not going to do her job for her. What the hell is she worried about anyway? Does she think I'm going to freak out? Oh . . . well . . . maybe she does. Maybe she has reason to . . . but I'm not that bloody unreasonable . . . although maybe I am. It would probably be a bad idea to grin now, so I'll just have to do it on the inside.

"Well, I . . . I know I promised, Gabriel, but I don't have a choice."

Oh, for goodness sake, what the hell are you scared of? Just come out and say it. I know you're going to have to drug me, so just get on with it, or you're going to put me in a coma from pure frustration. Oh, and next time you're trying to hide something from me, try not to think about it so hard.

I can practically hear her teeth grinding. Good. I can barely contain the self-satisfied smirk, especially as I feel Laurie's silent amusement.

There's a long pause, and when she touches my arm some inner devil takes over, and I open my eyes and grin at her. I was going to say *Boo*, but I don't need to because she skitters back with a gasp, dropping the syringe, which hits the floor with a tinkle of glass against the tile.

Clutching her chest, Elena pulls herself together and glares at me. "Have you been awake the whole time?"

"No." It feels weird to be talking with my voice again. "Only since I got too tired to stay asleep."

"That doesn't make sense."

"Oh, well." If I was straight, I might have noticed that she has very pretty brown eyes, and she looks a lot younger with her hair down. Dammit, I do notice that she has beautiful brown eyes, but they don't even come close to Laurie's, which I now find. They're sparkling, and there's a tight smile on his face. He sees the humour in the situation, but he also understands how brief it's going to be.

Recovering, Elena bends to retrieve the syringe. "You're lucky, the cap hasn't come off."

"How does that make me lucky?"

"Because I'm not going to have to go back to the lab to look for another one and have to explain why I'm there and what I'm taking."

"Hmm . . . I suppose that counts."

"Are you going to be pulling any more stupid stunts, or can I go ahead and save your hides now?"

"What stunts?"

"Gabriel." Laurie's voice is soft and neutral, but it makes me frown anyway.

"All right, all right. I'm sorry. I'll behave." What does he think I am, some fucking kid? I figure I deserve a little revenge, even if it is petty and aimed at the wrong person.

Elena prods my arm, looking for a vein, and it occurs to me to ask, "So, how are you actually going to get me out of here?"

"You're going to walk."

"But I . . . I thought . . ."

"I don't have to put your body to sleep to put your mind to sleep. It would be a pain in the arse to have to carry you, and I'm sure as hell not going to be the one doing it."

"But I . . ." Elena flicks off the needle, and before I have a chance to say another word, she sticks it in me. "Aw, that hurt. You could have been gentler."

"Yes, I could have. Are you ready?"

"I don't know. Am I?"

"Do you have all your things?"

"We don't have any things. If you remember, this was all very sudden."

"Oh . . . yes . . . Okay. Can you stand up, Gabriel?"

What the hell is she talking about? Of course, I can . . . Woah . . . maybe not. Blinking my eyes does nothing to clear them, and although I seem to be quite lucid, I'm finding it difficult to hear Elena and Laurie with my ears and not at all with my mind. I'm also finding it difficult to get my body to do what I want it to.

When I try to stand the first time, the ground turns soft and starts to ripple like waves on the deep sea, making me fall back. The second time, I'm expecting it, and although the ground is still soft and wavy, I can manage if I hang on to Laurie. Walking is going to be interesting.

Laurie's saying something to me, but I have to concentrate hard to hear him.

"Are you okay, Gabriel?"

I mean to reply, but it comes out as a load of garbled nonsense.

"Gabriel?"

I think Laurie's as startled as I am, but when I try again it's even worse and means I have to stop concentrating on walking, so I nearly fall over.

"Don't worry, Gabriel, the effects won't last long. Only until we get to the hotel — about half an hour."

It occurs to me to wonder what happens after, but I have too much on my mind right now for that to be an important consideration. Walking is taking up a lot of my concentration, especially when we get to the helicopter. To say it's hard to get up the steps would be like saying the sun's quite warm. In the end, Laurie has to bodily sling me across his shoulder and carry me up them.

I've never been so grateful to sit down in all my life. It's incredibly disorienting when the helicopter takes off. I can't hear the blades, and it feels as if we suddenly go from sitting on the ground to hovering way above it without there being anything in between. I must've made some kind of sound, because Laurie squeezes my hand. It feels strange, but I know what it is and squeeze back. He seems pleased.

It's easier when I have my eyes closed. It doesn't seem so weird. I'll just close my eyes for a while. Just . . . just . . .

"Gabriel, Gabriel." Someone is shaking me, but it's hard to respond. "Gabriel. Can you get up now? We're here, and we need to get out quickly so the helicopter can take off again."

Oh yes, it's her — Elena. There's a strange buzzing in my head, and I hear . . . I hear . . .

"It's wearing off."

"I know," she says, urgency adding an edge to her voice. "Another reason to hurry."

"But . . ."

"Gabriel, just get out of the helicopter and let me worry about what happens next."

"But . . ."

"Gabriel," Laurie says. He says it very softly, but I hear . . . him . . . I hear . . . Aw, that's really starting to hurt.

"I don't think this is the time to argue."

I think he's right.

This time it isn't so hard to get up, except that the buzzing is becoming oppressive and makes me stumble.

"It hurts."

"I know. Just get to the car."

"What good is that going to do?"

"Once you're in the car, I can give you something to help, but I can't carry you."

"Oh. Okay."

By the time I get to the car, I don't care what she does to me. I'd be happy if she just cut my head off. Worryingly, I'm starting to get that strange, detached feeling. It's coming on fast, really fast, and I barely make it to the car before everything winks out in a bright and painful flash.

I'm expecting there to be pain, but there isn't, not really. I have a bitch of a headache, and I'm thirsty as hell, but that horrible blinding pain is absent. The buzzing is gone, too. I . . . I hear them. They're talking softly about the place we're going, and she's thinking about it. I can *see* the wooden cabin on the edge of the woods. I can *see* the little girl running to the shore of the lake. Happy memories, warm and pure. They make me smile inside, just for a moment.

Laurie's not thinking about the cabin. He's thinking about me. He's always thinking about me. He's scared about the way I passed out and wondering whether Elena should've drugged me, whether it's hurt me, and if I should've been asleep this long. Again, it makes me feel warm, but only for a moment. Then it turns cold.

I realised something. I got out of the facility, and I'm probably safe here . . . but now what? I trust Elena to teach me to shut out the voices and then I'll be able to go wherever I want. The physical symptoms will go, but will anything have changed? We escaped, but they still want me. They know what's happened, and I know what they want from me. I'm still going to be on the run.

Okay, so I'm probably going to be able to protect myself better, and I'm going to know when they're coming, but I still have to leave everything behind. I still have to run.

I let Laurie run with me, but that was before I knew what he's been through. He's been running all his life, and if he stays with me, he'll never be able to stop. He's found a place to stop . . . to settle down, and he deserves that. I can't stop running, but he can. He can have security, safety, a good life—and without me, he will. Decision made. When I move on, I move on without him.

I must've made some kind of sound, because Laurie's instantly on the alert.

"Gabriel? Are you okay?"

"I hope I had a good time last night because the hangover's a bitch." Ouch. I'm not kidding. I should've sat up more slowly.

"Whoa."

Laurie steadies me, and for a moment, I rest my head against his shoulder—until I remember. I feel Laurie's hurt when I push him away. Good. I don't want to hurt him . . . not really. Not at all. But I need to. I have to.

"Where are we?"

The scenery flying past the window is wild—craggy mountains and scrubland, interspersed with breath-taking views of lush green valleys and sparkling lakes.

"Almost there," Elena says.

"Almost where?"

"You'll see when we get there."

This is starting to be annoying. Is she trying to piss me off? Oh. Right. Okay . . . bitch. She is.

"Are we there yet? Are we there yet? Are we there yet?"

"Oh, for God's sake grow up, Gabriel. I liked you better

when you were unconscious."

"Ditto."

"I haven't been unconscious," Elena snaps.

"Sorry, I didn't realise you were a member of the grammar police."

"Just be quiet and behave yourself."

Behave myself? Bitch. How dare she treat me like a kid? I'm not a kid. How dare she make assumptions about me like that! I am what I am, and most of that's what *they* made me. If I didn't need her, I'd get out of the bloody car right now. Actually, if I do get out of the car—if I stay here in the wilderness—I won't need to learn how to control this.

But I can't stay here forever. I do need her, and so I can't tell the bitch to fuck off. It would be to my advantage, I think, not to tell her that I know how she feels.

Laurie's getting frustrated with me, I can tell. Good. I'm sick, tired, abused, scared, hurting, and confused. I'm facing a future of running away from someone who wants to dissect me, with a head full of other people's thoughts. On top of everything, I have to drive away the only person I've ever really loved. I think I'm allowed a bit of petulance.

"What?" I snap at him, and he jumps, his eyes widening.

"What? I . . ."

"You were looking at me as if I was a nasty smell under your nose. If you think I'm a childish, spoiled brat, then just say so."

"Gabriel, I wasn't . . . Well, all right I was a bit, but . . ."

"But what? So I'm cranky. I reckon I have a right to be. If you don't like it, then just get out of the damn car."

"Gabriel?"

I hurt him. I know I did. I can feel I did. I hate myself.

"Just shut up, Laurie. I have a headache."

There's a horrible atmosphere, but I don't care. I don't feel like conversation, and at least I can sit back with my forehead against the cool glass and close my eyes without having to talk to anyone. I can feel they're both pissed with me, and it hurts my head. I wasn't kidding about that, either. It feels like there's a band around my forehead that's getting tighter and tighter.

"Can you stop being so angry with me, please?"

"You deserve it, Gabriel." Laurie snaps.

"I know" — I'm surprised by how weak my voice sounds, how exhausted. It's been a hell of a long couple of days, and I don't think those drugs Elena gave me are agreeing with me at all — "but it hurts."

"Hurts?"

Laurie's instantly concerned, all his anger disappearing. Elena's less prepared to let it go, but hey, half gone is good.

"Are you all right?"

Good question. "Actually . . . actually, I don't think I am."

Laurie puts his arm around me and draws me against him, resting my head against his shoulder. I know I shouldn't do this, but I feel like shit. Would it be so wrong to let him hold me for a little while? His arm's so strong, his hair so soft. It's falling over my cheek when he bends his head. He's worried about me, and I don't have the energy to tell him not to. I manage to smile, and that's the best I can do.

She's worried about me, too. I don't give a flying fuck about that, about her. It's her fault I'm feeling like this in the first place. This is her fault. Well, her and others like her. I must be crazy letting her take me to this place. Far away from everyone. Far from any help. Shit! I hadn't thought of that. Is that why we've come here? So that I can't get help? Panic gnaws me. Calm down. I must calm down. Panicking isn't going to help. Besides, she wouldn't have needed to bring me here. There was no help for me in the facility either.

But what if they wanted me to train first? But that would

be stupid because then I can fight back. But what if she's going to make it so I can't fight back? But that's stupid because they'd definitely have ways to stop me back there. But what if they don't? What if . . . Dammit. I'm going 'round in circles, and my head's so bad it hurts to think.

There's not much I can do about it now. I have to go along with it. I need to. But I can still be on my guard. I'm not going to let them take me without a fight. I just have to be . . .

Chapter Twenty-One

Hell, it hurts. Everything hurts. It's not *the pain* though. It's not overwhelming. I can . . . Wait, where the hell am I? Aww. Mental note . . . don't sit up fast.

It's cool and still. It smells of pine . . . ah, the cabin. I look around, but there's not much to see. A bed, a chest of drawers, a chair. There are dark blue curtains drawn across the window, and it seems like the sun is bright outside.

Everything's made of wood, even the floor. It's cool on my feet, feels nice. My head's not so nice, but it's not so bad I can't stand it. I've had worse.

The main room of the cabin is nicer than I expected. What had I expected? Don't know. It's really big, and it seems cosy but chic at the same time. Eew. It reeks of wealth and privilege. I should've known.

There's no one around. I wonder where they are. Meh. The kitchen is shiny and looks like it's never been used. The fridge is *huge*. What do I care? There's juice, and right now that's all I care about, except that I notice bottles of beer, lots of them. I store that knowledge away for later.

Large glass doors look out over a long lawn leading down to the lake. Pretty. I can imagine standing here in the darkness with a beer in my hand, watching the moon rise over the lake. Yeah, right. I'm getting poetic. I'll have to watch that.

The breeze from the lake hits me as soon as I open the door. It's wonderful. I didn't notice how hot I was until I was cool. When my foot touches the grass, I realise I don't have any shoes on. Okay . . . cool.

It's actually nice here. The grass is soft, the breeze is gentle, and the lake is beautiful. I'm almost relaxed. Now if I had a beer . . . At least my headache feels better.

"Hey."

Great, I knew it was too good to be true. Why? Why can't I stop feeling good at the sound of his voice? Why do I have to melt into his side when he puts his arm around my waist? Why can't I push him away? Why can't I . . .

"How are you feeling now?"

"Better. I'm sorry about all that."

"Sorry? What?"

"Yeah well, just shut up and hold me."

Why the hell did I say that? Why don't I resist when he turns me around? Why don't I stop him when he bends his head? Why am I putting my hands in his hair? Wow, it's so soft, and his lips are soft, too. *Oh, God!*

"No!" I stumble with the force I use to push him away. I can't let him get this close. I can't let myself get this close.

"What's the matter?"

"I can't do this. It's too . . ."

"What? What's wrong? What did I do? I thought . . ."

"Laurie, I–I know I want . . ." Fuck. Great. I've lost the power of speech. I don't want to say this. I can't say this. I can't see that look in his eyes. Dammit, I'm so fucking weak. "Oh, fuck it."

When I throw myself at him, I completely take him by surprise, and we both hit the deck. He doesn't know whether to fight me off or hold me close. We end up with me kneeling over him. He looks stunned, confused, beautiful—so goddamn beautiful. What can I do? I have to get up and walk away. I have to run. I have to . . . Oh God, it feels good to kiss him.

"When you two have quite finished . . ."

The cool voice breaks in on the heat of our kiss, and I almost growl at her. She's changed into jeans and a t-shirt and looks about sixteen. I hate her.

"What do you want?"

"I thought there'd be time to run you through a few exercises before dinner."

"Now?"

"The sooner, the better. I guess you've got a bitch of a headache, right?"

"Yeah, so?"

"So even the two of us are too much for you to handle right now. You're unconsciously trying to block us, and it's hurting you."

"No, that's ... that's just ..." Okay, I have to acknowledge that maybe, just maybe, she could be right. "Okay. What do I have to do?"

"Come inside." Without waiting to see if I'm following, she strides back toward the cabin.

"What's got up her nose?"

"You have."

"Me? What have I done?"

"Gabriel, sometimes you can be a complete jerk."

"Only sometimes?"

Laurie grins broadly and kisses me. It feels good. What the hell am I thinking? Abruptly I push myself up from him and hurry after Elena. I don't know if he follows. I don't look back.

"So what do I have to do?"

"First, maybe you can lose the attitude."

"Sorry, where I go the attitude follows. I'm kind of attached to it."

"For God's sake, what's the matter with you? I'm trying to help you."

"Yeah, trying to help fix something you broke in the first

place."

"That wasn't me."

"It was your kind."

"My kind?"

"That place you took me. The place where you work. The people you work with, they destroyed my life, my whole life! And they're still doing it, so don't fuck with me. Don't expect me to be grateful to you for trying to help me fix something that you did to me."

"It wasn't me. I'm trying to help you. It wasn't me who hurt you."

"Hurt me? You didn't hurt me. You destroyed me. You have no idea what my life's been like because of what you did to me. Hah. Life? I've *had* no life. And I've destroyed the lives of everyone close to me. You poisoned me, and now I poison everyone who touches me. You did that. *You did that!*"

"It wasn't me!"

"I might as well have been!"

"It! Wasn't! Me!"

I'm gripping her arms, and she's struggling, but I don't care. "Tell me you don't know about The Chair," I hiss, and she goes still. "Tell me." She turns her face away, and I'm so angry I want to rip off her head. "Tell! Me!"

"I can't, Gabriel. I know. I've seen."

I can't bear to touch her anymore, so I practically throw her away from me. I don't care that she stumbles and falls.

"I hate you." I try to shout, but it's just a whisper. My voice is too weak to sound like more than a croak. My legs are too weak to hold me. I'm too weak to stop my tears . . . no, sobs. There's nothing I can do, nothing but kneel on the floor and weep. And I hate her.

When she crawls across the floor and tries to put her arms around me, I try to fight, but I'm too weak and too full of tears. In the end, I've no choice but to let her hold me close, and I'm so tired I rest my head on her shoulder. But it's only because I'm tired. Only because I'm too weak right now to fight. Once I stop crying, I'm going to push her away. Once the pain in my head stops, I'm going to tear hers off her shoulders. I hate her, and I'm never going to stop hating her.

"I hate you." It's still a whisper.

"I know."

"Damn you . . . damn you to Hell. I *hate* you."

I try again to push her away, but she's holding on tight now, and the more I struggle, the tighter she holds me until I can't fight any more.

Eventually, the tears stop, leaving me empty and still. Elena's still holding me tight, and I feel helpless and hopeless. I won't look at her. I won't let her in. I hate her.

"I know you were hurt, Gabriel. I've read the files, and I've seen The Chair. I know what they did to you. And yes, it's still there, but it's locked away and not being used. I was brought in to try and undo this mess. I wasn't even out of school when this happened to you. I swear to you that I've done everything I possibly can to put this right."

"Put it right? No one can put it right."

"I tried to save you. I tried to save you all."

"Maybe it would've been better if you hadn't bothered."

"Would it?"

Would it? Would I rather be dead than here with her and Laurie and the chance of a normal life ahead? A life where I have to drive away the one person I love and have ever loved. Where I have to learn to have a semblance of normality in my life. Where I'll always be on the run, looking over my shoulder? Would it?

"Yes."

"Oh, Gabriel, I'm sorry. I'm so sorry. I couldn't have let you die. I couldn't have gone on if I hadn't done my very best for every one of you. I'm sorry if you hate me, although I don't blame you. I'm sorry that you don't feel you can get past this, because it's the last thing I would've wanted and something I will try very, very hard to remedy. But I'm not sorry—I can't be sorry—that I saved you."

"What do you know about me and what's best for me? What do you know about what I went through? What I've kept on going through, what I'm *still* going through? You know nothing." Now I find the strength to push her away and even manage to get shakily to my feet. She stays on the floor, and I'm glad. I don't want her anywhere near me.

"You know nothing about me. Nothing. You don't know how much I was hurt . . . broken. You don't know how many lives I've ruined, not only my own. You don't know what it's like going through your whole life looking over your shoulder and waiting for the axe to fall. Trying to make relationships with other people, only to have them poisoned by your fear, your anger. You don't know what it's like to watch people you love destroyed and not to care, not to feel, not to . . . You don't know anything about me—anything.

"Don't try and say sorry. I don't want to hear it. I don't want anyone to be sorry for me. I don't want you to say you understand, because you don't, and I don't want to hear you say that you're glad you saved me, because I'd rather be dead."

She doesn't try to stop me when I run for the door. Laurie does, but I just throw him aside with the strength of my anger. I hear voices calling as I run, but I ignore them. I have no idea where I'm going, no idea what I'm going to do when I get there. I just run.

I stop when I'm too tired to run any more. I'm too tired to think, too tired to move, too tired to care. It's still quite warm, even though the sun's getting low. I have such a headache, but that's just from crying. There is no buzzing, no intrusion. There's only peace. That's what I need . . . peace.

I find a tree and let it take me into its roots. There's a hollow filled with dead leaves, and it's as comfortable as a feather bed to me right now. Everywhere there's a stillness that's filled with the noise that isn't noise. If I listen hard, I can hear the rustling and whispering of the wind. I must be close to the lake, because I can hear the water, too, lapping against something. It distorts sound so that everything seems far away and there's a hush over everything that can only happen near a large, open stretch of water.

Here I can stop running for a while. No one's going to find me. No one's going to hurt me. Here I can just be me. I can just be Gabriel . . . Well, I could if I had any idea who the hell Gabriel is these days. My life's been turned upside down.

Okay, it wasn't much of a life, but I knew where I was. I was running, but I knew what I was running away from. Now . . . I don't know if I'm running away, and I don't know who I'm running away from. Is it Elena? Is it some faceless scientist who wants me back in The Chair—Oh God, I spare a shudder for that. Or is it me? Am I just running away from myself?

Am I afraid to stop? Am I afraid to be normal—to be me? Am I afraid that if I strip away the anger and the fear and pain, peel myself like an onion, that under all the layers there's nothing? That Gabriel doesn't even exist anymore? Do I really want to die? Hell yes. Am I going to do anything about it? Hell no.

I've thought more than once that I have masochistic tendencies. I'm in an impossible situation, and I want out. I want to die more than I ever have, but it's like a rotten tooth. I can't pull it out. I need to poke at it for a while.

Maybe she can teach me. Maybe I can get away. Maybe I

can make it . . . to what? Well, that's too far away to think about. And what do I have to lose? If it doesn't work out, there'll always be razor blades, always be pills from somewhere . . . always a way.

Yes, maybe I'll try for a while and see what happens. Right now, though, I'm too tired to do anything. I'm pretty sure I can find my way back if I follow the lakeshore, and I'll do it in a little while. Let her stew for a while. What about Laurie? He doesn't deserve my anger. No, but there's not a whole lot I can do about that right now, and if I want to drive him away, I've got to stop these twinges of guilt every time I upset him. No, Laurie can wait, too. Now, I'm going to rest here, maybe sleep for a while. Then . . . well, I can think about that later.

I must've fallen asleep. It's full night. It's hard to get to my feet because I'm stiff as hell. There must have been a branch or something sticking into me, because my back hurts.

Following the sound of water, I find the lake, and it's beautiful. I don't have much time to appreciate the beauty of the bright moon hanging like a lamp over the still water — yadda, yadda — because something else catches my attention. I do appreciate the stillness now as I stand and watch the light. It's on the other side of the lake. A beacon in the darkness — for me. I wonder if they've waited up or just left the light on.

Do I want to go back? I don't know. It would be easy to keep going, never go back. I won't have to hurt Laurie. Well, yeah, I'd hurt him, but he'd get over it, and I wouldn't be there to see the hurt. But . . . oh hell, who am I kidding? Of course, I'm going back. I know there's only one thing waiting for me out here, and maybe I'm not ready to die yet. Or am I?

Okay, so I made the decision to go back, but that was weighed against trying to go on, but what if it was weighed against stopping? The lake looks inviting for a different reason now. What if I just walk into the water and let it take me? The cool water would feel so good against my skin. It would cool the heat inside. I would be at peace. That's all I want—peace. Why not? What do I have to go back to?

I don't know why I take my clothes off. Maybe just to leave something behind—something of me. Maybe so someone will find them and know. And it's as easy as that—easy to stand naked on the edge of the water, curling my toes in the deep cold of the water's margin. There's a light breeze that raises the hairs on my body, making me shiver a little. The thought that it'll soon be over lifts a huge weight from my shoulders, and I feel light and free. It's been a long time since I've been without fear . . . such a long time. I feel empty but in a good way. At last, an end at last.

It's been a long time since I felt happy, but I'm close to it when I step into the lake. Suddenly I'm overloaded—the cold water, the bright moon, the sounds of the night, but it doesn't hurt. Nothing hurts anymore. The Chair isn't going to have me now . . . no one is. I laugh. It's such a free laugh. The sound of it surprises, almost shocks me.

I walk on. Then there's nothing beneath my feet. The shore simply falls away, and so do I. I can tell I'm in deep water. I don't resist as the water closes over my head. The peace is even greater here. There's no sound at all but the hammering of my blood in my ears. Now, all I have to do is take a breath—just one breath, and it's out of my hands.

An image of Laurie flashes through my mind, and I fight to shake it. I open my mouth and water floods in. It's not the dirty, muddy water I was expecting, but cool, clear water that in other circumstances would've been refreshing.

Damn, I'm coming up fast. I need to do it now. If I fill my

lungs with water, I'll sink. Simple as . . . Simple as that. Simple. *Laurie*. No, don't think of him. The water hits the back of my throat, and the gag reflex kicks in. This is it. I'm choking. Stop choking and take a breath. Just one. Just one breath. Breathe, now!

Oh hell, I'm out in the air. Can't breathe. Choking. Stop. Breathe in, just one breath. Do it, Gabriel—do it now. Just one breath. One. I'm going under again. There's water in my chest. It hurts like hell. I can't stop choking, but at least it'll be over soon.

Laurie. No . . . I . . . No! Stop fighting—stop. It'll stop hurting soon. *Laurie*. It'll stop soon. *Laurie*. Ah fuck.

With a powerful stroke, I break free and gulp a breath of fresh air. Before I can go down again, I fight for the shore and suddenly feel the side of the underwater ledge hit my chest. God, it's hard to drag myself out. I'm coughing like hell, and tears are streaming down my face. As if there isn't enough water.

I just about manage to haul myself out of the water and stagger to the shore before collapsing on my knees, vomiting the contents of my stomach mixed with a large quantity of lake water. After another coughing fit, I vomit again and collapse to one side, fortunately avoiding the puddle of sick.

God, my chest hurts. Damn, damn, damn. One breath. That's all it would've taken. One damn breath, and it would've been over. Just one breath. Damn him. Damn him. Damn him to hell! Just one. I don't think it would've hurt more than the breaths I'm taking now. God, my chest hurts. Coughing brings up bursts of water that come out of my nose and mouth. I feel half drowned. If only I could've got the other half right.

I'm getting tired now, and I have half an idea that falling asleep wouldn't be a good thing. Why not? Dying of exposure wouldn't be a bad option. It's hard to relax when my chest and throat feel like I've inhaled acid and I keep having coughing fits.

God, it's a mess. I'm a mess. Isn't there enough water around without these tears? Oh great. Now I can't stop crying. Huge wracking sobs bubble up and burst from me. There's no one to hear me, so I let it go, let it all out.

The crying makes me cough up more water. I don't care. This is such a mess. I'm making such a fuck-up of my life, and I'm even a failure at ending it.

I've absolutely no idea how long I spend howling, literally. Eventually, the cold seeps into my bones, and I have to get up. I can't even die by doing nothing. That son of a bitch won't leave me alone. He won't let go. Now he won't even let me die in peace. Right. Well, I'm not giving in to him. I'm damn well going to . . . What am I going to do? I can't even lie down and die. I'm pathetic.

I suppose I have to go back. What else can I do? The bastard's going to haunt me until I can get him out of my life properly. By then, who knows? Maybe I can find a reason to live or the balls to die. Right, well. If this world is so set on keeping me in it, it can bloody well prove it. I'm going to swim across the lake. I'm a good swimmer, but I'm sick and exhausted. Maybe I'll get lucky.

Chapter Twenty-Two

Laurie

It's been a long night already, and it's not even two. Where the hell is he, and what am I going to do if he doesn't come back at all? If only I knew what he's doing, what he intends to do. He's tried to kill himself at least once I know of and sincerely intended to at least one other time. I know he's capable of it. I believe he was going to try again at the hotel, and he was serious about ending his life if he didn't get what he wanted at the facility. What if he does something stupid? What if he's done it? I might never know. Ah hell, that thought hurts.

But what can I do? I've run myself into the ground, searched along the road, through the woods, almost halfway around the edge of the lake. There's no sign of him anywhere. It's as if he just disappeared. Not knowing which direction he took or how fast he was running, I realise he might as well have.

In the end, all I could do was come back here and sit and wait. So I've waited. I think I might have dozed for a while, but I wouldn't let myself sleep . . . just in case. I'm so stupid. I sit here, with the door open and the light on, thinking that perhaps it'll shine a beacon to him, call him home. That somehow, I'll be able to help him if . . . The truth is if he wants to find us, he will. And if he needs help, I'll never know.

I'm cold, even though it's a warm night and there's a blazing fire in the grate. I don't even know why I built it—it's too hot to sit anywhere near it. I suppose it's for comfort only. The cold's coming from the inside.

Maybe doing something will help. I wander into the kitchen and put the kettle on for coffee. At least that might keep me awake for a while longer. Elena's asleep on the sofa. I don't want to wake her. She was so upset.

I feel a bit better, having something to do, but the pain inside is still there—the nagging fear that I'm never going to see or hear from him again. The only thing stopping me from breaking down is a wild hope and the same fierceness that helped me through the bad times when I was with David. I have a feeling that when . . . if . . . that hope dies, I'll give myself over to a grief that will make what I felt after David died seem like just a pale shadow.

Picking up the coffee, I make my way back into the other room. Then I drop the mug. Fortunately, the scalding liquid misses everything but my boots. I bite back a scream as a dark shadow looms and pauses in the doorway.

"Gabriel?"

He practically staggers into the room, shedding water. It's streaming from his hair and puddling on the floor.

"Oh my God, what happened? Did you fall into the lake?"

He gives me a look that chills me. There's a kind of lost and stark vulnerability that changes quickly into anger and even something that looks very much like hatred. But that's stupid. Why on earth would he hate me?

"Yeah," he says sarcastically. "Let's go with *fell*, shall we?"

His voice sounds strange—hoarse and raspy—and he looks . . .

"Come sit by the fire. You look like crap. What happened?" I don't want to acknowledge the fact he's naked. You don't accidentally fall into a lake after taking your clothes off. He just gazes at me, and I'm scared of the expression in his eyes.

Finally, he seems to collapse in on himself, as if he's lost some kind of internal battle. He starts to cough, and it sounds painful. It seems for a moment as if he's going to be sick, but he manages to control himself and stalks to the chair. Elena's awake now, and she hovers uncertainly at his side.

"Gabriel, what happened?"

His eyes are hard when he looks up at her, but they don't have that same expression of anger and hatred that they held when they looked at me.

"I swam across the lake," he says, and for a moment, I'm weak with relief. He swam. He took his clothes off so he could swim across the lake. But there's something that won't let me accept. *Let's go with fell.* What could he have meant by that? He could have just said *I swam.* I know what he meant.

"Hell, Gabriel, you're freezing. What on earth were you thinking? I know it's a warm night, but still . . . Laurie, get him something warm to drink." She picks up the rug that was over her legs as she slept and tucks it around Gabriel.

He lets her, looking entirely defeated.

Why do I feel so sick? I know what happened. Of course, I do. So why is he here? I mean in the cabin and on the Earth. I have an idea about that, too. It would explain the look. Maybe he does hate me right now because he can't . . . leave me. I'm not stupid. I've worked out for myself from his reaction at the . . . whatever the hell it was—lab, research centre, whatever—that he still thinks there's a risk.

He's spent his whole life looking over his shoulder, and he's no fool, he knows it hasn't stopped. Whatever Elena might say, or even think, they know exactly what went on with Gabriel, and I think part of the reason they let him go was that they want something from him. They didn't know if Gabriel was serious about killing himself before allowing them to take him again. They know exactly what they did to him, so I guess they'd have a pretty good idea. Personally, I have no doubt he would've, and I think they know that, too.

But they haven't gone away. They'll wait until he's been trained . . . until he's the most that he can be. Then they'll hunt him down. They'll know he won't be able to do anything but fight to survive. That's what he's been doing for the past seven years, and that's what he'll do again. They'll keep hunting, and he'll keep running.

And now he's seen into my past. He knows what I went through when I was running, and what it meant to me to stop. He's going to push me away. He'll try to drive me off in any way he can, but it isn't going to do him any good at all, because I'm not going to let him. I'm just going to have to let him try, then hold on tight . . . just like I did before.

The fact that he came back to me—and I know damn well from where—has to mean something. It means I have an advantage I didn't have before. He cares about me. In fact, I think he cares about me as much as I care about him. He meant it when he said he loved me, and that scared him. He's scared to let himself love me, and so he won't allow himself to show it. He's going to fight me all the way, but I've been playing the game harder and longer than he has, and he doesn't know how to break the rules like I do. If he thinks he's going to drive me away, he's going to have his eyes opened the hard way.

When I hand him his coffee, I can see how much he's shaking. He keeps his head down and won't meet my eyes, but that's okay. He looks ill and exhausted. I take his coffee away, and he blinks at me, surprised and confused.

"You need to be in bed. You can drink this in there."

"What if I don't want to?" he snaps, rebellion flaring in his eyes.

"Then I can't make you, but you know as well as I do that when you get warm, you're going to crash big time, and if you do it in there, it'll be nicer for you and easier for us."

"Oh well, if it's easier for you," he says sarcastically, but there's something in his eyes that says he's glad for the fight, but gladder for the excuse to get up and go to bed. He gets to his feet and stalks across the room, only a little unsteadily. Elena stares at me and I wink.

Gabriel stops in front of one of the doors. He pauses for a moment. "Which one?" he growls.

"That one will be fine," Elena says. She's trying to speak lightly, but it's obvious the whole thing's upset her badly. Ignoring her, Gabriel opens the door and disappears, slamming it behind him.

Elena puts a hand on my arm as I move to follow with the coffee. "What happened, Laurie? I know there's more than he's telling. I think you know what it is."

I shake my head. That's not a road I'll be going down with her, but she deserves to know something if she's going to be working with him. I can handle him, but she seems so fragile now, so out of her element.

"I'm not sure, but he has a self-destructive streak. Don't worry, I'll take care of him."

"Will he let you?"

"I don't intend to give him a choice. Elena, he's going to fight us, both of us, every inch of the way—he has to. Let him push you away and keep coming back. I don't know if he'll ever let you in, but eventually, he'll stop shutting you out."

"I don't know how to deal with him. I've never had to work with anyone like this before."

"I don't think there *is* anyone like him."

She smiles and shakes her head.

The room is in darkness. Curtains block out the light, although a little leaks through, enough to show me a dark outline.

"What do you want?" the outline demands. He's even angrier because he knows I can hear the tears in his voice.

"I brought your coffee."

"Oh. Just leave it on the table and go."

"Not until I know you've drunk it and got warm."

"Who the hell do you think you are? You're not my mother."

"No," I say, trying to keep the smile in check. I'd expected nothing less. "But I'm still not leaving until you've finished the coffee."

"To hell with the goddamned coffee."

"Whatever. Drink it."

He growls as he takes the coffee. There's a moment when I think he's going to throw it across the room, but he's not that stupid, and he knows he needs it. He's still shivering. He takes a mouthful and chokes. I take the mug quickly from his hands as he goes into a full-blown coughing fit.

"Did you swallow a lot of water when you *fell* into the lake?" He struggles to control the coughing, swallowing repeatedly. I can feel his glare even through the darkness. "I know what happened."

"You don't know jack shit."

"Why'd you come back?"

I sit on the edge of the bed, and he goes very still. Now the door's closed, there's barely any light at all, but I don't need it to know what expression will be in his eyes right now. He's holding himself stiff as if, by keeping his body rigid, he can stop the pain from tearing it apart.

"I was cold."

"Don't talk bollocks to me, Gabriel. I know full well what you intended when you walked into that lake, and it wasn't to swim across it. Why didn't you do it? Why'd you come back?"

"It's none of your business," he says softly.

I reach out to touch his hand and just have time to ponder how cold it is before he jerks it away. "Don't fight me so hard. You know you need me right now. Tomorrow could be different, a lot different, but right now you need me."

"I don't need you. I've never needed you and I never will." He's blazing angry, and that's good. "You just won't leave me alone. You've never got the message, have you? I don't want you. I don't need you. I. Don't. Care about you. Leave me alone. Stop pulling me back. You just won't let go. Why didn't you let me go back at the facility? It would've been so much simpler if I'd never woken up."

"Simpler for who?"

"For everyone."

"Not for me."

"Yes, for you. You'd have been hurt, but you'd have got over it. You would've got on with your own life and been happy. You wouldn't have been here, in this fucked-up situation, with this fucked-up me. For God's sake, Laurie, why won't you just let me go . . . let me . . . die?"

"Because I love you." It's a simple statement, quiet and straightforward, and it completely floors him. Although I can't see them, I know his eyes are focused on me, blazing like a bonfire. He's full of emotion, full of pain. Then he breaks, like I knew he would.

He doesn't resist when I pull him roughly into my arms. He's so cold. His body shakes with emotion, reaction, and deep chills that worry me. He sobs into my shoulder until he starts coughing, then goes right back to it.

"You're going to have to be careful, babe, or you're going to get ill after this. Come on, let's warm you up."

Somehow, I manage to manoeuvre us so we're lying down, then pull the covers over us. This isn't as easy as it sounds, because now it's Gabriel who won't let go. Between the sobbing and the coughing, it doesn't take long for his energy to run out. Then he goes quiet, breathing hard.

"I tried to kill myself, Laurie. I really tried."

"I know you did." I hug him and kiss the only part I can reach—the top of his head. "Don't do that again."

He laughs bitterly. "I'll try not to."

"I know you will. I'll help you."

He's too tired to speak now, and his arms slowly release me as his body relaxes into sleep, with his head still on my shoulder. He's warm now, and the coughing has stopped. He's sleeping peacefully, so I can let myself cry.

I think I must have cried for most of the night, or at least one of us did. I don't remember, but the pillow's still damp, so I must have. Although . . . yeah, he was wet, wasn't he? Maybe it was his hair that wet the pillow. He's gone now.

It's bright outside and hot in here. I've no idea what time it is, but I do know that, after the stress of yesterday, and the fact I didn't get to sleep until it had gone two a.m., I'm dead tired and I don't want to get up. I will, of course. I have no idea what Gabriel's state of mind might be today, and I don't want to take any chances. He's so fragile right now. He doesn't think he is, but he is. When he gets his strength back, he'll want to fight again—he'll need to. But in the meantime, I have to make sure he doesn't give up.

Mmm. Despite everything, it's nice to throw open the curtains and bathe in the warm sunshine. I open the window and let the morning in. Actually, I'm not so sure it's still morning. There's no clock, and I left my phone on the table outside. Just as well I slept in my clothes last night.

Elena's in the kitchen. She hears me and comes out.

"You've missed breakfast. I defrosted some bread so we can have beans on toast or something for lunch. I'm going to need to go down to town for supplies this afternoon. The cabin's stocked with basics, but there's only so much baked beans and tuna you can eat." She's trying to be bright and normal, but it's easy to see she's still shocked and shaken.

"How far is the nearest town?"

"About fifteen minutes' drive. There are shops at campsites around the lake, but they're basic and expensive." I nod, taking the coffee she offers. She knows I'm not interested in shops. "He's down by the lake," she says softly. I smile and head out the door.

It's a glorious day, and the lake does strange things to sound. Everything is still and clear and fresh. It feels like a new start. I could really relax here.

I stand on the decking and stretch, looking down toward the lake. The sun's twinkling, and there's a heat haze shimmering over the surface. At first, I can't see Gabriel. It's only when I begin to wander down toward the water that I see him sitting, completely still, with his legs drawn up, staring out.

"I don't want to talk to you."

Why am I surprised that he knows I'm here? Of course, he does. He laughs, and I know why. It's because he knows I know. I refuse to go 'round in circles like this.

"Can you read my mind?" I sit down on the grass, about six feet away from him.

"No, not unless you're talking to me."

"How do you know what I'm thinking, then?"

"I don't." He turns to look at me, squinting against the sun. His eyes are very blue today. They seem to be lighter than before, more like cool deep water than the midday sky. His expression is veiled, but not as hostile as before. He sighs and runs his hands through his hair. It's lank and stiff from the lake water, but it's still beautiful. "I don't know how to explain it. It's not like voices in my head. Not anymore."

Turning the full force of those beautiful blue eyes on me, he bites his lip. He doesn't have to read my mind to know what I'm thinking right now. He sighs and turns his head away.

"It hurts me. It hurts a lot. It's like . . . like glass inside my brain. Crushed glass, filling it up and tearing it to shreds. It's unbearable. If there are only a few voices, I can hear them if they're speaking to me and . . ." He glances quickly up, then down again.

There's something going on behind those pretty eyes. "What are you thinking about?"

For a long time, he doesn't answer, and I just sit, sipping my coffee, pretending to watch the lake but really watching him. Does he know? Do I care?

"I don't trust her," he says at last. "I don't want her to know everything."

"Don't you think she needs to know everything to be able to help you?"

He considers. "No, I don't think so. She's going to show me how to shut things out. Does it matter what's left? If it isn't working, then I'll think again, but for now, I don't want her to know how much I . . . how much I know."

"How much do you know?"

He looks up again. "I can't read your thoughts, but I do know what you're thinking about, and how you feel about it."

"I don't understand."

"I know you're thinking of me, and I know how you feel about me, but I don't know exactly what form your thoughts are taking. I can tell things, like if you're lying, but not what you're lying about." He blinks at me. "I know you love me, and I know you think you can help me, but you're wrong. You can't. No one can. All you're doing is holding me back."

"Holding you back from what? From killing yourself?"

He gives me a long, calculating look, and I so much want to be able to read his mind right now. "Maybe."

"Would you? I mean, if the chance arose, would you try again?"

He frowns thoughtfully. "I don't know. There are always opportunities if you're serious. I'm going to give living a try, but I'm not making any promises."

He's being honest, brutally honest, but still . . . His words drive a knife through my heart. I knew it—of course, I knew it. But to hear him say it, that he still might . . .

"Gabriel . . ."

"Don't. I know what you're thinking, remember?"

"No, you don't. Really, you don't. I can't ask you to promise me not to die. I know it's not a promise you can give. I just want you to know some things."

"No."

"No?"

"I don't want to hear. I don't want to know."

"Well, I'm sorry, but you're going to whether you want to or not. It's easy to say, I know, but I've been there, and I can say it with conviction. I can't live without you, Gabriel. Don't think that if you kill yourself, I'll get over it, because I won't—not ever. It'll kill me, too."

"Don't be—"

"Listen."

"No. I don't want to listen." He gets up and turns away, but I'm faster. I grab his wrist and swing him around, wrapping my arms around him. He struggles for a while as I remain silent, letting him. Eventually, he realises he can't break free and stops fighting.

"Let me go, you bastard."

"Not until you listen to what I have to say."

"Then say it and fuck off."

"If you die, you'll kill me. My body will go on, and I'll even still be Laurie, but not the Laurie who's standing next to you now. I won't be the same. The Laurie I was when I was seventeen died when David did. He lay down in that dirty warehouse and died right there with him. The body that walked away was an empty shell, and it's taken a long time for it to fill up again. What it's filled up with is something and someone new. There's a black hole somewhere inside me that can never be filled. I fall into it now and again, and it's the space that David used to fill. If you leave me, there'll be an even bigger space . . . a deeper hole . . . and another part of my soul will die.

"I can't tell you or even ask you not to do it again. I know you're afraid, and sometimes you get desperate and think there's no future, but there is. I'm your future just as you're mine, and I don't care about anything other than that. I don't care what happens to us, as long as it happens to us both together. I can't tell you what to do, but I *know* you love me. I know you came back for me because you couldn't leave me behind, and I can't leave you either. I *won't* leave you."

"What if I want you to?"

"I don't care what you say you want or what you think you need to do. I know you're going to try to push me away. I'd be disappointed if you didn't, but it's not going to do you any good. I'm here, and I'm staying until you can look me in the eyes and tell me truthfully you don't love me. Can you do that?"

Gabriel turns his face up to me, and the angry expression drains out of his eyes. He seems dazed and confused, but then he presses his lips together and hardens his face. "I don't love you."

If he thinks I'm going to fall for that unconvincing performance . . . I have to laugh, and it makes him angry.

"What? Didn't you hear what I said?"

"I heard."

"So why are you still here?"

"Because I'm not a complete idiot. I may not be able to read your mind, but I didn't need to, to know you were lying through your teeth."

"I wasn't lying. I don't . . . I don't love you, and I just want you to go away and leave me alone."

He's trying. He's trying hard, and that's cool. He doesn't have the strength to fight right now, and that's cool, too. When I lean in and kiss him, he goes stiff, starts to struggle, but eventually gives in and relaxes into the kiss.

Eventually, I raise my head and smile at him. "Now *that* I did believe."

He struggles again, and this time I let him go. "Fuck you," he spits out as he storms off. I have to smile after him. This is going to be interesting.

CHAPTER TWENTY-THREE

Well, the last few days have been interesting. Gabriel keeps pushing me away, and I keep coming back. I see him watching me all the time. Sometimes it's with longing, and sometimes with hatred. Then sometimes . . . sometimes it's such an open look, filled with equal measures of pain and love, that it hurts me.

He hadn't got away unscathed by his escapade in the lake. By the end of the first day, he was running a high fever and delirious for most of the night and half the next day. I sat with him the whole time. I don't think he remembers, but there were times when he screamed my name and clung to me desperately, begging me not to leave him. Then there were times when he wept bitterly and moaned and raved that he needs to make me leave so I'd have a life and he won't drag me down with him when he has to go on the run again.

The most heartbreaking of all were the times he begged to die. He begged me, God, and the universe. He pleaded to be released from his pain and fear — to not be a danger to me, to have peace, to stop running. He broke my heart, and I think he darn near broke Elena's, too.

There were times when Elena stared at him as if she was in a trance — fascinated and repelled at the same time. There were times when she ran from the room in tears, and there were times when she took him in her arms and rocked him like a mother does her child and said "I'm sorry. I'm so, so sorry," over and over and over.

In those long hours — in short, burning, tearing bursts — he gave me all his fear. It's made me more certain than ever that I'm not going to leave him.

When he started to get better, he improved quickly. By the morning of the third day, he was clear-headed and back to his usual stormy self, albeit he was still weak and had a nagging cough that won't leave him.

The next day Elena started the training, and what seemed like relatively simple exercises when she explained them often left him curled up, moaning with pain, or even unconscious. When this happened, she looked as if she'd been beaten with a stick, but she persevered. Of course, Gabriel would never give up or admit he's struggling.

He seems almost to thrive on pain. He pushes himself way beyond his limits sometimes, with a strange sense of maliciousness, as if he's somehow trying to punish us. With Elena, he succeeds.

Today they're in the bedroom, and I haven't heard a sound for a good half an hour. It's not so nice a day today. The sky's grey, and there are low clouds over the lake bringing the smell of rain. I've been walking along the shore, encased in a fine mist of summer rain that settled on me, wetting me without being very wet at all.

I stand at the closed patio doors and gaze out at the rain clouds moving in from the far side of the lake, which gradually swallow the scenery, drawing it back behind the grey cloak of the rain. When the first spatters hit the windows, I close my eyes to breathe in the freshness and listen to the patter of raindrops on the glass.

A shiver ripples along my spine, but it isn't unpleasant. It's late afternoon, and the fire's burning in the grate. There's a pleasant feeling of being enclosed in warmth and cosiness, while the world outside turns cold and grey. I know that by the morning the rain will have passed, and the world will be made new.

Turning away from the windows, I wander over to sit in the armchair in front of the fire, even though I'm not cold. I sink down with a sigh and let my head rest against the back of the chair. I haven't been this relaxed in a long time. Even Gabriel seems more cheerful and focused today. There've been no tantrums, and he came out of the mental exercises Elena gave him to perform every morning with a confident smile rather than his usual scowl of pain. Things are looking up at last, and I'm cautiously optimistic about the way this whole thing's going to turn out.

Of course, Gabriel's still not letting me get close. For all he clung to me when he was ill, as soon as he became lucid, he drew back and has generally been cold and distant. He's allowed me to kiss him once or twice but pulls away from any kind of physical contact. There've been moments—a brush of our hands, a glance across the room, his head resting against my shoulder for a few minutes—but they pass quickly, and he almost seems to resent them, as if they're a show of weakness on his part that leaves him angry at himself. I'm riding the tide.

I glance up when the door opens and smile at Elena. She's pale and seems tired. She always looks tired, and her eyes are permanently haunted.

"Was it a hard session? Do you want a coffee?"

"Yes, it was. Don't worry about the coffee, I'll get it. I need to be doing something. It didn't go so well today."

I know what that means. Gabriel ended the session either unconscious or in agonising pain. I didn't hear any screams, so I guess he's out cold.

"I'll go and sit with him."

Elena nods grimly, a frown on her face.

Nervousness flutters in my stomach. "Was it *that* bad?"

"I don't know ... I ... there was something that just

didn't feel right, and it was . . . I don't know. I suppose I'm just getting tired. It all felt wrong."

"What do you mean *wrong*? Is Gabriel okay?"

"I don't know what I mean, Laurie. Things have been going well, and I'm beginning to feel as if he's starting to trust me. At least, not fighting me anymore. I think he's beginning to realise I'm not trying to deceive him and can see where these exercises are leading.

"I know they're hard. Sometimes they hurt, and they're always a struggle. That's the nature of the beast. But it's easier when he's not fighting it.

"He's got the basics down well, and it's just a matter of practising how to hold the shields in place and how to let things through selectively. The hardest part is already done. He can throw up a shield quickly when he needs to, which means he has protection against unwanted intrusions." She looks at me and smiles. "I'm sorry, Laurie. I mean he can shut out the noise when he wants to, so it doesn't hurt when there are people around."

I'm not that stupid. I knew what she meant, but I don't say anything, just nod and smile.

"All he needs now is practice to make it more complete and more effortless. It needs to become second nature, something that's as natural as breathing, or it'll dissolve when he's stressed, tired, asleep . . . and it will all come crashing in on him. There's nothing more I can teach him about that."

She pauses to run a hand through her thick, rich hair. It's more obvious than ever that Gabriel isn't the only one who's struggling and working themselves into the ground.

"But there are other things I can teach him, like being open to particular people, thoughts, key signatures . . ." Seeing my blank look, she presses on. "If there's a full shield up, he doesn't *hear* anything, and what's the point in that? There are two things I'm trying to teach him—one of them is how to turn the shield into a filter so if, for example, you're in a crowded room, he can remain open to you or pick up on any particular individual without having to let everyone in."

"Okay, I understand. I'm right with you, so what's the problem today? That doesn't sound particularly difficult. I mean, not enough to send Gabriel off."

"Well, the other thing I'm teaching him is how to *listen out*. I don't know how to explain it ... Umm ... say he's waiting for you somewhere, and he doesn't know exactly when you're going to turn up. You'll be outside his range so he won't be able to *tune in* to you. So he *listens out*. He leaves a window open so when you get within range, he'll know you're coming." She hesitates.

"He's particularly keen to learn this one because he wants to keep himself safe from whoever he still believes is after him. He simply won't accept that he's safe now, and no one's going to be hunting him down."

"Do you think he's safe?"

"Yes, of course, I do. I'm aware of all the projects being worked on at the facility and the people working on them. I have absolute trust in them. I think Gabriel's being entirely paranoid to think anyone would want to hurt him. Okay, I can't deny some of my colleagues desperately want to work with him, but he'd never be forced, not anymore. Things are so much more open these days they wouldn't dare, and I don't think anyone would want to. The initial project was a huge mistake, one that's never going to be repeated." She shakes her head and shivers.

"I can't blame him for being frightened and paranoid. Some of the things that went on, what happened to those poor children, were horrendous. I mean, the implants themselves. Who would perform brain surgery on thirteen-year-olds without their knowledge or consent?" She shudders.

"Be that as it may, I don't think he has anything to fear.

However, I do acknowledge he's afraid and that he has, at least in his own mind, grounds to be. So I'm trying to teach him how to keep a window open for anyone who approaches him wishing him harm, especially anyone who's thinking about the project or anything to do with it.

"Actually, it's more about listening out for feelings than trying to *hear* anything. Anyone who approaches with ill-intent will feel wrong to him and alert him so he can tune in and identify who it is and what they want . . . well, as far as possible," she finishes with a sigh.

"Okay, I've got the general picture . . . I think."

She smiles. "That's a very general picture. I don't think I have the strength to try and go into particulars. The technicalities are detailed and complex."

"But I still don't get why you're so rattled today in particular?"

She frowns. "I don't know, but the whole process felt wrong. Sometimes it's easier to put him into a light trance so I can direct him to open or close parts of his mind or consciousness without resistance. Today, it seemed as if he kept slipping too deep, and it was hard to get him to focus at all. And . . . and . . . I don't know, sometimes I was saying things that didn't make sense even to me, and when I tried to think about it, I couldn't remember what I'd said. Every time I said it, Gabriel seemed to slip deeper, and I had to keep bringing him back.

"What do you mean?" I'm even more nervous now.

"I don't know. Maybe it's just that we've both been working too intensely, and we're getting mentally tired. Sometimes I forget he's still not well. Don't worry, Laurie. He's fine. He's a bit out of it, but he'll be okay in ten or fifteen minutes. In fact, I think I'll forgo the coffee and get straight to making lunch. He'll be hungry when he wakes up."

I have no real understanding of what she's talking about,

and to be honest, I don't care. All I care about is that something went wrong, and no matter how many times she says Gabriel's okay, I'm not going to believe it until I've seen him and spoken to him myself.

The room is cool and dim, since the curtains are pulled over the window. They flutter a little and are spattered with water. The sound of the rain is strong, as is the smell, which mingles with the pine scent that's soaked into the fabric of the cabin. I love the smell of rain, especially summer rain that comes after a hot spell. I toy with the idea of closing the window, but the sound and smell are just too pleasant.

Gabriel's awake, and that surprises me, especially as he hasn't said anything or even acknowledged my presence.

"Are you okay?"

He doesn't answer or even stir, and those butterflies in my stomach start calling up a storm. He's lying on his back with one arm thrown up behind his head, staring at the ceiling, with heavy-lidded eyes. There's no expression on his face at all. He looks as if he's sleeping with his eyes open.

Sitting down on the bed next to him, I brush away some strands of long hair that stripe his face. Some of them are stuck to his eyelashes and must be irritating when he blinks. He ignores them, and he ignores me.

"Gabriel, are you okay? Do you even see me? Do you know I'm here?"

Clearly not, and that worries the hell out of me. What had she said about him slipping deeper and needing to be called back? I figure maybe this is one of those times, and I've no idea what do to. But if that had happened, surely Elena would have done something. Wouldn't she be here? Would she have left him if he needed her? God, I hate all this. He's making himself so vulnerable to someone I don't quite trust, and he doesn't trust at all. Are we doing the right thing?

As I stroke his cheek, Gabriel shivers and starts to speak.

It's very quiet, and when I bend close to listen, it doesn't make any sense. It's scary, because it's completely toneless, as if he's chanting a mantra or something. It sounds a bit like the incoherent ramblings that happened when he was delirious with fever. Quickly, I lay my hand on his forehead, but he's cool. He groans at my touch and turns his head on the pillow. The chanting falls silent.

"Gabriel, I'm getting worried about you. I don't know what's going on, but I don't like it. I'm going to get Elena because—"

A deep shudder runs through him, and, with a groan, his eyes roll closed.

"Shit. Right, that's it. I'm going to—" Again I'm stopped mid-sentence.

Gabriel blinks open his eyes and smiles sleepily. "Wassup?"

"Fuck, you scared me."

"Scared you? Why?" He drags himself up to sit with his back against the wall and regards me coolly, his head to one side.

"Never mind, you were just . . . out of it."

"Nothing new there. All this stuff's harder than I thought."

"Gabriel, do you trust her? Elena, I mean. Do you trust her?"

He narrows his eyes. "Why? What happened?"

"I don't know, that's the point. Something went wrong and . . ."

"Something went wrong? What went wrong?"

"I don't know, and neither does she. She was kind of . . . I don't know. She freaked me out. She doesn't believe you have any reason to fear the people at that place. She thinks it's all in your head, and she's just humouring you. It's . . . I don't know. It's not what she said so much as how she was saying it, I suppose. Then when I was sitting with you just now, it suddenly occurred to me that you're leaving yourself completely open to her and she could be . . . I don't know, it's probably stupid, but she could be doing anything to you."

Gabriel frowns. "Don't think I haven't thought about it. No, I don't trust her, but I don't think I have any choice. I need to learn what she has to teach me. I try to protect myself as much as I can, but I know full well there are times when I'm not in control, and when I don't remember what happens or what she says to me."

He looks thoughtful and bites his lip when he says, "Sometimes I do wake up feeling strange. It's as if something inside me has been . . . opened up . . . switched on . . . changed. Mostly I understand it when I practice, and I can do things I couldn't before, or it's easier to do things. But sometimes . . ." He shrugs. "Like today. Today I feel . . ." He raises his eyes to me and looks tired. Most of the time, he's strong and stubborn and even hostile, but at this moment he looks ill. "Vulnerable," he finishes and looks down again.

"That's how you looked . . . when I came in. You were kind of awake, at least your eyes were open, but you didn't know I was here, and you were talking . . . like talking in your sleep, really soft and not making any sense."

"Was I?" He looks startled and helpless. "I don't know what to do. I feel like we're close to something. The end? End of what? I don't know. I can't leave it like this. It's . . . incomplete. I don't feel any malice from her, any deceit. I suppose she can hide it, but she seems very open. I don't know . . ."

"I don't know what to say. I don't like this situation, not at all. I don't like the fact that I don't understand any of it so I can't help you. I don't like the thought of you putting yourself completely in her hands and not knowing what she's doing to you. I'm scared for you."

For a moment he stares at me with a completely open look. Then the shutters come down. "I can take care of myself. You don't need to understand, because I don't need your help. This is my issue, and I'll deal with it my way."

"And what way is that?"

"My way," he says stubbornly, and I know that there's no point saying another word.

He's closed up on me again, and he'll just stubbornly dismiss or ignore everything I say. I know it's because he's scared, but what can I do? If I try to hold him or comfort him or even talk to him about it, he'll push me away, and it will only make things worse. The easiest way to hold on to him is to let him go.

"Okay, whatever. Elena's making lunch. Come out when you're ready."

I feel his gaze on me as I walk out of the room. I know he wants to call me back, to ask me to hold him. And I know he's way too stubborn to do it. Sometimes he's so frustrating. Sometimes?

Elena looks up when I enter the kitchen. "Everything okay?"

"No, it's not." She looks a little startled at my tone of voice. I hadn't intended it to come out so sharp.

"Is Gabriel okay?"

"I think so. Now."

"I don't understand. What're you trying to say?"

"When I went in there, he was staring into space and talking nonsense. He didn't even know I was there."

"Oh. There's no need to worry about that, Laurie, honestly. He's just processing the things he's learned."

"He doesn't know —"

"Laurie . . . I know it's hard for you to trust me, for both of you. Gabriel has terrible memories of the things done to him at the facility and associates me with the people who did it, no matter how much I tell him that I'm different, that I don't mean him any harm, that I'm trying to help him. On one level, he's never going to believe that, and I know it. I accept it. But I swear to you, I'm not doing anything bad to him. I'm just trying to help.

"I've never met anyone like Gabriel before, and I'll readily admit to you that there are some things I'm learning and adapting to as I go along, but I've studied this subject for many years, and theoretically I know what I'm doing."

"Theory's very different to practice, and it's someone's mind you're playing with."

"I'm not playing, Laurie. I'm deadly serious about this, and I'm not doing anything that puts Gabriel at risk. I know that sometimes it seems as if he's being hurt, and sometimes I admit that he is . . . that the things he needs to do to learn the opening up process hurt. I can't do anything about that. The implant's opened up some areas and closed down others, which make some things that shouldn't be difficult hard for him, and that can hurt. I don't always know what they're going to be, and sometimes I lead him into something that hurts him, or we come up against a wall that he has to push through knowing it's going to hurt him. I don't do it intentionally. I never hurt him maliciously or unnecessarily."

"She's telling the truth."

We're both startled by Gabriel, who's leaning nonchalantly against the doorframe.

"Gabriel, are you all right?" Elena asks.

I hear the edge of real concern in her voice. Is it because she cares about Gabriel, or is it because she's not sure whether he actually is?

"I'm fine, you'll be glad to know. What happened to make you doubt it?"

"I don't . . ."

"I thought you've learned enough about what I can do to stop blatantly lying to me."

"I have. I'm sorry. Yes, there was something that made me doubt it. And no, I don't know what it was. I'll admit to you that there was a point when I lost control. I don't know why, and I don't know how, but I believe I got you through without any problems in the end."

"You believe?"

"Yes" — she looks him straight in the eyes — "I believe. And I never led *you* to believe there wouldn't be times when I was working blind and doing the best I could."

Gabriel holds her stare for a long moment, then shrugs. "True," he says, then turns and walks away.

When I follow him into the other room, he's slipping through the glass doors out on to the patio. For a moment I panic, images of the mist swallowing him and taking him away forever flashing through my mind. But that's just silly. He isn't pissed off enough to do anything stupid . . . is he?

Well, he does do something stupid, but not in the way I feared. In fact, maybe it wasn't *that* stupid at all. He stands on the patio with his face up to the rain and starts to dance. It's just a slow, swaying dance without any direction or finesse, but it's beautiful — because he's beautiful. On an impulse, I hurry across the room and follow him through the doors.

Gabriel opens his eyes when I put my arms around his waist, but he doesn't pull away. Instead, he smiles and relaxes so we're moving together, swaying in time with music that only Gabriel hears. He closes his eyes and lets his head hang back, so the rain falls on his face. His hair is soaked already and hangs almost to his waist. I long to run my fingers through it, but I figure they might get stuck, and I don't want to ruin the moment by pulling out a handful. Instead, I lean forward and kiss his throat.

Again, he doesn't pull away but raises his head, puts his arms around my neck, and kisses me back. It isn't a hungry kiss, as most of the few he's allowed me to steal these last few days have been, and it isn't a hesitant one either. It's sweet and gentle and perfect. Somehow I forget about the rain, and the cabin, and the world. All my worries float away, and there's only the kiss—only Gabriel. He sighs, and I pull him closer. He still doesn't resist, and it flashes through my mind that maybe . . . just maybe . . . he isn't going to push me away this time.

The flash develops into a wish, then a prayer. I feel Gabriel smile against my lips, and I wonder what it means.

When he pulls away, my desires turn to fear, especially when I can't read the expression in his eyes. He frowns and bites his lip, gazing up at me through eyelashes that are far too long, with eyes that are far too blue.

"I can do it alone, Laurie," he says, and my heart plummets. Tears spring to my eyes, and I'm glad the rain is heavier now and hides them. He chews on his lip again and gives a huge sigh. His gaze becomes more direct, and his lips curve in a little smile. "But I don't want to," he says, taking my hand and leading me back into the house.

CHAPTER TWENTY-FOUR

It's raining again, a light summer rain that seems to be falling from a cloudless sky. It won't last long, but it's washing away the oppressive heat of the last few days. The rain's too gentle to make a sound as it mists the grass and the patio and wets them surprisingly thoroughly, but the smell's still there, the scent of newness. Ha, I don't even know if that's a real word, but that's what it's like — as if the rain washes the world and makes it new. It's easy to believe right now because that's how I'm feeling about my own world — that it's been made new.

Two hands appear, sliding around my waist, and I feel the weight of a head on my shoulder. Gabriel makes me shiver whenever he touches me, which has been a lot lately. He doesn't do things by half. When he's holding himself back, he's the ice queen, especially when he's had a lapse and he's angry with himself for giving in. But once he decides to give himself up, he gives himself completely.

That day Gabriel took me by the hand and led me out of the rain, he didn't just take me into the bedroom, he took me to a whole new world, and I'm still living in it. I can hardly believe how different it is.

There've been times, especially when we make love, where he's hesitated and seemed to struggle with his inner demons. I always back off and wait, and he always comes back and gives himself up to me. Not that I'm always on the receiving end. With Gabriel, it's never been easier to completely surrender myself to another person, not even with

David.

Why am I thinking about David now? He has no place in my new world. There is only Gabriel. When we eat, sleep, sit, walk, play, he's always there—glancing shyly at me, touching me somehow. This is a whole new world for him, too, and I know it hasn't been easy for him. He doesn't know what to do, how to act, so he acts like a child experiencing something for the first time. At first, he's shy and hesitant. Then he throws himself into it almost obsessively.

He's calming down a little now. I can sit next to him without kissing him or having him sit on my lap. I can even look Elena in the eye without blushing . . . sometimes. I think she felt horribly awkward to begin with but has got used to it now and just leaves the room when he gets too . . . affectionate.

"Are you cold?" Gabriel asks.

"No. I'm perfect."

"You shivered."

"That was you."

He giggles gently. "I know."

"You know, the novelty of having a boyfriend who can read your mind could wear off very quickly."

"I'm sorry. I was only teasing. I don't . . ."

"Gabriel, I'm *teasing* you."

"No, seriously, I haven't thought about it until now. It must be hard for you. I think it would be hard for me. Who am I kidding? It would be bloody impossible for me. I'm too independent to stand not having that control . . . having someone else being able to see what's going on in my head. I've been kind of selfish, haven't I? I've been focused completely on myself."

"It's all right, you're allowed. This *is* all about you."

"No, it's not. Part of it's about me, but it's not *all* about me. A huge chunk of it's about us." He pauses a moment and nuzzles my neck. "There's never been an *us* for me before, not really. There kind of was with Daniel, but by the time I realised it, it was already too late, and as for Michael . . ." I feel him shrug. "I've been in love, kind of, but I've never had a proper relationship."

"You'll get the hang of it."

"I hope so. But it isn't right that I should know everything. I don't want to get used to doing something that might end up driving us apart. Everyone's entitled to their privacy, especially inside their own minds."

I turn around, still in his arms. "You're awesome, Gabriel. I'd like to say I'd be totally happy to be completely open to you, but I'm not sure I would, not always, not forever. Sometimes there are things that really shouldn't be said. I mean . . . for one thing, I'd never be able to organise a surprise party."

The slight frown that had begun to mar his face melts away, and his grin blinds me as he presses himself against me and kisses me.

It hasn't been all sunshine and roses, of course. For hours every day, Gabriel locks himself away, either alone or with Elena. It's hard not to break in when I hear him scream, but thankfully that's only happened twice in a week, and not at all for the last three days.

Some things aren't getting better, though. Almost every time he works, he either passes out or goes into that strange trance state where he talks nonsense.

In fact, he's now started to do it even when he's not working with Elena. It happened two days ago when we were relaxing in the evening. I was sitting on the sofa, and Gabriel was lying with his head in my lap. We were kind of watching TV, but Gabriel was mostly watching me. I can't say I was unhappy about that. Then something changed—

something about his eyes when he was looking up at me. He wasn't looking at me at all.

"Gabriel? Are you okay?"

His eyes were wide and unblinking, and my stomach dropped. After a few moments he started to speak in that same expressionless voice, and I freaked and called for Elena. She knelt on the floor and murmured to Gabriel. I don't know what she said, but it had a dramatic effect on him. He shuddered, and for a moment I thought he'd stopped breathing. Elena stroked his hair. "It's okay, Gabriel. Come back now, wake up."

With a deep sigh, he blinked, then looked at Elena in surprise. "What's going on?" he asked, turning his eyes back to me.

"You had a little slip. Maybe we should stop working like that. I think the basics are set solid enough."

"I don't understand. What happened?"

"You just went into a trance for a few minutes."

"I did?" He still sounded unfocused and . . . lost . . . and he carried on being confused for a while before shrugging the whole thing off and pretty much going back to normal.

The same thing happened yesterday, about ten minutes after he came out of the session with Elena. We were chatting at the kitchen table when suddenly all the expression left his face, and he just slid down onto the floor and lay there with his eyes fixed and staring, like before. This time I knew Elena was scared, even though she tried not to show it.

It took ages to talk him out of it, and he was shaking by the time he shuddered and blinked and asked what the hell he was doing on the floor. It didn't escape my attention that Elena was shaking, too.

They haven't had a session today, and I've caught Elena sending Gabriel nervous looks, especially when he decided to practice by himself. It all went smoothly, though, and he didn't pass out or anything at the end. In fact, he was very pleased with himself.

"I think I've got the hang of it at last. Can you try talking to me? Both of you? I'll see if I can filter one at a time."

Exchanging glances and shrugging, we did what he asked, and whatever he was doing must have worked, because he was beaming like a Cheshire cat by the end of it.

"I think that I'm pretty much done with you now, Gabriel," Elena said afterward. "It's purely a matter of practice. Maybe we can have half an hour, twice a day, doing what we've just done, all three of us, and you can spend another hour or so practising concentration techniques. Of course, even though I'm going to stop the actual training, you can stay here as long as you like. I thought maybe we can start taking short trips over to the camping sites and then down to town, building up the number of people you're shielding against, although a shield is a shield and you'll find that if you can shield against ten, you can shield against a thousand. Filtering is more difficult, though, when there are a lot of people."

"That sounds good. I never thought I'd say this, but it'll be nice to be around people again."

"I think it's time you started to get back to normal. We've been focusing inwardly too much."

"It's a bit of a relief, to be honest. I was starting to feel overwhelmed. Lately, it's been . . ." He shrugged. "I'll be glad to ease off a bit."

"Who said anything about easing off? Just because I'm not stuffing things into your head doesn't mean that you can ease up on working with what's already there."

"Nice way to put it."

"What can I say? I have a way with words."

Gabriel grinned. "So when can I go out?"

"No one's stopping you right now."

"You know what I mean. Where there's people."

He was all lit up, and it made us both smile. "Are you so bored with our company?"

For a second, he looked confused, then horrified, then mischievous as he said, "Can't stand either of you. I think I'm going to go insane if I have to spend one more day in your company. I'd sell you both for half a camel and a handful of tobacco."

Today he's not so keen to leave. He didn't even want to get out of bed. I have to admit I was with him there . . . in more ways than one. I don't think I'll ever get tired of waking in his arms, watching him wake, his eyes opening and his lips curving in a smile that tells me he's happy to wake in mine.

I can't believe that things changed so completely so fast. I'm still suspicious, expecting it to change back at any time, but the longer we go on, the more hope I have that it won't.

Oh, I know the intensity will wear off—no one can keep that up for long . . . except . . . well, with Gabriel I'm not at all sure that he can't. Gabriel has always been intense, and I think the change wasn't as sudden as it seems. I suspect it's something he's been wanting for a long time but has denied himself. After all, he did come back for me.

I feel warm. His kiss is so open and easy, it warms me from the inside out. There's no hesitation now, no holding back. Every kiss blows me away.

"If you two are quite finished trying to suck each other's faces off, maybe I could interest you in some lunch."

"I'm always interested in food," I say with a grin, and Gabriel smiles and follows me into the kitchen.

I wish I could say that Gabriel was as interested in food as I am. For as long as I've known him I've never seen him eat a full meal, but since we've been here, his appetite has been declining steadily. Now he does nothing but pick at his meals. He doesn't seem to be losing weight, but he's getting pale, and I worry sometimes. I don't know what difference eating a whole meal would make, but it would make me feel better.

Elena's made cheese on toast, and the smell is enough to make my mouth water. I've devoured two pieces before Gabriel is halfway through his first.

"Do you want another piece? One's fine for me."

"Oh no, it isn't. You don't eat enough to keep a bird alive. You're going to eat both pieces, and a piece of cake, or no more kisses from me today."

"That's not fair. Since when have you been the food police? What I eat's up to me." Now there's the old Gabriel, full of fire and indignation.

"True, and who I kiss is up to me."

He glares at me as if he wants to tear my head off. Elena turns to the sink to hide the grin on her face. I shrug at him as he stuffs the rest of his piece of toast into his mouth, immediately regretting it because the cheese is still very hot. When his eyes stop watering, he glares at me, picks up the toast, and stalks into the other room. Elena turns, and her grin splits her face. "He doesn't like being told what to do, does he?"

"Nope. Well, not all the time." I wink and saunter after Gabriel. He's standing at the glass door, nibbling his toast.

"Don't think you're getting away with not eating by walking away from me. I've brought your cake, and if you go out there and get it wet, I'll just get you another piece."

He spins and glares at me, but then he sags and sighs. "I'm just not hungry. I'm not ever hungry."

"I know, but you have to eat. You've been pushing yourself hard, and it's been taking a toll on your body. You've been ill, and you're not at full strength and never will be if you don't eat."

"I can't eat when I'm not hungry," he snaps.

"Who says you can't? We give you food—you eat it. Where does being hungry come into the equation?"

He sighs loudly. "I'm never going to win with you, am I? You're never going to leave me alone."

Putting the cake down on the table, I walk across the room and gently take the toast out of his hand. I push back his hair and gaze at him with fire in my belly that surely shows in my eyes. "I am never, ever, going to leave you alone. You'll never be alone again, not if I have anything to do with it." Gabriel smiles his slow, sexy smile. "Now eat the bloody toast, or I'll stuff it down your throat."

Gabriel allows me to put a corner of the toast into his mouth and takes a delicate bite.

"More."

"I can't . . ."

"Nope . . . no can't . . . bite off more."

With an exaggerated sigh, Gabriel takes a big bite and chews as I draw him over to the sofa, sit him across my lap, and feed him.

"You're treating me like a child," he says, pouting slightly.

"Are you complaining about that?"

The pout turns into a begrudging smile. "Nah . . . I'm quite happy to let you do all the work for a change."

"For a change?"

"What's that?"

We both look up as a dark figure looms at the glass doors. At the same time, the other door opens, and it seems as if people are pouring in from all sides. In truth, there are only six, but they fill up the room, if not the space in it. They're all men—all dressed immaculately in black suits—and all terrifying in their silence.

Elena comes out of the kitchen and screams. One of the men grabs her and holds her gently but firmly. Gabriel leaps off my lap and backs against the fireplace. I follow, standing slightly in front of him, in what I know is a futile attempt to protect him. Gabriel glares at Elena.

"You," he spits out. "You betrayed me. You set me up."

"I . . . I didn't. I swear."

"Then how did they know we were here? Why didn't I hear them coming? You bitch! You set me up." He's screaming by the end and pushes me out of the way to lunge at Elena. One of the goons catches and holds him. "Let me go, you bastard. You've no right . . . Let. Me. Go!"

I throw myself at the goon and try to pry him off Gabriel, but it doesn't take long for a pair of steel-clad arms to go around me, pinning my own arms to my sides and drawing me back. Gabriel's fighting furiously, still screaming at Elena, who looks stunned. He has no chance of breaking free, but I know him, and he must try. Right to the end, he needs try. But what will the end be? How far will he go? Will he choose death this time?

The door opens, and someone else comes in. He isn't dressed in black but in a casual lounge suit. He's older, his hair greying at the sides. His face is pleasant and smiling, but as soon as he sees him, Gabriel freezes.

"Hello, Gabriel. Are you going to be a good boy today?"

"No, I'm fucking not. I'm not a kid anymore, and I'm going to fucking tear your head off, you son of a bitch. Why can't you just leave me alone? Haven't you done enough to me?"

"Come, come, dear boy. If it weren't for me, you wouldn't be alive today. I wasn't expecting gratitude, but—"

"You son of a bitch. How dare you say that! Okay, you saved my life by taking that thing out of me, but it was you who put it there in the first place. If you hadn't, I wouldn't have needed saving. I would've had a life, you bastard. You stole my life!"

"You always tended toward the dramatic," the man says with a smile. There's something almost affectionate in his voice, but it only makes Gabriel even angrier.

He's scared—really scared—but he'll never show it, not to them. Now, more than ever, I'm sure that whatever happens, he'll go down fighting.

The man walks slowly toward Gabriel and stops in front of him. "You've grown up, Gabriel. You're a very beautiful young man. It's going to be a pleasure to work with you again."

"Like fuck you will. I'll die before I let you do that to me again."

"I think you probably mean that," the man says thoughtfully, then smiles broadly. "But to do it you have to have an opportunity, which I have no intention of allowing. Trust me, Gabriel, you will work with us. As I've told you a hundred times, it'll be a lot easier for you if you relax and cooperate."

"Never."

The man smiles again and pats Gabriel's cheek. Gabriel's response is to spit in his face. I'm trying furiously to come up with a plan, to somehow get away—to get him away. My mind's gone blank. There are seven of them and three of us . . . ah shit! There are eight of them and two of us. I never would've thought Elena would do this.

"What the hell's going on? I don't understand."

The man turns to Elena as if he only then realises she's here. "Ah, Elena. I have to give you my sincere thanks for looking after Gabriel so well for us. I'm sure you've trained him excellently, just as we told you to."

"I . . . You what? No one told me how to train him."

"I think you'll find we did."

"No . . . I . . . no. No one told me what to do. It was my own research."

The man smiles, and this time it isn't even trying to be a nice smile.

"Don't strain your mind too much, my dear. You won't remember, any more than you'll remember when we put the tracking chip into you."

"You did *what*?" She looks so shocked that I'm beginning to think maybe she didn't betray us after all.

The man leaves Gabriel and walks over to her. Even Gabriel has gone still and is watching in silence.

"Did you really think we were going to let him go that easily? That we would've had a second chance and just let it slip through our fingers?"

"But . . . but the project was shut down. The files were closed."

"If you remember, they were re-opened when the implants started breaking down. You've read them yourself."

"I know but . . . but that was different. That was just to save them . . . to try to save them. It was accepted that the original experiment was a terrible mistake—that it would never be repeated."

"Accepted by whom?"

"Well, by . . . by everyone."

"No, my dear, not everyone. That experiment cost the taxpayers billions, and the Ministry of Defence wasn't happy when it failed. From the moment the files were re-opened, they've been waiting for someone, anyone, to survive so we can try again."

"The . . . the Ministry of Defence? What . . . I mean, what does it have to do with them?"

"You are so naïve, my dear. Did you think that we'd go to all that trouble, spend all that money, break that many laws, for purely altruistic reasons? The project was undertaken on behalf of the Ministry of Defence and designed to identify possible military applications."

"M-military? You want to use Gabriel for military purposes?"

"Not at all. Although I'm sure Gabriel would make a wonderful soldier, I have no interest in anything other than what he has inside his head. Now that you've unlocked that glorious mind for us, we'll crack it like a shell, and suck out whatever's in there that makes him so special. We'll find a way to teach others to think like him—to do what he can do."

"But you can't! You can't duplicate what Gabriel has. He's unique."

"Hardly unique. But anyway, that's by the by. If we break him down far enough, we'll find a way to duplicate his mental processes."

"But you can't."

"Trust me, Elena, if we have to dissect his brain atom by atom, we will find a way. And we have you to thank for that. Thanks to the things you've programmed into his mind, he has no choice but to open up to us. He can't fight us."

"What? What do you mean? What did she do to me?"

The man turned back to Gabriel. "What did she do?" he asks softly. "She did exactly what we told her to do. Now, much as I've enjoyed this little chat, I don't have the time to stand around here all afternoon. I'm anxious to get Gabriel settled in and start working with him."

"What do you mean *working with me*?"

I was wrong. He *is* showing them how scared he is. He can't help it, and I've never, ever wanted to hurt anyone so badly.

"Come now, Gabriel. Are you really trying to tell me you don't remember all the times we spent working side by side, gradually peeling away the barriers that protect your fascinating mind? Of course, we had a different objective then, and not only has that changed, but you've changed. We've learned a thing or two along the way. I think you'll find the experience quite different this time."

"No . . . no . . . you won't take me back there. I'll die first. I'll kill myself."

"How?"

"I . . . I'll find a way. Somehow, I'll find a way. I'll make my heart stop. I'll . . ."

"My dear, Gabriel, haven't we had this conversation before? I have no intention of allowing you the slightest opportunity to do anything of the kind." He lays his hand against Gabriel's cheek. Gabriel hisses and tries to turn his head to bite it. "Oh dear, Gabriel. I'd like to say that I was hoping we could do this the easy way, but to be honest, I really wasn't. My scientists went to great pains to train Elena how to program certain things into your mind, and I'm dying to test out how effective they are."

"What . . . what have you . . ." He gazes up at Elena with eyes that are wide with horror and hatred. "What have you done?"

"I don't know. I swear to you, Gabriel, that if I've done anything to you, I didn't know I was doing it. I swear it."

"I wouldn't strain yourself to justify your actions to him, Elena dear. In a few moments, it isn't going to matter."

"What do you mean?"

It seems as if everyone holds their breaths as the man turns back to Gabriel. "Well, it's been nice talking to you again, Gabriel, and I look forward to working with you. I'll see you back at the Institute later. We've updated The Chair, you know? It's almost unrecognisable, as I'm sure Elena would confirm . . . if she could remember."

"What?" Elena gasps.

"Consider your project concluded, Elena," he says, not taking his eyes off Gabriel. "Why not take a nice long break? We'll contact you if we have anything further you can help us with." Quickly, before Gabriel has a chance to react, the man leans forward and murmurs something into his ear. Gabriel's body jerks and stiffens for a moment before going completely limp in the arms of his captor.

"Gabriel!" I'm not even aware that I've shouted. I'm fighting mindlessly, kicking, biting, using every trick I've learned over the years, but I might as well have been fighting a bronze statue. The man who holds me doesn't react in any way. He doesn't try to hurt me or subdue me—he simply holds me.

The goon holding Gabriel scoops him up in his arms and heads for the door. As Gabriel's head lolls back over his arm, I see that his eyes are open but completely empty. What the hell have they done?

The man turns and heads for the door. All but three of the goons follow him. At the door, he pauses and turns to the three remaining, two of whom are the ones holding Elena and me. "Keep hold of them for ten minutes, then let them go. Take their car and meet us at the rendezvous point for transfer."

The goons nod, and he disappears.

Chapter Twenty-Five

Gabriel

I feel . . . Well, I don't know how I feel. I may be dreaming, but I don't think so. I think I was dreaming and now . . . now I . . . I'm not. I'm quite comfortable, I think, warm, too. Do I usually go through this inventory when I wake up? Am I waking up? Was I asleep? Am I still asleep?

I hear someone speaking, but it seems to be coming from a long way away, so they are probably not talking to me. I think I should probably open my eyes now. I'm not sure why, because I'm quite happy lying here with them closed. It feels good. Strange but . . . for some reason, it seems important not to open my eyes.

"Come on, Gabriel, I know you can hear me. Wake up, it's time to get to work."

Gabriel? What's that? It sounds kind of familiar. Gabriel. Hmm. Oh . . . oh, I think it's not a what. It's a who. I think it might be me.

"Gabriel?"

"Hmm?" Maybe those voices are talking to me after all, because that one sounded a lot closer. Why is it saying my name? It is my name, isn't it? Didn't I establish that it's my name? I think . . .

"Wake up, Gabriel."

Okay, the voice sounds cross now. Am I doing something wrong? Is he . . . Is . . . Oh shit. Oh shit! I remember. No . . . no . . . "No . . ."

"That's right, Gabriel, you remember now, don't you? You remember who you are and where you are."

God, I wish I didn't.

Those lights. I hate those lights. I've always hated those lights. They hurt my eyes, and they've haunted my dreams for years.

Looking at the lights may hurt, but at least it means I don't have to look at anything else. I don't have to look at the straps, the needles in my arms, the electrodes, the equipment, the sharp instruments, the smug faces.

"Hello, Gabriel. Do you remember me?"

"I wish I didn't."

"Oh, Gabriel, let's not get off on the wrong foot. We have a long way to go."

"I'd rather not get off on any foot. Why don't you just let me go, and I won't spend the rest of my life thinking of a way to syphon acid through your ear and melt your brain. Oh, sorry . . . too late."

"Well, well, our little Gabriel has grown up. You're a lot feistier than you used to be."

"Feistier? Who the hell uses words like that these days?"

The man laughs, and I hate him even more. Oh God, how I hate him. I have to hold on to that. I need to let my hatred drown out my fear or . . . or . . . I don't know or what, but I will not show him I'm scared. I *will* not.

Shit! I hate it when they tilt the chair back. I particularly hate that he's looking down at me. I want to face him eye to eye. I don't know what difference that would make, except that it would make a difference to me.

"We have a lot of work to do, Gabriel, and I think you'll find that things are very different this time. You always were a fighter, and I can see that nothing has changed there, but fighting is pointless now. You can't keep us out because, thanks to your programming, there are doorways right into the core of you."

"What do you mean?" I don't like the sound of that. I don't like it at all.

The hateful face bends closer to mine. "Did you really not suspect a thing? Not have any idea what she was doing to you?"

"No." I'm scared now. What does he mean? What did she do to me? I try to think back, but it was all new and strange. How would I know if any of it was wrong?

"Don't worry, Gabriel, it's nothing for you to be concerned about. You won't know a thing about it, but it's going to make life a lot easier for us, and if you remember anything about the way it was before, I think you'll realise that it makes things easier for you, too. I don't want to hurt you. I've never wanted to hurt you, and now I don't have to. All you need to do is lie back and let it all happen. You won't be able to fight, so there's no point trying, and in a little while you won't be able to.

"It's going to be a long and very weird ride, but I promise you'll survive it. I can't promise that your mind will, though. I'll push it until it gives up its secrets, and if I break it, so be it. As I've told you many times . . . if you relax and cooperate, it'll be easier and less likely I'll have to rip apart your mind to get at the information I need."

Ah hell, I didn't need to hear any of that. I'm scared. I don't want to think about what's going to happen next. I remember what it was like before, and I know this is going to be worse. I've sat here so many times in my dreams, and every time I woke screaming, but this time the screaming isn't going to wake me up.

God, I'm so scared. I can't breathe . . . I can't . . . I have to calm down. I can't let him see how scared I am. I won't let him see. I won't give him the satisfaction. I won't . . . Ah hell . . .

"Don't be afraid, Gabriel. I'm going to take good care of you. I won't hurt you any more than I have to."

"Fuck you."

He smiles. He knows. He knows how scared I am. He knows, and he smiles. I hate him. But I can't hold on to the hate. I can't let go of the fear, especially when he starts doing something behind me and my whole body starts to tingle as the electrodes send tiny bursts of electricity through it. It doesn't hurt, but it scares the crap out of me.

"What are you doing?"

"Nothing for you to worry about. I need to get baseline readings for everything so that I know what's happening to you when I start playing around."

"Playing around?"

He bends over me, smiling. "Are you quite comfortable, Gabriel?"

"What the fuck do you think?"

The smile broadens. "Good. I'm going to send you on a little trip. We'll start gently enough, but it's going to be quite a wild ride. I'm sure you'll be much more cooperative by the time we've finished."

The man turns away, and when he turns back, he has a syringe in his hand.

"No. Please don't. Wait." Dammit. I swore I wouldn't beg. I won't . . . I won't beg. I bite my lip, hard. My eyes widen, but I can't stop that.

"You disappoint me, Gabriel. I thought you would've had more pride. You know it isn't going to do any good."

I feel shame, and I think I'm actually blushing. Hatred floods me, thankfully washing away some of the fear. If only he'd lean a bit closer, I'd spit in his face.

"Surely you're not afraid of this little thing." He holds up the syringe, and I force myself not to close my eyes. "It's just a little piece of glass and metal. It's not even as if I'm going to have to put the needle into your arm—that's already been taken care of. You won't feel a thing."

I can't help my fingers curling into fists. They'd grip the arms of the chair if they weren't strapped palm up. "Fuck you to hell." Damn my voice for shaking. Damn the tears that are leaking from the corners of my eyes. Why do I have to be so weak? Why can't I fight through the fear? Why can't I—

"Don't worry, Gabriel. You've no need to fear this. It's going to have very little effect except to help you relax. It's not as if you haven't been getting armfuls of drugs for the last couple of hours."

"What? No, I . . ." Bite your lip, Gabriel. Bite it hard.

"Now that's better. That's what I was expecting. You were always the fighter—always a pain in the arse. I was expecting nothing less. You've had plenty of time to perfect that attitude."

"You have no idea what I've been doing all this time. No idea what your experiments did to me. You stole my life. You took everything away from me—my family, my friends, my mind. You turned me into something less than I was . . . than I could've been. Thanks to you, I have nothing— nothing. I have no home, no friends, no support . . . nothing."

"Seems to me you have something." He smirks as he injects the drug into my arm. I force myself not to look. I'm ready to meet his eyes when he raises his face again.

"What? What do I have?"

"Well, I may be wrong, but I assumed that the pretty boy who was so concerned about you when you were last here— and who we found in the cabin with you—was your boyfriend."

"Laurie." Damn, how could I have forgotten about Laurie? Some boyfriend I am—selfish to the last. I *knew* I shouldn't have let him in. But he would still have been there, wouldn't he? He would still have been in the cabin . . . and they wouldn't have known. At least we had the last few days. "What have you done to him? Where is he? What have you done?"

The man's smile changes and I notice it but can't think about what it means. "That's for me to know and you not to worry about."

"Please . . . please don't hurt him. This is nothing to do with him. He's not involved in any of it. He doesn't know . . . he . . ."

"Oh, but he is involved, Gabriel. You've let him in. You involved him."

"I know . . . I know I did, but he's . . . please . . . please don't hurt him." I have no problem begging for him. I'd do anything for him.

"Struck a chord, I see. Don't worry, Gabriel . . . seriously. You have enough to worry about already. Now, I think it's time to move this on."

"But . . . I . . . I . . ." I can't finish the sentence. I can't make another one. It was sudden, this thing that happened to me. I can't put my finger on exactly what it was. I don't think it's the drugs. I've taken enough to know what it feels like to be drugged, and this isn't it. Not quite. Oh, I can feel the effects of the drugs on my body. I'm relaxing despite myself. The knot of anger and fear inside me is unwinding, and I'm getting heavy, sinking into the chair. But it's not my body I'm concerned with right now — it's my mind.

I'm still aware of what's going on around me. In fact, I think it's clearer than before. I'm aware of every sight, every sound. The world around me is crystal clear. The colours are brighter, the outlines sharper. It's such a weird sensation. I see people moving around me, making adjustments, preparing equipment, touching my body, and although I know exactly what they're doing, none of it makes any sense at all. It's as if it just doesn't matter.

The Chair's been raised pretty much upright again, and I look down at myself with complete dispassion, noticing without embarrassment that I'm naked, and that my torso and legs are dotted with electrodes. If I think about it, I can feel the buzzing of the electricity as mild shocks make all the hair on my body stand up. I wonder if the hair on my head is doing the same—surely there's too much of it. It's a brief thought, and my mind wanders away from it. There are electrodes on my arms, too, on the inside of the wrists and elbows, either side of the IV lines. I wonder why, but this thought, like the last, flies like a butterfly from my mind.

I'm aware of someone sitting down next to the chair, and I turn my head to see a pair of dispassionate blue eyes regarding me seriously but disinterestedly. His lips are moving, but I don't hear what he's saying. That strikes me as a little strange, but I'm not very interested, so I let my mind move on.

My attention is drawn to his fingers, pressed against the inside of my wrist. I can feel the throb of the blood beneath the firm pressure. The speed of the pulses seems to be increasing. I don't know why, and I don't care. It's the only evidence I have that anything is changing in my body, and it really isn't important—although it should be, shouldn't it? Shouldn't I be worried that they're making my heart speed up without doing anything to me, at least nothing I'm aware of? They hadn't injected anything else into me, and I know the drug I had before was making my muscles relax and slowing down my heart rather than speeding it up.

I turn my attention to the man again. He still seems to be talking to me, and I find it strange that I can't hear him. Suddenly it seems very important that I close my eyes, and so I do. It's quite interesting with my eyes closed. I see swirls and tunnels and words that turn into pictures. I feel as if I'm speeding down the tunnels, deeper and deeper inside my mind, and the words are following me, the pictures playing out, showing me scenes from my past, getting faster and faster until they're nothing but a blur—then it stops.

I'm floating upside down over a swirling mass of clouds, my arms and legs spread out, my hair floating out around me, ticking my shoulders. Pictures are floating up through the mist, resting briefly on the surface and disappearing again. Daniel, Michael, Carrie, Elena . . . and Laurie. Time and time again, it's Laurie. Laurie smiling . . . Laurie frowning . . . Laurie crying . . . Laurie reaching for me. I should reach back. I need to reach back. I need to touch him—if not with my hands, then with my mind. They've taken him, hurt him. He needs me, and I have to reach him.

My mind and body are straining, trembling with the effort. Reaching, reaching, reaching. I have to—I need to—I have to—I need to. Is there something? Is there . . . Is there . . .

Abruptly the pictures of Laurie are gone, and the intense desire to touch him goes with them. I'm exhausted. I want to sleep. I want to . . . want to . . . I want to . . .

A new picture emerges from the mists. It's someone I recognise. It is *him*, the man who brought me here, the one who hurt Laurie. This time I don't need to be prompted to reach out, but I don't reach—I thrust. All my anger, my pain, my fear, my sorrow. It streams from me in a torrent of emotion that I focus on that hated face. I feel a tension, and I throw myself against it. Again and again, I batter against the barrier, which doesn't stand for long. With a pop, the barrier is gone, and I rush into the shocked mind and . . .

No . . . no . . . I don't want to stop. I don't want to pull back. I want to . . . I want to . . . I want . . . The picture fades, and I hang limply, exhausted. Everything begins to slip away — the mist, the tunnels, the images, the words ... and my awareness. But something yanks me back. It hurts. I don't want to be here anymore. I want to sleep.

The pictures start again, flickering over the surface, rising and falling. One face rises and settles on the surface of the mist. I recognise this face — it had been hovering over me a moment ago. Again, the tension rises and I ... I ... The anger leaks away and I feel nothing. I feel the need to reach out and touch the mind, gently. No, it's not a need, it's a compulsion, and I have no choice but to obey.

Gently, my mind brushes against the other, and rather than push against the barrier, it simply waits to be allowed in. As soon as I feel the resistance weaken, I allow my consciousness to seep in and for the first time fully experience what it's like inside another mind. I'm assailed with so many sights, sounds, and emotions that I'm completely overwhelmed. I cry out and struggle to hold on to myself, to anything around me, but it's like smoke slipping through my fingers.

"No ... no ..." Everything's spinning, spinning, spinning.

With a gasp, I jerk and find myself opening my eyes back in my body, in The Chair. What just happened? I turn my head toward the man who's sitting next to me, but he isn't speaking any more. He glances up, nods, then rises and moves away. I turn my head the other way and blink up at the other man, the hated monster who's responsible for all this. He looks a little shocked.

"That was impressive, Gabriel."

"It was? What was?"

"You have an amazing mind, and I'm going to find out how it works if it kills you. Can you do that consciously?"

"Do what?"

"Enter someone else's mind and become part of it, implanting your thoughts and absorbing theirs. What do you see? What do you experience? What's it like, to see what someone else has seen, to experience what they've experienced?"

"I . . . I don't know. I . . . I didn't know I could."

"I'm sure you didn't. That wasn't part of your training. We didn't want anyone else to know it was possible. We didn't know the full extent ourselves. It manifested a little while you were unconscious when the implant was being removed. Your pain was transmitted to the doctors who were working on you.

"We suspected you were unaware of this ability and that you had no idea how to access it consciously. So we had Elena build into your training a susceptibility to surrendering your control over your mental and psychic processes when in a deep trance. It was more effective than we could have imagined. It still has limited parameters. You weren't able to reach your boyfriend, but I'm sure the barriers can be shattered once we've opened up your mind."

"What . . . what do you mean? What have you done to me? What are you going to do to me? What did I just do?"

"Quite simply, we've established that you can not only impart words into another's mind, and receive their words, emotions, and directed thoughts, but you can actually enter their minds, by force if necessary but more easily with invitation. Experience everything they've experienced and inject your own emotions, cause pain, and presumably anything else you want.

"The possible connotations are astounding. Potentially, you can look inside anyone's mind and access their thoughts, emotions, and knowledge. You could take information from them without them even knowing you were there. And not only can you take from them, but you can give—you can literally change their minds and make them feel whatever you want. The possibilities are endless. You'd be the perfect spy, the unstoppable assassin — killing with a thought, without being anywhere near the target. It's astounding."

"No . . . no, I won't . . . I won't do any of those things. You can't make me. You can't."

"I can make you do whatever I want. With the auto-suggestions built in, all I have to do is put you in a trance, and you'll have no choice but to do what you're told. For now, we'll have to keep your body immobilised while we explore your mind, but eventually, we'll be able to control that, too. Well done, Gabriel. You're everything I hoped you'd be and more."

"No! I won't do it. I'll find a way. Somehow, I'll find a way."

"You may as well accept it, Gabriel. It makes no difference either way, but you'll cause yourself far less anguish if you accept the inevitable."

"Never."

"Whatever, it makes no difference to me. Now, let's take another trip into that glorious mind of yours, shall we?"

Chapter Twenty-Six

Time after time after time my mind was violated, assault-ed, battered, and used. Repeatedly I was taken on journeys into the minds of others. At first, it was the people who were physically present in the lab. Then with people who were brought in, introduced to me, and sent to locations at increasing distances from the lab until they got to a place that was beyond me.

I was forced to experience again and again the overwhelming sensations of entering someone else's consciousness. At first, I got lost every time. I was completely overpowered by the sheer weight of another person's thoughts and experiences. I constantly found myself emerging from the trance screaming with agony, then losing consciousness abruptly for minutes? Hours? Days? I had no way of telling time.

The scientists became impatient with me and tried various methods of forcing my mind to retain control, to be able to keep hold of itself while it sifted through the data that swirled around it. They shocked me, drugged me, inflicted pain, and imparted pleasure, but nothing changed.

So they switched directions and had me forcing my consciousness like a spear into other minds. This was in some ways easier and some ways harder. Curiously, I had no problem holding integrity when I entered with the purpose of imposing, rather than absorbing. I suppose I didn't need to be as focused. I didn't need to make sense of what was going on around me in order to locate a particular point and draw it out. I had no need to know my way around the garden, or even what kind of flowers it contained, to plant my own seed . . . or set fire to the grass.

I hated this. It didn't hurt like the other . . . not me, but I was made to hurt others, and that killed me. At first, I simply had to implant a word, an idea, a picture into someone else's mind. I did it over and over and over for what seemed like weeks but could have been hours. Gradually the images became more complex and were accompanied by emotions. Then I started to change the way they felt about things . . . made them see a picture and feel the opposite of what they should have felt seeing it. Pictures of flowers provoked feelings of anger, baby kittens were terrifying, rotting corpses erotic, torture humorous, etc. Then I started to hurt them.

I didn't get to choose the pictures or the feelings. They were implanted into my mind, either by auto-suggestion or images flashed in front of my eyes by a visor that I remembered well from the first time . . . and feared.

These experiments were more successful and were pushed further and further, harder and harder. I don't remember whether I was ever forced to kill anyone. I'm glad.

I'm asleep right now. I'm pretty sure I'm asleep. These days it's hard to tell. I hope I'm asleep. I see Laurie. He's reaching out to me. His lips are moving, but I don't know what he's saying. I'm dimly aware of others with him, blurred shadows at his shoulder.

I love you. I hear that. It's a faint echo in my head. *I love you. Hold on. Just hold on.* The echo hurts, so I let it go.

Lately, they've been doing a lot of things that hurt me. I don't know why.

Oh . . . wait . . . I . . . I think . . . think maybe I heard someone say that they want to dissect me. No, that's wrong. It has to be. If they dissected me, I'd be dead, right? No . . . dissect . . . dissect my . . . my processes. I think that's what they said . . . *processes* . . . the way I process things.

I'm numb now. They've battered my mind so hard, for so long, it's hard to think . . . hard to picture anything clearly.

They've stopped the experiments . . . they had to — they weren't working anymore. Yes, the memories are getting clearer now. They said I was tired — mentally exhausted — I needed to recharge or be permanently damaged. I felt tired. I feel tired. My head hurts all the time, even when I'm asleep. Am I asleep? Laurie's gone now and I'm sad . . . I think.

"Gabriel. Gabriel, listen to me. Listen."

"Okay." It's a whisper. I haven't spoken in anything louder for days. Days? Years?

"We're going to do something a little different today. I know what you can do, and now I need to know how you do it. I need to know if I can teach anyone else to do it. I'm sorry, but it's going to hurt. There's nothing I can do about that. You've been asleep for a while, and I've done what I can physically. I can't do any more without damaging you, and I don't want that. I need you alive and whole. I've looked inside your body as far as I can, and now you have to wake up and let me into your head."

I don't understand his words. I haven't understood anything for a long time. My head hurts, and my thoughts are like treacle. I have no motor control and very little control over my mind. I can only speak in one or two syllables and nothing above a whisper. My sight and hearing are distorted, and I can barely feel anything. Surely there isn't much else they can do to me.

"I'm going to inject a drug into your arm, little by little, that will make your body relax and fall asleep very slowly. At the same time, I'm going to flash a succession of lights and images into your eyes. I'm taking constant readings of everything I possibly can to see how your mind and body process everything I'm doing to you. It will be uncomfortable to begin with and then get more and more painful. I'm sorry I can't do anything about that. Try not to panic. It might feel like you're bursting apart, or even dying, but I won't let you, okay? I'll keep you safe, I promise. Don't be afraid."

I don't understand what he's saying or what's happening to me, so how can I be afraid? Nevertheless, I have to admit to a twinge of unease as the chair tilts back and I feel hands on me. I don't know what they're doing. I close my eyes and begin to drift. I'm so tired, and it's a pleasant feeling—just drifting. I'm ready to sink into it and let it take me away. Unfortunately, that's not allowed.

When the man starts to talk, I'm too drowsy and distant to take much notice and none of it sinks in. The slap shocks me back to awareness.

"It's not time to sleep yet, Gabriel. All in good time." My body is fizzing, and it's the strangest feeling. Not uncomfortable or painful just . . . strange. "I'm going to put the visor down, and I want you to keep your eyes open as long as you can, okay?" I don't answer, and he doesn't expect me to.

I stare upward and watch with vague interest as the visor is swung out and lowered over my face. From the outside, it's just a piece of moulded metal, enamelled in white. It's like the masks that used to be worn to masked balls, but without the eye holes. The inside looks just like the smooth, black, reverse side of the mask. When lowered, it fits snugly over the face from hairline to mid-cheek, arching over the bridge of the nose. It always makes me feel horribly claustrophobic, even though it leaves my nose and mouth free.

The inside of the visor is close enough for my eyelashes to brush it when I blink. All outside light is shut out, and I can't see anything. In the darkness, the feeling of floating away is more intense, and I don't want to fight it. I suppose he must be giving me the drug by now, but it doesn't seem to be making any difference.

A light comes on—two lights, actually, small pinpricks, one in front of each eye. Sparks of fear shoot up and down my spine and a gnawing ache starts in the pit of my stomach. I know what's going to happen now. I remember, and I'm scared. I'm really scared.

Gently at first, the lights start to flicker. Then little starbursts surround the points which expand into circles, which become more intense, then slowly begin to flash brighter and faster and bigger and more intense, building up so gradually my brain barely registers it, until it starts getting uncomfortable. My eyes are burning, and I close them, but it doesn't make any difference.

"Keep your eyes open, Gabriel." How does he know?

Everything's getting confusing. I think my mind's given up trying to process anything. There are little flickers of pain from somewhere in my body, but that's so far away it doesn't matter. There are pictures now, flashing past too quickly for me to see. I don't know how many of them. They come between the flashes. Brighter and brighter, faster and faster.

It's hurting now, stabbing into my brain like needles. I couldn't keep my eyes open if my life depended on it. The lights keep getting brighter and faster, sending kaleidoscopic patterns over the inside of my eyelids, and they consume my world. Something's happening to my body, something that makes me feel suddenly very claustrophobic, and I start to struggle, to panic.

"Steady, Gabriel. Everything's all right. Don't worry. Don't panic. Remember, I told you not to panic, that it's all going to be all right. It's going to get painful, but I don't want you to worry I . . . Shit . . . What—"

Bang! Was that on the inside or the outside? Aah . . . No . . . *No!*

Screaming pain tears through my head. The lights and colours and pictures flash past in a never-ending blur of pain, pain, pain—lancing into my brain and setting off explosions all through my head. No. *No!* If I could scream, I would. I'd scream and beg and crawl on my belly if I had to. Just stop . . . stop . . . please stop. My brain is on fire, burning with thousands of tiny supernovas pouring molten rock into the core. No, no, no, no, no. Then . . .

I hear a voice. I don't know how I hear the voice, because I haven't heard any others, well, apart from the man. Oh God, I can't think. Help me . . . please help me. Stop . . . stop . . . Oh hell, oh hell.

A name floats to the surface of my imploding brain. Laurie. *Laurie, help me! Please help me!* I scream, but it's a silent one, and lights keep flashing and the pictures speed past, and the pain goes deeper and deeper until . . . Bang! Gone.

No more lights. Darkness. Cold. Pain. Touches. Voices. Movement. Darkness. Pain. Touches. Voices.

"Gabriel? Gabriel, are you okay? Can you hear me? Gabriel?"

Voices. Voice. Touch. Pain. Darkness. Light. Touch. Voice. Laurie.

Laurie. No sound. No . . .

"Gabriel, hun, please wake up. I don't know what to do. I'm so scared to move you, but we have to get out of here. Gabriel."

Lights. Voice. Laurie. Pain. Touch. Darkness. Movement. Pain. Laurie. Voice. Darkness. Light. Movement. Touch. Laurie.

"L-L-Lau-Laurie." Sound. Voice . . . my voice.

"Gabriel, thank God. Open your eyes, Gabriel. I'm going to get you out of here, but you have to open your eyes."

Voice. Light. Pain. Movement. Laurie. Touch. Light.

Sound. Feel. Feel. Feel.

"Laurie." It's a croak, but it's my voice. It's my voice? "Laurie."

"Yes. Yes, it's me. Come on, Gabriel. Open your eyes. Tell me you can hear me. Tell me you're okay."

"Laurie." It's coming back now. It's all coming back.

"Gabriel . . ."

"Wait. Just . . . just . . . wait."

There's a pressure on my chest, the weight of a head, and the sound of soft weeping. Laurie. It takes a huge effort to lift my hand and rest it on his head. I'm free. The thought is dull and not important. It's worth marking, though. I'm free, and there's no more pain, at least not on the outside. I mark with slightly more interest that the electrodes are gone, and it feels different. That's what the fizzing must have been.

My hand slips off Laurie's head when he raises it. He wipes tears from his face and smiles . . . kind of.

"I've been so scared, Gabriel. All this time, not knowing where you were or what they were doing to you. It's been too slow. I've tried everything I can to get you out, but it took so long. I thought I would die with frustration. I was so frightened they would have . . ." He takes my hand and squeezes it hard. "I know they've hurt you. I saw. I'm sorry I wasn't in time to stop it but . . . but . . . please, Gabriel. Please tell me they didn't do anything too bad, that they didn't . . . didn't . . . change you."

Change me? I don't understand. Everything . . . hard. My body is . . . heavy and my mind . . . slow . . . heavy. Laurie . . ."Tired."

"I know. I know you're tired. You can rest soon, but we have to get out of here first. Can you walk?"

"Walk?" I think I know . . . I understand . . . I can . . ."How?"

"Gabriel, I . . . Does it hurt? Does it hurt to move?"

"Hurt? No. Not hurt, just . . . hard."

"I don't understand. Can you hear what I say? Do you understand? Do you know who I am?"

He sounds scared. Why? "Why?" Everything is . . . slow. Even . . . my words. "Why? Yes, I do."

"You do what?"

I'm confused, losing track of the conversation. I'm struggling hard to understand, to answer, to be . . . be what he . . . what he wants . . . what I . . ."Laurie."

"I'm sorry, Gabriel. I'm asking too many questions. You look so confused." He rests his hand against my cheek, and I close my eyes. It's cool and feels so good. "There'll be time for questions later. Try to stand up."

He slings my arm around his shoulders and put his around my waist, hauling me up off The Chair. I slide, and my feet hit the ground, but my legs won't hold me. I know what I'm supposed to do, but my body just won't do it. I feel like a lump of unformed clay.

"Help me here," Laurie calls. I know he isn't talking to me, so I don't try to raise my head. "Get him out of here. I'll meet you at the gate."

"Are you sure—"

"Just go. Cameron will stay with me and help me get things done here."

"Laurie—"

"Just take care of Gabriel."

I don't understand. I don't understand any of it . . . except that Laurie is . . ."Laurie, no."

"Hush, my love. Go with John. He'll take care of you. I'll be with you soon."

"Please, Laurie . . ."

"I'm not going to let this place haunt you anymore. I'm going to make sure you're free—that no one will come after you, ever again. I want to make a life with you, a safe life with no running, no looking over our shoulders. I'm going to protect you now, whether you want me to or not. You'll never get rid of me. Never." He kisses me, gently, on the forehead, before a giant of a man sweeps me up in his arms and the world swings dizzily.

"Laurie." I close my eyes against the blinding flashes of light and colour that tear into my brain. "Laurie." But the second time there's no voice left to make a sound.

I didn't see Laurie at the gate—I was unconscious. I didn't see him on the journey or in the hospital—at least I don't remember. I don't remember much at all. They tell me I was raving, that I didn't know who or where I was. That I couldn't move consciously, couldn't think, couldn't speak anything that made sense. They tell me it went on for a long time—weeks—and they thought that's how I'd be forever. They tell me a lot of things. They? The doctors, the psychiatrists, the counsellors.

They're always there, gnawing at the edges of my consciousness. In some ways, they're as bad as the government scientists. There've been times when I've wondered if they were the same—working for the same masters, doing the same experiments, torturing me, raping my mind.

Thankfully, I was unaware of most of it, and now I don't remember. I wish I didn't remember the facility. That, unfortunately, is clear enough, at least as much as I was aware of at the time . . . right up to that last day.

The pain stayed with me for a long time. It's still there now, lurking, waiting to explode if I try to probe it, if I try to think too hard, to stretch my mind.

It didn't take long for my body to come back online, but not so my mind. I've been poked and probed and tested and treated, and now I think I've put up with it for long enough. For such a long time I haven't cared, but I feel better today and I'm going home.

They don't like it, of course. They hate it because they weren't the ones who told me I'm ready. They don't want to let go of me that easily. I wonder more than ever whether they've been told to keep me here, or has all this left me wholly paranoid? I was bad enough before.

I don't feel well, not really, but I'm well enough to know that being here isn't helping me anymore. I'm restless, and I've started taking longer and longer walks, sometimes out into the garden. It's still hot, too hot sometimes—too hot to lie in a sticky bed in a stuffy room and let strangers into the most intimate parts of my . . . my head. I don't want to talk anymore. I don't want to try to think anymore—all it does is give me a headache. I have a lot of headaches. Not like before, but . . . strange.

A lot of the things I feel are strange. Something is nagging at the back of my mind. If I could get my mind working again, maybe I could see what it is.

I'm sitting in the garden. It's a hot day, and the sky is blue, very blue. I'm thinking of Laurie's eyes and wondering why he hasn't come to see me. No one has come to see me. No one but Laurie knows I'm here. There've been times when I've thought that Laurie was part of it. That he left me here to be tortured by these people, but that's stupid. He saved me, right? He won't leave me alone . . . not for long . . . not forever.

I'm going home soon. They don't want me to leave. Maybe they're right. Maybe I'm not ready. I still feel like there's a blanket drawn over my thoughts, a mist inside my mind, that won't go away no matter how hard I try to dispel it. They've given me a hundred possibilities—shock, PTSD, neurosis, physiological or neurological damage. Sometimes they say it'll get better, sometimes they say it won't. Frankly, I don't care. I just want to get out of here and start living my life again. I wonder why Laurie hasn't come.

They tried to tell me I couldn't leave until they said I could. That I wasn't here because I wanted to be, but because they said I had to be. They said they could force me to stay, but they've spent so long telling me I'm not a prisoner anymore that it didn't take much intelligence to use their arguments against them. Maybe that's what changed their minds. Whatever.

There was never any question of me staying. I knew that—they knew that—everyone knew that. So they *agreed* to let me *try* to *rehabilitate* at home. Bollocks. They think I'm going to stay with my family. As if. I'm going to find Laurie, find out why he left me here. God, I wish this fog would get out of my head. I have my memories back, so why can't I . . . can't I . . . what? Dammit . . . what!

A nurse is walking toward me. It's the smug nurse. I hate the smug nurse. She speaks to me as if I'm five. I haven't been five for fifteen years . . . give or take. I don't even try to smile. I haven't bothered for ages. Why would I? I don't feel like smiling.

"There you are. I wish you wouldn't keep running off. The doctor wants to see you. He has some things to go over with you, and if he's happy, then you can go."

I tilt my head and look at her. She's middle-aged, with auburn hair twisted up in a tight chignon. Hey, I know such a lot of random words. In other circumstances, I might think she was pleasant, motherly. Right now, the last thing I need is a mother.

"Quite frankly, I don't give a gnat's bullock whether he's happy or not. As soon as my ride shows, I'm out of here."

"Come on now, Gabriel, be reasonable." Now that's better—frustration and irritation. Honest emotions at last.

"Reasonable? Why on earth would I be reasonable? I feel like I've been a prisoner here, and I'm hardly going to want to speak to the chief gaoler before my parole."

"I never understand you."

"You never try."

"Just get your arse back to your room, young man, and talk to the doctor before he sends someone more persuasive to bring you back."

I stifle a grin and bite my lip. She's getting more motherly by the minute. Of course, I have to go back to my room — *my room?* — but I don't have to like it, and I don't have to make it easy for anyone.

With a sigh, I roll my eyes and get to my feet. Physically, I'm pretty much back to normal now, so I lengthen my stride, making her half walk, half skip to keep up.

Chapter Twenty-Seven

The doctor was a twat. He's always been a twat, but it took me a while to realise it. He asked me a whole load of stupid questions, and I was strongly tempted to give flippant answers, but that would've been stupid.

What would I have done if he'd changed his mind? This place is like a fortress. I'd never be able to force my way out, although I've often enough convinced myself I could if I had to.

I tried hard to hide my frustration at his stupidity. He was treating me as if I was some kind of retard. I know I've had problems, but you'd swear I was mental from some of the things he asked.

Yes, I know who I am. Yes, I know where I am. Yes, I know who he is . . . well, his name and qualifications at least. He's never given me the chance to get to know the man behind the white coat . . . not that I would've wanted to. No, I don't know what day of the week it is because I've had no point of reference for a long time. No, I don't know who the prime minister is because I've never had the slightest interest in politics, and I wouldn't know David Cameron if he bit my arse at a party.

In the end, I think he was as frustrated with me as I was with him. He pushed his glasses up onto his forehead, peered at me with a tired sigh, and told me he was happy to *give it a go*, as long as I promised to be sensible, not push myself, and came back at the first sign I was about to crack up. Is he insane? I've never been sensible, I always push myself to the limits, and if I feel like cracking up, this is the last place I'm ever going to go.

He arranged a follow-up appointment with a doctor I've never heard of and have no intention of keeping, and I think he knew that. I guess he had to go through the motions. Then he looked at me again, a real look, not one that made me feel I was on a dissecting table with his scalpel in my brain.

"You worry me, Gabriel. You fight everything, and that's not a bad thing, except when you're fighting those who are trying to help you. I don't think you realise how ill you've been." *Oh, I realise. I don't think he knows why.* "You've made a very fast and promising recovery, but that concerns me. You're not well yet, and I know you're hiding a lot from me. I wish you'd be more open." *Well, we all have our wishes and dreams.*

I watched him steadily and could tell he knew what I was thinking. He knew that as soon as I left the room, I'd try my very best to forget he ever existed.

"Will you at least promise to take your medication?"

"Of course, I will."

"Will you keep the promise?"

I shrugged, and he knew it was a no. He sighed. "Gabriel, in all honesty, every shred of professional experience is telling me to keep you here, at least until we've stabilised your medication and are sure you're taking it regularly. That alone makes me very uneasy."

My stomach flipped. Maybe I shouldn't have been so cocky. It crossed my mind—forcefully—that if they tried to drug me, I was going to make a run for it, no matter where it got me. I wasn't going down that road again without a fight.

"Take it easy, Gabriel. I'm not going to detain you. I know something of your history, and I know that's the last thing you need, but you *have* to understand you're not as well as you think you are. The things that happened to you have damaged your mind. We've put you back together as best we can, but there are pieces missing, and until they're filled, you're unstable and could regress very quickly. Please, take your medication, try to keep stress to a minimum, and get help if you need it."

"I-I'll try."

"At last, a straightforward and honest answer."

I had to smile at that. He's not as stupid and dry as I thought he was—still a twat, though. He handed me a bag of pills with a prescription for more, then escorted me to the door. He held out his hand, and, after a moment's hesitation, I took it. And that was that.

Now, I'm sitting on the bench outside the hospital, waiting for my lift. I have nothing—no clothes, no wallet, no personal belongings. Even the bag of pills is sitting at the bottom of the nearest rubbish bin.

Where will I go? I suppose I should go back to the flat. The boys will probably be worried. I'm sure someone will have told them what happened. Truth is, though, I don't want to. They're part of my past—a past I don't want to revisit. So where do I want to go? Who knows?

I feel strange, restless. My past is lost in the mist, my future uncertain, and my present uncomfortable. What a fuck-up. Now when have I thought that before? I can't sit around anymore. I get up and wander up and down, the gravel crunching under my feet. There's something about this place that bothers me. It always has, and now it's overpowering. I have to get out of here.

I start to walk toward the gate and am almost run over by the car that takes the turn a little too quickly. I fling myself to the side and lie on the grass, shocked. The car skids to a halt, and a door opens. I blink up at the figure leaning over me, just a dark outline against the sun.

"Gabriel, fuck, are you all right? I didn't mean . . . I was so . . ." The familiar voice fades, then begins to laugh. "I couldn't wait to see you and then I try to kill you. Fine boyfriend I am."

"Laurie?"

A hand reaches down, and I take it to haul myself to my feet. He's just as I remember him. Just as beautiful, just as . . . I begin to smile, but it freezes on my face. Slowly I turn my head to look back at the building I've just left. Fuck. How could I have been here all this time and not realised? Fuck. How could I have been here at all?

Suddenly, shockingly, painfully, the mist is blown away . . . no, ripped out of my mind. Everything comes into clear focus and drives me to my knees. I sag forward with my head in my hands, blinding pain crippling me.

"Oh my God. Gabriel, are you okay? Shit . . . I'll go and get someone."

"Don't you fucking dare." I manage to raise my head. He's crouching at my side, looking scared, worried, confused. Fuck him.

He's completely taken by surprise by my fist when it smacks into the side of his head. Slightly stunned, he falls sideward, and I throw myself on him. Pinning him down and ignoring the pain in my head, I punch him again, and again, until he grabs my hands and flips me over so he is on top, pinning my arms behind my head.

"What the fuck's wrong with you?"

"You bastard. You left me there, in a fucking mental hospital. You had me committed, you bastard. How could you? How dare you? No wonder you never came to see me. No wonder there was no word, no message, nothing. I thought . . . I don't know what I thought, but you left me there. You bastard, you left me there."

He lets go of me and sits back. I simply lie here, staring up at him, shock and anger making mincemeat of my guts.

Then I start to cry. "You left me there."

"You don't understand. It wasn't like that."

"Then what was it like?" I spit at him, traitorous tears still running from my eyes. "What was it like to abandon your *boyfriend* in a place like that and walk away?"

"I didn't abandon you."

"Then what? What do you think you did? Send me to a holiday camp?"

"No," he says softly, and at that moment, I want to hit him so, so badly.

"Get off me, you bastard. Just take me back to the flat and then piss off out of my life. I hate you. Do you understand? Are you going to get it into your thick head this time? I hate you, and I don't want you in my life."

"Please, Gabriel, I . . ." He sounds so sad. He's so beautiful, so . . .

"*No.* I don't want excuses. I don't want anything from you. Just get off me. Get! Off! Me!."

"Will you just shut up and listen for a minute? I did *not* abandon you."

"Well, it feels like you did."

"*Shut up!* Just shut up and listen for once." He falls silent.

"Well," I say after a while. "I've shut up, so either get off me and leave me alone or talk and then get off me and leave me alone."

"You have no idea, do you?"

"No idea about what?"

"When you got out of that place you were . . . were . . . You couldn't walk, couldn't talk, except to rant nonsense. You didn't know who I was, or who you were, or where you were. You went crazy. You were like a baby, not able to do anything for yourself.

"We took you to the hospital, and they kept you there for a few days until we were sure you were physically okay and then . . . They had to drug you to stop you fighting everyone, and you were completely off the planet. What were they supposed to do? Your mother came to see you and got upset, then they came and took you away. No one would tell me anything.

"In the beginning, when you were in the . . . other hospital, I sat with you every minute of the day. I did everything I could think of to get through to you, but you had no idea I was there. When they brought you here, they wouldn't even tell me where you were. They told me it was better for you if I didn't see you for a while, to let you get settled in and start *therapy* and then . . . then all the doors closed on me. I couldn't find out anything. It was worse than when I was trying to get you free from the facility. At least then I was doing something.

"I tried, Gabriel. I swear I tried. I tried everything I could think of, everything I could. I was desperate, crazy. I had no idea what they were doing to you, and no way of finding out. When your mother rang me to tell me you were coming home, it was like a huge weight lifted from my shoulders. She didn't want to come because she was afraid of how you'd be, so here I am. I was scared, too, Gabriel. I was so damn scared."

I can tell from the expression in his eyes that he really is scared. I suppose . . . I suppose it must've been pretty bad for him. To be honest, it hadn't been that bad for me, not really.

"Okay, get off me."

"Gabriel, I . . ."

"I'm not going to hit you. Just get off me."

He gives me a long look, then hangs his head, that beautiful hair almost brushing my stomach. He scrambles to his feet, turning away to put his hands on the roof of the car. His shoulders are slumped, and he looks so dejected.

I lie here in the grass and watch him for a while. He doesn't move. He knows I'm watching. There's no mist in my mind now, and the headache's fading. I'm clearer than I've been in a long, long time—clearer about a lot of things.

A slow smile spreads across my face, and I'm warm inside. Slowly I get to my feet and notice that the sun is high and hot on my shoulders. I lift my face and realise I can go wherever I want, do whatever I want. The freedom is intoxicating. I feel good.

Laurie stiffens when I put my arms around him, then relaxes as I lay my head on his shoulder.

"I'm really sorry, Gabriel," he says in a choked voice.

"I know."

He turns in my arms, and his face is terrible. He's crying harder than I did. As he looks into my face, then away, great big sobs start to bubble up from deep inside of him. I pull him close and just hold him as he sobs out his fear and hurt.

It feels strange to stand here with my Laurie sobbing in my arms—strange and horrible. I did this. I think about him getting the call, being lit up and excited . . . Then I crushed him. Now I think about it, I can see he's taken time and trouble over his appearance, which is more than I have. *God, you're such a selfish fuck, Gabe.*

"Laurie? Laurie, stop. I–I'm sorry. I didn't mean to hurt you. It's just . . . I just needed someone to hit out at, and you were here. I know it's no excuse, and I'm such a stupid, selfish fuck-up but—"

I'm cut off by Laurie. He raises his head, his eyes blazing. "You are not a fuck-up. You are strong and brave and . . . and . . ."

"Ssh." I pull his head down onto my shoulder and stroke his hair as he slowly calms down. He's shaking. I did that. Well . . . maybe not just me. I guess he's been scared and frustrated and angry just like me. I suppose he's just letting it all out. "I'm sorry."

"No. No, don't say you're sorry. You had every right . . . have every right to be angry with me. I should've held on tighter. I shouldn't have let them take you away again. I should have . . ."

"You did what you had to do, Laurie. You did the best you could—for me."

"I tried to."

"I'm such a stupid fuck. No, Laurie, don't say it. I was . . . I am. You did so much for me. I'm so grateful."

"I don't want you to be grateful," he says with a frown.

"I know. I know why you did it. You did it because you love me, and I don't deserve it. I don't deserve you. You don't deserve to have it thrown back in your face, so . . . I'm sorry . . . and I'm grateful."

At last, he meets my eyes. There is so much fear in him.

"Do you . . ." he says tentatively. "Do you still . . ."

There's no need for me to answer—if he doesn't see it in my eyes, he feels it in my kiss.

Later, when we're driving along leafy country lanes, Laurie asks in a subdued voice, "Was it terrible for you, Gabriel? Was it truly awful?"

Despite everything we'd said and done, we'd still been travelling in a tense silence, and his question catches me by surprise. I need to think about it for a moment.

"In the facility, yes. Yes, I suppose it was. It's like a dream now, a horrible nightmare. But I remember, and yes, it was terrible." I can't help shuddering at the memories as, for a moment, the pictures flash through my mind, causing something, somewhere, to fizz and pop. Impatiently I push them away and frown, thinking carefully. "At the hospital? No, not really. To be honest, I don't remember very much. I remember faces, tests. Sometimes it felt like I was back at the facility and I panicked. On the whole, though, I suppose it wasn't all that terrible.

"I didn't know where I was until I came out and looked back. It was like . . . like there was a fog in my head, and nothing was clear until it lifted."

"And has it lifted now?" He sounds anxious, and I reach out to lay my hand over his.

"Trust me, I couldn't be clearer right now. I'm very focused."

"Focused on what?"

He glances over at me, and I give him my sexiest smile. It's lucky we're on a straight and quiet stretch of road because he almost puts us in the hedge.

"So where are we going?" I ask innocently, trying to lower the temperature a little.

"I thought I'd take you back to my house. You can see my work, and when you're up to it, I'll show you the gallery."

For a moment, excitement thrills through me, but it doesn't last long before I crash. "Laurie, I–I'd love to but . . . but I–I don't know."

"Don't know what? Don't you want to come back with me? To stay with me? It's okay if you don't. We can go anywhere you want."

"Laurie . . . I–I can't . . . I . . ." The fear is surging through me, and it's stealing my ability to speak. I'm so angry with myself for being so stupid but . . .

"Whoa." Laurie pulls in to the side of the road and turns to me. He looks anxious. "What's wrong? Why the freaking out?"

"I'm sorry. It's just . . . I so, so want to settle down with you. I want to leave this all behind and start again." *That's funny . . . start again? When did I ever start?* "I want to stop running and start living but . . . They didn't let me go, Laurie. They didn't stop. They're still going to be hunting me. I can't . . ."

"Oh, is that what this is about?" He's laughing.

"I don't understand."

"Trust me, Gabriel. They won't be coming after you again."

"How do you know?"

"Well, for one thing, the research centre doesn't exist anymore."

"What?"

He grins at me with a strange light in his eyes. "Didn't they tell you? There was a terrible accident. The whole place went up in flames. It was completely destroyed. All the files, the papers, the research. The computer drives were wiped. The tapes and discs were melted. It was a huge mess. No one's ever going to work there again. No one's ever going to work on those projects again. It would just be too expensive to set it all up, and the political climate isn't the same as it was then. It's over, Gabriel."

"Over?" His words aren't sinking it. My mind just can't comprehend what he's saying. *It's over?* What does that even mean? "I don't . . . How? How did that happen?"

"How do you think?" There's something in his voice, something hard and cold that I've never heard there before.

"What? What . . . you?" Something occurs to me. "How *did* you get me out of there?"

His smile is feral, and the expression in his eyes makes me shiver.

"I called in a lot of favours. I have a lot of friends, and not all of them are crooks and street trash. There are plenty of people in much higher places who'd rather it not be known that they are my *friends*, or ever knew me. It's probably best not to ask about that."

"You . . . um . . . Do you mean that when you were . . . um . . . with David . . . that they . . . Okay." God, that's embarrassing to think about. So I won't. Whatever he had to do to survive in the past, he's *mine* now.

"Yeah . . . So, don't worry anymore, okay? You're coming home with me and that's that. I'm going to take care of you now."

"Take care of me? Dream on. No one takes care of me. I can take care of myself." My old fire's still there. Better set the ground rules from the start. "I am not weak. I don't need anyone to take care of me. I don't need anyone to do anything for me."

"Of course, you don't *need* it, but what has that got to do with anything?"

"What? I . . . You confuse the hell out of me sometimes."

"I don't know why. It's very simple, boyfriend. I like taking care of you. I liked taking care of you when we went on the run. I liked taking care of you at the cabin. I liked taking care of you when I burned down the research centre, and I, being the selfish bastard that I am, am going to thoroughly enjoy taking care of you for the rest of your life, which, incidentally, you're going to be spending right here with me."

"And of course, I have no say in that at all."

"Of course not."

There was a time when I would've kicked off at that. I don't need anyone. I've never needed anyone. I'll never need anyone. But I do. I do need someone. I need Laurie. So I smile. It's a smile that starts deep inside and blooms like a rose.

"Well . . . okay, I think I can live with that, although . . ."

"Although what?" Laurie asks, a smile on his face.

"I'm not confident you can live with the consequences."

"Consequences, eh?" Laurie's still smiling, and he's moving closer.

"Yeah, serious ones. First, I'm going to make you kiss me. Every. Single. Day." I lean in a little closer and lick my lips. "Better make that every hour." Laurie kisses the tip of my nose. "Uh-huh . . . there's more."

"There is?"

"Oh yeah, lots more. Second, I'm going to make you touch me . . . at every possibility."

"Touch you? Where?"

I lower my head and look up at him through my eyelashes. I know it drives him crazy, and I'm rewarded when he runs his tongue over his lips, finishing by sucking his bottom lip into his mouth. There's a hungry expression in his eyes.

"Everywhere," I purr and move closer, shifting so I'm perching on the central console. "But especially here." I pick up one of his unresisting hands and slide it around my back to cup my buttock. He squeezes gently and smiles a sexy smile. He opens his mouth to speak, but I stop him with a finger on his lips. "And here." I almost lose it when I release his hand on my thigh, and he decides to take back the control.

Gasping, I let my head fall back as he runs his hands over my body. Things are getting quite . . . strained . . . and I push him back. "One last thing."

"Really?"

"Oh yeah." Hell, I'm breathless.

"And that is?"

"Well, seeing as you're taking care of me so well . . ." It surprises me that I still have the flexibility, but I somehow manage to manoeuvre myself around the gear stick to sit on his lap, facing him. I put my arms around him and kiss him, and it's as if it's the first kiss we've ever shared.

I just let it happen for a while. It's too good to spoil with words.

"And?" Laurie gasps at last.

At first, it confuses me because I'd forgotten everything but the kiss.

"Oh, yeah . . . I almost forgot. Well . . . with all the touching and the kissing, with you taking care of me so well, I'm going to have to return the favour and . . . take care . . . of you." As I speak, I slide my hand down between us, and Laurie whimpers.

"I think I can live with those consequences."

Our gazes meet and the smiles fade, the car fades, the world fades. There are only two people who exist in the world.

"I love you, Gabriel."

"I know. I love you, too. You're a bossy, infuriating, arrogant stalker but" —I shift position so I can put my hands on his shoulders and smile down into his eyes—"I love you. I fought like hell against it, but you wouldn't let me go. Thank God. I don't know what I would've done without you. I'm pretty sure I'd be dead."

"You're too strong for that. You would've found a way."

"Maybe I could have, but I don't think I would've wanted to."

Laurie shivers and his eyes darken. "That's over now, isn't it? It's in the past. You're not going to try to kill yourself again, not ever?"

"What can I say? Forever is a long, long time. I can't make a promise that lasts forever. I don't feel that way now. At this moment, I can't see that it's ever going to be an issue . . . but I can't say forever."

He looks at me with the damnedest expression on his face. I wish I knew what he's thinking. Whoa. Wait. What the . . .

"What's wrong?"

I don't know how long I've been staring at him. It must have been a while. He looks . . . concerned, scared.

"Laurie I–I can't . . ."

"Gabriel?"

He puts his hands either side of my waist and supports me as I sag. I don't know why, but it's a huge shock. I never wanted it, but . . .

"I can't hear you."

"What do you mean? What . . . Do you have something wrong with your ears?"

"No . . . no, not my ears . . . my . . . my . . . I can't hear you . . . in here." I press my fingers against my temple. "I hadn't even noticed it before. I don't even think I remembered it was ever there. When I was in the hospital, the mental hospital, they did all sorts of tests, all sorts of things that seemed strange to me at the time. I must've forgotten about it. How is it possible that I forgot? And now . . . now . . . It's gone."

I'm numb. I don't know what to do, what to think. I can feel my head shaking, but I'm not doing it. It's shaking itself . . . no, no, no, no, no. And I don't even know why it's such a blow. I never asked for it, never wanted it, but . . . but it was part of me, a part of me that's gone.

"It might come back. Maybe it was the stress and trauma, and when things settle down, it might come back."

I'm looking at him, but I'm not seeing him, not really. "Maybe."

"Would it be so terrible if it didn't?"

I force myself to look *at* him. I gaze into those incredibly blue eyes and see what's behind them. I have no idea where the smile comes from, but suddenly it's there, bursting out of me like warm sunshine. Laurie looks a little stunned, but he's not as stunned as I am.

"It's okay, Laurie. It's going to be okay. I'm going to be okay. It's gone. It's *all* gone. I can be normal. I can . . . I can be whatever I want to be."

"You always could, babe."

"But now . . . now . . ." I'm so excited. Why am I so excited? Maybe I am insane. Maybe I should turn around and go straight back to the hospital, but . . . I mean . . . for God's sake, this is so good. This is crazy. "Laurie, it's over. It's all over. I'm free. I don't have to run, or hide, or pretend to be something I'm not, or hide something I am. I don't have to shut myself off from the world, protect myself from people. I don't have the temptation to poke about in your head to find out what you really feel . . . I know it, just like everyone else . . . with my heart."

"Slow down, Gabriel. I'm confused. Are you happy about this or not?"

"Happy? I don't know. I don't know if that's the right word but . . . Hell yeah, Laurie. *Hell* yeah, I'm happy."

Laurie grabs me and holds me so tightly my ribs creak. We kiss until our lips swell and our jaws ache. The kiss is salted with tears — his and mine — but they're not sad ones.

Panting, I lift my head and grin down at Laurie. I've never seen him look so beautiful. I've never seen anyone look so beautiful. His hair's all over the place, and his face is flushed. He looks stunned, and I don't need to be able to read his mind to know what's on it.

"Oh *God*, you're beautiful, Gabriel."

"Thank you. You're not so bad yourself."

"Do you remember when you wouldn't let me tell you that you're beautiful."

"I was an idiot. Feel free to do it whenever you want."

"You're beautiful, Gabriel. You're more beautiful than anyone I've ever seen. More beautiful than any one man has a right to be. You're perfect and I —"

"Okay . . . maybe that's enough. Too much sweetness rots the teeth, and mine aren't used to it."

"You're crazy, do you know that?"

"Sure do. I have spent time — however long it was — in a nut house to prove it."

"Don't say that, Gabriel." His expression is serious—his eyes dark and stormy, a frown on his lips.

"It's not the first time, Laurie. I'm not ashamed of it. I'm angry that I didn't know what was going on, but I wasn't . . . I didn't have a problem being there, just not being able to leave."

"Well, now you have, so let's put it behind us."

"Aren't you worried I'm going to freak out and go psycho on you?"

"Worried? I'm counting on it."

He makes me smile—a smile so hard my face hurts. A few months ago. I'd never have believed I could feel so free. It's intoxicating. I want to shout—to cry—to scream to the universe . . . *I'm free!*

"What are you thinking about? You've got that smile on your face."

"What smile?"

"That one." He's making me smile again. I bend down and kiss him.

"I'm free." I don't need to say any more. I know that I don't need to say any more because he understands—he understands perfectly.

"So is this really the end?"

"What do you mean, *the end*?"

"The end of all of this—the running, the fighting, the fear."

"End? I suppose it's the end of something." That sunlight bubbles up again, and I hug him tightly. "But it's the start of a whole new something else."

ABOUT THE AUTHOR

Cheryl was born and brought up in a very conservative working class Welsh mining valley. For generations, her family had been farmers and miners, and she was very much the black sheep. The first of her family to attend university, she broke the mould, becoming a lawyer, an artist, and, of course, a writer.

When, at thirteen, her daughter became very open about the fact she was gay—and having known for years that her brother was—Cheryl became far more aware of the problems facing young gay people generally. Over the years, speaking to her daughter, who is an enthusiastic campaigner for gay rights, and her friends, Cheryl realised that there was very little *out there* in the world of literature for young gay people. It seemed that what gay literature existed was highly erotic and sexual in content. She therefore set out to write m/m stories that were about romance and not sex, aimed at older teens and young adults.

Since that time, Cheryl has become totally addicted to writing gay romances, thrillers, adventures, fantasies, and all kinds of other genres, with little or no sex to get in the way of the story and the characters. She finds it extremely rewarding and has had a lot of positive feedback from young people who have read her works.

Cheryl continues to live in the Welsh valleys with her son and two cats. Her daughter has left her for the lure of her long-term girlfriend and the lights of the big city. She fills her days with the important things in life, such as writing and painting. She is a committed pagan, and unconventional mother, but, over and above it all, an obsessive writer.